THE PROFESSOR'S MISTRESS

THE
PROFESSOR'S
MISTRESS

A Novel

Thomas T. Thomas

THE PROFESSOR'S MISTRESS

Copyright 2013 Thomas T. Thomas

Cover photo by Rick Hyman via iStockphoto®
Cover design by Kimberly Killion

ISBN: 978-0-9849658-8-5

Contents

October 1952

1.	Putting *Galatea* to Bed	3
2.	The War of the Drums	6
3.	Nights on the Town	10
4.	Letter from Home	15
5.	Homecoming	21

Spring 1958

1.	Toeing the Party Line	27
2.	Dani's Diary	32
3.	The Shoe That Did Not Fit	33
4.	Bruised Fruit	39
5.	Dani's Diary	43
6.	Every Word a Lie	44
7.	Superman's Downfall	47
8.	Things That Go Bump in the Afternoon	49
9.	Beyond Her Control	51
10.	A Note from School	53
11.	Fear and Loathing	57
12.	Dani's Diary	58
13.	Spring Fling	59
14.	The Stalker	62
15.	The Affair	66
16.	Dani's Diary	70
17.	The Discovery	72
18.	The Accusation	75
19.	Thirty-Six Hours (I)	78
20.	Thirty-Six Hours (II)	83
21.	Thirty-Six Hours (III)	87
22.	Thirty-Six Hours (IV)	90
23.	Thirty-Six Hours (V)	94
24.	Thirty-Six Hours (VI)	97
25.	Thirty-Six Hours (VII)	100
26.	In the Emergency Room	104

27. Primary Diagnosis   107
28. Learned at Her Mother's Knee   116
29. The Daily Call   122

Winter 1968

1. Professor of Logic   127
2. Christmas Dinner at Home   130
3. The Shadow in the Trees   134
4. The Enigma in the Library   139
5. Resolution of the Faculty Senate   146
6. Hunting Among the Trees   148
7. Hunting in the Stacks   150
8. Resolution of the Faculty Senate   152
9. Reunion of the Old School   155
10. Return of a Potential Buyer   158
11. Changes to the Curriculum   161
12. Resolution of the Faculty Senate   163
13. The Enigma on the Mall   165
14. Finding a Kindred Spirit   167
15. Daughter of the Revolution   171
16. The Wreck Under the Tent   174
17. Dani Brings Home a Friend   177
18. Resolution of the Faculty Senate   182
19. Eviction Notice   183
20. Rivals of the Old Firm   185
21. Sealing the Deal   188
22. Resolution of the Faculty Senate   193
23. Work for a Handyman   195
24. Helping Them Understand   200

Spring 1968

1. The Paperwork   205
2. The Elective   207
3. Watching the Professor at Work (I)   210
4. Overheard at the *Marat/Sade* Rehearsals   213
5. The First Rally of Spring   214

6. Repairing the Engine 217
7. Watching the Professor at Work (II) 220
8. Overheard at the *Marat/Sade* Rehearsals 222
9. Sharing Her Happiness 223
10. A Trivial Virtue 225
11. Mending, Bending, and Brazing 228
12. Overheard at the *Marat/Sade* Rehearsals 231
13. Blind Date with Fusillade 232
14. Weak at the Knees 236
15. Too Much Too Soon 240
16. Overheard at the *Marat/Sade* Rehearsals 243
17. The War of the Squirrels 244
18. Refloating *Galatea* 246
19. A Night of Watching 249
20. Overheard at the *Marat/Sade* Rehearsals 262
21. Testing the Engine 263
22. Moving Day at the Cottage 266
23. Time to Wind Things Up 268
24. Nowhere to Be Found 271
25. *The Persecution and Assassination of Jean-Paul Marat as Performed by the Inmates of the Asylum of Charenton Under the Direction of the Marquis de Sade* 273
26. The Leveling of a Lifetime 276
27. Homecoming 278

Summer 1968
1. The Reason Why 285
2. Getting to Know You 288
3. Extending Her Horizons 291
4. Dinner with the Family 295
5. Doing a Deal 300
6. A Summer Cruise 307
7. *Bon Voyage!* 312
8. Crosswise in the Trough 318

9. Change of Name   326
10. Filling Up   329
11. Appreciation for *Galatea*   331
12. First Hurdle   332
13. Sister, Wife, Whatever   335
14. Age Turns to Beauty   341
15. Alerting the Authorities   345
16. Appreciation for *Galatea*   348
17. Couple of Days Behind   349
18. Halfway Mark   351
19. First Time in Ten Years ... and Counting   353
20. A Miss by Less Than a Mile   355
21. Appreciation for *Galatea*   359
22. Squall Line   360
23. Interlude Ashore   366
24. Scraper   378
25. Appreciation for *Galatea*   381
26. Catching Up With the World   383
27. Change of Plan   388
28. Georgian Bay   395
29. Catching Up With the Money   399
30. Treatment for a Gunshot Wound   409
31. A Hazard to Navigation   412

Fall 1968
1. Mother and Daughter   419
2. Done Roving   422

About the Author   425

There is a smile of love,
And there is a smile of deceit,
And there is a smile of smiles
In which these two smiles meet.

—*William Blake*

OCTOBER 1952

1. Putting Galatea to Bed

George and Marian Kirkeby stood on the dock at the Lakeshore Yard, near Byzantium, New York, and watched their ship come in. The couple had driven up from Rochester for the annual ceremony of bedding her down for the winter while the paid crew, Captain Emmet Gallagher and First Mate-Engineer Andrej Haraszthy, brought the steam launch *Galatea* along Lake Ontario's southern shore, a trip of sixty miles from her summertime berthing in Irondequoit Bay.

"I still get a thrill seeing her from the land," George said. "We don't get this view of the grand old vessel—coming into dock like this—when we're already aboard and picking up our guests."

"Emmet's hung out all the bunting, I see," Marian remarked, pointing to the string of pennants flying on the forward stay, from the bowsprit to the top of the first mast, then all the way back to the second mast. "What do they say?"

"Spell it out, darling," he urged.

"You know I'm no good with signals."

"But you should recognize a few by now."

"Well, I see two of those blue-with-white-squares. Is that the 'blue peter'?"

"Yes, and that stands for …?"

"Peter … Papa, the letter P!"

"Speaking of blue peters, gosh, that wind is cold!"

"You came out here without your long johns, didn't you?"

"I didn't think wind off the lake in October would be so keen."

"A couple more days like this and we'll be seeing ice on the creek."

"Back to your spelling lesson."

"But *you* distracted *me!*"

"Two Ps together?"

"Well, I see just two flags before them," Marian went on. "The first one's white-and-red, so that's either Foxtrot or Hotel. And the second is white-and-blue, which I'm sure is Alfa. It can't be F-A-P-P-anything, so it must be 'happy.' "

"Very good, m'dear!"

"Now give me the rest."

"After that comes 'ending' and the numbers one-nine-five-two," he said. "Then 'golden,' 'summer,' and 'days' in 1953."

"What a lovely thought, George! Did you put him up to it?"

"I may have had a hand," he said modestly.

As *Galatea* came parallel with the dock, the first mate jumped ashore with a line while Captain Gallagher finished up his business in the wheelhouse. They each greeted the owners with a nod, then went off to confer with the yard manager, Mr. Gibbs.

As George and Marian stepped aboard, he carried the picnic basket that had been at their feet. They went down into the main cabin, where Haraszthy had already put dust covers over the furniture and cleaned out the galley. Further forward, Gallagher had blown down the boiler. Whatever else they might need to do in preparing engine and hull for winter storage could be done once the boat was drawn up on shore.

George retrieved a vacuum bottle from the basket. "May I pour you a libation, darling?"

"Of course. About time, too!"

He unscrewed the cap, which did double-duty as a plain metal cup, and filled it with a clear liquid. He offered the cup to her.

"No ice?" Marian said, taking it. "Mmm, cold!"

"Ice seemed redundant today," he replied.

"And why dilute the good stuff?"

"Sorry about the olives," he said. He tipped the container's mouth toward the light coming in the cabin windows. "They appear to be stuck at the bottom."

"I don't see why we bother with them anymore."

"It's traditional, darling," he said. "People would miss them."

"People don't miss the vermouth in your martinis—and what's your recipe now? One drop? Or is it two?"

"I tip the vermouth bottle ever so slightly toward the shaker, being careful not to spill any. Besides, you don't need any of that wormwood-flavored wine when you serve really good gin."

"Nobody's complained yet."

"Well, Gretchen Meyers ..."

"Gretchen wouldn't know a good time if it fell on her."

"She likes drinks with floating fruit and a little parasol."

"Enough said," Marian agreed.

"Excuse me, sir—ma'am?" Captain Gallagher said from the entry. "We're about to pull her over to the ramp."

"Do you want us to go ashore?" George asked.

"It might be more convenient, sir."

So the owners went back onto the dock and walked the long way around, to the other side of the yard and out onto one of the concrete piers flanking the boat ramp. By the time they arrived, the workboat had maneuvered *Galatea* over to the ramp, and Mr. Gibbs's crew had ropes on her for aligning bow and keel with the notches and supports of her cradle, which was already down in the water.

At the top of the ramp, a tractor started up and slowly backed away, pulling two lengths of iron chain out of the water. The cradle followed, and the men with ropes pulled the hull forward until it settled into the timber skeleton with a series of muffled groans. A few minutes later the long, white hull with its dark-red underbelly was out of the inlet and freely dripping water and a summer's growth of hanging weed.

"Excellent," George said, "just like delivering a baby."

"And what, pray tell, would you know about *that?*"

"Why, just the usual—I mean, hypothetical—"

"Oh, hush! Say goodbye for another year."

"Sleep well, my beautiful *Galatea.*"

And he blew a kiss to the boat.

2. THE WAR OF THE DRUMS

THE OUTHOUSE STENCH had struck the moment his plane from the States landed at Kimpo Airfield in Korea. It was a sense memory of place and time that William Henry Wheelock carried to his dying day. The Koreans fertilized their rice paddies with human waste, politely called "night soil," and the odor had dug itself into his brain and never let go.

Through all seasons the foul vapors slipped under the flaps of his tent at night. They fought with the taste of his eggs at breakfast and smothered his steaks for dinner. Among the troops it was said that only kimchi could stand up to the smell coming off the paddies, and kimchi was disgusting. The only time the odor seemed to diminish was now, in October, when the paddies froze with the onset of winter. The farmers still spread their steaming muck, of course, but it had a chance to freeze before making headway on the wind.

But now the smell was coming back stronger as his jeep followed the Honton River up to the southern edge of the Iron Triangle between Ch'orwon and Kumhwa. The terrain on all sides was really too hilly and arid for rice farming, but Wheelock knew well enough that night soil could fertilize any kind of field. Perhaps his nose was playing tricks, and the smell only seemed stronger. Over his months in country Wheelock had become a connoisseur of stenches, and he could now identify something more. From somewhere close at hand came the sweet miasma of bodies left too long above ground and then buried in shallow graves with too little lime. And—yes!—mingled with the smell of bodies was a lighter, more penetrating aroma that he knew well.

God, he was going to be glad to get out of this country!

"There's one, sir," said his driver Binns, who could also smell the difference. The man pointed to a dark, square-shaped mound along the side of the road.

Wheelock sighed. "Pull over, Sergeant."

Operating this close to the nearly static front lines, they went fully armed. In addition to Wheelock's Colt Model 1911 side-arm, he had laid an M1 Carbine across the jeep's back seat with the stock ready to hand. Just in front of it, with stock and barrel reversed, was the standard M1 Garand rifle issued to Binns. The driver also carried a couple of grenades clipped to his belt. Of course, none of this weaponry meant much if they came upon a probing Communist patrol. Still, as the jeep skidded to a stop on the muddy road, William Henry reached back for his carbine before getting out.

The blocky cache was covered by a tarpaulin weighted with rocks and stood much taller than a man. Wheelock could count by the semicircular bulges along its upper edge that it was nine wide by five deep. He could estimate the height of the stack as three tall, because he knew exactly what he was counting: fifty-five gallon fuel drums.

But before he became too excited by the find, Wheelock had to make sure this wasn't an unregistered storage dump of full drums. He lifted the bottom edge of the tarp. Up close and freshly released, the sweetish, knifelike smell of gasoline and the deep, bitter scent of lubricating oil again cut through the stench from the fields. He rapped on a drum in the lowest tier and got a hollow *boom* in return.

They were *empty* fifty-five gallon drums, left by someone at the roadside for the Drum Fairies to come along and collect. ... That would be Wheelock and Binns.

He made a notation on his map: 135/55, with an estimate in yards to the last milepost he and Binns had passed. Now all he had to do was coordinate this sighting with the other pencil notations that stretched from here back to Inch'on. Then he could fashion a truck route that would pick up all the drums in the shortest distance with the least amount of unladen travel. In this way the effort would take the least time and consume the least fuel. It was just a matter of linear programming, really.

Wheelock had landed in country in the summer of 1951, immediately after the Allies had beaten off the last of the Communists' spring offensives around Seoul. On his collar tabs flashed the gold oak leaves of a major, which he always suspected had been a consolation prize for the unglamorous duty to which he had been assigned. Packed in his luggage were folio-sized page proofs of a book titled *Methods of Operations Research*, co-authored by one George E. Kimball and based on work the man had done for the U.S. Navy during the war. As the text had recently been declassified and was about to go on the presses at MIT, Wheelock carried a mockup of the book pages "rather than carting classified documents all over the Pacific Theater"— as the colonel in charge of Stateside petroleum operations had explained at the time.

The Quartermaster Corps must have figured that a graduate student in the classics, who could read fluently in two dead languages, would find the statistical abstractions of operations research a breeze to decipher. Wheelock tacitly agreed to treat the analysis of resource allocations as just another form of esoterica and plunged himself into the study of probability theory, strategical kinematics, operational experiments in logistics, and gunnery problems. The book was filled with diagrams and tables—some of the latter reminding Wheelock of fragments from Cretan Linear B. Well, at least it had kept his mind occupied while he waited for transportation to the Korean peninsula.

And so it turned out that William Henry Wheelock's war in Korea had been a war of the drums. A modern army marched, not on its stomach, but on wheels and tracks turned by gasoline and diesel fuel, anointed with lubricating oil. These materials were brought into Inch'on's treacherous harbor, which was plagued by thirty-foot tides, in small coastal tankers. They were offloaded at a transfer station for petroleum, oils, and lubricants—or POLs, as the armed forces knew them. Avgas went out by pipeline or rail car to the airfields. But fuel for the forward areas went by truck in fifty-five gallon drums and, less often, in five gallon jerry cans. The trouble was, maintaining the POL supply was under the joint jurisdiction of the Quartermasters Corp, the Corps of Engineers, and various units of Transportation.

Everyone wanted to see as much gasoline and diesel moved to the front as quickly as possible. Not everyone saw returning the empty drums for future refilling as a priority. The limiting factor—as Kimball's book had taught Wheelock to think—was not the supply of fuel, but the availability of empty drums to carry it. Shipping out an endless supply of new drums from the States, even for an organization as rich and wasteful as the U.S. Army, was not an option. Wheelock's assignment, before he ever set foot in Korea, was to establish a system that would get the empty drums back to the depot with the least effort and inconvenience to all concerned. The system that seemed to work best was for Major Wheelock and Sergeant Binns to drive around the forward areas—the rear of the front, as it were—locate caches of empty drums, and mark them for return.

From the back of the jeep, he took a can of white paint and a flat brush and marked a large I-in-a-circle on the front of the tarpaulin facing the road. That was the agreed-upon mark with his drivers: "I" for return to Inch'on.

"Not too many, are there?" Binns said.

"Enough," Wheelock replied.

"Fewer than before."

"What are you trying to say, Sergeant?"

The man stared off to the horizon. "Maybe we're getting ahead of the game? Fewer caches this month than last. More barrels must be finding their way back to base."

"We're still a few thousand short," Wheelock grumped. "At the very least."

"But … when we find them all, they'll let us go home, right?"

Wheelock thought about that for two seconds.

"Nope," he said. "Not a chance."

3. Nights on the Town

JANE WHEELOCK STOOD in her stocking feet before the mirror on her closet door. She wore only a black nylon slip—the one with a line of uneven stitches under her left breast where the lace of the bodice had come apart. What, she wondered, from her diminished wardrobe of party dresses, would she be able to wear this evening? The blue was out, because she had worn that on Monday. Of her two black dresses, one had a tear—she supposed from brushing up against a loose screwhead along the zinc-coated bar, and she hadn't gotten around to mending it—and the other really did need to go to the cleaners.

Which left the red satin with the shawl collar and plunging neckline. It was the exact color of a maraschino cherry, which set off her pale skin and the reddish highlights in her hair. With the matching pumps, that dress had set Jane back a week's wages plus tips. It would be perfect—except for a brownish stain the size of her thumb in the fabric of the belt. She didn't have time to fix it, but maybe she could substitute her old, wide, black-leather belt. The effect of that combination would be striking.

With ten minutes to go before her ride was due to arrive, Jane knelt and began digging through the bottom drawer of her bureau, looking for that belt.

"Mommee!" came Dani's voice from the doorway. "Mommy, where are you?"

Jane lifted her head above the edge of the bed. "Right here, darling."

"You disappeared!" the three-year-old girl exclaimed.

"No, I just—ducked down." Jane dipped her head again. "See? I was looking for something."

"I thought you'd gone away!"

"No, I've been here all along."

"But you *will* go away."

"I work tonight, yes."

"Stay with me!"

"I can't."

10

"Please!"

"Mommy has to go to work," Jane said reasonably. "You know that. And you get to stay with Mrs. Obmanchikov. She gives you borscht and blintzes, doesn't she?"

"She smells," her ginger-haired daughter insisted.

"Danielle! That's not a nice thing to say."

"But it's true!" the girl replied.

"Still, we don't *say* it."

"O-*kay*," Dani sulked.

"Now I have to finish dressing. Did you go potty?"

"Mother!" The little girl was outraged.

"Just asking. Go put on your shoes and socks. We're late."

Jane found the leather belt, slipped on the red dress, and cinched in the waist. She looked like a pirate, but there was no time to change now. She went to help her daughter tie her shoelaces. Then she got her scarf and her long, black cloth coat.

By the time they got out the door of Jane's apartment and down the hall to Mrs. Obmanchikov's, Lou Fiacco was in the driveway pounding on his horn. The middle-aged Russian woman, wife of a professor of Slavic languages whom Jane had never met, or even seen, answered on the first knock.

"Mrs. Wheelock!" The woman looked surprised.

"Hello, Mrs. Obmanchikov." Jane paused. "This *is* the night you said you would take care of Dani—isn't it?"

"You are going out again?"

"I work evenings, you know."

The woman looked down at Jane's feet. "Such nice shoes ... *krasnie*."

Jane thought she had said "crazy" and opened her coat. "They go with the dress."

Mrs. Obmanchikov studied her. "You always look so fancy when you go out."

"Thank you. I try to keep up appearances." Jane would not tell this woman, the biggest gossip in the apartment house, that the only work she could find was as a cocktail waitress. Anyway, it was none of her business.

The horn sounded again.

"That's my ride." Jane urged Dani forward, but the girl clutched her hand and hung back.

Mrs. Obmanchikov took Dani's other hand and drew her through the doorway. "Come, *devochka*. Tonight we make potato pancakes."

Dani smiled uncertainly up at her, turned to give her mother a worried look, and went inside.

"Good-bye," Jane said as the door closed.

Downstairs, she opened the passenger door of Lou's car for herself and slid onto the bench seat.

"We're going to be late," he said.

"You always say that. We never are."

"Jimmy gets off at six sharp, whether I'm there or not. If the bar's unattended, the county could lift our license. Then both of us would lose our jobs."

Lou was the night bartender at the Ace of Spades. He was always worrying. Harry Benson, the owner, was the worrying kind, and he made it infectious. Because the bar was so close to campus, they got scrutiny from both the Byzantium Police Department and the University of Lake Ontario administration. The first thing Harry had taught Jane was how to spot fake identity cards and to be polite but firm about refusing to serve the underage boys and girls.

Now Jane briefly considered what it would be like to lose this job. The hours were bad, and she usually did not get home until after two in the morning. The pay was good, compared with her previous jobs, but the tips—according to Sheila, the other waitress, who had been running drinks for twenty years—were only so-so. That was because of the clientele. "College kids and academic types are lousy tippers," Sheila told her. "But there *are* compensations."

The compensations were that the two women seldom had to deal with the really sullen, hard-core drunks, never had to hide out during bar fights like you got with the blue-collar set, and didn't worry much about taking physical abuse. The students were too shy to pinch Jane's bottom, while the professors were too refined. And at least the company was adult. After a full day of caring for a toddler, even a child as bright as Dani, Jane yearned to get out of the house, to chat, however briefly, with people more than two feet high, to dress up and feel pretty, and yes—if the job called for it, if she felt like it—to flirt a bit.

But there was no one to flirt with this evening. The Ace emptied out sometime after nine, and by midnight Lou had sent Sheila home. At one o'clock, when they were the only two people left in the place, he said to Jane, "Let's lock up."

"We're open for another hour, aren't we?"

Lou walked down to the small front window and looked out past the blue-and-yellow neon glow of the Pabst sign. "Stoplight's gone to flashing red at the corner. Not a car in sight, passing or parked, for two whole blocks. And no pedestrians, because they've rolled up the sidewalks."

Jane giggled, then sobered. "Harry won't like it."

"Harry won't know," Lou said, dead serious.

"Another hour's pay ... I need the money."

"You vouch for me. I vouch for you."

She started to say that was cheating, but Lou had already turned off the sign.

While he cashed out the register and stacked chairs on the tables, Jane washed up the last of the glasses, dumped the peanuts back in the tin, and swabbed down the length of the bar. Then he took her out back to the car and opened the passenger door for her, like a gentleman.

When they reached the street, however, he turned left instead of right.

"Where are you going?" she asked. "I live the other way, remember?"

"We've got time, don't we?"

"Time?" Jane was confused.

"Before you pick up the kid."

"Sure, but since I'm going home early ..."

"I thought we could go over to my place."

"Oh?" Jane froze on the seat. "Why would we do that?"

Lou's right hand came off the wheel, settled on the cushion between them, and scuttled sideways, like a crab, toward her left leg. She put her own hand over his, to stop him. She was suddenly conscious of the diamond on her third finger, winking dimly in the dull light from outside. She felt the weight of her engagement ring and wedding band.

"I've seen how you look at me," he said tightly.

"And what kind of look is that?" she asked.

"Like you want it—like you want me."

"I'm a married woman, you know."

"And he's been away how long?"

"Lou … you're a coworker … a friend."

"I could be a lot more," he said, but his hand was already pulling back.

"I know you could," she sighed, "but that would spoil it."

"Just for the night. Just this once."

"That would make it even worse."

"Yeah." In the come-and-go light from the streetlamps, she could see that he was biting his lip. "I guess so."

After he turned the car around, Jane let him drive until they were almost in front of the apartment house.

"Lou?" she said quietly. "No offense?"

"Sure. None taken."

"In a way, I'm kind of flattered."

"I'm … glad."

"Pick me up tomorrow?"

"Sure."

4. LETTER FROM HOME

THE OTHER MEMORIES from Korea that Wheelock would carry to the end of days were the texture of the paper, color of ink, and complete text of every letter he received from home during his tour of duty. While he loved his wife Jane with every fiber of his being, William Henry had to concede that their relationship was on a wholly physical plane. While he himself was literate—almost hyper-literate—and adept at putting his thoughts and feelings on paper, addressing them in imagination to his absent wife, Jane turned out to have no such ability. When he was not physically present, or within the sound of her voice or a local phone call, she apparently felt little need to remember or communicate with him. So Wheelock treasured any awkward and ungrammatical scrawl she might dash off and send his way, hoarding those few lines against the periods when she gave him nothing.

Wheelock had married Jane Dobray at his father's house in central Pennsylvania during the winter months of early 1949. She agreed to have him only on condition that William Henry go back to school and make something of himself, rather than selling Buicks and Chryslers to farmers and shopkeepers—his job after demobilization from the war in Europe. William Henry had finished his remaining undergraduate courses, which the war had interrupted, that same spring and taken his baccalaureate degree. And then, before their little Danielle was born later in the year, Wheelock started graduate studies. By the time his reserve unit was called up for Korea, he had completed coursework for his doctorate of philosophy—always in the classics, with emphasis on Greek rather than Roman art and literature—and was choosing among possible topics for his dissertation.

All the time William Henry was studying, Jane worked to put him through school and keep their small family together: store clerk, office telephonist and receptionist, checkout at the local A&P—whatever paid a good hourly wage while he attended classes by day and sat up through the night reading dead texts in Greek and analyzing them in sometimes even deader prose.

When the baby came and Jane could no longer work, they subsisted on his stipend as a graduate teaching assistant. Sometimes they slipped on the rent payments and let the phone company disconnect them for a month or two. Together they ate tons of macaroni and cheese. Jane openly fretted about money and compulsively counted the pennies in her purse, but she never regretted choosing William Henry for a husband, or his hope of becoming a college professor one day. Still, it was only when he was called up again and had an army paycheck to send home that Jane's and the baby's living situation improved.

When William Henry and his driver arrived back at the POL depot in Inch'on, he was still cherishing his wife's last letter: she had covered the whole side of one page but with handwriting that was loopier—Jane's word for it—than usual. So it came as something of a surprise when the company clerk, Donnelly, called out, "Hey, Doc! You got a letter!" as William Henry passed his desk. Donnelly was waving a light-blue, entirely civilian-looking envelope.

"Really?" Wheelock said. "Maybe it's from my congressman."

"Yeah, your draft board made a mistake," Binns quipped.

"The typing's not good enough," Donnelly sniffed.

Wheelock took the envelope. The weight of the characters was irregular, the sign of a hunt-and-peck typist striking with uneven pressure. Some of the closed loops were also filled in, indicating a poorly maintained machine. The return address was from his own apartment building in Byzantium, New York. He thought on that for a moment. Had Jane ever learned to operate a typewriter in any of her jobs? If so, he wasn't aware of it. And the address the sender used for him was barely adequate to work its way through the Army Post Office system, because it showed the wrong theater of operations. If there had been a Wheelock anywhere in Europe, then he would be holding this letter right now instead of William Henry. So far as he knew, Jane had never made that mistake.

Wheelock glanced pointedly at Binns and Donnelly, who were standing on either side of him, studying the envelope as he was. William Henry walked off to his own desk to read the letter. He slit the top of the envelope, and a half sheet of the same blue paper came out, covered with the same uneven typewriting.

> Dear Mr. Wheelock—
> This is hard letter for me to write to soldier overseas who has not seen his dear wife in so long time. I know you must miss her terribly, but you must not feel like that. Your wife is not good woman.
> Every night for weeks she dresses up to nines and goes out. She is always going with same man, driving away in big automobile and leaving your daughter Daniela with me to take care of. She never returns before midnight and sometimes not until small hours of morning with her dress sometimes torn and the smell of liquor about her. Your wife says she has job, but I don't know what kind of job makes you to drink and rip your clothes and cavort with men. At least not honest job.
> I sit babies only for the sake your little girl, only because I love her and I respect you. Not to help this woman who wrongs you. For her God has made a special circle of Hell.
> Come home soon and save your marriage.
> Your friend,

There was no signature. Wheelock turned the paper over, but there was no note, no other marks. He studied the outside of the envelope again. He read the letter over three times.

And all the while his mind whirled, battered by the hurt and humiliation of these accusations. His brain frantically tried to absorb the shock of finding out, simultaneously, that Jane, as loving and caring as he remembered his wife to be, was now acting like a prostitute, and his marriage, as much as his emotional stability depended on it, had just vanished like a desert mirage under the edge of a dark cloud.

Or … was she? Had it? What was the truth here? And did he have to accept this letter at face value? Almost reflexively, Wheelock began to fight the letter's implications with the deductive logic in which he had trained and which now formed his daily work.

Someone, who apparently lived in his apartment building, had written the letter but neglected to sign it, refusing to declare himself—or, more likely, herself. And why? For fear of disclosure and retaliation? From whom? From Jane—who would never see the letter, who was never meant to know of it? Or from William Henry—who could do what, exactly, from half a world away? Or, rather, was it because the mischief-maker was a coward, pure and simple?

That the writer had only rudimentary command of English was obvious. Diction and syntax suggested a person of foreign extraction, an immigrant, of which several lived in his building. William Henry thought of Ahmed Sayyedin, an elderly Arab scholar, but he was a quiet man who spoke to no one—besides, how likely was he to "sit babies"? Mrs. Laquelle upstairs, a bone-thin black woman from sub-Saharan Africa, spoke better English than Wheelock did himself, and she was native in French. The Obmanchikovs—he a professor of Slavic literature, she a housewife—were Russian expatriates, dignified people, whom he was sure would never stoop to this kind of vicious gossip. So the letter writer must be someone who had moved in after Wheelock had left for Korea.

This person, whoever it was, claimed to be babysitting Danielle while Jane went out in the evenings. And Jane was said to be coming home late, although the exact hour was not given and the time might well be exaggerated. These were presented as facts.

The rest was supposition. The writer said Jane drove off with a man, but this man was never identified or described. It was reasonable to assume that, if she had taken a new job at further than walking distance, Jane would need a ride. Wheelock had left her with an apartment and an income, but not enough money to buy a car. If the driver was always the same person, then it might as easily be a coworker as a boyfriend, given that this escort was punctual enough to allow Jane to arrange for a babysitter. An affair was therefore presumed but not shown to be fact.

As to what kind of job might require Jane to wear fancy dress, drink liquor, and occasionally get her clothes torn or disheveled … well, Wheelock himself could think of several. She might have found work as a fashion model—Jane certainly had the face and figure for it—in a dress shop that stayed open in the evening for private showings. Or she might have joined an amateur theatrical group—they were popular in university towns—with evening performances that naturally meant staying out late. Either job might involve Jane's having to change her clothes quickly and, occasionally, rip them. And either might involve the presence—although at some remove—of liquor.

Jobs like that did not even have to pay real wages. Jane did not need the income, not with his army paycheck to see her through. However … what Jane's definition of actual "need" might be, or how her and Dani's situation might have changed since he went away, William Henry had no way of knowing.

Finally, was Jane, by nature, a "not good woman"? After two years of marriage he could say that he knew his wife. She was loyal. She was loving. She was honest. She would not hurt him, even if she thought she could act in secret and get away with it.

William Henry Wheelock weighed the letter and its contents. The details were found wanting. The story was thin and mostly based on conjecture and assumption. The allegations were contrary to what he knew to be fact. And, most damning of all, the writer had chosen to remain anonymous. That meant Wheelock was automatically barred from following up, from asking questions and seeking clarification—except by publicly confronting his wife with what was most likely a tissue of lies.

But still, deep in a corner of his mind, there was doubt. Could one person truly know another? Could any man really be sure of his wife? Especially a woman as bright and beautiful as Jane? Left alone for more than a year?

He put the letter back in its envelope. But he did not throw it in the wastebasket, where someone else might find it. He did not burn it, as it deserved. Instead, he put the letter in his desk drawer and turned the lock on it. And there it would wait.

5. Homecoming

When Willie came home the following spring, Jane took her daughter to meet his train at the station in town. As the local pulled in from Syracuse, Jane scanned from window to window on each of the cars, methodically searching for his handsome face under the peak of a dark-green uniform cap with the gold insignia in the center. She didn't find him there, or among the streams of men climbing down from the vestibules.

Jane was turning this way and that, frantically searching the thinning crowd on the platform, when she felt a tap on her shoulder.

"Daddy!" shouted little Danielle at her side.

"Hello there!" said a familiar voice behind her.

Jane turned to find her tall, fair-haired husband, who instead of an army uniform was wearing a gray felt hat and khaki-colored raincoat, but he still wore Willie's face with its strong nose, long jaw, and sad, scholarly eyes. It was now a deeply tanned face that had a few more lines around the eyes and mouth, but it was his own.

"You're not in uniform," she said, confused.

"I'm not in the army anymore," he replied. "They discharged me yesterday down at Fort Dix."

Before Willie could explain further, she dropped her daughter's hand and grabbed him. She wrapped her arms around his neck, planted her mouth on his, and hung on tight.

He responded with a bear hug and a deep, hungry kiss.

After an eternity, the pressure released and their lips parted.

"Whew!" she said.

"It's good to see you, too."

Then Jane took her family home. She let Dani play in the living room, closing her ears to the occasional bang and crash and the resulting howl, while she diligently made love to her husband all afternoon.

At half past five she rose, had a shower, and began dressing for work. She had taken her strapless, black taffeta dress with the chiffon skirt out of the closet and was holding it against herself for inspection when Willie rolled over and opened his eyes.

"Where are you going?" he asked, somewhat sharply.

"I have to go out," she said vaguely.

"But where?" he asked.

Jane turned to face him, still holding the dress. "I'm going to work."

His face held the beginnings of a scowl. It was more than the face of a man losing out on a final bout of lovemaking. Willie's expression had turned opaque and distant. The way he paused was suddenly cautious. And he looked—just a little bit—scared.

"Dressed like that?" he asked in a tone that said he might not believe her answer.

"I didn't want to tell you in my letters, because I thought it might worry you, but I have a job serving drinks at a bar downtown."

"Oh," he said. Then again, with relief, "Oh!"

Jane tried to figure out what he had been thinking—what he had been fearing—and she didn't like her conclusions.

"It's just a job," she said defensively. "Like being a waitress, but with alcohol."

"I didn't think you would need a job," he said. "Wasn't my army pay enough?"

"It gets me out of the house." She shrugged.

"In the evening," he said slowly.

"That's when people drink."

"Why don't we stay in tonight?"

Jane shook her head, "I'm on the clock. They expect me."

"This is my first night home," he said reasonably.

"But what would we do if I stayed?"

He smiled and patted the bed.

"Didn't you get enough of that already?" she asked.

"Then let's go dancing. You've got the dress for it."

"But Lou will be coming by for me in ten minutes."

"Lou?" She didn't like the way his eyebrow arched.

"He's the bartender. He always drives me to work."

"Tell him you just quit, that you're going dancing."

"But ..." Jane discovered she did not like being ordered around by her husband. "But I don't have a sitter for tonight. I thought you'd be taking care of Dani. Still, if you really want to go out, I could call Mrs. Obmanchikov. She—"

"No!" William Henry said sharply. "Not her!"

Jane was perplexed. "Well, why ever not?"

"I've changed my mind. Let's stay in."

"This is too confusing." She raised her arms and slid the dress down over her head. "I've got to get going."

"Stay with me," he said, pleading now.

"Sorry, fella. You just botched it."

"When will you be back?"

"Don't wait up," she said.

Three weeks later, Jane learned that Willie had put a down payment on a house without first talking the matter over with her. It was more of a cottage, really, one of three identical structures nestled into a stand of second-growth pines on the university campus, just north of the library. Jane was going to protest but, when he showed her the cottage, she fell in love with it immediately.

It had walls of cream-colored matchboard, more like a summer place than a real house, and a peaked roof of rain-darkened wooden shakes. The door and the shutters on the windows were painted a deep green—the same color that the groundskeepers painted fences and signposts all around the campus. It was charming and quaint and everything she had dreamed of. But still, Jane felt she had to put up a fight.

"Aren't these cottages reserved for faculty?" she asked.

"I'm going to be faculty," he said, "soon enough."

"That's not certain, is it? You haven't finished your dissertation."

"My thesis advisor is very encouraging. Besides, the administration already took my check."

"We can't afford it," Jane said, but she put her hand out for the key.

"When you figure how much we were paying in rent, it makes financial sense."

"What if you get a professorship someplace else?"

Jane opened the front door onto a small parlor. The house was unfurnished, of course. Light patches on the walls showed where the former occupants had hung pictures. Jane decided they would have to repaint the whole place inside before moving in. The windows had drapes made of cheap cotton in a faded cabbage rose pattern, and those would have to go as well. There was no carpet, but the floor boards were good, blond oak with an inlaid strip of some other, darker wood—maybe cherry—running around the edges of each room. The floors needed a good scrubbing and waxing, too. Jane could see she had her work cut out for her. But still she had questions.

"What happens if we have to move later?"

"Well, then we'll have an asset to sell."

"Back to the university," she pointed out.

"That's in the deed papers," he admitted.

They toured the separate dining room, the small but adequate kitchen, which had a range and refrigerator included in the sale, the tiny spare room downstairs, which would make a sewing room for her—or, more likely, a study for Willie—and the two bedrooms at the top of the narrow, twisting stairs that curved up and around the fieldstone fireplace. Its chimney was the center post of the house and would keep them warm and cozy through the winters.

"It's totally impractical," Jane said.

"But ...?" he prompted.

"I love it."

Spring 1958

1. Toeing the Party Line

William Henry Wheelock did not usually get to socialize with faculty outside the Classics Department, but across the bottom of the big red heart that was his invitation to the annual Valentine's Day party thrown by the chairman of the Sociology and Political Science Department, Fred Goerlich had scrawled: "And bring that lovely wife of yours."

No sooner had they gone through the front door, shed their winter coats, and accepted drinks from a tray than someone took Jane's arm and led her away to a group of women by the avocado dip. Someone else pressed William Henry's hand and turned him around in conversation. And the party was on.

Perhaps half an hour later, the associate professor with whom he was chatting—a sour little man named Michelson, with a tiny patch of beatnik beard on the knob of his chin—looked across the room and said, "Ah, the mating rituals of the educated elite." The comment brought to William Henry's mind the image of chalky fingers fumbling under folds of rough tweed. Then he saw where Michelson was looking.

Jane and a man who was indeed wearing a tweed jacket with gray flannel slacks were head-to-head as they bent over the host's new "stereo." From a distance, the machine looked like a turntable and panels with knobs and dials that somehow got built into a cocktail cabinet veneered in cherry wood with pink fluorescent tubes mounted inside. The man was showing Jane how to put on and play a record.

After a certain amount of amplified scratching, the strains of an orchestra floated out over the chatter in the room. The first few bars were racing, energetic music that William Henry thought of as "madcap." Then the music broke into a wistful tune, heavy on the strings, that was familiar from the radio: the overture to *My Fair Lady*.

"Bastardized *Pygmalion* in musical-comedy drag," Michelson said.

William Henry decided that he did not much care for Michelson.

Across the room, he saw Jane and her friend raise their heads from the machine and smile at one another. And William Henry got the point of Michelson's earlier sneer.

For this party, Jane had chosen to wear a skin-tight Cheongsam dress of red-satin covered with Chinese embroidery in gold thread. The top had a high, round Mandarin collar and the narrow skirt had a slit that went all the way up to her hip. It was so tight and revealing that William Henry, who did not happen to see her put the thing on while they were dressing, now could not imagine what she might be wearing underneath. The skirt left no room for a girdle or garter belt, and the slit showed no top welt of a stocking on that side. So perhaps she was wearing nothing at all!

For the man she was standing next to—indeed, for every man in the room, even her husband after almost ten years of marriage—Jane in that red dress exerted a powerful influence. Pervasive as musk. Obvious as a mink.

William Henry went over to the pair by the stereo set, unavoidably trailing Michelson. When they got within earshot, Michelson said out loud to him, "*Pygmalion,* of course, is the story of how a brilliant man takes up with a totally unsuitable woman, thinking he can make something out of her that she can never be."

Jane looked at Michelson and gave a ladylike grunt, a clearing of her throat that started well below the diaphragm. "That's usually the goal of every woman who takes up with a man," she said aloud.

From nearby came appreciative laughter, all of it female, none of it male.

"Why don't you go away now," Jane said pointedly to Michelson, "and let me dance with my brilliant husband." She raised her arms to William Henry, and they stepped briefly through a tight circle to the reprise of the wistful tune.

Further into the evening, the music had stopped and the party settled into knots and clusters of serious conversation. The topic around them turned to *Explorer 1*, the rocket that the United States had sent into orbit just two weeks earlier, after several well publicized launching pad disasters. "*Sputnik* is still the first," someone said, referring to the Russian satellite from the previous October. "That was truly a fantastic scientific achievement."

"The product of a superior civilization," Fred Goerlich said smugly. It was well known on campus that the advances of Russian socialism and the shortfalls of western capitalism were his particular hobbyhorse.

"And look at how fast the Soviets developed nuclear technology," said a professor of sociology, one of the chairman's sycophants.

"They've gone from a backward, hierocratic culture to the pinnacle of modern physics in just over a generation," added another.

At William Henry's elbow, Jane made a soft raspberry. The learned professors turned to look at her. Jane said out loud: "Thugs."

"I beg your pardon?" from the first man.

"Okay, thugs with missiles that can now reach around the world," she replied. "Is that better?"

At the fringes of their circle, the room broke out in whispered side conversations: "Who is she? ... What impertinence! ... What's she saying?" The hiss of suppressed outrage caught William Henry's attention.

"Well," said the second man to the room at large, "the average Russian, the workers, are certainly better off under their Soviet form of democracy."

"Who's 'better off'?" Jane asked. "You mean with guns to their heads? Do you actually believe that the Russians build walls to keep the envious Europeans *out*? Ask the Hungarians about that!"

"My dear," Goerlich intervened, "some measures may be necessary—temporarily necessary—to overcome the recalcitrant elements in society."

"Then I guess 'recalcitrant' means people who don't want to be shipped off to Siberia?" Jane retorted, now confronting her host directly. "Stalin did that to whole populations, didn't he?"

"Stalin was a great leader," the first professor said. "He singlehandedly brought Russia into the twentieth century."

"A great butcher, you mean" Jane shot back. "Any part of the twentieth century the Soviets now have, Stalin's spies stole from us—either from us or the Germans. And that includes your precious atomic weapons and the rockets to deliver them with."

"Well, that was then," Goerlich said. "Stalin is dead now. And these new men, Bulganin and Khrushchev—"

"Thugs again," Jane replied. "Born into thugdom, apprenticed to thugs, successors to a thug, and practicing thuggery. What's to choose from? It's thugs all the way down the line."

Goerlich turned away, saying ironically to his audience, "How can I argue with logic like that?"

Half-amused and half-admiring, William Henry wondered what had made his wife so bold, to take on the chairman of the department and thrash him at his own party, surrounded by his academic minions. Could it be she'd had too much to drink? No, William Henry did not remember seeing more than two glasses of wine pass through her hands all evening.

And then he realized that Jane could speak so bravely because she was the freest person in the room. She had no ideological position to defend. Communism, socialism, capitalism were just words to her. But she could spot a fraud and a thug when she saw one. Moreover, she also had no position on the faculty to protect. These were people outside her and William Henry's sphere. What the wife of a junior professor of classics said or did had no resonance in the Sociology and Political Science Department. And if anyone did take offense, they would put it down to Jane's status as a certified ignoramus, a woman with only a high-school diploma, William Henry's beautiful but bumptious wife.

Later, having said their goodbyes to the host and hostess—admittedly with some trepidation on William Henry's part—as he was helping Jane with her coat, he leaned close to her ear. "You were feisty tonight," he whispered.

She turned to look at him over her shoulder. "You really think so?"

"I mean, the way you cut through their crap and all."

"Does that 'crap' pass for critical discourse on campus?"

He considered. "Well, yes … a lot of the time."

"You're in the wrong business, my man."

Much later, after paying off the babysitter and checking that Dani was soundly asleep, he took his wife into their bedroom and she showed him just how little she was wearing under that red dress. Jane was bolder, more imaginative—and more aggressive—than she had ever been in their lovemaking. William Henry was by turns fascinated, then enthralled, and finally just a bit intimidated.

It was only later, and upon reflection, that he was also starting to worry.

2. DANI'S DIARY

SATURDAY, FEBRUARY 15: Sometimes I wake up at night and hear sounds through the wall by my bed. They are Mommy and Daddy on the other side, in their bedroom. I know it's wrong to listen when people are talking in another room. Mommy says so. Mostly, I can't make out words, just voices. But I can tell when Mommy is crying. She doesn't cry with tears and sobs, because mommies never cry that way. But she makes moaning sounds out loud, like she is sad. Then all of a sudden she gives a big shout, like something surprised her. Or sometimes she gasps like she is being hurt. I asked Daddy one day, and he said no, she is not being hurt at all. But he said it really fast and seemed embarrassed about what's going on. And I know there's only Daddy in there with her when she cries. So ... is Daddy hurting her? Would he tell me if he was? I hope he's not doing anything bad to Mommy, because I love Mommy. I love Daddy, too.

3. THE SHOE THAT DID NOT FIT

IT WAS SOME kind of cruel joke, the way Jane figured it. After all these years of waiting, she was finally going to be inducted into the prestigious Faculty Wives Club. But could they just invite her to one of their meetings, give her a corsage or something, and show her the secret handshake? No. They wanted to throw an elaborate afternoon tea.

Or rather, they expected *Jane* to throw an afternoon tea.

For one hundred and thirty ladies.

In the Garden Room.

Well, at least she didn't have to buy all the tea, the cakes, and everything herself, because that was a pretty big group and her family was still on a tight budget. When Jane asked the FWC president, Lorraine Lombardy—who was also wife of the chairman of the Classics Department, wouldn't you know, and that was Willie's boss—about paying for the party, the woman had actually laughed out loud. "Oh, no, my dear! That's why we have a *kitty*. You just tell the cook, Mrs. Grayson, what you want her to serve and she'll see to everything. You don't go out of *pocket*. Dear me, no!"

So all Jane had to do was decide. That should have been easy enough. But when she called up this Grayson woman, a comfortable three days before the scheduled event, their conversation went like a chat with the idiot of a very slow village.

Jane began directly: "I would like to arrange a tea for the faculty wives on the afternoon of the twenty-sixth."

"I'll have to see if the club facilities are available that day," said a gruff voice.

"It's the regular meeting," Jane replied. "Mrs. Lombardy said—"

"Lombardy don't run the club," the woman replied.

"Then can you tell me who does?"

"I do," was the answer.

"Ah! And is the Garden Room going to be open that day?"

"I'll have to check." In the background Jane heard a *plop!* She imagined a heavy ledger hitting a countertop. "Nope," the voice said eventually. "Not available. The Faculty Wives Club has a meeting that afternoon."

"I know," Jane said under tight control. "And Mrs. Lombardy asked me to arrange tea. For the members. In the Garden Room. She said you would help."

"Well, why didn't you *say* so?"

"I thought I just did."

"Not to me."

Jane decided this whole thing had to be done in person, so she could make eye contact, or slip the woman a sawbuck, or brain her with a heavy spoon, or something. They agreed to meet at ten the following morning to work on the details.

But when Jane walked up to the huge, paneled, black-painted outer door of the Faculty Club—the *Wives* part was just the social auxiliary—she suddenly felt more than a little intimidated. The club occupied what used to be a private mansion on a side street just off campus. Behind a broad lawn with impeccable shrubbery under its mantle of snow, the building rose an imposing two stories in blocks of gray sandstone decorated with fluted columns, dentil moldings, fanlights, gables, and Grecian urns: architecture that Lorraine Lombardy proudly reminded everyone was "the Palladian style." Years of the university's proceedings in eminent domain had gobbled up the surrounding properties, until the mansion was now flanked on one corner by a classroom building cast in concrete during the federal public works boom of the thirties, and on the other by a modern brick women's dormitory that had opened just three years ago.

Jane was dying for a cigarette to calm her nerves, but they were a vice she had only recently discovered and still kept secret, even from her family. When she felt herself becoming too pressed or stressed, she would take her pack of cigarettes out of hiding and go for a walk in the woods around the cottage. Afterward she would wash her hands and, if necessary, change her clothes because of the smell. If she now entered Mrs. Grayson's kitchen carrying the fume of tobacco about her person, Jane believed she would be giving this complete stranger access to one of her deepest secrets—and so a kind of leverage to use against her.

In the kitchen, the size of everything took Jane's breath away. The gas range had about twenty burners and a griddle bigger than the top of her own stove at home. The smallest pot she could see looked to hold about twenty gallons. And there wasn't a fist-sized paring knife in sight, just a rack of cleavers suitable for butchering a cow and a circular contraption for slicing cold cuts that would take your hand off at the wrist.

Mrs. Grayson was in her sixties, shaped like a frog and looked like one, in her mint-green uniform with the frilled white apron, and with eyes that seemed to bulge sideways out of her head. But now she was all smiles and cheerfulness, greeting Jane like a sister and offering her a cup of coffee and a piece of fresh cinnamon cake.

"Oh, yes," she said with a laugh. "They always make the new members arrange their own teas. It's like a rite of passage. But don't worry, you'll do *fine.*"

The two of them quickly settled on the main item: a choice of Earl Grey tea—Mrs. Lombardy's favorite—and the regular China black "for those who don't care for scented teas," Grayson said. Jane suspected she was among the latter.

"I'll make my famous scones," Grayson said. "They're everyone's favorite. And *petits fours* always go over well. Now, were you thinking of a high tea at all?"

Jane smiled and waved broadly. "Of course!"

"So you'll be wanting sandwiches, too. Water cress, cucumber and brie, and some of that thin-sliced Polish ham—for spice. I know just what ladies like to eat." Grayson paused. "Now, do you want me to cut off the crusts, ma'am?"

"Um …" The question was one Jane would never have considered. Dani used to be finicky about her sandwiches, no crusts, always wanting them cut clean off—but only back when she was a toddler. "Oh, I don't think so," Jane said. "These are grown women, after all. They can deal with the crusts."

"Whatever you say, Mrs. Wheelock," Grayson replied with a smile.

On the day of the event, Jane dressed conservatively in a charcoal-gray wool skirt that didn't have too much flare, a sweater twinset in a delicate French gray that hovered on the border of the visible spectrum between gray and pale green, and the string of natural pearls that William Henry had brought back from Japan at the end of his last tour of duty.

She arrived at the Faculty Club at three-thirty in the afternoon, half an hour early, and walked past a signboard in the lobby announcing the tea in her honor. She left her winter coat and scarf in the cloakroom and went on to the kitchen. There she found Mrs. Grayson with flour on her apron and elbows, probably from working the dough for her scones. The cook was standing before a lineup of young college women in matching green uniforms, giving them final instructions on the serving.

"How is everything going?" Jane asked when Grayson came to a stopping point.

"Oh, ma'am, ever so well," the cook said. "You just go on in."

In the Garden Room, she found a number of the members already in attendance, including Mrs. Lombardy. The club president came over to Jane immediately.

"Ah, my dear! So delightful! How *did* you get Grayson to make her scones? She will never make them for *me*. You must have the *touch*."

Jane smiled and murmured something inconsequential.

"Now there are some people you absolutely must meet," Lombardy went on, taking her by the elbow toward a group of women. And so Jane was introduced, one by one, to more than a dozen different women whom she had known, if at all, only from Willie's occasional mention of their husbands' names.

The scones were a great success, with many compliments to Jane. And her choice of teas was praised extravagantly. But when those college girls carried the trays of sandwiches around the room, the assembled faculty wives fell silent. After much inspection and choosing, only two of the wives accepted a sandwich onto their plates. The rest refused with polite but forced smiles. Jane saw one of the women who had taken a sandwich start to pinch the crust off with her fingernails, as if she were peeling a boiled shrimp. The wife in the chair next to her glanced over and shook her head the tiniest bit, and the woman dropped the sandwich.

Mrs. Lombardy looked left and right, to gather in every eye. And then she gave a great and knowing smile. "*Froo-stah eh-yam froos-traht*," she pronounced solemnly.

Several of the women tee-heed at this.

Jane put down her cup, clinking into the void. "What's that about fruit?"

The women who had tittered now laughed quietly.

"It's Latin, my dear," Lombardy explained. "I said *frusta*, the crusts, nominative plural, have frustrated you, from *frustrari*, the irregular infinitive."

Infinitely irregular, that was what this snooty woman was saying about Jane. The whole thing, this tea party, everything, had been a setup, from the beginning, from Grayson's question about crusts as they planned the menu to Lombardy's quotation now—worked out ahead of time no doubt, and in Latin no less. They had all set out to ridicule her. Jane could see how she had been caught, cleaned, and cooked. Well, it was too late to back out gracefully. Still, there was no sense in taking any of this lying down.

"Are you saying I'm frustrated?" Jane demanded.

"If the shoe fits ..." Lombardy began less than graciously.

"I'm sorry you don't like the crusts," she said loudly, turning to address the room at large. "Neither did my daughter—when she was about four years old! But if that's what's keeping you from eating, then I'd say *you* were the ones who were frustrated."

It sounded weak, even to her own ears, but Jane was beyond caring.

Still, the room went dead quiet. No one, apparently, had ever challenged Lorraine Lombardy on her own turf before. Half the eyes were fixed on Jane, almost fearfully, the other half on the club president, begging her to rescue the situation.

Mrs. Lombardy opened her mouth.

Jane held up her wrist and looked at her watch. "My goodness! Is that the time?" She stood up, balled her napkin and dropped it on her chair, and collected her purse from the floor underneath. "Don't get up," she urged the assembled ladies. "I've had *such* a lovely time."

And then Jane beat a graceful, unhurried retreat to the front hall, the cloakroom where she gathered her coat and scarf, and on to the huge outer door of the old mansion. Unfortunately, the door was too large and well balanced to slam effectively. So Jane just let it shut quietly on her career as a would-be Faculty Wife.

4. BRUISED FRUIT

WILLIAM HENRY WAS in his study at home, working on an article he hoped to publish about naval warfare in the ancient world, sticking his professional oar—figuratively speaking, that is—into the controversy about the quinquireme. In the Greek and Roman texts that survived to the modern age, all the authors presumed their reader's familiarity with ship design and the mechanics of rowing. It was commonly accepted by modern scholars that the Greek trireme had three banks of oars, placed one atop the other, although no one had ever discovered an intact warship, and everyone was working from pictures painted on vases, carved into bas reliefs, and such.

When the inevitable arms race set in, however, with heavier rams and thicker armor, new ship designs required more rowing power, and the quinquireme was born—mostly used by the later Romans. But no one among modern classicists could quite say how five banks of oars might work. So the notion arose that the "five" must refer to the number of rowers per oar, rather than the number of banks. And the more dogmatic among them applied this reasoning backward, to argue that therefore the Greek trireme must also have had, not three banks, but three rowers to an oar in a single bank.

Now, marshalling references from Thucydides, Herodotus, and Diodorus, William Henry was preparing to wade in. He had been fascinated by ancient navies and tactics since first reading about the Battle of Salamis as an undergraduate. The notion of these long, lithe boats, made of light pine and white fir, dashing about in tight formation, armed with striated beaks of stout bronze and guided by huge painted eyes, made his blood race. He once thought that, if he had not joined the army in the Second World War, he might have been happier in the navy, perhaps commanding a torpedo boat or even, one day, a destroyer.

William Henry was just coming to the point of his article when the front door of the cottage slammed. He supposed that Jane was home, bearing the fruits of victory from her first tea as an official Faculty Wife. A glance at his desk clock, however, showed it was not quite four-thirty—too early for her to be returning from a social triumph.

The door of his study burst open. Without pausing to knock, Jane stormed in, red faced from the cold, still wearing her coat and carrying her purse.

"It was a setup!" she rasped. "Start to finish!" She flung her hands in the air, suddenly noticed the purse dangling by its strap from her forearm, and slung it onto the sofa in rage. "They were all out to get me and—oh!—they got me good!"

"Whoa, Jane!" he said, perplexed. "Who was it got you?"

She glared at him, panting heavily. William Henry guessed she had run all the way back from the Faculty Club. "The wives. Your precious faculty. The *ladies!* It was a duck hunt—and I was the duck!"

"Now, look," he said reasonably. "I'm sure they didn't mean to be—"

"Don't you tell me what they did!" she exclaimed. "You weren't there!"

"Well, then ... what happened?"

"They wanted those fussy little green sandwiches, and the cook asked me if she should take off the crusts. She had everything else worked out, the whole menu, down to the choice of tea, but she had to ask *me* about the crusts. And I said no, of course not, because only little kids are squeamish about crusts. So when they bring out the sandwiches, everyone starts picking at the crusts, like the sight of 'em just makes these women sick. And then that snotty Lorraine Lombardy makes a joke in Latin at my expense. Just to ridicule me. And everyone gets to laugh. Like they all know Latin. It was a setup, and everyone was in on it. Just to humiliate me!"

"Jane," he began. "Why don't you sit down?"

She dropped into the chair in front of his desk, then popped right back up. "I'm too angry to sit down."

"You might be less angry if you tried to relax."

"Are you telling me what to feel?"

"Not at all. It's just …"

William Henry knew he should have seen this coming. Jane was an unpredictable commodity in any polite social situation. He could remember an incident at their wedding reception, as they were unwrapping a gift of silver service, settings for twelve in Damask Rose by Oneida, from his mother and father. Jane had at first exclaimed over the many pieces, dazzled by the luster of the metal and the intricate floral pattern of the handles. But within two minutes she was making fun of the demitasse spoons, as being too small to eat with. Then she pretended to jab William Henry's side with the wide, blunted blade of a fish knife, asking what it was good for, having neither a point nor a sharp edge.

He understood that Jane had not been brought up as he had—under the Judge's stern precepts and Libby's gentle hand. Jane's values were good, of course. Her sense of right and wrong was strong. She was a decent person. But she did lack an appreciation for the finer things. She was inclined to make fun of anyone having too many spoons and to believe that sandwich crusts were an issue only for children.

"I think you may have to apologize to Lorraine Lombardy," he said quietly.

"What!" She stared at him—glared, actually. "Never!"

"Clearly, there's been a misunderstanding. If you could patch things up—"

"No, you don't understand." Jane took a deep breath. "They don't like me. They know I'm lower class. But instead of just letting me go on about my business, they had to bring me in and humiliate me. They made a point of it. It was malicious."

He sighed. "Do you really think they care that much about you?"

This thought seemed to catch Jane off guard. Obviously, it had not occurred to her that she might not be the center of their attention. "But … it was a tea in my honor!"

"And would they do that in order to humiliate you?"

"To show how much they didn't want me."

"That sounds pretty complicated."

"But …" Jane slumped into the chair, visibly wilting, and withdrew her chin into the collar of her coat. "You don't understand at all. You're just taking their side."

"I know you feel vulnerable, darling. And you don't like it. But these people are important to our life here. A university is like a village. You have to make peace with the people around you. These women have, for some reason, made you miserable. But you can be a good sport about it, show them you don't care—"

"Oh, I showed them that already."

He could imagine how she showed it, too. Jane was nothing if not inventive.

"Yes, I'm sure you did," he went on. "But now you have to be nice and pretend that nothing happened."

"Hah! … Why?"

Someday there might come a time for him to lecture Jane about exhibiting grace under pressure, but he could sense today was not that day. "If not for yourself, please, just do it for me. It's important to my career."

"Your career," she repeated dully. "I see, it's on your account."

"Then because I ask you? Because I love you?"

"Well, when you put it like that …"

"Thank you," he said gently.

5. Dani's Diary

Tuesday, March 4: Today there was a funny smell in our house. It was nasty and stinky, like burning leaves after they get raked up in the fall when the undersides are all wet. Only this smell was indoors. And it's not fall. When I asked Mommy about it, she just waved her hand in front of her face and said I was imagining things. Then she told me to go up to my room for telling lies. And that's *totally* unfair! Because I did smell it. It was stinky and awful. Like burning garbage. I think she smelled it, too. But she was afraid to talk about it.

6. Every Word a Lie

Only because Willie wanted it, Jane eventually called Lorraine Lombardy and invited her to lunch at the Continental Arms in order to make peace. The restaurant was in a half-timbered, colonial-style inn on the edge of town, whose décor included polished copper pots and pitchers, flintlock rifles hanging with their buckskin pouches and powder horns, suitably blackened with age, and windows with panes of genuine bull's-eye leaded glass. All that, and planters filled with spidery jungle foliage that might have been ferns. The man behind the solid-oak bar served a monstrous martini in a two-handed crystal goblet with a skewer of pickled Brussels sprouts instead of an olive.

Jane was working on her second martini when Lombardy came through the door.

"Yoo-hoo!" Jane whooped and waved at the older woman.

Lombardy smiled uncertainly and came over.

"I got us a table," Jane said.

"How nice, my dear."

"It's over here."

Jane slid off her stool, secured her drink, remembered to pick up the little paper napkin from underneath it, and made her way across the dining room on an intercept course with the maitre d'. She let the man seat Lombardy and pulled out her own chair. She took another sip from the goblet before sitting down.

"Mmm, that looks good," Lombardy said. "May I have one?"

"Certainly, madam," the maitre d' replied suavely.

Jane decided she could get to like the old gal.

As they opened their menus, Jane determined to plunge right in. "Look, about the tea party, and what happened, I just want to say—"

"Did something happen?" Lombardy asked brightly. "I don't remember—"

"The sandwiches," Jane pressed onward. "With the crusts—"

"Oh, yes. Grayson left them on, didn't she?"

"Only because I told her to."

"Did you?" Lombardy affected to show surprise. "That wasn't very clever."

Jane suddenly remembered why she didn't like this woman.

"She asked me specifically about them," Jane said.

"Well, she shouldn't have. Grayson knows how to make tea sandwiches."

Jane was confused. "So you're saying ... it wasn't ... a test?"

"A test? Good heavens! Of what?"

"My social skills."

"But every social encounter is a test of skill, my dear," Lombardy said smoothly. "It is by the social graces that we separate ourselves from the beasts, gnawing on their bones and growling to warn each other away."

"Oh?" Jane felt the blood rushing to her head.

"Of course. The Japanese make a religious ritual of tea. While, for us westerners, there is a special, human grace in knowing how to fold and hold your napkin, which spoon to use, and whether and when to dip it in the sugar bowl. And, yes, there is ritual in having your sandwiches pressed thin, cut into dainty squares no larger than a single bite, and rendered crustless. That is how we social animals recognize and honor each other—and how we keep out the beasts."

Jane sighed. "By which you mean me, I guess."

She sensed that she was truly lost.

"Oh, no! Not at all."

"But I—"

"You handled yourself very well at the party. Indeed, with great poise. I myself was being a pest, both condescending and rude—I freely acknowledge that—while you responded with grace, even with a sense of humor. That certainly made an impression on the other members. In fact, I accepted your invitation today in order to have a chance to apologize."

"You're apologizing to *me*?"

"Yes, my dear."

"That's really very ... kind."

"Oh, but I do have an ulterior motive. I want you on the Planning Committee for our annual Spring Fling. It's a little charity thing we do: part spring cleaning, part benefit auction, and always loads of fun, I promise you. I want that great organizational head of yours working on it this year. Do say you'll help out."

"Well ... yes, of course."

"There! I knew you would."

Jane picked up her menu, more to hide her thoughts than anything.

A waiter brought the martini goblet for Lombardy and she hefted it immediately. "I really do need this. You have no idea how much I was dreading this meeting."

Jane looked her in the eye. "Me, too."

But inside she was seething. By being first to apologize, Lombardy had taken the upper hand completely. Sneaky old bitch! Now Jane was at a disadvantage all over again. And working on this Spring Thing would get her in even deeper with the faculty wives, offering her ten thousand new ways to lose face again. It was all a plot to put Jane in her place.

Damn it!

7. SUPERMAN'S DOWNFALL

BILLY CHARDON WAS in Dani's fourth-grade class at school. Everybody—or all the girls, anyway—said he was a nerd, with those black-rimmed glasses, those plaid shirts, and carrying all those books home every night. But when Billy sat up straight, and that little curl of black-black hair fell over his pale forehead, and the sunlight hit him just right, Dani thought she could see a resemblance to Clark Kent. And everybody knew what that meant.

Not that she was going to do anything about it, of course, because Billy pretty much ignored her. The way all the boys ignored all the girls, even when the girls wished they wouldn't. It was so frustrating, knowing this secret about Billy Chardon, and still having him treat her like she was a poison rock from Planet Krypton. Or worse, from Planet Nowhere.

One day toward the end of March, with the days getting warmer and the snow going slushy on the ground, everyone was feeling, well … itchy. On that day Dani had decided to do something about Billy Chardon.

And then, as if she planned it, Superman went running right past where Dani was standing. They were at the edge of the playing field, where the weeks-old snow was particularly rotten and the mud was coming out in patches. Billy was running blind, full out, head turned back over his shoulder, looking into the sky for a ball or something. Dani's leg, just kind of on its own, came up from the ground and got caught in front of his shins. She didn't actually kick him. It was more like a nudge. Just a tap.

Billy let out a yell and went face down in the wet snow. He fell so fast and so hard there wasn't time to break the fall with his hands. More like with his nose. The crusty surface blasted away in all directions, revealing a rich, dark mud. Billy flew across it like a base runner sliding home.

When he stopped skidding, he lay there a moment, then stood up. His whole front, his chin, his unzipped corduroy jacket, his flannel shirt underneath, and his khaki pants to the knees were slicked down with black mud. Dani thought he would start to bawl, but he only looked puzzled. Then he found his glasses, five feet beyond in the unbroken snow, and put them on. It was as if only the glasses let him see how messed up he really was.

"Crap!" he muttered.

Then louder, "Boogers!"

"God damn it!" he shouted.

Suddenly he looked around. Not so he could find out who had kicked him—because, wouldn't you know, he didn't even realize he had *been* kicked—but to see if anyone had noticed his fall. He saw Dani looking at him and scowled at her.

She shrugged and turned away.

She was still from Planet Nowhere.

8. Things That Go Bump
in the Afternoon

Jane had heard it said that old houses speak to you. Privately she supposed the great house where Willie grew up in Roulette had a whole encyclopedia to recite. But the cottage in the woods where they lived now—maybe a pamphlet or a handbill. And so, one afternoon in March, as Jane was resting with her feet up in the living room, with a magazine across her lap, although she wasn't really reading, with a forbidden cigarette held between her fingers, although she hadn't taken a drag in the last five minutes, the house did speak.

Of course, after half a dozen years, Jane knew all its natural sounds. She knew the click and thump the furnace made when it started up in the basement. She knew the tick-tick the refrigerator gave when the compressor first came on. That had been a hard one to figure out, until she asked Willie about it one day. And there were the various creaks and groans from the floorboards— more creaks from upstairs, more groans from the ground floor— as her small family moved around in the house. And the stairway had its own percussion section: kettle drums when Willie went up and down, snare drums for Dani.

But this was a different voice. This was not a click or a tick, a boom or a thud. This was a wood wind. It started as a sigh. A sigh with a little hum at the end, like her mother used to make when passing judgment without actually saying anything.

Jane lifted her head. "What?"

But there was no answer.

She sat still, listening.

Click-whump, and the furnace started up. After a moment Jane could feel the warm breeze from the register by the dining room door. But that wasn't it—not the source of the sigh.

In the sudden cocoon of silence created by the air coming from the register, Jane listened for the sound again. The ash on her cigarette grew long and gray, wobbled in the draft, and fell off on the carpet. Still, she did not move.

Nothing ... nothing.
And then, from somewhere, an indrawn breath.
Jane waited.
Her mother's voice said, very distinctly, "Fish knives."

9. Beyond Her Control

Dani was daydreaming, barely aware of her surroundings, when her fourth-grade teacher, Miss Shelby, called out the names of students to come up to the blackboard and solve the arithmetic problems she'd written there. Dani certainly did not hear Billy Chardon's name called—but she could feel his presence as he came up the aisle behind her, even though Dani's desk was at the front and she wasn't looking for his reflection in the classroom window or anything. He was just *there*. She could feel him coming like a heat at the back of her head, growing warmer and brighter and redder, as if she was backing up to a hot stove.

When the pressure was too great, Dani turned in her seat, and her leg shot out from the opening at the side of her desk. The meat of her calf crossed the sharp bone of Billy's shin, and that hurt a bit. But it hurt him more.

Billy Chardon was flung forward as if kicked from behind. His face collided with the front panel of the teacher's desk, and his glasses flew off in two different directions, broken across the bridge of his nose. Billy rebounded from the desk and rolled onto his side on the floor. His hands went up to his face, and blood came out from between his fingers.

If he had been badly hurt, he would have stayed down. That was what Dani figured. But no, he popped up like a cartoon character. He stared at the blood on his hands and then balled them into fists. He looked around for the source of his trouble, and right away he found Dani.

She smiled at him. That's what you were supposed to do, her mother always said, to make people like you—smile at them. But smiling at Billy Chardon only made things worse, because it only made him madder.

He reached across the top of Dani's desk, grabbed her white blouse in one bloody fist, and yanked her halfway out of her seat. Before she could duck, his huge right hand came up fast and hit her in the face. The blow landed across the left side of her face, catching on the eyebrow above and the cheekbone below her eye.

Dani saw stars and fell back, missed her seat, and ended up sitting on the floor.

From the other side of the room, Miss Shelby moved faster than Dani would have believed possible. Almost before she was on the ground, and with Billy still coming after her, the teacher appeared behind him, grabbed his arms, and swung him away, lowering him onto his knees in the empty space at the front of the classroom. Then, when Billy was under control again, Miss Shelby turned him around, took his face in her hands, and assessed the damage to his nose.

"Rebecca!" she called to the girl standing closest to the door.

"Becky!" she repeated when the girl didn't move.

"What, Miss Shelby?" Becky quavered.

"Go and get the school nurse. Bring her back here, no matter what she tells you to do. The rest of you"—this was to the students standing by the board—"return to your places." Then Miss Shelby turned and looked directly down at Dani. "And you, Danielle Wheelock, you get back in your seat and don't move. I saw *exactly* what you did."

"But I didn't—!" Dani began hotly. Her eye was beginning to throb.

"Be quiet! You're in enough trouble as it is."

10. A NOTE FROM SCHOOL

WHEN WILLIAM HENRY came home after holding office hours on campus that afternoon, he found his wife in the living room, sitting in the wing chair that he normally thought of as his own. Jane had her arms crossed so tightly they were practically wrapped around her body. She only unclenched long enough to bring a lit cigarette out of the space near her armpit, take a long drag, and return the glowing butt to its hiding place. He only hoped the upholstery would not catch on fire. He decided not to comment on the fact that, from anything he could smell—aside from the acrid stench of cigarette smoke—there was no sign of dinner in the offing.

"Hi there," he said, sounding as cheerful as possible.

"Hello," she replied stonily, not looking up at him.

"I didn't know you had taken up smoking."

"It calms me. It helps to soothe my nerves."

"I see. And what is making you nervous?"

"Ah! We come to the question now, don't we?"

"Why are you being so mysterious?" he asked. "What's going on?"

Jane made eye contact with him for the first time. There was a gleam in her eyes that he found distinctly unsettling. "Nothing," she said. "Except that our daughter turns out to be a cold-blooded killer."

"What?" He was taken aback. "Who says so? What happened?"

"The school people," Jane said, suddenly sounding tired. "The principal sent Dani home with a note three hours ago."

"Well, what did she do?"

"Does that matter?"

"Of course!"

"Humph!"

"Jane!"

"All right! They say Dani—in front of the whole class, mind you, and with the teacher watching—tripped a boy, hard enough that he fell into the teacher's desk. She hurt him bad enough to

53

need a dozen stitches, maybe even gave him a concussion. And they say all this was—here I'm quoting—'an intentional action, meant to cause bodily harm.' "

"Oh my!" was all William Henry could think to reply. "Where is Dani now?"

"Upstairs. In her room." Jane sighed. "I sent her there as punishment."

"What does she have to say about the incident?"

"Nothing. Not her fault. Doesn't know what they're talking about."

William Henry went to the foot of the stairs and called, "Dani!"

Muffled, from behind her door, at great distance, "What?"

"Would you please come down here?" he said.

A pause, which stretched on in silence.

"Right now," he said more sternly.

He heard footsteps and a door slamming. His daughter stood in the shadows at the top of the stairs. Then she descended into the ruddy, late-afternoon light coming through the living room's west-facing windows. William Henry could immediately see something was wrong. Dani held something grayish—a wet towel—to her left eye. She stopped in front of him, staring up with her good eye. Her normally pretty mouth trembled on the edge of strong emotion—maybe tears but also, possibly, rage.

"Let me see your face," he said gently.

She took away the cloth to reveal a shiner, a real doozy, more purple than black. It went all the way around, from the bridge of her nose, up to her eyebrow, down through the socket, and deep into her cheekbone. The white of her eyeball had flecks of blood like garnets around the iris.

"Who did this to you?" he demanded.

"Billy Chardon."

"Who is that?"

From across the room Jane answered: "The boy they say she assaulted."

William Henry turned. "He struck our daughter in the face?"

"Well, exactly!" his wife flared. "Dani's got the black eye. How can they blame her for all this? It doesn't make sense!"

William Henry tried to remain calm, think the matter through. "Perhaps the boy thought he had provocation," he said.

"Oh! Right! You take the man's side!" Jane huffed.

"When did Billy hit you?" he asked Dani quietly.

"I really don't remember," she said evasively.

"Well, was it before or after he fell down?"

"Umm ..." Dani looked guilty. "After."

"Why did he fall? Did you trip him?"

"I *didn't,*" Dani insisted. "He fell."

"And is that the truth?" he asked. "You so swear?"

She hesitated fractionally and nodded. "I swear."

"You know what happens to people who perjure themselves?"

Behind him, Jane cried out, "Look at her, for God's sake! *She* has the black eye. That proves she's innocent."

"I would think it proves rather the opposite," William Henry said quietly, almost to himself. "In any event"—he turned to address his wife—"if the boy could apparently strike back like this, he was not actually killed. Or even rendered unconscious."

"The principal's story is confused," Jane agreed, taking a drag on her cigarette.

"Still, what are we going to do about all this?"

"I've already punished her," Jane said dismissively.

"You sent her to her room. Do you think that is sufficient?"

"I don't know, you can beat her if you want to. I guess Billy's black eye made a pretty good impression on her."

"But don't you think—"

"Do whatever you want, Willie!" Jane shouted. She stubbed out the cigarette and stood up quickly. "I'm sick of this whole conversation. I'm going to bed." She pushed past them at the foot of the stairs and went up. A moment later, another door slammed.

William Henry looked down at his daughter.

"I really didn't trip Billy on purpose," she said.

He wasn't so sure about that, being well able to imagine the confused urges of a prepubescent girl, at least where boys were concerned. "I know you didn't—at least not on purpose," he said. "Let's see what we can do about dinner, shall we?"

11. Fear and Loathing

Up in the bedroom, Jane tossed her pack of cigarettes onto the nightstand, arranged her pillows against the headboard, and lay down without taking her shoes off. She stretched out on her back, arms straight at her sides, like a soldier at attention. She stared up at the dim outline of shadows on the ceiling.

After a minute of lying quietly, when nothing up there could help sort out her feelings, Jane pulled herself up into more of a sitting position and stared across the room at the wall.

After another minute, when she found herself becoming really agitated, Jane reached over for the pack, shook out a cigarette, and struck a match.

In the brief flare of yellow light and the biting smell of sulfur, something moved in the room.

"You can't control her, can you?" said a familiar voice.

Go away, Jane pleaded silently.

"Whatever made you think you could be a mother?"

I don't know. Please go away.

"But then ... Dani's just a bad seed, isn't she?"

Takes one to know one, Mother.

"Sticks and stones, darling," Margot said.

You know she's only a little girl.

"But you never attacked a classmate."

I don't know ... if he was cute ...

"You never had that kind of guts."

No, I was always too scared.

"Too prissy and proper, missy."

Whatever you say, Mother.

"Good night then, darling."

12. Dani's Diary

Thursday, April 3: My mother is getting so weird! Like that thing at school, with Billy Chardon. Okay, I goofed up. I know that now, because Dad and I had a talk about it after dinner. He said sometimes people get feelings—impulses, he called them—and they are sometimes the right thing to do but mostly not. And my wanting to see Billy fall flat on his face and get mad about it was a *bad impulse*. Okay, I get it. I shouldn't have done that thing with my foot. But still, Dad was very nice about it.

Mother doesn't act that way at all. As soon as she saw the note from the principal, she got angry. Not disappointed angry, like when my report card has a C, or impatient angry, when the table isn't set by dinnertime. The note made her plain furious—as mad as Billy was, right before he hit me. Her face got all red and puffy. She put her hands on my shoulders and dug her nails into me hard. But I don't think it was me she was mad at. She said something under her breath that sounded like "foggers." Maybe it was "fathers."

And then, last night after we had all gone to bed, I heard her in the bathroom. She had the light off, because I couldn't see the bright line under the door. It sounded like she was crying in there. I did the bad thing, and she's the one crying about it. That's just weird!

13. Spring Fling

JANE HAD CHOSEN the clothes she would donate to the Spring Fling with great care: nothing too old, nothing threadbare, nothing that looked like she didn't want it anymore. Three blouses, one with a nice bow and ruffles. A cream-colored wool suit with black trim that only a fashion expert could tell wasn't a real Chanel. And a cocktail dress in dark green taffeta that she had brought back from the dry cleaners just the day before the sorting party at Melissa Bogosian's house.

When Jane showed up with her clothes hung neatly on hangers in a garment bag, Missy herself met her at the door and led the way into the living room, where the others were already gathered.

"Why, dear, don't you look nice!" Missy cooed, smiling around at everyone.

Jane had paid special attention to her own personal appearance that day, wearing her best suit, pastel linen the color of sunrise, one step below Easter Sunday church quality, with a white silk blouse and a favorite scarf covered in tiny pink-and-yellow tea roses. But something in Missy's manner when she gave the compliment made Jane pause: too enthusiastic, too bright-eyed, too many teeth in that smile. What she was really saying was that the linen had wrinkled at the elbows and across Jane's lap from the drive over. Or maybe Missy's gimlet eyes had spotted a stain that Jane had missed. Something was wrong. And this woman, by being so sweet about it, was inviting the whole room to notice the fact.

Nothing Jane could do but be sweet in return. "Don't we all?" she replied. And she gave a big smile around the room, the same way Missy had.

One of the women came forward to take the garment bag from her.

"Why don't you help with the sorting, dear?" Missy said, taking Jane by the arm across the hall and into the dining room. There the table and chairs were piled with skirts, sweaters, and blouses in no particular order. "The first thing to do is separate things we can sell directly from those that need some mending or cleaning."

Jane saw immediately that the two women already at work here were among the lowliest members of the Faculty Wives Club. But she could hardly refuse on grounds of status. "Of course," she answered, smiling at the two. "Sell, mend, or clean. Gotcha!"

For half an hour she inspected other women's cast-off garments. It was a solitary process: one by one unfold, check front and back for stains and spots, sniff the collar from a ladylike distance for tell-tale odors, pull at the seams and hems for hidden rips and tears, and then refold and place in one pile or another. The job required no discussion, and so the three drudges in the dining room got to overhear the running commentary, exclamations, and laughter from the living room. There, Jane presumed, her betters were dealing with clothing that had already passed as saleable.

"She's always trying too hard, if you ask me," someone said.

"I remember when she wore that two years ago."

"Not quite an afternoon dress, is it?"

"Too dreary for cocktails."

"*Brown* taffeta?"

A rippling laugh.

"Is this a *Chanel?*"

Suddenly Jane's ears pricked up.

"If it's a real Chanel, we can get a bundle for it."

There was a breathless silence in the other room.

Then, "It's not Chanel."

"Oh, yeah, the label."

"Not even close."

Another laugh.

Jane dropped the article she was holding. They were talking about the clothes *she* had brought. They were making fun of her best cream-colored suit. They were laughing at her. Clenching her fists, Jane ran across into the living room, ready to give them all a piece of her mind.

Missy was holding up a bright silk scarf, the white patch of its label still caught between her fingertips. The scarf had the right colors, the unerring simplicity of style, so that it might certainly have come from Chanel.

"Yes?" Missy asked, looking over at Jane.

"Um," Jane said inanely. "We're about half done in there."

"Good to hear it. You're not being too critical, I hope?"

"Oh, no. Lots of good merchandise. Lots of keepers."

"Excellent, dear."

Jane retreated in confusion. One of the other women still at the sorting gave her a sympathetic look.

But they *could* have been talking about Jane's cream-colored suit. Between the time everyone had laughed and the time Jane made it into the living room, Missy might easily have set her suit aside and picked up the scarf. In fact, if she heard Jane coming, that's exactly what she would have done. And pulled out the scarf's label like that, just to cover her tracks and confuse Jane.

They were still laughing at her.

They would always be laughing at her.

Everything Jane did would be a joke to them.

It was intolerable.

"I can't stay," Jane said aloud.

"What, dear?" said one of her fellow drudges.

"I really have to go."

"But you said yourself, we're only half done."

"You two can finish up."

"It goes much faster when there's three of us."

"Yeah, well, now there are two."

Thankful she had brought neither coat nor hat that had to be retrieved, Jane made her escape through the connecting hall and out the front door before anyone in the living room could call out and stop her. The first clue they had was Jane's slamming the heavy door behind her, so hard that it rattled windows across the whole front of the house.

14. THE STALKER

"Now, here's a thing," William Henry's wife said, rattling her part of the paper over the breakfast table. He looked up from the section he was reading—the world news and an analysis of the Russian and U.S. space probes to date: two *Sputniks*, an *Explorer,* and a *Vanguard*—and saw that Jane was holding the pages covering local affairs and social issues. "What is it, my dear?"

"This reporter has done a study of housewives," Jane said. "He followed them around, in fact. From home to school and drop off the children. Then home to grocery store and do the shopping. Store to beauty parlor and then more shopping. And so on ... Hmm, no one stops at the library, he says."

"Is it some kind of time-and-motion study?"

"No, he just follows them. Doesn't talk to them, apparently, because none of them has anything to say. Or nothing worth saying, is what he means."

"What is the argument of the story?"

"That's just it! No one says *anything.*"

"No, I mean, what is this man's point?"

"That housewives are boring," Jane said.

"I don't think that's generally true."

"You're obviously not a housewife."

"But your life isn't boring—is it?"

"Not always. Just most of the time."

"You have Dani to play with," he said cautiously.

"She's a little girl. And most of the day she's in school."

"And when she gets home, you talk to her, read to her ..."

"She has her own friends. She doesn't want Mother around."

"Well then, you have *your* own friends. The Faculty Wives Club."

"Oh," Jane said. "Them."

"Is there something wrong?"

"I've stopped going, is all."

"But I thought you liked them."

"Willie, really, it's all right."

"No, I mean, it's important to me—" he began.

"To your job?" she asked scornfully. "To your standing on campus?"

"No, that you have company, and things to do, some purpose in—"

"Some purpose in my life? Like a rummage sale? Please! ... Really!"

"They do it as a benefit, to help other people."

"They keep most of the money themselves, you know," Jane said. "None of it really goes to charity. It's all hypocrisy with them."

"I didn't know that. I'd always understood—"

"There's a lot you don't understand, Willie."

To show that the conversation was closed, Jane raised the newspaper in front of her face. She sat in silence, but he could see the pages tremble with the tension in her hands. His wife was really upset.

Then, after a moment of silent reading, she let out a squawk.

"What is it?" William Henry asked quietly.

"The bastard was following *me!*"

"Who was?" he asked, confused.

"The reporter in this housewife story!" She thrust the paper at him.

"No, really? Did you see him? Did he bother you?"

"No, I didn't *see* him. They're too clever for that. They hide in the bushes with their cameras and microphones. They keep just beyond the edge of your sight. But I've caught glimpses."

"I think you're imagining things."

"Oh, am I? The evidence is all down here in black and white. Tuesday I was at the A&P, and then I went to the Sterling Dress Shop, and then picked Dani up at school. The reporter had to be following me."

"Does he describe you in any way?"

"No, just 'an average housewife' is all it says."

"Did he name those places specifically? The A&P? The dress shop?"

"He didn't have to, did he? How many grocery stores are there in town?"

William Henry thought he could name three. "I don't know. How many?"

Jane faltered. "Well, the A&P is the best place for produce, everyone knows that. The Sterling is the only shop that has really nice clothes anyone would buy. And there's only one elementary school."

"So ..." He tried to sum up an alternative explanation. "So because these places are so popular, or unique, isn't it possible he was describing several different women?"

"But I didn't see any of *them* out on Tuesday," she said triumphantly. "Therefore it must have been me."

William Henry was perplexed. Was Jane really insisting she was being persecuted by a simple newspaper article? All he could think to say was, "I don't think that logic holds."

"Logic has nothing to do with it! That man was stalking me!" She went over to the kitchen window and pulled the drapes closed. "He could be out there now, watching the house."

"Spying on 'an average housewife'?" He tried not to smile.

"Who knows what that man wants?" Jane replied darkly.

"Evidently a story in the paper—but it's one he's already published."

"Just you wait and see." She gave him an infuriatingly self-satisfied smile.

"It's getting too thick in here," William Henry said, standing up. "I've got a class to teach."

But as he was pulling his notes together in the study, little bits of the conversation kept coming back to him. He knew Jane had always been self-conscious and sometimes even a bit vain. She was a beautiful woman, after all, and she knew it. But this seemed to be more than vanity, or female self-absorption. Men hiding in bushes? Stalkers watching the house? That sounded like a full-blown case of paranoia.

William Henry wondered if he should look up someone over in the Psychology Department. In the interest of acquiring knowledge, he could make a few noncommittal inquiries. But whoever he talked to would ultimately want to meet and examine Jane. And how would he explain that? The thought that, behind her back, her husband was even thinking of discussing her mental condition with a psychologist would make Jane truly angry. And that would only make things worse, wouldn't it?

Better to hope that this was a rough patch, a phase.

His wife was experiencing a dark mood.

It would blow over, eventually.

15. THE AFFAIR

JANE WAS OUT and about in town on a brisk, sharp-edged day in the middle of April. The air seemed to be full of charged particles. The clouds in the sky shone brightly, white and hard, not looking fluffy at all. And rising from the damp earth came—perhaps not the actual *smell* of flowers, but the possibility of the flowers themselves.

She had an hour to herself before she needed to collect Dani at school. And that weighed on her mind. These idle moments were the most dangerous, exactly the times when that social-gossip reporter could pick up her trail and follow Jane and her daughter home. So it was with relief that Jane spotted the bar.

The front window was dark, and the place almost looked closed—except that the neon Pabst sign was lit against the greenish-colored glass. After taking a glance up and down the street and seeing no one she knew, Jane went inside. The reporter had never mentioned her going into a such a place, so it must be safe.

The interior was as dark as the evening on an overcast day. Indirect lighting on the ranked bottles behind the bar made it an oasis of muted colors—the reds, browns, and greens of their labels—floating amid a roomful of shapes and shadows that might have been patrons but were in fact only the empty chairs and partitions between booths. Jane made her way over to the bar and lifted herself onto a stool, grateful for the obscuring gloom. She shrugged off her coat and let the sleeves dangle behind her. She put her purse on the bar, found her cigarettes, and lit one, conscious of the yellow flare of the match against her hands and cheeks.

The bartender came over. "What can I get you, miss?"

Something in the voice was familiar. Jane fixed the man with a hard stare, then instantly looked away. She knew him. It was Lou ... somebody. Pinocchio? Finocchio? Some Italian name. So this must be *that* bar, she realized. And did he recognize her? In a plain dress, without the evening makeup, and with her hair all pinned up?

"A beer, please," she said without looking at him.

"Any special brand?"

"Whatever's on tap."

"Coming right up."

If he knew her, he wasn't letting on.

Jane said a small prayer of thanks.

"That's not very friendly," spoke a voice at her elbow.

Surprised, Jane looked over with a jerk of her head.

Margot was sitting on the next stool. She was slender and beautiful, just as she had been in Jane's youth, with the same glossy black hair and lustrous, bright eyes. But on closer inspection, Jane could see that Margot's skin was leathery, stretched taut over the bare curves of cheekbones and chin. As she watched, the skin turned black as if burned by all-consuming fire. Red highlights glowed in her dark hair, as if patches of it still smoldered. Tiny flames danced in her eyes.

Why are you all burned, Mother?

"Why, it's the hellfire, darling."

Did you go to Hell, then, after—?

"You sent me there, many times."

When Margot spoke, little puffs of smoke came out of her mouth, as if the air had suddenly turned frosty. Her lips appeared rough and chapped, caked with ash instead of lipstick. Jane could smell the sulfur of burned match heads.

You know I didn't mean it, she said. *I was just an angry little girl.*

"But words have an effect, you know. Every word. Every curse."

Lou returned with Jane's beer, set it on a napkin in front of her. His eyes never made contact, even when he brought over a dish of peanuts.

Why did you say I was being unfriendly just then? He doesn't know me.

"Of course he knows you," Margot said. "You slept together many times."

It was just the once. ... No, wait—

Jane had never slept with Lou, not even once. She was sure of that—well, almost sure—although she had known all the time they were working together that he wanted to take her to bed. He had offered to, at least once, and would have followed through on it, if she had let him.

No, Mother. That was your slutty behavior, not mine.

"It takes one to know one, darling."

I was a good girl. I never cheated on my husband.

"You only remember it that way, kiddo."

You're wrong about me, and you know it.

"Oh, my brave girl!" Margot laughed, and papery flakes blew out of her mouth. "You had the itch. You always did. You are as horny as a pussycat in heat. You did it with Lou. You scratched that itch. You did, too."

That's not true. I don't think it's true.

"But it *feels* true, doesn't it, darling?"

Jane sipped at her beer. It was cold, sharp, definite, with the spike of the alcohol, the sting of tiny bubbles. That was reality. The things she remembered—or told herself she remembered—had a liquid, hazy quality. She might not have been as chaste as she remembered. So many nights ...

"Why don't you ask your husband?" Margot suggested.

About what? My infidelities? Really, Mother!

"He never talks about the war years, does he?" Margot grinned, and her lips cracked. "He never asks about the jobs you took, the people you saw, the things you did."

Willie doesn't have to. And anyway, all that is in the past.

"He doesn't dare to, you mean. Because he knows what you did."

He couldn't know. He was thousands of miles away. There was the war—

"But he knew *you*, didn't he? He knew your nature. He could suspect the rest."

Willie never gave the slightest hint. He never made insinuations or accusations.

"And he never demanded punishment, never gave you the release of retribution with a black eye or a swollen lip. He never offered you the chance to close off the affair. He never allowed you to forget about it, either."

There—was—no—affair, Mother!

"So you say, darling. So you say."

To get away from that smirk and from the smell of sulfur, Jane pushed the beer across the zinc-covered bar, slid off the seat, gathered up her coat and purse.

The bartender came over. "Is something wrong, miss?"

She pulled out a couple of bills and slapped them down.

"Keep the change," she snarled—and ran for the door before anyone could speak another word.

16. Dani's Diary

Friday, April 18: I'm getting scared. Mother is acting really crazy. And *strange,* like she doesn't know Daddy or me anymore. But *mean,* like she sure hates our guts. I don't know what I'm doing wrong. Daddy told me not to worry. He says it's not my fault. And it's not his fault, either. He says Mother is having a difficult time right now, and she's feeling really sick. But she doesn't sneeze or have a runny nose. He said no, she has a sickness *inside.* I asked where inside. He said—real slow, like he wasn't sure—he guessed it was her heart, or maybe her head. I said, oh, you mean like a headache? He said no, more like she was having bad ideas. I don't know about that. I have bad ideas all the time, and when people find out about them, they don't say I'm sick. They say I'm a bad girl and I should know better. Has Mother been a bad girl?

Jane found the notebook under a stack of folded underwear in the top drawer of Dani's dresser. She didn't mean to snoop. She just wanted to know how long she had before the laundry was due again, and counting the family's clean things was easier than picking through the dirty things in the hamper. Anyway, who said nine-year-olds had a right to privacy?

She was halfway through reading when she got mad. She got madder as she read to the end.

"Dani!" she yelled, in a voice that rattled the cottage's rafters.

"Yes, Mom?" from down in the dining room.

"Come up here! Right now!"

Her daughter clumped up the stairs and came into the room. She froze when she saw the diary in Jane's hands.

"What is this?" Jane demanded, shaking the notebook at her.

"It's a diary."

"Who said you could write this?"

"Well, no one. I just thought, you know … like Anne Frank …"

"This is a bad thing to do!" Jane shouted. "You're writing about people. That's mean and cruel." Jane tried to control herself. "And you're writing about me!"

"I'm *sorry!*" the little girl wailed. She reached for the book. "Please, can I have it back?"

But Jane held onto it. "Oh, no!" With sudden inspiration, she ripped the book down its spine. Then she ripped the pages across. Smaller and smaller pieces. And when they got too thick to rip, she wadded them up, dropped them on the floor, and stamped on them.

"You're never to do this again!" she shouted at her daughter. "You've done something terribly, terribly wrong!"

But Dani had already fled from the room.

17. THE DISCOVERY

As PART OF her spring cleaning ritual, Jane always rearranged the closets. If the cottage in the woods had one drawback, it was lack of storage space. Instead of playing musical chairs, she played an endless game of musical shelves, and the last pile of clothes or books or bundled magazines left standing had to go up into the crawlspace among the rafters that extended over the two upstairs bedrooms. And that space, too, was getting full.

To see what she had to work with, Jane carried the stepladder up from the kitchen closet, set it in the hallway, climbed up five rungs, and pushed up the trapdoor in the ceiling. For light, a single bulb hung on a cord, and when she pulled the chain it danced back and forth, sending half-shadows spinning and dodging around the attic at the edge of her vision.

Near the opening were the stacks and bundles she had put away on previous trips. Jane climbed over and around them to see what might be salvaged in the jumble beyond. In the third rank, she found a dark-green tin box, reinforced at the corners and bound with straps of canvas webbing. On the upper surface in black stencil was her husband's name, preceded by the word "MAJ." It was his footlocker from the war.

Although Willie was proud of his service, he was a relatively unsentimental man, she knew, unlikely to keep souvenirs or place any great value on the folded uniforms this box would contain. Perhaps it was time to open it and see what space could be made for the things he treasured more, like a few bales of his precious *National Geographic*s. Jane settled back on her heels, worked the straps loose, and lifted off the lid. The sides made a deep, muffled screeching.

Inside, as she suspected, were khaki shirts and slacks, a tunic in olive-drab wool, a metal Band-Aid box that rattled with Willie's insignia, and two manila-brown envelopes that probably held the letters she had written to him and his discharge papers. To make certain she would not be throwing away anything official, Jane opened the first envelope and slid out its contents.

On the very top was a light-blue Air Mail envelope, addressed to Willie in Korea, with a return address from the apartment building where she had been staying with Dani at the time. It was not one of her letters, because it was typewritten. Curious now, Jane opened and read it before she gave a thought to invading anyone's privacy.

The words lifted off the page, hardly touching her eyes and brain, to pummel at her heart: "not good woman" and "special circle of Hell." The words held such loathing and contempt, it frightened Jane to think she could be their object. It angered her to think Willie had to receive them and must have been distressed by them, even for an instant. Of course, she knew who had written the letter: that Russian woman who used to babysit Dani while Jane was out working. But Mrs. Obmanchikov had always been so smiling and so helpful. So like a grandmother to Dani. And such a snake to Jane herself.

"You see?" said Margot's voice. "He knew all along."

But it's a lie! Jane wailed inside her own head.

"Everyone knew about your whoring."

But I didn't! I'm not a whore!

"Can you prove that?"

Her mother was right. What objective evidence could there be that you had *not* spread your legs for a man? Chastity left no bruises. Faithfulness made no stains. Jane had only her memories, and now they were failing her.

"You can see the knowledge in his eyes every time he looks at you. Your Willie knows he married beneath him. It was bad enough that you had no breeding, no culture, no schooling. But you didn't even have any morals."

But I've always tried to be a good girl, Jane said.

"And isn't it odd that he never confronted you?"

He didn't have to. He never believed any of it.

"He never gave you a chance to explain."

Explain what, Mother? This pack of lies?

"And yet he kept the letter, didn't he?"

It's just some junk he never threw out.

"He's always checking up on you."

No, he trusts me, really he does.

"Asking what you do all day."

That's just him being nice.

"Who you had lunch with."

He wants me to go out.

"And fuck your brains out, darling!"

Margot's high, silvery laugh rang around the narrow attic space. Jane tried to fight it by quickly stuffing the papers and clothing back into the box. Only when she replaced the metal cover did the laughter fade, melting into the tin screech as it slid into place. The canvas straps muffled it entirely.

Jane climbed over the piles surrounding the trapdoor, the way back home.

But the light-blue envelope and its letter were still in her hand.

18. The Accusation

Jane kept the awful letter with her all afternoon. It was folded back into its envelope and secured in her apron pocket. Toward evening, she kept one nervous eye on Dani, who was cutting out daffodils in yellow and green construction paper on the dining room table. When Willie at last came through the door, Jane told her quietly, "Dani, go to your room."

"But—Mother! I'm not done."

"I'm counting to three. One."

"Why? What did I *do?*"

"Nothing, dear. Two."

"Well, can't I—?"

"Three, and scat."

Dani gathered her things and ran for the stairs.

"Close the door up there," Jane called after her.

"Is there some kind of trouble?" Willie asked.

Jane followed him into his study. She pulled out the envelope and laid it on his desk blotter. "You tell me."

He glanced at it, obviously not recognizing the return address. "What is it?"

"You don't remember getting this letter in Korea? I find that hard to believe."

He looked more closely, picked it up, opened it. "Oh!" was all he said.

"Oh?" Jane repeated. "What kind of 'Oh' is that, Willie? As in, 'Oh, *that* letter, which I've kept safely hidden all these years'? Or is it, 'Oh, the letter that makes me such a superior person compared to my whoring wife'? Just tell me what 'Oh' means, please."

"No," he said calmly. "It's a letter which I thought I burned long ago."

"And yet you kept it. Why? Was it to use against me one day?"

"Now how could I do that, if I thought it didn't exist?"

"But it did exist, you know, lying in your trunk, on top of *my* letters."

75

"In the first place, why were you going through my army things?"

"This is not about your privacy, Willie. That letter damages me."

"No, it doesn't. Because I never believed a word of it."

"Then why didn't you share it with me?"

"To what purpose?" he asked.

"Why, so that—" She stopped.

"So that you could get all hurt and angry—as you are now?" he answered for her. "So that you could defend yourself against charges we both know are wrong but can't be proved, one way or the other? So that we could *laugh* about it? Really, Jane! By the time I got back to the States, what was the point?"

"You can twist my words a thousand different ways—" she began.

But another voice cackled, "You're twisted like a pretzel!"

Be quiet, Mother! I can handle this, Jane replied.

"You've really got yourself a scholar there."

Just go back where you came from.

"Too bad he's such a sissy."

What do you mean?

Willie's handsome face wavered in front of her, momentarily becoming Margot's charred ruin. "Some soldier your boy must have been!" the face said. "A real man would have rushed home to fight for you. Or beat you bloody for fooling around like that. But this one just stayed away and acted hurt. And now all he does is make up excuses for his cowardice."

"I can't argue anymore," Jane said finally—to whoever was standing there. "I have a terrible headache." She turned blindly away, feeling for the chair in front of her, then groping for the doorjamb beyond.

———

William Henry did not know what to make of the conversation. Clearly, after finding that poisonous old letter, Jane had been spoiling for a fight. And she was working herself up to deliver a good roundhouse punch, too, when suddenly—*pfft!* She gave it up, became sick of the whole thing, and couldn't wait to get out of the room. Women were such strange creatures.

But did he have that punch coming to him? Did he perhaps deserve her anger? Well, no. Because, as he had tried to tell Jane, he never believed the accusations. Not then. Not really. And certainly not now.

As if the thought were stimulus to a reflex, William Henry tore the letter and its envelope across. He doubled the pieces and tore them again. He repeated this process, fingers moving faster and faster, until the paper was a scuffed blue wad that he could hardly bend, let alone tear. Finally, he dropped it into the wastebasket. As he should have done so many years ago …

Almost like a thief, William Henry tiptoed up the stairs and crossed the short hallway, conscious of a dull psychic heat pouring from behind the closed door of his and Jane's bedroom. He tapped softly at Dani's door.

"What is it?" his daughter asked.

"You can come out now," he said quietly

"Did you and Mom have a big fight?" she whispered.

"No, and yes. Did she say anything to you about it?"

"No, but she looked pretty steamed."

"She was upset, is all."

"Uh-huh."

They made macaroni and cheese for dinner, and William Henry left a plate of it warming on the stove for Jane. Shortly after eight o'clock, he went upstairs and knocked on her door.

"Go away," his wife said distinctly.

"Are you feeling all right?" he asked.

"Sure, I'm peachy. Now just go away."

William Henry went downstairs again to work. Some hours later, when he went up to prepare for bed, his wife was sleeping soundly. However, so as not to wake her, he took a pillow and blanket from the linen closet and made up the sofa in his study.

19. THIRTY-SIX HOURS (I)

JANE SLEPT THAT night—or rather, she believed she must have slept, for she woke the next morning after nine o'clock. But she had no memory of falling asleep. She could only remember lying fully clothed on the bedcovers, curled up on her right side, hugging her knees to her chest, breathing in darkness, locked in silent struggle with her anger, her sense of outrage at her husband, her mother, her life, her fate, and her fear of the coming daylight and what it would make her do.

Even at that hour of the morning, with the sun not yet high in the sky, the day was hot and still, hazy and muggy, with not a bird to sing or a breath of wind to stir the trees around the cottage. It felt like the worst days of summer, brought on unseasonably soon. Jane woke up—although she would not remember, later, how she came to be awake or in what state—with sweat damp in the creases of her clothes and beads of perspiration on her face and in her hair, like dew. Her body felt as if she had been beaten. Her face was puffy and tender across the cheekbones and throat. In the bathroom mirror, her eyes were ringed with dark circles that might have been a mixture of tears and yesterday's mascara, but they might equally have been bruises because of the dull pain they caused her.

The house was empty. Jane stumbled from one small room to the next, looking for her family. Her daughter's bed was empty and neatly made up, with the blanket tucked under at the corners. Her husband's side of their bed had not been slept in. If Willie and Dani had eaten breakfast, then he had so thoroughly cleaned the kitchen as to leave no trace of their meal. Even the coffee pot was empty, clean, and cold.

Jane appeared to be alone in the house.

"They've abandoned you," Margot said.

Shut up, Mother, Jane replied tiredly.

There was a grayness all around her, like fog drifting through the room where she ended up sitting. The fog muffled her thoughts and put the outside world at a distance.

"But that's a *good* thing, darling," her mother went on. "At least he won't try to beat you up. Count your lucky stars. He should have beaten you bloody. He *would* have beaten you bloody."

Willie never beat me, you know *that.*

"Oh? And what about those bruises?"

Jane had a sudden vision of an eye blackened from the bridge of the nose around the rim of the socket and down into the soft flesh underneath. The eyelid was puffed out like a rotten grape. But whether it was her own eye or somebody else's she could not say. It *felt* like her eye.

Willie never … he never meant to … he wouldn't …

"Whatever you say, dear. But think about your daughter."

He loves Dani. He never hurt her. He could never—

"Then where did that black eye come from? Hey?"

Yes, Jane remembered now. The eye that had been hurt so badly was Danielle's. Someone had hit her in the face. And William Henry had been involved somehow. He'd been *concerned*, she remembered. Perhaps without realizing it, he had been the cause of her daughter's disfigurement.

"You have to get out before he comes back."

Take my daughter and go, Jane agreed.

"That's the spirit! Go! Go now!"

Jane was on her feet and in motion before she knew where she was going.

"You'll need money, of course. A lot of money. A lifetime's supply."

They have lots of money at the bank, Jane thought to herself.

"That's right, darling. There's your savings account."

Without stopping for her hat or purse, Jane was suddenly out the door. She did not even pause to take her house keys but left the front door hanging open. It did not matter. She was never coming back.

———

"Mr. Stephenson?" said Eileen Wendover, one of the tellers, who had left her station to come over to Joseph Stephenson's desk. "Would you join me at the counter, please?"

Something in her voice alerted the assistant manager of the Byzantium branch of the Farmer's and Merchant's Bank of New York to expect a situation. The last time a teller had spoken in that tone, an unmasked man with an unspecified weapon had just presented a note demanding access to the vault. Stephenson glanced at Eileen's station: just one lone woman, rather pretty, with short auburn hair. But from the way the woman was looking around the bank's lobby, nervously—no, distractedly—she well might be part of a gang waiting outside.

"What seems to be the problem, Eileen?"

"Mrs. Wheelock wants to make a withdrawal, sir."

"And?" he prompted. Withdrawals were routine business.

"She wants all the money in her accounts, both checking and savings. And they're held jointly with her husband."

"Then he'll have to co-sign to close them."

"I've already explained all that to her, sir."

"And …?" This was becoming tiresome.

"She told me to …"

"Told you to what?"

"To f-f-fuck myself."

"Oh! Language!" he scolded the teller.

"It's true, sir! Now she wants to speak to you, sir."

"All right," he sighed. "I'll come."

The closer Stephenson drew to the woman at the counter, the more cause he could see for concern. She was not merely distracted but also disheveled. Her clothes appeared to have been slept in. Her face was haggard, her eyes darkened to the point of bruising. Her hair, which from a distance had appeared wind-blown, was simply uncombed and, well, matted. She had a lit cigarette between the fingers of her right hand, even though he disapproved of smoking in the bank and had posted signs to that effect.

"May I be of service, Mrs. Wheelock?" he asked.

"Only if you can get me my money."

"I understand you want to close your accounts."

"No—just take the money out."

"I'm afraid that amounts to the same thing. As Eileen here has told you, these are joint accounts, so you'll need your husband's signature to do that."

"Shit!" the Wheelock woman said.

"Tell her she needs to bring in her passbook, too," Eileen whispered in his ear. "That's for the savings account. And she has to make out withdrawal slips."

Stephenson turned. "Hasn't she done any of that?"

"I don't *have* the passbook," the Wheelock woman answered, taking a long drag on her cigarette. "My husband has it. I can't get it either, because I'm leaving him, and he can't know until I'm gone."

"This is most irregular," Stephenson grumbled aloud.

"Welcome to my life, pal!" Mrs. Wheelock said with a grimace.

Out of the corner of his eye, he saw Eileen nodding in sympathy.

On an impulse of human kindness, Stephenson hesitated— usually a fatal error in banking. Considering the woman's physical state, especially the bruising around her eyes, he suspected his responsibility just possibly might lie elsewhere. "Are you in distress, madam?" he asked.

She gave him a disbelieving look. "Well, yeah! What do you think?"

He turned to have a word in private with Eileen. "How long have the Wheelocks been with us?"

"Oh, years and years, sir! Maybe eight? Long as I've been here, anyway."

"Let me see the records." Together, they went to the filing cabinet and consulted the transactions posted against the accounts in the ledger sheets. The Wheelocks appeared to be excellent customers: a tidily growing account balance, never overdrawn, everything regular. They had a mortgage with the bank, too, and always paid in full and on time.

He returned to the counter with the teller trailing behind.

"Here is what I'm prepared to do, Mrs. Wheelock. We can't close the accounts without the proper signatures, that's final. But I can authorize a small loan against the balance. A personal loan, you understand. Made on your signature. With the accounts held as collateral."

"How small?" she asked.

"Well—two hundred dollars?"

"Shit! How far will that take me?"

"Then would, um, three hundred suffice?"

"Make it five and you'll never see me again."

That was definitely the wrong thing for her to say under the circumstances, he thought. But then, Stephenson understood the woman's motivation. And the bank would always have Wheelock himself—a professor at the university, with a reputation to protect and possible tenure in his future—to make good on his wife's loan. Considering the black eyes that man had already given her, he was due for some trouble in his life. "Just let me get the forms," he said.

Not until an hour after Mrs. Wheelock had left the bank, with the cash folded into her purse, did Stephenson think it was safe to call Professor Wheelock's office and give him the bad news.

20. Thirty-Six Hours (II)

THREE DOORS DOWN from the bank was a drug store, and luckily so. Jane discovered that she had left the house without her cigarettes, and now her body craved the soothing smoke. She went in and asked at the counter for the brand she liked, Chesterfields. She paid with a crisp twenty from the wad she had taken from the bank, accepted her change, and picked up a clutch of free matchbooks from the display beside the cash register. Still standing at the counter, she tore off the cellophane and the foil end of the package, shook out a cigarette, and lit up. When the clerk at the register made a face at her, she stuck her tongue out at him.

Then she closed her eyes as those magic fingers reached down into her lungs and smoothed out the tangled skein of her nerves. Opening her eyes to the world again, Jane discovered that she was thirsty. Not only that but, despite the fact that the morning was going well and she was on her way to freedom, there was still a dark spot in her mind. She was still feeling low and depressed. Well … a drink would set her up right. But she did not want to go into a bar, because of the people she might meet there. Her eye caught on a display behind the counter, not unlike the display behind the bar where she had worked.

"A fifth of Jim Beam—black label," she told the man.

As he reached up to the shelf, she changed her mind.

"No, make that a quart."

She paid for it with change from the twenty and accepted the bottle in its slim, tailored paper bag. Holding the burning cigarette in the corner of her mouth, she stripped off the bag and cracked the seal on the bottle.

The clerk was scandalized. "You can't drink that in here!"

"Why not? I won't spill any."

"It's state law, ma'am."

"Okay, okay."

Out on the sidewalk, Jane opened the bottle and took a stiff drink right from the mouth. The whiskey burned her throat only a little, but it landed in her stomach with a jolt like a thrown

83

punch. She took a step backward and let out a gasp. And then, as soon as she breathed in again, her mood brightened. The gray cobwebs were fluttering and tearing away with the new breeze inside her mind. The morning sun seeped in past her eyeballs and made everything golden. She had her escape money. She had the necessities of smoke and comfort. Now, the only thing she needed was ... lunch.

Jane could not just go home and make a meal for herself. Not with Willie out and about and probably looking for her. Then she remembered that it was Thursday, the day the Faculty Wives held their weekly lunches. Jane hadn't shown up in a long time, and so it would be a pleasant surprise if she appeared today. Besides, there were a few things she wanted to say to Lorraine Lombardy and the rest of them before she left town forever.

––––––––

One of the waitresses who served the Thursday Get-Together at the Faculty Club came to stand nervously behind Lorraine Lombardy's place at the head table. After a minute had passed without the woman saying anything, Lombardy turned in her chair. "Yes? What is it?"

"There's someone asking for you, ma'am."

"And does this someone have a name?"

"It's—uh—Mrs. Wheelock, ma'am."

"Well, she's a member. Show her in."

"I ... I can't, ma'am. No, not really."

"Why ever not?" Lombardy asked.

All she got in reply was a glazed look.

"Well then, where is Mrs. Wheelock?"

"In the foyer," the waitress said, relieved.

Lombardy put down her napkin, excused herself to her luncheon companions, and strode out toward the front of the building. The sight that awaited her caused Lombardy to miss a step and almost walk off her own high heels. Jane Wheelock might have been many things—arrogant, brazen, cunning, deceitful, excitable, foul-mouthed, gauche, hotheaded—her social faults had become legend among the members. But she was always impeccably groomed and beautifully dressed. The wretch who stood in the middle of the hallway now, chain smoking and dropping cigarette ashes on the carpet, looked like she had been kept out in the rain overnight and left to dry. Her hair was a mess. Her face pasty and bruised. Her clothes wrinkled and stained. And, as Lombardy approached, there was a definite whiff—no, a reek—of whiskey.

"Jane!" Lombardy exclaimed, then paused. For anyone else, she normally would have held out her arms and invited a hug. But not to this woman, not in her present state. "How are you, my dear?"

"I'm hungry," Jane said shortly.

"That's good to hear, dear," Lombardy said inanely.

"They won't let me in. Thursday lunch, you know."

"Well, you see, dear—" What was there to say?

"Did you blackball me, Lorraine?"

"What? I? No, it's just that—"

"Do I embarrass you girls?"

"It's not that. It's just—"

"You kicking me out?"

"I think it's best."

Jane Wheelock's face twisted then, like a rubber mask in the hands of a child. Her eyelids closed down into hard slits. Her lips curled back on themselves and quivered, like a dog trying to show all of its teeth at once. A raw screech started in the back of Jane's throat and gained volume, second by second. Flecks of foam formed behind her teeth and actually blew out of her mouth on the waves of sound.

Simon, the club's majordomo, was instantly standing at Lombardy's side. "Do we have a problem here, ma'am?"

"Mrs. Wheelock is having—" A what? A fit? Temper tantrum? Attack of *delirium tremens*? "—a difficult day. Please show her outside."

The man took Jane firmly by the elbow. She quickly rounded on him; Lombardy thought she was going to throw a punch. But

Simon deftly manipulated her arm, and Jane sagged down on one knee in pain. The screech turned into a short, surprised shriek.

"Gently, Simon. As you would a guest."

"Yes, ma'am," the man murmured.

Rather than watch the humiliating end of this, Lombardy turned to go back to the dining room. She resumed her seat and her meal, which was now cold.

Ten minutes later, Simon was hovering behind her chair.

Lombardy gave him a tired look. "What is it now?"

"Trouble, I'm afraid, ma'am. After I showed Mrs. Wheelock the door, I decided to keep an eye on her, considering her present condition."

"Very sensible."

"Well, I don't know where she could have gotten the bottle. Maybe it was hidden in the bushes, stashed there before she came in, you understand. Anyway, by the time I looked out the side window, she'd poured it all over the balustrade, covered a good ten feet of the railing. She put a match to the stuff while I was watching. Looked me right in the eye and lit it."

"What stuff?" Lombardy asked. "Lit *what?*"

"Whiskey, ma'am. Fairly good brand, too."

"You mean she tried to set the club on fire?"

"That she did. Or singe the paint, anyway."

"You put it out, I trust." Lombardy said.

"Oh, yes, ma'am. With the extinguisher."

"And so, where is Mrs. Wheelock now?"

"She left while we were fighting the fire."

"She commits arson, and you let her go?"

"It wasn't by choice, ma'am. We were busy."

"Well, call the police," Lombardy instructed.

Simon bowed stiffly and turned to leave.

"No, wait! That's harsh. No real harm done."

"Ma'am?"

"Call Professor Wheelock. If he's not at his office, have the switchboard take a message. Tell him he'd better go find his wife before she does actual damage."

21. THIRTY-SIX HOURS (III)

WHEN THE FACULTY Club's huge, black-painted front door slammed open and a man burst out, Jane threw her empty bottle into the shrubbery and ran off diagonally across the lawn and then down the sidewalk, not stopping until she reached the corner. When she looked back, she saw it was only the butler, Simon, and he was carrying a fire extinguisher. So he would have no time to chase her down the street. Still, she thought it prudent to keep on going. After another block, all thoughts of lunch, Lombardy, the fire, and the Faculty Wives were gone from her head.

But there was one more thing Jane had to do. If she was going to leave town, she wanted to find her daughter.

At first, she only wanted to say good-bye. As there was no telling where Jane's escape from her husband and her marriage would end up, it would be cruel to subject the girl to the uncertainties of life on the run. But as she thought about Dani, her pretty face and her clever mind, Jane's resolve began to waver. After all, daughters belonged with their mothers. Who else would teach her what she needed to learn from the world? Not her father, certainly. With his scholarly detachment, he could hardly remember to feed Dani, and he knew nothing about buying her proper clothes. And when the time came, he wouldn't be able to guide her through the changes that were coming in her body and her life. No, Jane could not leave Dani behind. Wherever Jane was going, they were going together.

But, if there were two of them, they had better take the car.

And the car was still parked at home, Jane realized.

With her keys still on the hook by the door.

Things had suddenly become confused.

She took a deep breath, looked around to regain her bearings, and set off across a lawn in what she imagined was the right direction.

"Wait there, Dani," she said breathlessly. "I'm coming!"

———

"Yoo-hoo!" sang a disembodied voice in the office of the Maple Street School. It might have been a female voice, but it might equally have been a parrot or mockingbird. "Hey there!"

Deirdre Jordan, the school secretary, looked up from her typewriter. The machine was placed on a desktop behind the counter that separated the public from the private areas of the office. From where Jordan was sitting, the counter was up at eye level. Still, if the speaker was on the other side, then she was either very short or crouching below the far edge, trying to hide. Jordan stood up and leaned over. Nobody down there, either.

"Yes? What is it?" Jordan called uncertainly.

"Out here," said the voice, coming now from the hallway.

Jordan suspected a joke by the sixth graders. "Show yourself, please!"

"Is it safe?" the voice asked timidly.

"Of course it's safe! Come in here!"

A petite woman with tangled auburn hair and a pretty, if smudged, face looked around the doorjamb. Jordan thought she seemed familiar: a mother, or maybe an older sister, of one of the school's students. But which mother or sister? After so many years, the faces all ran together. "Can I help you, ma'am? Or is it 'miss'?"

"Miss ... Dobray. Yes, that name will do for now."

"Do I know you?" Jordan asked suspiciously.

"I'm Danny's mother," the woman replied.

"Which one? We have seven boys named Danny here."

"No, Danielle ... Or Dani ... She's a my little girl."

"Oh, Dani Wheelock? You're Mrs. Wheelock?"

"Shh!" the woman hushed. "Don't tell anyone, will you?"

"Look, what do you want?" Jordan asked, tired of these games.

"I've come for my daughter. I'm going away and taking her with me."

"Well, she's in class now, of course. Where do you plan on taking her?"

"Just ... away," the woman said vaguely. "I don't know where myself yet."

"This is highly irregular," Jordan said. "To release a child, even to a parent, we would need a reason and a destination."

"The reason is … It's not safe for her anymore. Or for me. You see—"

Deirdre Jordan had a sudden insight. What she had thought were smudges on the woman's face might just as easily have been bruises. And her hair looked as if someone might have been pulling on it—yanking it out by the roots, in fact—in a scuffle. "Is this in the nature of an emergency?" she asked gently.

Mrs. Wheelock looked at her with large, shining, lost eyes.

"Is it your husband?" Jordan asked, even more gently.

Mrs. Wheelock nodded slowly, saying nothing.

"Wait here. I'll go fetch your daughter."

22. THIRTY-SIX HOURS (IV)

WHEN WILLIAM HENRY returned to his office on campus after his last class of the day, he found a pile of pink message slips lying beside his phone. Helen, the Classics Department secretary, always put his messages in inverse chronological order, with the most recent on top. That one, he saw, was from the Byzantium Police Department, asking him to call a Sergeant Dominic Benelli, with the subject line left tactfully blank.

A sudden cold chill went through William Henry. Given the muted argument with Jane the night before, particularly the strange way she had broken it off, and considering his wife's increasingly volatile and strained behavior over the past couple of weeks, a call from the police could mean any number of things, none of them good.

Before he dealt with that one, which was likely to take the most time—and to give himself a chance to work his way up to it, as it were—William Henry glanced through the other messages. The earliest was from a Mr. Stephenson at the bank, on the subject of "loan against your accounts." But William Henry didn't recall having any loans. The second was from Lorraine Lombardy, on the subject of "vandalism and arson." That was very odd, because he associated the wife of his department chairman with purely social matters. And then he remembered she was also president of the Faculty Wives—and that, he realized with a sick feeling, might have something to do with Jane. The last message before the call from the police was from a Mrs. Jordan at the Maple Street Elementary School, on the subject of "release of your daughter to ..." with the rest a scribble. Helen's message-taking abilities tended to fade out after a few words, regardless of the subject matter or its consequence.

If there was a pattern to all of this, William Henry could not read it. Yet he knew it must have to do with Jane. She would be the binding link in what appeared to be a random series of catastrophes.

90

He checked his watch: four-thirty in the afternoon. He could try the bank and the school, but both would be probably closed by now. He called the number associated with the Lombardy woman, and got the reception desk at the Faculty Club.

"Is Mrs. Lombardy there?" he asked.

"I'm sorry, sir. She left some hours ago."

"Is this ... Simon?" That was the concierge.

"Yes, it is, sir." Followed by an expectant pause.

"This is Professor Wheelock. I have a message from—"

"Ah, Professor," the man's voice dropped an octave. "That will be about the slight altercation we had this afternoon. Please don't worry about it. There was hardly any real damage, and the club management has decided not to press charges."

"But what happened, man!"

"Your wife, sir, appeared at the club in a state of some—disorder. She exchanged words with Mrs. Lombardy, and we were required to show her out. Upon leaving the club, Mrs. Wheelock did set a small fire, which was quickly extinguished."

"And where is my wife now?" he asked.

"I hardly know, sir. All this happened at midday."

"Thank you, Simon. You've been most helpful."

"Not at all, sir." And the line clicked off.

William Henry set aside the others and picked up the message from Benelli. He took a deep breath and dialed the number.

"Byzantium Police," came the response, although it was more like "*Zantyum.*"

"Sergeant Benelli, please," William Henry said.

"One moment." *Click. Click.*

"Benelli here," said a deep voice.

"Sergeant, this is Professor Wheelock."

"Oh!" A long pause. "Thank you for calling back, Professor. I wanted to let you know we found your car."

"My car?" William Henry was confused.

"You own a '49 Plymouth Club Coupe?"

"Then this isn't about my wife?" he asked.

"Ahh ..." Another pause. "Was she driving the car, sir?"

"Probably. I mean, she usually has it during the day."

"Well, sir … You see, a passing motorist sighted it about fifteen miles west of here on Highway 104 and called it in. We sent a patrol and verified it."

"Why would a motorist notice my wife's car? What did you verify?"

"That the car was up against a tree, sir. Left the road at a fairly high rate of speed, too. No skid marks, bounced through the ditch, and came up in the woods."

William Henry gripped the phone. "Is my wife all right?"

"No, sir. That is, there's no sign of your wife."

"But she—was my daughter with her?"

"Oh? Yeah, we thought it might be something like that," Benelli said. "You see, the driver's side was clean, but the officer on the scene reported seeing blood on the passenger side of the front seat. Looked like maybe a head impact against the dashboard. So we deduce a second party was in the car."

"Oh, God!" William Henry said. "Where are they now? Which hospital?"

"I don't think you heard me, sir. We found the car but no bodies, no people. We figured you ran off the road, had that accident, scraped your head, then hitched back to town. That scenario, more or less—except for the blood being on the wrong seat."

"You didn't search the surrounding area?" William Henry said slowly.

"No, sir. No need to. People who wreck their car and can still walk away, you figure they went for a tow, not off wandering in the woods."

"So what happened to my wife?"

"You tell me, sir," Benelli said reasonably. "Did you try calling at your house? After a thing like that, most women go home for a cup of tea and put their feet up."

"I'll …" William Henry closed his eyes. "I'll call home."

"Good idea, sir. The simple answer's usually the right one."

After he hung up, William Henry dialed the cottage. He let it ring ten times. And then, on the off chance he had misdialed, he tried once more and let it ring twenty times, just in case Jane and Dani had gone to bed after their presumed ordeal. Still no answer.

He thought about calling the police again. He would order a search of the area around the car. Or he could make a missing person's report. But, either way, they would likely refer the case back to Sergeant Benelli. William Henry was sure he could not endure any more of the man's plodding, infuriating matter-of-factness.

Instead, he decided to go home and wait for his wife.

He might even put his feet up and have a cup of tea.

23. THIRTY-SIX HOURS (V)

JANE HAD HEARD that, when you were out in the woods, when you couldn't see the sky or track the sun, then you could always tell north by the moss. Moss grew on the north side of trees. And she had been using this knowledge to travel west, keeping the mossy side of the each tree to her left—that is, keeping the north side of the tree on her south side—or keeping the bare side, which would be the south side, to her right side, or the north side. That way, her front would always be pointing west, and that was the way she walked.

"Where are we going?" Dani asked for the hundredth time.

"West," Jane replied shortly. "We have to go west."

"I know. You said," Dani sighed. "But why?"

"West is the way to new adventures."

"I don't want any adventures."

"But you will someday."

"I want to go home."

"Well, we can't."

"Why not?"

Jane thought about that for a while. Because life at home had gotten complicated. Because your father will beat you. Because he will beat me. Because I can't live at home anymore. Because I can't live anywhere else without you. Because ...

"I don't know," she said at last. "We were driving west. Now we walk."

"We were driving until you crashed the car," Dani said accusingly.

"No, you pulled on the wheel. You made us go off the road."

"That's because you were swerving across all the lanes!"

"I was not. I'm a good driver. How's your head?"

"It hurts. It's still bleeding, you know."

"I know. You're a brave girl."

"I'm tired. I'm hungry."

"We'll eat soon."

"Eat what?"

Jane considered that question for a dozen paces. She had her purse with her. There was always a roll of Life Savers in the bottom. Almost always, that is, if she remembered to buy more when the roll ran out. Jane stopped, rooted around, and came up with a stubby cylinder with the foil and paper wrapper folded over the end.

"Look, dear! Wintergreen. Two for you and one for me."

"Is that what we're going to *eat?*" Dani exclaimed.

"Sure. Sugar for energy, and wintergreen for …"

"For what?" the girl asked suspiciously.

"For luck. We just need some luck."

"No, Mother, we need a *map!*"

"Nonsense. We have—"

Jane was going to say "the moss." But suddenly she saw a tree standing directly ahead of them. It had moss on both the right and left sides. She went up to it, touched it, walked completely around it. The moss grew in vertical stripes: the bright green of moss, the muted gray of bark, all the way around the tree. Now, what did that mean? That north might be anywhere. That they were not walking west after all. That they were lost.

"We need a map," she agreed bleakly.

"See? I told you so," Dani said.

Jane looked up, past the high boughs of the trees, to the sky. It was more gray than blue. She thought she could see a star up there.

"It's getting dark," she said.

"Where are we going to sleep?"

"I don't know. Here maybe."

"In the woods? On the ground?"

"There's no place else," Jane said.

"I'm cold. I'm hurt. I want to go home."

"Well, we can't go home. We're lost."

"And whose fault is that, Mother?"

"Shut up!" Jane said. "Shut up! Shut up!"

Suddenly, Dani was cowering before her, hiding her face in her hands. And Jane realized that she had her hand raised, ready to slap her daughter. She pulled her hand down with an effort. She knelt on the ground and began putting together a bed of dried leaves and forest duff. She took off her sweater and laid it on top of the pile.

"Here, lie down on this."

"What are you going to do?"

"I'll—I'll lie here beside you."

Dani knelt next to her, took the measure of the meager bed, and tried to lie on just half of it. Jane took the other half, nestling into her daughter like two spoons, and put her arm around the girl.

"Good night, Mother."

"Good night, dear."

24. THIRTY-SIX HOURS (VI)

WHEN WILLIAM HENRY arrived home at the cottage in the woods, Jane and Dani still had not turned up, despite the sergeant's assurances. He decided to take matters into his own hands—but that was more easily said than done. It cost William Henry nearly two hours, working from his address book and being mindful that it was now the dinner hour, to locate one of his faculty colleagues who both owned a car and was willing to loan it on short notice. He did consider at one point calling for a taxi but wasn't sure how he would put the instructions to the driver: "Just head out along Highway 104 until we find something …"

It was dusk and turning to dark when William Henry finally got out on the road. For the last few miles he wondered how he would ever find the car. Beyond the ditch along the side of the highway there were only shadows, and they were deep enough to hide anything. In the end, though, he was drawn to a pattern of flashing lights. When he pulled over and stopped, he saw it was the dome light and blinkers of a tow truck. Beyond it, sitting hubcap-deep in the grass, was his car. Someone, perhaps Sergeant Benelli, had called for the tow truck to retrieve it.

"Excuse me!" William Henry said, coming up just as the driver hooked a chain to the rear bumper. "I believe that's my automobile."

"Yes?" the man replied blandly.

William Henry recited the license plate from memory.

"Sure enough," the man said. "You were driving this?"

"No, my wife and daughter. I understand they were hurt."

"Nah." The man waved. "This looks worse than it is."

"The police said there was blood inside …"

"Really? Here, let me get a light." The tow truck driver went to his cab and came back with a nine-volt flood lamp. It lit up the interior of the car like a magnesium flare. There was a spot, more like a smear, on the metal dashboard that might have been blood—or shoe polish. It looked black in the harsh light. The caramel-colored mohair upholstery showed a pattern of dime-sized spots that might have been blood—or grease. None of it looked too bad, to William Henry's intense relief.

"Where are they now?" the driver asked.

"I don't know. The police say the car was abandoned. Did you see anyone …?"

The man shrugged. "They just told me to come out and take it to the garage."

"Is it drivable?" William Henry asked, not sure about handling the two cars.

"Yeah, for about a mile. Radiator's busted. She'll seize up, going that far."

"Then you'd better give me your card, so I'll know where to pick it up."

"Oh, we'll find you! It's twenty bucks for the tow, you know. Plus costs to fix."

"Whatever it takes," William Henry said, ready to leave the man to his chain and winch. Somewhere, along the road, on the edge of the woods, maybe wandering around inside, were his wife and daughter. They might be hurt. Jane was clearly confused, not thinking straight. Perhaps some passing motorist had given them a ride home. But then where were they? If they had taken Dani to the hospital, someone would have called long before he left the cottage.

As the truck pulled his car backward through the ditch and up onto the shoulder, the glare of its headlights made the shadows shift and dodge under the trees. William Henry went up to the edge of the undergrowth and tried to discover any kind of trail Jane and Dani might have followed. There was nothing.

"Jane?" he called. "Jane!"

And then, after a moment, "Dani!"

Not even his own echo came back to him.

The woods were so thick, the pair might be a hundred feet away and not hear him.

William Henry went to stop the tow truck driver, asked to borrow his flood lamp, and ended up paying ten dollars for it. After the truck went off with the Plymouth, he plunged into the woods with the light.

He tried to be systematic about searching, moving in straight lines, counting his paces, sweeping the beam of his lamp carefully left and right so as not to miss one of their huddled, unconscious forms in the underbrush. He remembered reading about search patterns at sea and something called a "box search," with sides that became longer and longer on each pass. Using the road as one side of the box and the crash site as its center, he tried to execute the pattern on three sides, each time going further along the road in either direction and deeper into the woods. He kept calling their names, "Jane! ... Dani!" until the sounds became meaningless yelps and his voice a hoarse croak. He kept this up for two or three hours, until his legs were trembling with fatigue and the bulb of the flood lamp started to go dim.

At last, even William Henry had to give up. All he could do then was go home and wait for his wife and daughter to show up.

25. THIRTY-SIX HOURS (VII)

EVERY JOINT WAS aching when Jane woke up. Her knees, her hips, her back, her neck, all protested the hard ground and the cold night air. The crick in her neck was sending waves of pain up into her brain. Jane put a hand up to her head and found a cold crustiness that she only slowly realized was frost in her hair. She dropped a hand to Dani's shoulder. It was stiff and cold, like a piece of wood under the thin fabric of her sweater. Jane shook it but got no result. She felt her daughter's forehead, and it was as cold as marble.

"Dani!" Jane called. Her voice came out more croak than shout. "Wake up!"

Her daughter lay in her arms, head at an angle, mouth slightly open. The patch of dried blood above her left eye had a white rime on it, like ice.

"Oh, Dani," Jane wailed. She sat up, with a hand to her mouth. She had killed her only child through madness and neglect.

"What? Mom?" the girl stirred and answered sleepily.

"Oh! Dani!" she said. "You're alive! You're okay!"

"Well, sure." Dani frowned. "I mean, why not?"

Now that the matter of her daughter's life was resolved, Jane knew they had to go on, had to keep moving. Otherwise they would starve and freeze to death in these woods. The shock just now had only been a warning. But, since the trick with the moss had proved unreliable, she had to find another way to guide them. Well, with the sun just coming up, she could easily find their way west, at least for the next hour or two, by keeping the sun to their backs.

"Come on," she said, pulling Dani to her feet. "We have to get going now."

"Where? Where are we going anyway? I'm hungry. I want breakfast."

"We'll get breakfast when we get there, dear," Jane replied.

"Get where? I'm tired. I'm cold. And I want to pee."

"No time for that. We must hurry or they'll ..."

100

"They? Who? What will *they* do?"

Jane didn't have an answer.

"Come on!" she said.

Before Dani could put up a fuss, Jane charged off through the trees. Where bushes blocked her route of march, she counted her steps while going around, so many south, so many north. She wasn't about to get lost again. Not this time. Every hundred steps or so, she looked back to see that her daughter was keeping up. Dani wasn't always at the same distance, but she was always in sight. A frown marked Dani's beautiful face, reluctance dragged at her feet, but she was always there. Good girl!

"Just like yourself at that age," said a breathy voice at her shoulder.

Shut up, Mother! Jane said automatically, not looking over.

"Of course, I never marched you through the woods."

No, but you did lose me in Central Park. Twice.

"Not lost, dear. You ran away. Remember?"

What a lie! I looked and looked for you!

"And we found you at the boathouse."

What? I was sleeping, Mother.

"You were hiding, dear."

Well … maybe I was.

Before Margot could gloat over this, a darting shape moved just beyond the trees, distracting her. Jane stopped and peered. Another dark shape—like a great, hunched-over bear, but with a gleam of silver on it. It moved with an eerie silence, maybe with just a sigh of wind. Jane hesitated, then took a step closer.

Dani passed her at a dead run. "Mother! It's a car! That's the road!"

"Don't go out there!" Jane was suddenly afraid. "Please, no!"

"They can help us!" Dani shouted. "We're rescued!"

"But they'll see us! You don't want them to—"

"You don't, but I *do!*" the girl told her.

Before Jane could catch up to her, Dani ran out through the screen of underbrush, crossed the grassy verge, and leaped the ditch alongside the road's shoulder. She was running along the edge of the pavement, waving her arms and yodeling a wordless "Hey-yay-yay-yay!"

The car they had seen at first was too far down the road. But another was coming along almost right behind: a black car with a shield painted on its door panel and a rack of lights on the roof. Dani turned to face it, and the car slowed. Almost at the same time the lights began flashing and the siren whooped.

Dani waited patiently for it to come up to her.

Jane turned and tried to force her way back through the brush.

An amplified voice behind her called out: "Mrs. Wheelock? Please, stop!"

She turned to see one man get out of the car and go to Dani. The other man, the driver, crossed the ditch and came after Jane.

"We're the police, Mrs. Wheelock. We've been looking for you."

Jane would have gotten away, except that the sleeve of her sweater was caught on a dead branch. Before she could twist free, a hand came through the leaves and closed on her other shoulder, gently but firmly.

"You really have to come with us, ma'am," the policeman said. "Your daughter's hurt, you know. Her forehead's bleeding. And you don't look so good yourself."

Jane tensed, ready to turn, to bite the hand, to fight the man. But the brush was too thick. She couldn't reach through it to get at his face and eyes with her nails. She couldn't break through it to run. She was trapped. With a shrug, she went mentally limp and let him draw her out into the open. The policeman was talking fast now, babbling to her, about how worried her husband was about her and Dani, how scared everyone had been when they found the wrecked car, but everything was going to be all right now. Those were just words. He was going to take her back. Back to Willie. Back to the trap.

She allowed him to lead her to the car, settle her into the rear seat with Dani, and close the door on them. Jane would bide her time. Soon. Soon these men would make a mistake. Soon they would leave an opening. And then she would grab her daughter and make a run for it.

In the front seat, the policeman who wasn't driving radioed the dispatcher, told her to call Professor Wheelock, and have him meet his wife and daughter at the hospital.

"They're taking you right to him," Margot said from the seat beside Jane. "Too bad. You should have run when you had the chance, dear."

But they already had Dani. I couldn't leave without her.

"I always said you have to make choices."

That's not a choice I can make.

"No courage at all," Margot sighed. She crossed her arms and slowly faded away. Through the window, beyond her vanishing reflection, Jane could see they were coming into town. Soon enough, they turned into the circular driveway of the red-brick county hospital and stopped by the double glass doors of the emergency room. The radio-talking policeman came around and took Dani out one side of the car, while the driving policeman came to the other and took Jane. She noticed that they always kept their bodies between her and her daughter. Still, it was just a matter of time until they made a mistake.

26. In the Emergency Room

When the police called the next morning about finding Jane and Dani, William Henry still had his friend's keys from the night before. Rather than stop to ask if he could borrow the car again, he just drove it away. He wedged into an on-street parking spot opposite the hospital and ran across the lawn to the ambulance entrance. An empty patrol car was already standing there. He shoved open the wide glass doors and ran through the hall to the waiting room. When he found that empty, too, he ran down the short corridor toward the treatment bays.

There was a curtain pulled across the first bay, and he pushed it back to reveal his wife, a doctor and nurse, and two uniformed patrolmen positioned around his daughter on the examining table. Dani saw him before anyone else.

"Hi, Daddy!" she exclaimed.

Jane turned stiffly, her face showing alarm.

William Henry gathered his wife into his arms. "Oh, my darling! I was so worried about you both ..." That was as far as he got. Jane had gone limp—not melting with love, but suddenly lifeless, like an animal that decides not to resist the tug of a snare. She did not rise to embrace him. When he drew back to study her face, she would not look up at him. He held her at arms' length, his hands on her shoulders.

"Jane?" he asked softly.

She would not answer.

"What's going on?"

"She's been kind of quiet," one of the officers volunteered.

"Both your wife and daughter are suffering from shock and exposure," the doctor said. "Dani has a possible concussion, probably mild, but it should have been treated right after the accident. So I'd like to keep her for a day or two, just to sort things out. For Mrs. Wheelock, I'm going to prescribe a mild sedative, and then you can take her home."

"I understand, Doctor," William Henry said.

"No!" Jane grunted. It was almost a growl.

"But, darling, they have to check your—"

"No!" Jane repeated, now with a shriek.

She struggled against him, then past him. William Henry thought she was moving toward Dani on the examining table, to comfort her, to cuddle with her. So did everyone else. But in mid-stride Jane slipped sideways and spun around. She ended up behind the nearer of the two patrolmen, having pulled his revolver out of its holster. She held it with both hands wrapped around the grip and her index finger inside the trigger guard. The end of barrel was pointed directly at William Henry.

"You're not taking us. You're not taking me. You're not taking Dani." She said this like a chant, as if repetition would make it so. But it was the venom—her voice low, determined, brittle to the point of breaking—that caught William Henry's attention. Where did this anger come from? Why should she hate him so? "You're going to leave here without us," Jane went on. "You're going to leave us alone. You're—"

After the initial moment of shock had passed, the patrolman she had disarmed managed to react to the situation. He flashed one hand toward Jane's eyes, to distract her, and batted the gun down with the other, hitting her across the wrists with enough force to make Jane drop the heavy weapon. From his military service, William Henry knew enough about weapons to appreciate the risks the officer was taking—with Wheelock's life. The revolver was police issue and likely a double-action design, which meant that even with the hammer down, it would cock and fire if Jane pulled the trigger with enough force. Having the gun knocked out of her hands might or might not provide that force. At any rate, the gamble paid off.

The patrolman let the gun clatter away across the tiles. Throwing one of Jane's arms wide and catching the other one close, he neatly whipped her around and pinned her hands behind her back. The other officer tossed him a pair of handcuffs, and he secured her with two quick movements, the ratchets making sharp, rasping noises as they tightened.

Jane had gone limp again. She was breathing hard but saying nothing. She glared around at them like a trapped animal.

"Take her to the station, Steve?" the arresting policeman asked his partner.

"I think ..." the doctor interposed slowly, "we should hold Mrs. Wheelock here for observation."

"But, Doc!" the policeman protested. "She pulled a gun on him! My gun!"

The doctor seemed to notice the darkness in Jane's eyes for the first time.

"I was going to suggest upstairs," he continued. "In the psychiatric ward."

The two policemen looked at each other.

"Oh, yeah," the first one said. He bent to retrieve and holster his gun. Then the two of them led William Henry's wife away, one holding each arm, with Jane hesitating and stumbling between them.

"Daddy?" his daughter quavered.

"It's all right, dear. Mommy's all right now."

But, deep in his heart, he knew that was far from the case.

————

As her police captors escorted Jane down the hospital corridor to the elevator, they passed a familiar figure. Jane twisted to look back at her. Margot was leaning against the wall. As soon as she knew Jane was looking, her mother lifted her hands and silently applauded her daughter. Little puffs of ash rose with each clap of her hands.

27. PRIMARY DIAGNOSIS

TO GO ON the psychiatric ward to visit his wife, William Henry first had to make an appointment through her psychiatrist, Dr. Frederick Barlow, who was one of the residents on the hospital staff. At the appointed time on Monday afternoon, he had to sign in at the nurse's station in the open corridor outside the ward, empty his pockets of keys, coins, wallet, comb, and penknife—suffering a long, hard stare when he produced the latter—and take a receipt for these effects. Only then would they let him through a locked door. It had a window of pebbled glass, the kind that sandwiched chicken wire into the layers.

Beyond, he found himself in a windowless room, a booth actually, barely bigger than a closet, facing another door with more chicken-wired glass. As soon as the latch clicked behind him, the one ahead released on some kind of electrical circuit, and he could pull the door open. Like an air lock, he thought, only this was a people lock, and he suspected it would not work so automatically going in the other direction.

William Henry did not know exactly what to expect inside. His mind conjured up medieval visions: iron rings set in stone walls, floors covered in straw and offal, rooms lined with kapok and mattress ticking, wretches in canvas and leather jackets buckled up the back, flapping their elbows and gibbering. But he knew that was just his imagination.

What he found was a normal hospital ward, like any other in the building, except that the main area was not set up with beds but instead arranged more like an institutional living room: waxed tile on the floor, couches and armchairs in cracked leather, dinette-style tables and chrome chairs with vinyl seats and backs. It all seemed pleasant enough. Except for the white-painted metal slats across the insides of the windows.

At first, he wondered where the ... patients ... slept at night. Then he noticed the two interior walls were lined with doors, and a couple of them stood open. Inside were individual rooms: single bed, night table, chair, chest of drawers. It was all very

107

civilized. Except the rooms had no windows, and the doors had knobs and bolt locks—but only on the outside.

The patients themselves—he counted nine heads, looking for Jane's distinctive auburn hair and not finding it—all wore identical blue-serge bathrobes and khaki-colored canvas slippers. They all seemed incredibly subdued ... for crazy people. One woman, gray headed and vacant eyed, looked up at him without curiosity, not even registering a presence.

"May I help you?" asked a voice from behind him. William Henry turned to find, tucked into the corner opposite the entry door, the high barricade-like counter of another nurse's station. The counter hid all but the woman's head in her stiff, white cap, as if she had been decapitated and left on a shelf.

"I'm looking for my wife, Jane Wheelock," he told the head.

"She's in the bathroom," the head said, tipping her cap to a nearby door labeled RESTROOM. "Be out in a minute."

William Henry stood just inside the entry door, fidgeting and waiting.

After a minute there was a rap on the bathroom door. The nurse got up, pulled out a bunch of keys jangling on a fine chain at her waist, and unlocked the door.

Jane stood just inside. Her hair was in rattails, as if someone had tried to brush it inexpertly and given up. She wore the same blue robe as everyone else—except that hers hung open to show the short hospital gown underneath, white cotton with tiny blue flowers—and the canvas slippers. Her face held the same vacant expression as the old woman's. Behind her, William Henry could see that the bathroom had no mirror, no windows, and no interior door.

"Christ sake," Jane said to the nurse, but listlessly, without her old fire. "Lock me in there like I'm going to escape or something. Only there's no place to go ... Oh!" She paused, noticing her husband for the first time, looking at him, then through him. "Hello, Willie." She looked down at herself, pulled the robe together, and knotted the belt.

"The lock's for your own protection, dear," the nurse said.

"Hello, Jane," William Henry said. "My, you're looking—"

"Another damn lie," Jane told the nurse. "Like shit," she said to him.

"Just a little tired, I think," he substituted, "but not at all—"

"Crazy? In-sane? De-*men*-ted?" Jane supplied.

"I was going to say 'sick.' "

"Sure you were."

William Henry led his wife over to one of the couches. Jane took the extreme end, forcing him to sit in an armchair positioned perpendicular to the way she was facing. She held the throat of her bathrobe closed with one hand, the other tucked away under her elbow.

"What do you want?" she asked guardedly.

"To see you. To find out how you're doing."

"So you see. I'm locked in the psycho ward with crazy people."

"It's just for a few days, until you get your—"

"Mind back?" she finished.

"Well, your composure. Then they'll let you come home."

"Home." She did not sound convinced. "With you."

"Of course. Isn't home where you belong?"

"I don't belong anywhere anymore."

William Henry did not know what to say to that. He did not think it was good for Jane that they were fencing with words like this. She did not appear to be agitated—just too tired to continue. Jane stared at the baseboard on the other side of the room. Then she looked at the windows, as if she could see beyond the metal slats. Then she seemed to be waiting for something, and he realized she was waiting for him to go.

"Well," he said. "I guess—"

"Yes, why don't you?"

"Go," Jane meant, as if they had read each other's minds. He stood up, and she made no move to follow. He walked uncertainly away, toward the nurse's station. The disembodied head regarded at him with an expression of total understanding: the woman must have seen many defeated husbands pass through here. She tipped her head toward the entry door, and as he approached to put his hand on the knob, it buzzed and clicked.

William Henry turned to look back at his wife. She was smoothing a fold of the blue robe across her knee, apparently unaware that he was gone, or perhaps that he had ever been there.

He let himself through into the people lock. The opposite door clicked, and he went out into the empty corridor beyond.

———

The psychiatrist, Dr. Barlow, was an old man with thick, white hair and a lined, sagging face that suggested he had seen too many of the world's tragedies. His office was spare and neat, threadbare in the way William Henry expected of a county hospital. The desk had no papers lying around, nothing to link the doctor to any specific patient, not even Jane. He offered William Henry a guest chair upholstered in a coarse-weave fabric that was jade green at the corners and back. The seat cushion was the ghostly green of Chinese celadon pottery, faded by wear and by sunlight coming through the uncurtained window. The room smelled strongly of floor polish and cigarette smoke, although no ashtrays were in evidence.

"I understand you've had a chance to visit Mrs. Wheelock," the doctor began.

"What have you done to her?" William Henry demanded.

"Merely kept her under observation."

"She's barely awake!"

"Ah, yes. That's the Thorazine. It helps keep her calm."

"Comatose, you mean."

"Would you rather she were agitated?"

"Well, no, but—"

"Mrs. Wheelock is having difficulty dealing with reality," Barlow went on. "In her present state, she appears to hear things, perhaps even see things, that are not present for the rest of us. These are called hallucinations. Some of my colleagues believe they result from a deterioration or scrambling of sensory inputs in the brain so that, for example, the rustling of fabric becomes a whisper, or the creak of a door hinge becomes a human cry. She also appears to imagine events in the past, or assigns unusual meanings and interpretations to remembered events, then clings to these interpretations despite all rational argument. These are called delusions. Quite often they are paranoid in nature, which means that your wife feels persecuted and reacts with suspicion. For example, she has the idea that you beat her—that you beat both her and Dani."

"That's absurd! I've never laid a violent hand on either of them."

"I'm not saying that you did. But she has this idea firmly in her mind. Perhaps it is a form of transference. She may feel guilt over a real or imagined wrong—something she did, for which she is worthy of being beaten—and so she imagines that you indeed have beaten her. Do you follow me?"

"No, not really," William Henry admitted.

"The point is, we cannot know where these ideas come from. I will do my best to understand them, and help Jane understand them, in order for her find her way back to reality. But neither you nor I should take them at face value. They are, in truth, figments."

"Is there anything I can do?" William Henry asked.

"It would help to know how long she's been having these delusions."

"Well ... since the last couple of days, I guess. It all seemed to start with an old letter that Jane found."

"The accusation of adultery?"

"Just a mean piece of gossip."

"And yet she reacted strongly to it. Perhaps that was the source of her guilt."

"I never believed a word of it. I am convinced in my own mind that Jane never—"

"Ah! But remember—figments? Misremembered events? It is not in *your* mind that we find the guilt."

"Well, yes, of course."

"And there was nothing before that?"

"Jane has been going through a difficult phase. There was some friction with the other faculty wives. It isn't always easy for someone with her education and background fitting into an academic setting," William Henry explained. "That's made her moody."

"How long has she had these feelings?"

"Oh, two or three months now. More, I guess."

"Then it can hardly be just a mood swing, can it?"

"You're saying this was part of her illness?"

"We can't subdivide the mind like a chest of drawers. Each part separated neatly."

"But she hasn't always been crazy. Not like the last couple of days."

"No," the doctor admitted. "But her condition is known to be progressive. This disease usually strikes during the patient's late teens but—especially in young women—sometimes not until the middle to late twenties. It appears to come out of the blue. Then it develops in an ever-tightening spiral, until there's a psychotic break, and then you have events like those of the past few days."

"What condition is that, Doctor?"

"Well, we used to call it *dementia praecox,* Latin for 'premature dementia.' But now the illness has another name, one that more completely describes the symptoms of personality dissociation and separation from reality ... schizophrenia."

"And now you have a cure for it?"

"I'm afraid there's no cure."

"But this Thorazine—"

"Merely a sedative."

William Henry paused, trying to absorb all this. Finally he said, "What will I do?"

"I suggest you let me arrange to have Mrs. Wheelock transferred to the state mental hospital for a period of observation and treatment."

"You mean, have her committed."

"They can care for her on a long-term basis," Barlow said. "Sometimes—but I don't want you to get your hopes up—after a length of time, the disease appears to burn itself out. Then the patient recovers her sense of reality and some—but not necessarily all—of her ability to function in a normal, rational capacity."

"How long, Doctor?"

"Months. More like years. Quite possibly never."

William Henry took this calmly enough on the outside. Inside, however, his mind, his heart, his whole being shuddered, lurched to a stop, and tilted sideways, like a moving ship striking on a submerged rock. At first he had thought Jane was simply angry, and then he had tried to accept that she was ill, but he never imagined the illness might be permanent. It was as if the doctor had told him Jane had cancer or a terminal condition. He realized now, for the first time, that he might lose his darling Jane, his wife, the woman he loved.

"Oh!" was all he could think to say. But inside, his mind was straining, dashing about like a mouse in a box, trying to evade the awful possibilities. He had a duty to his wife, but also to his daughter. Who would care for Dani? Who would teach her to be a woman? Their world together was about to change—no, about to collapse.

"What," he said finally, "what am I to do? And my daughter …?"

"You can hope for the best. Pray for your wife, if that's your choice."

"And there's nothing more you doctors can do?"

"We will watch. Try to keep her calm. Protect her from herself."

"For years …" William Henry said, still trying to absorb it.

"For the rest of her life, if necessary."

———

That night William Henry made a long-distance call to his parents at home in Roulette, Pennsylvania. He had delayed informing them of Jane's breakdown until he had a chance to talk with the doctor and learn the true state of affairs. Now he spoke with his father Robert, who was sharing the telephone's earpiece with his wife Libby. William Henry briefly described Jane's bizarre actions around town during that terrible day and a half, ending in her final flight and the car crash. No, he glossed over them, actually, made them sound less desperate and crazy, so as not to alarm his mother. And he left out the incident with the policeman's gun entirely. He went into more detail about Dr. Barlow's diagnosis, *dementia praecox,* schizophrenia, and his terrifying prognosis: years of insanity, perhaps a lifetime of isolation. Both for Jane and for himself.

"Oh, my boy, I'm so sorry ..." his mother said.

His father was silent for a moment. The static on the line stretched out in the hollow rhythms of steady breathing. Then Robert began tentatively: "I think ... there may be a legal remedy ..." Robert was a lawyer and had been the county judge.

William Henry shook his head. "I don't want to contest the commitment."

"Not what I meant," Robert said. "I know the statutes are different in New York State, but there must be some provision about mental illness."

"I'm not following you."

"Your state's pretty tough about granting divorces, but you can seek an annulment on grounds of insanity ... especially something like this. The doctor did say the condition develops slowly, so it may have been present when the two of you were married."

"I'm not going to divorce Jane!"

"You say that now, Willie."

"She's my wife. I love her."

"Just consider it," his father urged. "For your daughter's sake."

"It seems so cruel," William Henry said. "Just abandoning Jane like that."

"Tell me what you're feeling ten years from now."

"Ten years from now I will love Jane as my wife."

———

He waited until the next day after school to try to discuss Jane's diagnosis with Dani. The girl had been ominously quiet after her excursion through the woods with her mother and then being under observation for her concussion. *Waiting for the other shoe to drop,* was how William Henry interpreted his daughter's silence.

"Your mother will be staying at the hospital for a while," he began.

"Is it because she hurt her head?"

"Yes, she's had some confusion. She's actually pretty sick."

"Do we have to go and visit her?"

"Well, of course we can—don't you *want* to visit her?"

"I don't know. Not if she's going to hurt us."

"You know she didn't want to hurt you. Or me. She just can't control herself. And the doctors are going to watch her very carefully."

"Because she's sick," Dani summed up.

"Yes. The doctor makes what's called a *diagnosis,* about what's wrong with your mother, and then a *prognosis,* about what will happen to her. Right now, she has a kind of mental disease called 'schizophrenia.' And they expect it will take a long time for her to get better."

Dani absorbed that. William Henry tried to think back to his own childhood and what "a long time" meant to a nine-year-old. He could remember a month being almost forever. "They're going to keep her very safe," he added.

"Rachel Lee says they've got her locked up in a padded cell at the booby hatch," Dani said. "Is that like being in jail?"

William Henry was shocked. "Who is Rachel Lee?"

"One of the girls at school."

"Well, you tell Rachel your mother is sick and needs medical attention. She's in a hospital—not that other place."

"But is she? Locked up, I mean."

"There are some restraints," he agreed. "But it's not like Rachel said."

"Good!"

Only later, after this conversation, did he wonder if Dani was approving the fact that her mother wasn't in jail—or that she was under restraint.

28. Learned at Her Mother's Knee

AFTER THE THIRD day in the psychiatric ward, Jane suddenly realized that the muzzy feeling in her head—like she had been pounded with a large, velvet-covered hammer—wasn't because she was tired, or bored, or worn out from worrying about being locked up and unable to foresee any kind of future for herself, for her marriage, for her daughter.

It was the pills they gave her.

"Thorazine," the nurse had called them.

"Chemical lobotomy" was Jane's name for them.

A shrunken head was only the most pronounced effect, she learned. Over those three days, she also noticed her mouth feeling gummy and tasting like she was sucking on a galvanized nail. At odd moments her vision went blurry and her sense of balance failed, so that she suddenly reeled and stumbled. Her bowels had also clamped up. Her face came alive at odd moments with uncontrollable grimaces. Her hands and legs went into spasms of twitching and jerking.

Putting all this together took great effort on Jane's part. She had it worked out that the pills equaled sickness. She had to remember that, hold it in her mind. Yes, remember ... Remember what? Pills equal sick. Pills make you stupid.

Jane Wheelock wasn't stupid. She wasn't going to let them make her sick. If she put up with that, then the next thing you know they would give her a real lobotomy. Cut the brain right out of her.

Years ago, as a little girl, Jane had learned to take the pills her mother forced on her—the bitter ones that she didn't like. Jane learned to make a swallowing movement with her throat, even accept a glass of water and drink it down. But she had already moved the pill around and under her tongue, where it was safe and dry and didn't make a taste. And then, when Margot wasn't looking, she spit it out into her palm and put it down the toilet.

The trouble with the psych ward was, you couldn't go to the bathroom without asking permission. So she had to find someplace else to put the pills. Sticking them deep in the seat cushions of the old couch would only work for so long.

Well, that was just for starters. She would also have to fake what the pills did to her: the vacant stare, the slow and shuffling walk, the twitches and drooping of her head. But faking was easy, because she only had to look around at the other patients. It was then she suddenly understood that they were all being given Thorazine. They weren't just lazy and stupid, like she had thought at first, or not all of them. They were simply being drugged.

After two days of sliding the pills under her tongue and stashing them around the ward—in the couch, under her mattress, in the planter of the dying rubber tree—always careful to avoid being seen by the eyes watching from the corner—Jane began to wake up. By the fifth day, she was alert enough to start observing the hospital's routine, noting its weaknesses, and begin working on a plan.

The first thing she noticed was that the hospital staff, even the nurses assigned to the ward, made an unconscious distinction between people and things. The people they watched, kept track of, counted, and recounted. But the things that came into the ward—food carts from the kitchen, the medication cart from the pharmacy, wheeled baskets from the laundry—these things they took for granted. The carts were not going to run away. After the trays of food had been handed around, the medications administered, the beds made and the old sheets loaded into the baskets, the staff pushed the carts into an empty bedroom just beyond the line of sight of the eyes in the corner. And, because there was nothing on the empty carts worth stealing, they never locked the door on them.

The second thing she noticed was the tempo of activity in the ward. The days and nights were always empty, uneventful to the point of suffocation. Sometimes Jane would welcome one of the patients going off in a screaming fit, just for the diversion. She even thought of trying it herself and had to guard against it, because then the staff would know she wasn't taking her Thorazine. But, in all that boredom, all that empty time, for one hour of the day—half an hour, really, just before dinner—everything started happening at once. Some lucky conjunction of the hospital's schedules brought the dinner trays and the cart with the take-before-food medications into the ward at the same time the orderlies were changing the bed linens. So, for that brief window of time, regular hospital staff were coming and going, and a confusion of carts entered and left that unused bedroom.

And that was also when Jane noticed the third thing. The food and med carts were lightweight boxes of sheet metal on small castors. Each cart was partitioned into shelves and cabinets. Empty, they rattled and banged like a collection of old pots. But the laundry carts were solid wooden platforms with pipe frames built to support stiff bags of heavy canvas. They had big, thick wheels that rumbled the same way all the time, whether the carts were full or empty.

By the sixth day, Jane had worked it all out. Toward the end of that window of time, she drifted alongside the door of the bedroom, which someone had left ajar. After checking for those watching eyes, she slipped inside the room. Two of the laundry carts were there—one full, the other only half full—while the third was still being wheeled around the ward by the orderly making up the last of the beds. Jane pushed aside the tangle of sheets in the half-empty cart and climbed in. She wriggled down to the bottom and pulled the sheets over herself, holding her breath against the fetid odor of crazy people's vomit and urine stains.

If she had been a big girl, Jane's plan would have failed. But she was petite and small boned, weighing not quite a hundred pounds. When the orderly pushed the cart out of the ward, maneuvering it through the double set of doors, the wheels would just roll a little more solidly than usual.

For a long time—so long that Jane lost count, first of her heartbeats, and then her breaths—the cart did not move. Finally, she heard the room door open and felt a pair of strong hands clamp onto the pipe frame, shifting the bag slightly with her inside. Then the cart moved—backwards, it seemed. Stopped. It moved again, in the other direction. Bumped something. Moved. Stopped. Bumped again. Moved for so long that Jane could no longer feel the movement. Stopped abruptly. Moved, bumped, and stopped. Then the floor gave way beneath the cart, and Jane thought they might be in the service elevator.

After another equally long series of movements and bumps, there was nothing. She counted heartbeats again and, when she got to two hundred, began to dig herself out of the basket. The air above the top layer of sheets was hot and steamy. She was in the hospital laundry. She lifted her head over the cart's rim and looked around: bright lights and white-jacketed pipes overhead, gleaming steel machines that would be industrial-strength washers and dryers. But no one operating them, no one around.

Jane climbed out and rearranged the sheets to conceal her nest. It took her no time at all to find windows—high up in the wall, at ground level, but without any bars—and the door into the corridor, without a lock. The corridor was not for either patients or the visiting public; it had a natural cement floor and white-painted cinderblock walls. But at this hour it had no people, either. Jane knew it would be difficult to explain herself down here: a patient in a blue bathrobe and canvas shoes. But she could tell from the piles of laundry around her that bathrobes in all the wards were blue. So there was nothing special to mark her as a mental patient. If she kept her head and smiled in a normal way, she might be able to pull it off.

At the far end of the corridor was another door, and this one had a lock. But it was for outside, to keep people out there from coming in. On her side, there was just the knob that turned the dead bolt. She turned it.

The air outside was warm and still, a foretaste of summer. Beyond the door were a short flight of eight concrete steps and the staff parking lot—half empty at the end of the day. Jane climbed the steps and crossed the lot, moving casually, stopping once or twice to look at the parked cars, as if she was thinking of buying one. This was for the benefit of the hospital windows overlooking the lot, where people would be watching her. But always she headed for the trees along the back of the hospital property.

Once inside the screen of the trees, Jane moved fast. She wasn't tracking the sun, which was almost down in the west, or studying the moss, which grew on every side of each tree. She just moved as directly as possible away from the hospital building.

In a hundred yards she came out the other side, along a road. By now it was dark enough that the passing cars mostly had their headlights on. Two by two, the lights appeared over the rise, approached, and passed, never pausing. But then a solitary light appeared, jiggling up and down in a way that no car headlight jiggled. As it approached, Jane heard the high-pitched roar of a motorcycle engine.

The light slowed, swerved toward her, and stopped just short of the gravel strip alongside the road. The exhaust note settled down to a comfortable *blah-di-blah-di-blah-dip-dop-dip*, with an occasional *blip* thrown in when the rider twisted the throttle.

"Hello, beautiful," said the rider. From what Jane could see in the backwash from the headlight, he had blond hair and a beard that framed strong, white teeth. He wore a peaked leather cap and aviator-style goggles that hid his eyes with reflections.

"Hello," she said softly.

"You just get out of bed, darlin'?"

"Can you give me a ride on that thing?"

"Sure. Where are you headed?"

"Nowhere. Anywhere. Away from here."

He laughed. "You got that right, baby! Climb on!"

Jane looked at the tiny rear seat, a stuffed leather pillow sitting on the shiny black fender. She pulled up the hem of her bathrobe, put a leg over the fender, and squatted on the seat. The rider reached back and, going by feel, adjusted her feet to the pegs attached to the frame on each side. Jane clamped her naked thighs against the denim at his hips, spread her hands against the leather front of his jacket.

The rider turned his head, so that his face was at right angles to hers. "My name's Eric, by the way," he said.

"Jane," she answered.

"Well, hang on, Jane!"

He blipped the throttle again, but this time the bike's engine did more than warble briefly. The whole machine roared, bucked, then leapt. In half a heartbeat it was hurtling down the road, following the cone of its own headlight.

Over Eric's shoulder, Jane watched the road unreel before them. The wind made tears in her eyes and sent her hair into a frenzied electric dance. But it also blew the last of the Thorazine cobwebs out of her head. She had never felt so alive. So clear. So sharp.

29. THE DAILY CALL

EVERY DAY FOR the past month the call came in just ten minutes after five o'clock. Mike Greer, desk sergeant at the Byzantium Police Department, figured that was when the man got home from the office. Come home, fix a drink, call the police for any news. Among his other duties, Greer compiled the police blotter, which included the Missing Persons reports and any action concerning same. By now, he was on a first-name basis with the caller.

"Hello, Professor. What's new?"

"Well, Mike, I thought you could tell me."

"Nothing on your wife. You gotta know that by now."

"But you're still looking, right? You have, what do you call, *leads?*"

"Ahhh …" Greer tried to turn his exclamation of disgust into an audible yawn.

"What?" Wheelock demanded.

"Willie, there *are* no leads. No clues. The department's got nothing to go on. One minute, your Jane's checked into the psycho ward, all snug and tight. The next—*poof!* Gone. No one sees her go. She doesn't leave a trail of breadcrumbs. There's no glass slipper or wrecked pumpkin. Cinderella just disappears. So … unless she gets picked up in another jurisdiction and uses her own name—but why would she, when she doesn't have any ID on her?—then she's just another white female with no distinguishing features. She's gone, man."

"But you're still looking?"

"You see, after thirty days …"

"You're *not* looking."

"We'll keep the file open."

"But where does that leave Dani and me? I mean, things like, are Jane and I still married? Does she have custody rights? What about our bank accounts?"

"I don't know, Professor," Greer said. "Talk to a lawyer. I think, if Jane doesn't turn up after seven years, you can get her declared legally dead. Then you do what you want."

"Dani will be sixteen by then! How do I raise a daughter all alone?"

"Don't ask me. We're the police. We just arrest drunks."

"I'm sorry, Mike. I shouldn't burden you—"

"Not to worry. You're a good man, Willie. You'll figure this thing out. Now look, I've got to go catch some criminals."

———

After they hung up, William Henry sat in his study for a long time, until it started to grow dark. Dani, up in her room, was probably doing homework. Maybe she was too scared or too worried to ask him about dinner or bedtime. The house was deathly quiet.

Greer had called him a "good man"—but was he? Really? William Henry thought back over the incidents of the past spring, leading to Jane's psychotic breakdown. He had known about her anxieties dealing with the Faculty Wives Club, her feeling threatened by Dani's troubles at school, her suspicions about being watched, her anger at his keeping that horrible old letter, her suddenly taking up the cigarette habit, her flashes of rage and resentment. Jane had always been a strong-willed person, opinionated, often volatile. But this was a new Jane emerging from some kind of chrysalis—and not as a butterfly.

All that time she was deteriorating, he had watched from the sidelines, had met her arguments from his own position of sweet reason and sober logic, and had convinced himself she was simply being moody. Was that what a "good man" was supposed to do? Shouldn't he instead have rushed Jane off to see a doctor, taken her for some kind of examination? But at what point, exactly? And would she even have gone? Or would she have refused with contempt? More anger. More paranoia.

And what about Dani and her future? Since talking with Dr. Barlow a month ago, William Henry had started reading about schizophrenia and related mental illnesses. One thing he learned was that a susceptibility or tendency toward schizophrenia—if not the disease itself—seemed to be inherited. William Henry's side of the family had no history of it, but Jane's background was the great unknown. So would Dani become strange and change as she grew older? Would she suddenly develop the same innate suspicion, the tendency toward anxiety and fear, and then the sudden onslaught of crazy, disconnected thoughts? William Henry vowed to guard against letting such imaginings bear upon his affection for his daughter. He would not be the catalyst for a reappearance of the disease in her generation.

But then, had Jane herself really been so sick? Was she actually such a lost cause? Despite the doctor's confident diagnosis, how sick had Jane been? Her disappearance from the face of the earth clearly proved that she had preserved enough mental acuity to escape from a locked ward, evade a police search, and hide herself under a new identity. Those weren't the actions of a crazy person, were they?

Outside his window, at the edge of the woods, the first of the summer's fireflies were coming out of the shadows. They blinked their on-on-off pattern of yellow-green light, wandering across the margin of his lawn like the spirits of the hovering dead.

Where was his wife now?

And was Jane even alive?

How would he ever know?

WINTER 1968

1. Professor of Logic

William Henry hated galoshes, those great, floppy boots of black, rubberized canvas that pulled on over his shoes, wrapped around his pants legs, and closed with tricky little clasps of black-enameled steel that were impossible to work if you were wearing gloves. But when the snow lay several feet deep and drifted, as it did in December all along the southern shore of Lake Ontario, and when his class was halfway across campus at eight o'clock in the morning, before Buildings and Grounds had a chance to plow and sweep the walks, then he really had no choice. He might have been happier if he had someplace to leave the boots once he got inside, but this morning class was in an amphitheater which had no closet. So he had to fold his overcoat and stuff it onto the shelf under the lectern. He couldn't do that with his dripping galoshes; so they stood off to one side beneath the chalkboard, forlorn, leaning together, making puddles as they warmed in the steam-heated air.

An amphitheater filled with three hundred faces—even the stupid, sleep-deprived faces of students taking a first-period class—was beyond the wildest dreams of a young professor in the Classics Department. But today he was not teaching the classics, except in the most tangential and derivative sense.

"So," he went on, "a disjunctive sentence is true so long as any component is true. Thus, if both p and q are true, or if p is true and q false, or vice versa, then the disjunction is still true." William Henry used a long wooden pointer with a rubber tip to indicate the first three lines of the second truth table that he had drawn on the board. "Whereas, if p and q are both false, then the disjunction itself is false."

He looked over his shoulder and saw nothing but bored faces. Even he was bored with the subject. Only a hopeless pedant and cataloguer like Aristotle could possibly love truth functions. But the structure and nature of conjoined statements was an essential part of the material, and so all three hundred of them and their professor had to plow through the material.

127

Last year the College of Liberal Arts had dragooned William Henry into teaching this class, Philosophy 001, Introduction to Logic. The subject was tedious, obscure, and empirically useless. If any of his students remembered even one discreet fact or function from the sixteen-week course, he would count it a success. But the curriculum gods had decreed that Introduction to Logic could satisfy a full three credits of the liberal arts math requirement. In the third year of an undeclared ground war in Asia, with the Selective Service breathing down the neck of every male student, waiting for the missteps that would revoke his 2-S deferment and send him off to the jungle, a college math course for English majors that did not involve algebra, analytical geometry, or—heaven forbid!—calculus was a godsend. That alone made Philosophy 001 the most wildly popular, if disdained and misunderstood, course on campus.

Conversely, in this new Age of Relevancy, with its preternatural focus on things that were "now" and "happening," student interest in the classical literature of supposedly dead societies like ancient Greece and Rome had almost vanished. At the same time, the Classics Department was populated by older, more established professors who had cut their teeth on Aeschylus and Ovid in the original Greek and Latin while William Henry was still pushing the Red Ball Express across northern Europe. So the courses available to a still-untenured professor were few and far between.

He did have one course in his field—Language Arts 167, Beginning Greek. While William Henry might be barred from teaching the literature, he loved teaching the language. The thirteen students enrolled in his course included four children of Greek immigrants, who had imagined it would be an easy fulfillment of their required language credits. But now, where everyone else struggled bravely with the unfamiliar tenses of the Greek verb, those brought up with Greek at home struggled with pronunciation, which differed between ancient and modern Greek. That class met Tuesdays, Thursdays, and Saturdays at eleven, and the only dissatisfaction William Henry felt was the fall off in attendance on Saturday during football season. Still, Beginning Greek was the one bright spot in a teaching load that otherwise resembled a treadmill. By contrast, Introduction to Logic was the low point of his week.

"Has everyone got that?" he now asked his eight o'clock class. For emphasis, he tapped his pointer on the truth table chalked on the board as he recited: "True-true, true-false, and false-true are all true. False-false is false. … Right?" In return he got some sleepy nods and a few scowls. The most animated reaction was from one of his galoshes, which fell over with a little splash.

Well, he knew they would start having fun—the students, not the galoshes—when the course got into the fallacies. Everyone liked those.

2. CHRISTMAS DINNER AT HOME

THE TURKEY WAS the smallest that Dani Wheelock had been able to find at the A&P, four and a half pounds, and looked if anything like a really big chicken, except with whiter skin. Still, it was too much for just her and her father. They would be eating leftovers—sandwiches, some kind of fricassee, and soup—for the better part of a week. At least that took care of menu planning.

This was to be their first Christmas dinner at home since her mother had left, ten years ago. Every year, her father took Dani out to holiday dinner at the Colonial Arms. But now, because Danielle considered herself a grown-up, in her sophomore year at the university, and because she already did all the family cooking anyway, she insisted they celebrate at home.

Wanting to get everything just right and, to be honest, being a bit intimidated by the naked bird carcass, she had called long distance to her grandmother in Pennsylvania to ask about cooking times and stuffing recipes. Even with all the details she scribbled as fast as Libby talked, Dani was still uncertain. The bird's chest cavity would only take about half of the bread-crumb-and-celery mix she made, and she had no idea where to put the rest of it. Libby's references to the "gullet" had sounded reasonable over the phone, and Dani had accepted them with a couple of "Uh-huhs." But in practice she found they were anatomical nonsense: where the neck had been there was nothing but a flap of loose skin and no way to keep the stuffing inside it. She decided instead to cut the skin off and bake the extra stuffing in a bowl. More leftovers.

That morning, after breakfast and before she had started working on the bird, they had exchanged presents. Dani had bought her father a set of six monogrammed socks, dark burgundy with a script "W" in gold-colored thread just above the ankle. She had looked for any with the initials "WH"—for his full name, William Henry—but the clerk at the department store didn't think they could do that, even on special order. Her father had liked the socks anyway and promised to wear them every day.

For Dani, he had bought a new slide rule of a unique, circular design. Its different scales were printed in concentric circles on a disk of heavy white plastic. Instead of just one hairline cursor, this machine had two, etched on separate, transparent arms anchored to a rivet in the center of the disk. To solve a problem, the user would set the cursors to different numbers on the scales, then lock them at the prescribed angle and move them together to arrive at the answer. Dani had promised to learn how to work the device and to use it every day.

While the turkey cooked and the house filled with smells that brought back the Christmases when Jane had been with them, Dani cleared her books and papers off the dining room table. This was her preferred study area when the Barker Engineering Library was closed, because her bedroom upstairs was too small for a full-sized desk. She set out the good china and her mother's silverware from the sideboard. When she brought out the turkey, mashed potatoes, peas, and her first attempt at gravy, her father was lavish with his praises.

But then, as they started to eat, the conversation faltered and stopped—as usual. What were an abandoned father and daughter supposed to talk about at this happiest of times for all happy families?

"Everything going well in your course work?" he asked.

"Yes, Dad. I've got a lock on a three-five average."

"You're not worried about your calculus final?"

"Um, calculus was last year. No more math."

"Oh, right. Right. So it's all engineering?"

"Design, metals, drafting, structural."

"This is still what you want to do?"

It was the old question. Dani knew that her father had never fully understood her choosing the College of Engineering and specializing in mechanical engineering. He was a classics scholar. His father had been a lawyer. They were both trained in the liberal arts curriculum—and so word people. Dani was a numbers person. Maybe that came from her mother's side of the family—the mysterious side.

"It's what I'm good at," she told him now. "And I can make a name for myself, too, because there aren't many women engineers. Besides, the pay is really good."

"Making something of yourself—that's admirable." But he seemed uncomfortable with the thought. "Supporting yourself ... isn't that the function of a husband?"

"Oh, I don't want a husband. I plan to live alone."

"And what about ... well ... love?"

"I'll have lots of affairs."

"And children?"

"With the pill, that's not a problem."

"But sometimes they happen anyway," he said with a smile. "The vital force has a habit of getting in the way."

Dani wondered about that. No "vital force" had gotten in the way for her father, who ever since her mother left had lived as solitary as a hermit. From the one English course Dani was required to take, where they read Shakespeare's *The Tempest*, she had come to think of him as Prospero. He was the wise and mysterious man, living alone with his daughter in the cottage in the woods, cut off from the rest of humanity. It wasn't that William Henry disliked women, but he never spoke of them. He did not seek out their company, never went out on a date, never held parties or dinners that required a female companion. He simply, quietly remained faithful in his love for Jane, to the memory of Jane, wherever she was. In one way it was noble and good. In another, just pathetic.

"Life will find you, Dani," her father was saying. "And at some point, almost without realizing it, you'll help things get started. Then there will be children."

"Then I'll just have to work extra hard, so I can support them as well."

"I'm afraid you won't have a very good reputation."

"Fiddlesticks to my reputation!"

"But you won't have a *family*, either," he said. "Our culture's modeled on that—the sharing between a man and a woman, both of them working together to bring up their children, instill their values, prepare them to make more families in the next generation. I don't think that, as a society, we're quite ready for women to go it alone, taking lovers, dropping children, each with a different last name, who are conceived in just a moment's pleasure and then raised wild in the world, like a litter of bear cubs. It doesn't ... doesn't *lead* anywhere. Humans should aspire to something more lasting and permanent. It's our nature to build for the future."

"Well, what about you? You don't live with Mother. You don't even know where she is. And yet did I turn out wild, like a bear cub?"

"From the way you talk, apparently so," he replied sadly. "And our situation is different. Your mother got sick, and then she ran away before she could get help. It's almost as if she died. She and I didn't just ... have sex and move on. Some families are broken, but not by choice. And it's not a model on which to build a society."

"I don't care about society. I'm talking about my own life."

"And that, my dear, is the first step toward ending society."

In the silence that followed her father's last remark, Dani heard a soft pattering against the window. She looked up and said, "It's starting to snow again."

3. THE SHADOW IN THE TREES

WILLIAM HENRY FELL in love for the second time—after lifelong devotion to his wife Jane—on New Year's Day. It was not his intention to fall in love; he just wanted to get outside after a particularly snowy week over the long Christmas holidays, when he had no classes or office hours to take him out of the house, and no research project that needed a visit to the library. It had been a week of storm clouds and gloom. The walls of the cottage in the woods seemed to be pressing on the very air around him. And so, when the day came up bright, with a hard blue sky overhead and the sun dazzling on the new snow, he got in the car and went for a drive.

Or maybe love was calling him away.

He drove his old Volvo west along Lakeshore Road, watching for patches of slush and ice on the roadway with one eye and gazing out across the vista of Lake Ontario in winter with the other. Cold, gray waves rolled in, churned by the winds out of Canada, and struck at the stony beaches just out of sight below the modest lakeside cliffs. Occasional dashes of spray, already freezing to sleet, topped the banks and reached the edge of the road to fall like jeweled snow. If there had once been a protective barrier of ice extending out from the shore, the waves had already smashed it and carried it away.

At the point where the road turned inland to bypass the low area around an inlet, trees rose up and obscured his view of open water. William Henry picked up speed. He was now paying more attention to the road, especially where it crossed a bridge over the creek and the pavement waited with black ice. And then something beyond the leafless trees caught his attention. He turned his head to glimpse a low, angular shape, like a large box, but the size of a house. It was not a building, because he could see no windows or doors, not even complete walls. No, it was a tent made of brown canvas. Two poles stuck straight up through it, spaced along the tent's spine. Another long pole, this one a dull black, rose at a shallow angle out of the tent's open end.

William Henry slowed down to look back over his shoulder. Within that opening he could just see a curve of something hard and white. It was a delicious curve, with its own perfect proportions: out and then in, like the smooth, tapering muscles in the hindquarters of a horse. He guessed it must be the bow of some kind of sailing ship, and the pole above it would be the bowsprit. Even to his landsman's eye, that was a beautiful shape.

Just a little way beyond the tent in the trees was a side road, freshly plowed. On impulse, William Henry turned off. Within ten yards he came to a chain-link fence and a gate. The sign beside it read "Lakeshore Yard," and below that, "Bill Gibbs, Prop." with a local phone number. The gate stood open, and he went through it.

He drove slowly past a small office and a row of open sheds that contained the fat, squared-off sterns of cabin cruisers and the tall, blade-thin silhouettes of sailboats. Off to his left was a concrete ramp leading down to a stretch of the inlet. Next to the ramp was a traveling crane, apparently used to lift boats out of the water in fall and return them in spring. But at this season the inlet was solid gray with pockmarked ice. William Henry turned up an avenue between two of the sheds, following his nose toward the tented object he had seen from the other side of the screening woods. With no great trouble he found it and parked just behind the graceful white curve of the fantail stern. Below it hung the thick, loop-shaped rudder and, further back in the shadows, the three dull-bronze blades of a single, large propeller.

In the brown gloom under the canvas he could see the long, white hull propped on a series of rough wooden cradles. The hull stretched away, bellying out from the narrow stern, then gradually disappearing in the ghostly gleam of light at the far end of the tent. Two-thirds of the way down from the upper edge of the hull—what was it called? the gunwale?—the white paint stopped and a dull red began and went on to cover the bottom curve—the bilges?—and the shallow box keel. Just above this discontinuity he could see a faint, greenish-black line, as regular as a ruler but not painted on. He guessed this was the waterline, written in dried algae from a summer on the lake.

He gently touched the dusty paint on the white part of the hull, then rapped it lightly with his knuckles. There was no resounding echo. He struck it with the flat of his hand and got a satisfying *thunk!* This certainly was a solid ship.

"Can I help you?" asked a voice from behind him.

William Henry turned to find a tall man in a winter jacket, waiting beside his car. The man's face had the light brown, smoothly bulging features of the cartoon character Jiminy Cricket. His ginger-colored hair receded to the top of his head, completing the effect. The man was neither unsmiling nor uncertain, he was simply waiting for William Henry to explain himself.

"I was driving along and the, uh … boat here caught my eye."

"She does that," the man agreed proudly.

"Sailing ship, is it?"

The man laughed. "Not with that keel. She's a motor launch."

"A launch?" William Henry was perplexed. "Aren't they supposed to be small boats? This ship's has got to be … what, fifty …?"

"She's sixty-two feet at the waterline. Nearer to eighty feet, when you add in the bowsprit and the overhang at the stern. But size isn't what counts. *Galatea* is a day boat, with no accommodations. So, technically, that makes her a launch."

Galatea … William Henry of course knew the reference: the female statue from the Pygmalion legend.

He stepped up on the beam end of the nearest cradle, reached for the gunwale, and raised himself on tiptoe. Peering into the tented shadows, he could just make out the roofline of a low structure. Its matchboard walls were painted mustard yellow with dark-green trim. Along the side was a row of narrow sash windows, more like those in a house than portholes, except their tops were rounded into arches. They were made of varnished mahogany with brass fittings. Somehow, he had expected portholes.

"You said, 'no accommodations'?" William Henry recalled. He pointed up into the shadows. "Isn't that a cabin up there?"

"Well, yes," the man said, "but it's just a saloon, and the galley is hardly more than a pantry. This vessel was a rich man's toy, for taking guests out to watch regattas and sailboat races, but not to live aboard. There wasn't even a head until a later owner added one in the thirties. He had no place to put it but the engine room. It's just the toilet bowl sitting there next to the triple-expansion cylinder block, with a shower curtain for privacy. Like I said, a day boat."

"When was she built?" William Henry asked.

"Eighteen eighty-five. On Long Island Sound."

"Can I look inside?" He felt a sudden curiosity to see a "saloon" out of the Gilded Age of New York Society.

"I don't know if I can let you aboard." The man frowned. "Wait a moment."

He went off to one of the sheds and came back with a nine-volt flashlight and a short ladder nailed together from two-by-fours. Strips of old carpeting padded the legs at one end. The man set down the light and carried the ladder past William Henry into the tent. "I'm Bill Gibbs, by the way," the man said, stopping and sticking out a hand.

He shook it. "William Henry Wheelock. I teach over at the university."

"I figured as much. Watch your step around these cradles. They can be real toe-stubbers."

Halfway down the length of the hull Gibbs set the ladder's carpeted end against *Galatea's* side. He anchored it with one hand and gestured for William Henry to climb up. "You can see most of it from here."

Three steps took William Henry's head above the level of the deck, which was just a narrow walkway about six inches wide, without railing or hand line, between the side of the hull and the cabin trunk. The roof was low in this part of the boat, four feet or so above the deck. Obviously, the floor inside would be much lower, pushed down inside the hull. The cabin appeared to occupy practically its entire width and, from what he could see, most of its length. He took another step up and pressed his face to the glass. The interior was just more shadows in the darkness under the tent.

"Here, you'll need this," Gibbs said, passing up the flashlight.

William Henry switched it on and looked down into elegance from another age, glimpsed in circles of sharp white light a foot and a half wide. Ghostly sheets covered a settee, two wing chairs, and paired ottomans, but where the sheets had slipped he could see richly tufted, sea-green leather. Tables with marble tops and clawed feet. An oriental carpet with intertwined fish in deep reds and blues, patterned to fit the cabin's narrow width. Bronze lamp stands with Tiffany glass shades showing the faint green outlines of water lilies. More mahogany woodwork, including panels cut with scalloped edges, doorways flanked by fluted columns, and rosettes carved into corners. The cabin's width and length, its richness, and the arrangement of its furnishings reminded him of private railway cars from the same era.

"It's beautiful," William Henry said, finally switching off the light and climbing down. "Thank you for showing me," he said to Gibbs.

"She's for sale, you know."

"I didn't know that ..." William Henry paused. "You understand, I didn't actually come here looking ... I mean, I ... Well, I wouldn't know what to do with such a thing."

"Few people do, nowadays," Gibbs said with a sigh. "That's the problem."

"Thank you again."

William Henry got back in his car and drove out onto the icy roads. After having seen those glimpses of true splendor, he found the real world around him to be a grayer and bleaker place.

4. The Enigma in the Library

Danielle Wheelock fell in love for the first time—not counting her crush on the boy who had tried to beat her up in the fourth grade—on the day after New Year's. She had no intention of falling in love; she was simply in the wrong place at the right time. Despite the long holiday week, Dani had a research paper due in ten days, and that took her to the general stacks at the main library, the Theodosian Library at the center of campus, rather than her usual hangout at the Barker Engineering Library.

As a sophomore majoring in mechanical engineering, she did most assignments on scratch paper with a pencil, slide rule, and lots of erasers, except when she went into the shop and worked out solutions with a lathe and milling machine. But for her one course in structural engineering the professor actually wanted his class to turn in a paper, written in English, and preferably typewritten, with footnotes mandatory. The subject she had chosen, only because she had thought it would be short, was a history of the Golden Gate Bridge in San Francisco.

If anyone had asked Dani to calculate lateral stresses produced by the prevailing winds on the north and south towers and along the roadway deck, she could have done it with a ruler and calipers working from an old photograph. Loading on the cables? She would have asked whether he meant the horizontally looping suspender cables or the vertical support cables, and with or without cars, then answered within minutes, accurate to a few hundred pounds. But Professor Anderson wanted them to provide biographies of the architect, the chief engineer, construction superintendent, and leading fund raiser. Historical stuff. Word stuff.

And so Dani, who could build a model of the bridge out of yarn and toothpicks faster than write a paper about it, had gone to the card catalog three levels down in the annex to the reference hall and written out her list of Dewey decimals. Now she was wandering around the stacks looking for a book about Joseph Baerman Strauss, 1870-1938. *Died just a year after com-*

pleting the bridge, she realized, having already done some reading on the subject. This fact made her wonder briefly about the psychological stresses of designing and building controversial structures that would eventually become internationally famous.

Unlike the wide-open shelves at Barker, the stacks of the Theodosian were just plain creepy. From floor to ceiling, each level was less than six feet tall, which meant four of them would fit into two floors of any other building on campus. The gray steel shelves started an inch off the poured concrete floor pad and ended at book height, plus one inch, from the underside of the pad above. The long, shadowy aisles between the shelves were lit with spaced fluorescent tubes inside wire cages so that tall people, and Dani was tall for a woman, did not break the tubes with their heads. She was also aware that, with so much flammable paper around, the stacks had no sprinkler system. Instead, at the end of every aisle were a fire extinguisher—carbon-dioxide, not water or foam—and a red bucket filled with sand. Sand, to fight a fire in this place! When she looked into one of the buckets, she found a bottle cap, two gum wrappers, and three stubbed-out cigarettes. It was enough to make her heels itch.

But the creepiest part of the stacks in the Theodosian was that they seemed to go on forever: level on level, aisle after aisle, like an unexplored cave. In the distance, like the clamor of miners' hammers, you could hear the thud of snow boots on the funny little circular steps that threaded from one level up or down to the next. Nearer, like the flutter of bat wings, you could hear the rustle of pages coming from the semi-enclosed study carrels that were situated in free space at the ends of the aisles.

Dani drifted along the shelves of the 920s, the Dewey Decimal System code for "general biography," looking for her particular author. At the end of the row she turned the corner, with her eyes still focused on the book spines—and tripped over a pair of size eleven sneakers thrust into the passageway from beneath a carrel. The sneakers were attached to a pair of jeans-clad legs crossed at the ankles. She lurched, did a fast double-step, and caught herself before falling.

"Hey, watch it!" came a voice from behind the carrel's side partition.

Dani looked at the owner's placard: "Reserved for Professor E. J. Watkins, Ph.D." That was a friend of her father's, an elderly teacher in the History Department. Not a man to wear jeans and sneakers. She looked over the top of the partition and came into focus with a startlingly blue pair of eyes: the blue of late afternoon sunlight through sapphires, the blue of sky after a sudden rainstorm, the blue of clear lake water. She saw something free, open, glitteringly hard, and ... self-aware in those eyes. They dominated a face with dark, beautifully curved eyebrows, smooth cheeks, a sharply defined jaw, rounded chin, small mouth, and a nose that she thought was called "Roman." It was the face of a boy—or man, really—in his middle twenties. Definitely not Professor Watkins.

"Could you move your feet?" was all Dani could think of to say.

"I was here first," the young man said. But he grinned, refusing to take offense.

"Oh, well ..." This conversation was going badly, and for some reason she could not name, Dani wanted it to continue and for herself to be brilliant. "Well, look ... Since you're such a *fixture* here—and this is my first time in the library—could you help me find my book?"

"What book is that?"

She showed him the card.

He reached for it, studied it, uncrossed his legs, and stood up. He was taller than Dani by an inch or two, and that was a promising sign. He also appeared to be in good shape, athletic, judging from the muscles that showed through the white tee-shirt he was wearing under a navy blue pea coat. She looked around but saw no hat, scarf, or gloves anywhere. Unlike everyone else, who was bundled up for winter, he seemed to be dressed for a perpetual springtime.

"It's a biography," he said slowly.

"Yes. Well, I mean ... obviously."

"The book number is … um …"

"Around here?" she suggested.

"I think that's right," he agreed.

"Don't you study in this area?" Dani glanced down at the carrel's desktop. When she interrupted him, the young man had put down a library book, notable for the white numbers painted on its spine. Her brief glance only caught part of the title: "*Stalin, An Appraisal of …*" and, below that, "by Leon …" before he picked it up and turned the cover face down.

"Actually, I just came in here to get out of the cold," he said with another grin. That was when Dani noticed the backpack, leaning against the chair's rear leg. It was a serious hiker's pack, with a metal frame, sporting both shoulder straps and a belt, and lots of snap pockets on the sides. A blue nylon sleeping bag was rolled tightly and strapped against the frame's top curve.

"Lot of room for carrying your books," she observed.

"Actually, I carry my whole life in that pack."

"Looks like you just arrived on campus."

"Week ago, in time for the holidays."

"Pretty late in the semester …"

"No, I'm early for spring."

"You're enrolled here?"

"Something like that."

Dani could hear doors closing on the conversation. She didn't know how to keep it alive, and she felt sad about that. She took back her card and walked away to continue looking for her book.

"Wait a minute!" he called behind her.

"Yes?" She said, turning hopefully.

"Do you want to go for coffee?"

"I'd love to!" Dani replied.

They left the austere, steel-and-concrete, egg-crate environment of the stacks and exited through the library's huge reference hall and reading room. This space, three stories tall with a ceiling of inlaid marble and gilt fretwork, was supported by Corinthian columns as big around as sequoia trees. Dani and her new friend went out through the huge bronze doors—cast in imitation of Ghiberti's baptistery doors, except these bore industrial and agricultural scenes from Upstate New York—and down a magnificent triple set of granite stairs to the concrete walkway of the Mall. The young man shouldered his pack by one strap. Dani slipped the reference card for the Strauss biography into her pocket.

Since he was new to campus, she took him down to The Corner Room. This was a coffee shop on the first street in town that intersected the Mall, right across from the gates of the university. They settled into one of the high-backed booths, and he deftly shoved the pack under the bench.

Dani ordered coffee—"with a fresh pitcher of cream, please," after she had looked into the one on the table. Yellow with a film of butterfat. Gross! At the same time, her new friend was ordering a full breakfast, even though it was past two o'clock: eggs over easy, bacon, pancakes, hash browns, biscuits, strawberry jam, and coffee.

"Do you want a melon slice with that?" the waitress asked, deadpan.

"Sure, why not?" her young man replied with a straight face.

"Golly!" It was the only thing Dani could think of to say.

"Isn't breakfast the most important meal of the day?"

"Yeah—all of them." She meant it as a joke.

"Sometimes all I get." He looked away.

"So ... what are you going to be studying?" she asked.

"Excuse me?" He gave a startled glance with those blue eyes.

"I mean, what classes will you be taking ... in the spring?"

"Oh ... Political economics, I think. What do you study?"

"I'm in mechanical engineering," she said proudly.

"I would have guessed more civil engineering."

"What? Oh, you mean because of the Strauss book? That's just one course."

"You know what they say, don't you? Mechanical engineers make weapons—"

"—and civil engineers make targets," Dani completed the old saw. "Yeah."

"So you've chosen to make weapons?" He sounded disappointed.

"Not really. Mechanical engineers design lots of things, like automobile engines, railroad locomotives, printing presses … elevators …"

"All the toys of twentieth-century western civilization."

"More than just toys … Why political economy?"

"Excuse me?" He turned as if startled again.

"Your course of study *is* economics?"

"It seems like the best way to understand human nature, don't you think?"

"I thought that was the reason we have art, books, all of literature."

He made a face. "Those only show the mind of the novelist."

"Or the poet," Dani said, thinking of her father's Homer.

"A political nonentity. Usually an aristocrat—or one who pretends to be."

"Well," she said, not wanting to fight. "I'm an engineer myself. Just give me the numbers, please, and leave the fancy theory to somebody else."

"So … you don't care what happens to the world?"

"Of course I care!" Dani straightened. "That's not fair! You're making fun of me, and you don't know me. … I don't even know your name."

"I'm sorry. I was being rude." He reached across the table. "Nicholas Carr."

She took the hand. It was warm and soft, smooth, almost without callus. "Danielle Wheelock."

"Pleased to meet you." And he shook her hand.

They finished their meal—he with a collection of plates before him, she with just a cup and saucer—talking now of nothing so dangerous as ideas. When the check finally came, he picked it up, looked at it, and bowed his head. "I hate to say it, but I can't cover this."

"But you invited—oh, never mind." She dug out her wallet. "Look, you can pay me back when your allowance comes in, or whatever."

"I'm good for it," he said.

"*If* I can find you again ..."

"You know where to look."

"I don't—you mean—the library?"

"Yeah, anytime. Back in the stacks."

Dani's was puzzled. "But, if you're not a student, what do you *do* there?"

"Read," he said. "It's where the books are." And he laughed out loud.

5. Resolution of the Faculty Senate

"WHEREAS, AMERICANS OF African descent, other ethnic minorities, and women have suffered historic discrimination in accessing employment, education, housing, political power, public accommodation, and social services, creating for them a lower standard of living and reduced opportunity in the dominant white, male-dominated, European-based society of the United States; and

"WHEREAS, such historic discrimination has fostered a climate of unfair advantage for members of that white, male, European society; therefore

"RESOLVED, that the University provide direct, compensatory, and promotional advantages to minorities and women, so that they may achieve equal representation in undergraduate and graduate admissions, access to services, on-campus housing, academic remediation, and other supports necessary to ensure their success, and further that the University become a 'Discrimination-Free Zone' where everyone is treated with respect and courtesy."

This measure was enacted by the Faculty Senate on January 3. Although it passed unanimously, William Henry overheard a flurry of comments in the cloakroom as the members gathered their coats and hats and pulled on galoshes.

"What do you think it means by 'compensatory' and 'promotional' advantages?"

"I guess we're meant to overlook any lack of academic achievement."

"You mean, in admissions? Isn't that out of our hands?"

"I believe we have just set policy for the deans."

"But how are they to judge applicants?"

"Award extra points for race?"

"And for ethnicity."

"And gender."

"Does it really mean we have to house equal numbers of students in the dorms?"

"Not 'equal,' so much as 'adequately represented,' I should think."

"Then that would imply using some statistical measure?"

"You mean, going by population numbers?"

"Probably based on the census."

"It would be a start."

"I'm all for respect and courtesy. But how are we to maintain standards?"

"I think you're going to find standards are 'discriminatory.' "

"It's the business of the university to *teach*. Period."

"*Whom* do we teach? That's the question."

"We have a duty to unfortunates—"

"Tut-tut! 'Under-served'!"

"Yes, I meant that."

"This one really opens up a can of worms."

6. Hunting Among the Trees

Toward the end of his first week of classes after the holidays, William Henry decided to take another drive in the country. That old boat stored under a tent, *Galatea,* had stuck in his mind. At odd moments during the day she had come back in image fragments of faded, Gilded Age grandeur: chalky white paint, dusty mahogany scrollwork, tarnished brass fittings, worn oriental carpet. The notion of a pleasure yacht, its own self-contained little world, so gloriously appointed yet still surviving into modern times, fascinated him. He wanted another look.

Although he followed his nose west along Lakeshore Road, William Henry was quickly lost. Of course, he knew where he was, personally, to the mile on his odometer, but he had forgotten where *the boat* was. He could remember the yard being in a dip or swale in the landscape, with the road jogging inland around a creek or small river, but he never realized how many little creeks drained the southern shore of Lake Ontario. Each one claiming its own tiny valley filled with winter-bare trees. And the road crossed each creek on the same kind of two-lane bridge with cast-concrete abutments and yellow warning signs about the bridge freezing before the road surface.

He remembered his first sight of *Galatea,* seen out of the corner of his eye, had been the curve of her white bow, hidden among the trees. But that day the sky had been clear and bright, and the crisp, white paint had caught the sunlight. This day was overcast and threatening snow. The trees were dark and closed down. Nothing that he could see suggested the long canvas tent or the white bow.

He remembered, just after he'd spotted the boat, there had been a side road with a chain-link fence and a sign with the proprietor's name. Gibson? Hibbs? If the sign had a phone number, he couldn't visualize it. But without that, he would just have to search the phone book—or several of them from surrounding exchanges, because he had no idea in which little township he might have seen the boatyard. It certainly had been outside the

Byzantium city limits, perhaps even in the next county. But if so, he wouldn't know where to start. ... If the matter was even worth pursuing ...

After driving much farther than he had gone on New Year's Day, William Henry decided to turn around. Perhaps he would see something in the trees when he was headed in the other direction. ... Not that it mattered.

Seeing the old boat again had been a whim.

It wasn't as if he was going to *do* anything.

7. Hunting in the Stacks

Even though she had completed all the research for her term paper on the Golden Gate Bridge, Dani went back to the Theodosian Library later in the week. She told herself she wanted to check whether a book from her research list might have been returned to the shelves since her visit just after New Year's. But a young woman as honest as Dani had to admit there was another reason as well.

She went first to the biography section, 920, even though that wasn't where the Dewey Decimal System said the book she wanted should be. And sure enough, what she was actually looking for wasn't there, either. Then she recalled the biography he had been reading, something about Stalin and the Soviet Union. She went to look in the 940s, the history of Europe, with a slow pass through the Eastern Europe section. But she didn't find her mystery man.

She remembered their discussion at lunch and his interest in political economics. That took her down to the 320s and 330s, but a fast walk through the narrow aisles didn't turn up any sign of Nicholas Carr, nor anyone else wearing jeans and sneakers on a cold and dark winter's day.

Dani was about to give up when she turned the corner and came upon the last row of shelves along the eastern wall of the building. The metal shelving units were all a standard width, but this row had to be longer than all the others, because it stretched across the aisle that transected the middle of the stacks. So a gap of perhaps twelve inches separated one unit from the next. But that was not the odd thing about it.

She looked around and took her bearings. Dani counted the aisles behind her, estimated their width, and added the depths of the bookshelves between them—double depth, of course, because they held books facing into the aisles on either side. She knew the library structure's physical dimensions, because the previous week she had studied the layout posted in the room that held the card catalog. Then she divided in her head. She came up with almost, but not quite, enough space for one more row of shelves beyond the one she was facing. That explained the shadowy darkness she could see through the gap between the shelf units, where one expected to find only a concrete wall painted green.

Without quite knowing why, Dani slanted her shoulders and slithered through the gap. She found a long, narrow space only twenty-eight inches deep. It was dark except for the light that filtered through the bookshelves. To the right, after just a foot or so, a vertical beam—obviously part of the load-bearing structure—was cast into the concrete wall. That would explain the architectural need for this empty space, rather than simply leaving a wider aisle outside. To the left, however, the space stretched for a good ten or twelve feet and created a convenient cubbyhole. At the far end, in the dim light, she saw a blue nylon sleeping bag rolled out on the floor. Beside it, leaning against the wall, was a serious hiker's backpack on an aluminum frame.

Dani suddenly understood that Carr didn't just hang around the library because he liked to read. He was living here, tucked away into this architectural oddity of the stack structure. He probably bathed and washed his clothes in the restrooms after hours. No wonder he had been so hungry that day she met him.

She didn't know whether to pity him for being so poor and alone, or admire his ingenuity at being able to live without paying rent and utilities, or fear a man who could live so resolutely outside the structure and norms of society. The one thing she did not feel was disgust. She still hoped to meet him again, but today was obviously not the day.

Without touching his things—and before he might come back—Dani quietly withdrew from the nest.

8. Resolution of the Faculty Senate

"WHEREAS, the current South Vietnamese government of Nguyen Van Thieu obtained power through usurpation in a fraudulent election;

"WHEREAS, United States' political support of the Thieu government represents an act of imperialist repression against the local right of self-determination, in violation of the Geneva Agreements of 1954; and

"WHEREAS, United States' military support in South Vietnam constitutes an undeclared war, in violation of Article I, Section 8 of the U.S. Constitution; therefore

"RESOLVED, that the University end support for the so-called 'War in Vietnam' and deny aid and comfort to U.S. military forces and to the government in furtherance of its aims."

This measure passed the Faculty Senate on January 10 by a vote of 186 to 2. One of the "nay" votes was cast by the delegate from the U.S. Army Reserve Officer Training Corps on campus, Captain Edward Lewis Belton. The other vote was from the Classics Department, currently represented by Professor William Henry Wheelock.

After the session had adjourned, Professor Andrew Michelson, the delegate from Sociology and Political Science, cornered William Henry in the cloakroom. "What the hell's gotten into you, Wheelock?"

"What do you mean?" he asked.

"That Vietnam resolution was supposed to be unanimous."

"Never happen, so long as Captain Belton has a vote."

"Him, we can explain. But what about *you?*"

"I just didn't care for the measure."

"What? Do you *like* the war?"

"No ... not particularly."

"So vote against it."

William Henry wondered how he could justify his reasoning to a political animal like Michelson. For one thing, the obvious falseness of the resolution's wording stuck in his throat. While

Vietnam might not be a "declared" war, it had been duly authorized by Congress with the Gulf of Tonkin Resolution in 1964. While the Republic of Vietnam might not be the most upright of allies, they were a damn sight less repressive than the Viet Cong guerillas who were infiltrating across the 17th Parallel. As far as he could see, the mission in Vietnam was not much different from the mission he had supported in Korea, to protect a republican south against a totalitarian north.

Still, William Henry disliked what he saw in the creeping escalation of hostilities and the piecemeal involvement of U.S. troops without any clear objective. Although his prior service had been as a noncombatant with the Quartermaster Corps, he understood something about the limitations of military power. The use of armed force boiled down to two objectives: "take ground" and "hold ground." In Vietnam, the army's newfangled "air cavalry" units were flown into remote districts, where they shot up the infiltrators. Then they packed up and flew back to base, leaving the battlefield available for recapture. That was taking ground without holding it. And in any case, the war's overriding aims—"sweeping back the tide" of a determined cadre, propping up a corrupt and self-serving regime, "winning hearts and minds" out in the countryside—were political objectives, not military.

Perhaps, too, William Henry was reacting not just to the resolution itself but to the emotions that lay behind it. The most impassioned arguments of the delegates shaping the wording had focused less on the specifics of Vietnam than on the horror and injustice of all wars in general. But armed resistance was a necessity in certain circumstances. It had been necessary in Europe against the Nazis. It was necessary now in Asia against the Communists. And it had crossed his mind that the same people who cried for peace, peace at all costs, were mostly the same crew who had admired the Soviets and their achievements a decade ago. Peace for their side. Peace so they could win.

But overall, William Henry regretted the growing politicization of the campus. Respectful discussion and reasoned debate about these issues were becoming impossible. Chants and slogans were now the dominant rhetorical mode. And those who would not howl for peace were being branded as warmongers and enemies. Lines were being drawn. Reputations were being made and broken.

William Henry took a breath. "For one thing," he told Michelson now, "I really don't see how taking a stand on international politics falls within our charter. The Faculty Senate exists to advise the President and Board of Trustees on the university's academic functions and welfare."

"Keeping students out of war isn't part of their welfare?"

"You know the resolution won't accomplish that."

"No, but it's a moral stand we have to take."

"I also don't believe in futile gestures."

"When the people stand together—"

"But we're not 'the people.' We're supposed to represent the best thinking of the faculty. We are, supposedly, the older and wiser—"

"Are you speaking for the Classics Department? Or are these personal views?"

"You know the war resolution came up so quickly there simply wasn't—"

"Then it's personal. ... Say, weren't you a colonel in the army?"

"Only a major, and in the Quartermaster Corps. I was brevetted as a lieutenant colonel upon retirement."

"Whatever. You're voting along with Belton and the military."

"That's hardly fair, Andrew! There are many reasons—"

"No, there's really only *one* reason, Wheelock."

"What exactly are you trying to say?"

"Just be careful, Wheelock."

9. Reunion of the Old School

Nicholas Carr had found a working-class bar within walking distance of campus with the wholly unoriginal name "Ace of Spades." He had instructed his colleagues to meet him there at three o'clock on a Thursday afternoon, when they would likely have the place to themselves. He inserted himself through the narrowest crack of the heavy oak door with its diamond-shaped peephole, but he still let in a blast of cold air and a flurry of snow. Carr was stamping his feet and brushing snow off his jacket when Glynda Jacobs waved to him from a booth along the wall.

"You really should get some boots," she sai+d as he slid onto the bench. She stuck her own foot out to show off a black para-troop boot that laced halfway up her shin, with her jeans bloused over it. "You need to protect your feet around here."

Jacobs, who had come up from Cornell and was dressed for a bitter season on Lake Ontario, also wore a quilted nylon jacket stuffed with duck down and a knitted cap with ear flaps. Her companion, Randall Noyes, who had come out from Dartmouth, was similarly dressed in a thick corduroy coat, fur-lined hood, and leather gloves. They made Carr's pea jacket of unlined wool, his bare hands, and his high-top sneakers seem positively spring-like by comparison.

"We don't know from winter back in Berkeley," he explained.

"So buy yourself some boots and a coat," Noyes said.

"Funding's for operational use, not personal."

"Be hard to operate if you take sick."

"I have a strong constitution."

"So … what's the campus like?" Jacobs asked, changing the subject.

The bartender came over. Carr noted the two of them were drinking beer, asked for a ginger ale, and waited until the man walked away. "It's like any other school," Carr said with a shrug. "The faculty thinks they're really progressive because they wor-shipped Kennedy, voted for Johnson, and support civil rights and 'the Great Society.' They're full of good intentions."

"The students?" Noyes asked.

"Nice, white, middle-class kids. Earnest. Hard working."

"So our work's cut out for us," Jacobs said. "What about the administration?"

"Asleep," Carr said. "They imagine they're running the show."

"Where do you want to start?" Jacobs asked.

"Usual place. We'll take a table at Student Organizations Day, of course."

"When's that?" from Noyes.

"Spring registration. Big meet-and-greet, held in the gymnasium. We should have a serious-sounding name, but innocent—the 'Student Social Policy Forum' or 'Students for Social Change'—something like that."

"I'll get to work on a banner and flyers," Jacobs said.

"What are the wedge issues?" Noyes asked.

Carr considered everything he had heard and learned in the last couple of weeks. "The faculty is well prepped on the war and civil rights, so we'll want to echo them, of course. Still, those issues won't split the students off from the faculty and administration. ... I think we should push for a pass-fail grading system. Down with numerical grades and hierarchical rigidity. Down with unfairness, pitting student against student competing for grades. Down with making young men sweat to keep their 2S deferments. A lot of good arguments there."

"Can we actually get them to adopt a pass-fail system?" Noyes asked.

"Not the point," Carr said. "The issue will touch everyone— even female students, who all have boyfriends facing the draft. And it will be absolute poison to the faculty, who get their power through the grading system, and the administration, who think they have to maintain standards. It's a cause worth fighting for— on both sides. In fact, it would be counterproductive for us if the university actually bought into pass-fail. The game would be over and then we'd have to come up with another issue."

"The war," Jacobs said. "That's our main driver everywhere else. Everyone gets angry but nobody can do anything about it. And anxiety about the war drives the draft and deferments, too."

"Oh, no question," Carr said. "We'll use the war. Racial issues as well—I've got a whole list of courses and activities where blacks and women are under-represented. But grading will hit home the hardest."

" 'Students for Social Protest,' " Jacobs murmured.

"Too obvious," Carr said. "Gives our hand away."

"Can you be too obvious with these people?"

"No, but let's try to stay professional."

"Something subtle—and oblique."

"That's the ticket," he said.

10. RETURN OF A POTENTIAL BUYER

WITH THE SUN still going down around five o'clock in the afternoon, Bill Gibbs had just about decided to close the office early and head for home when the same dark-blue Volvo drove into the Lakeshore Yard. Gibbs remembered the driver: tallish, fair-haired, soft-spoken, a professor over at the university ... name of Wheelock. Gibbs remembered him, even after a couple of weeks, because the man had been looking at *Galatea*. Most visitors to the yard glanced into the tent just once, made some admiring little comment, and went on to look at the modern power boats. This man had actually asked for a ladder and a lantern and peered inside. Gibbs had known then that he would be back.

"What can I do for you?" he asked as Wheelock got out of his car.

"Oh, yes, Mr. Gibbs. It's just that I ... Well, I was wondering ..."

"Do you want another look at *Galatea*?"

"If you could arrange it ...?"

"Sure thing."

Gibbs went back into the office for the keys and led Wheelock across the yard to the tent. The makeshift ladder was still inside it, propped against the hull. He repositioned the ladder nearer to the stern and climbed up, over the gunwale, onto the deck. He offered Wheelock a hand.

"Won't we need the flashlight?" the man asked.

"I've run shore power in here," Gibbs said. "The circuits are all one-twenty volt. We keep a bulb burning in the bilges to knock down the condensation." He unlocked the double doors at the aft-end of the cabin and switched on the lights.

Wall sconces in the shape of bronze dolphins holding up yellow-glass seashells in their beaks lit the interior with a soft, warm glow. A second switch turned on table lamps and a brass chandelier above the small, built-in dinette, all with shades of green-and-brown stained glass. Gibbs found the whole thing a bit gaudy, but apparently it was to Wheelock's taste.

158

"Wow!" the man said. He walked down the length of the cabin, lightly touching marble tabletops, the backs of richly padded armchairs, the scrolled woodwork. "Wow!"

"The settee over there"—Gibbs pointed—"pulls out to make a bed."

"So you could sleep aboard her," Wheelock said.

"I guess. Like a studio apartment."

At the forward end of the lounge area Gibbs opened a paneled door into galley. Like the main cabin, it spanned the width of the hull. "One sink"—he tapped inside the basin—"made of solid brass, with hand pump. The freshwater tank holds eighty gallons."

"Are the counters black marble?" Wheelock asked.

"Soapstone," Gibbs said. "More durable." He pointed to the three-burner stove. "That's been converted to propane from the original naphtha. Much safer." He opened various cupboards and storage bins. "You could cook a whole meal in here, if you were frugal—and clever."

A plainer door of painted wood led them next into the engine room. Gibbs pointed out the dome-shaped boiler, the wedge of the engine block, and that unfortunate toilet bowl.

"That's a steam engine!" Wheelock exclaimed.

"Yes, no internal combustion in 'eighty-five," Gibbs said.

"What does she burn?"

"Originally naphtha—now jetted for oil."

"You mean, like diesel?"

"Bunker C, used motor oil, grease from the fryer." Gibbs shrugged.

Beyond the circular domed boiler, another plain door and three steps up took them into the tall wheelhouse with its three cathedral windows around the curved front. Gibbs put a hand to the mahogany-spoked wheel and gave it a slight turn to port. Somewhere back near the stern the linkage that moved the rudder gave out a hollow groan. He explained that the brass valve next to the wheel adjusted engine speed through a loop in the live steam line from the boiler. The lever and control rod that ported back through the aft bulkhead worked the engine's reversing gear. "All you really need with this setup."

"She seems perfect," Wheelock breathed.

"Well, she does need some work."

"Oh? Like what?"

"Patching, paint ... some tinkering. Mostly."

"I see."

"I told you the owner's interested in selling," Gibbs said.

"I remember. Is that because of her physical condition?"

"Oh, no! He bought the boat with his wife—they liked to hold parties aboard—but then she died." Gibbs dipped his head. "Now the man can't bear to go aboard. So he's prepared to let the boat go for a very reasonable price."

"What's 'reasonable'?"

"Twelve thousand ..."

"Yikes! That's a lot!"

"Not for a piece of history."

"I don't hold that many parties."

Gibbs smiled sadly. "Few people do."

11. Changes to the Curriculum

WHEN THE NEW course postings for spring semester came through interoffice mail from the Classics Department, William Henry saw that his one course in Beginning Greek had been cut. The chairman had penciled a notation that it might be reinstated in the fall, but there was no decision yet about which of the department's eminently qualified professors might teach it.

Apparently as a consolation prize his philosophy course, Introduction to Logic, had been expanded to two sections. It was definitely proving popular as a surrogate mathematics requirement. Well, with nearly six hundred freshman faces hanging on his every word, Wheelock could claim to be teaching more students than anyone else in the department. The university administration was certainly getting its money's worth out of his salary!

Also on the course list was a new offering, and he was assigned to teach it as well: Political Science 142, History of Social Protest, as part of the new Colloquium series in the College of Liberal Arts.

At first he was perplexed. William Henry had no experience of protest—political, social, or otherwise. He studied the typed paragraph of description, as it would appear in the spring catalog: "Examines contrary views of society and authority, focusing on social criticism through selected writings of Sophocles, Socrates, Plautus, Comedia Dell'arte, Defoe, Twain, and others." He would be team-teaching this monstrosity with a professor from the English Department, Agnes D'Angelo. William Henry thought he might have met her once—perhaps in a big, noisy crowd, perhaps at a football rally—but now he could not put a face to the name.

Where had all this nonsense come from? Before that thought was even formed, he remembered remarking to the dean, last fall, after a disappointing session of the Faculty Senate, that if they were going to keep genuflecting to the campus radicals, they might as well put political protest on the curriculum. At the time, he'd meant it as a joke—one that was not particularly well received. He remembered a glower from under those brilliant white eyebrows and a "Harrumph!" in the baritone that once had so famously lectured on Chaucer in the original Middle English. But evidently the thought had stuck, and William Henry's name along with it.

"Be careful what you wish for," he muttered to himself. "Or even *whisper.*"

Well, it was certainly not too early to pay a visit to Professor D'Angelo. He could only hope she wouldn't be too young, too hip, or too immersed in celebrating "political awareness" and "cultural relevance" along with her students and disparaging the classics and the traditional culture of "dead white males."

As a not-quite-yet-dead white male himself, William Henry wondered how long his career with the university, which he had once considered a life's ambition, would actually last.

12. Resolution of the Faculty Senate

"WHEREAS, WOMEN HAVE experienced unequal treatment in these United States in terms of political access, legal representation, and health care and reproductive services under a paternalistic, male-dominated society;

"WHEREAS, women constitute fifty (50) percent of the general population but are under-represented in federal and state government, professions, general business and management positions, graduate education programs, and the University population as a whole; and

"WHEREAS, women experience a special social burden through their traditional role as child bearers and child rearers; therefore

"RESOLVED, that the University declare solidarity with the aspirations of all women everywhere, promote abortion and reproductive rights, support equal pay, and foster equal rights commensurate with men."

The Faculty Senate passed this measure unanimously on January 17. However, the following comments were heard later in the cloakroom.

"Didn't we already pass this resolution?"

"That was about minorities. This one's for women."

"This one references both 'health care' and 'reproductive rights.' "

"Has anyone asked the women what they think about this?"

"Sixteen are in the Faculty Senate, don't you know?"

"So I'm guessing they were behind the measure."

"Well, clearly some of the menfolk helped."

"What does 'solidarity with aspirations' mean—really?"

"It's just feel-good language. It won't cost a thing."

"It might require a whole new course of study."

"Women's issues? Like home economics?"

"Think political. Legalized resentment."

"Well, there goes *in loco parentis*."

"Will we have co-ed football?"

"No, varsity field hockey!"
"That'll fill the seats."
"Yeah, bummer."

13. The Enigma on the Mall

THE NEXT TIME Dani Wheelock saw Nicholas Carr it was from behind, as he was walking up the Mall in mid-afternoon, between fifth and sixth periods. She only recognized him because of his dark-blue pea coat and white sneakers. What she did not recognize was the slender woman with an arm linked through his. This woman had long, blonde hair tied in a ponytail that poked out from under a knitted cap of soft, beige cashmere, and she wore skin-tight, black jeans that tucked into a pair of lace-up combat boots. Dani felt her heart sink.

Still ... as Dani had not seen her mystery man in nearly a month, what could she expect? That he would be hiding under a rock? He was a handsome guy and not shy with the ladies, as she had found from experience. The only question now was whether she should acknowledge him or cut him dead.

"Hey, Nicholas!" she called, running to catch up.

Carr turned—and so did his new young lady.

Well, not so young, maybe late twenties.

Not so pretty, either, without makeup.

In fact, she looked ... weathered.

"Hello there!" Carr said, his face lighting up, but he spoiled everything by saying, "Um ... It's Danielle, isn't it?"

"Yes, Dani Wheelock. Are you going off to class?"

"Well, not yet. Getting registered for spring, remember?"

"Won't you introduce me to your friend?" the woman asked.

"Oh, yes," Carr said. "Glynda Jacobs—Dani Wheelock."

"Pleased to meet you," Dani said, offering her hand.

The woman just looked at it, then looked away.

"So are *you* going to class?" Dani asked her.

"Glynda is a teaching assistant," he said.

Jacobs laughed and punched his arm.

Dani assumed he meant the woman was one of the graduate students who helped with a professor's teaching load or handled the lab sections in big undergraduate survey courses like chemistry or physics, but she didn't see what was so funny about that. "Are you studying political economics, too?" she asked.

The woman laughed harder, then sobered. "Yeah, that's right ..." She gave Carr a look that Dani thought might be called "knowing." There was something going on that she did not understand.

The clock tower over on the quad chimed the hour.

"Well, I've got to be running. Class in five minutes."

"I hope we can meet up again sometime," Carr said.

Dani glanced at Jacobs, but she seemed not to notice.

"That would be great. You're still in the library, right?"

"You know where to look," he said with a bright smile.

14. Finding a Kindred Spirit

William Henry went over to see Professor D'Angelo during her posted office hours. Along with the rest of the English Department, she had an office in one of the newer buildings on campus: a barren, three-story box with exterior walls of red brick cut every ten feet or so by window slits no wider than the spread fingers of a human hand. The slits reminded him of arrow loops in a castle wall, except that these ran floor-to-ceiling all the way to the roof. He couldn't wait to see the effect from inside the building.

There he found hard surfaces that were all modern and shiny: beige-colored vinyl floors polished to high gloss; wall panels covered in glossy, beige-colored Formica, punctuated with pads of beige cloth that might have been intended for sound control but were everywhere used as tack boards; and fluorescent lights behind beige-painted waffle grids. Strips of bright aluminum held everything together. Movable panels were clearly designed to turn open floor space into some kind of industrial egg-crate office system. The space allotted to Professor D'Angelo was fixed by three panels and an opening intended to serve as a doorway. Her possession was announced by a card in an aluminum bracket.

The office's proportions did not match the intervals of those arrow slits: the nine-inch-wide window nearest to her work space fell all the way at one end of it, along the far edge of her modular desk, and put the afternoon sun right in her eyes. She had to squint at the student paper she was reading.

William Henry tapped lightly on the frame of the wall panel. "Agnes D'Angelo?" he asked.

"That's me ..." she said, glancing over her shoulder, then turned to take a better look at him.

Somehow he had expected a woman with a name like "Agnes" to be older: gray haired, dressed in avocado- or cranberry-colored gabardine, bulk-knit sweater, clunky shoes, and eyeglasses on a dangly chain. Instead, he found a young woman, trim and athletic, barely out of graduate school, wearing a tight, black miniskirt, a sleeveless, ivory-colored silk top, and ankle boots. A leather motorcycle jacket was thrown over the back of her chair. She looked too much like one of his students.

Which made him feel particularly ancient.

"I'm—uh—Wheelock. We're going to be teaching a class together."

"Oh, yeah. That." But she was smiling. "Come on in and sit down."

The office space had two guest chairs and one free-standing metal bookshelf. Since an English professor, like a professor of classics, worked with nothing but books, the shelves were double-slotted with books, the two chairs stacked with books, the available floor space overflowing with books. D'Angelo helped him move them off one of the chairs.

William Henry was silently giving thanks that his own department had stayed in an older building constructed of concrete and marble. His office had fixed walls of plaster with real, painted woodwork, and was sized to pre-war conceptions of professorial space. He had his own door and window, and two whole walls that were nothing but built-in bookshelves—and still he managed to overflow them. So what, really, had changed? Books seemed to expand to fill the space available.

"I understand we have you to thank for creating this course," D'Angelo said as he settled into the chair and took the typed description from an inside pocket.

"Well, I suppose, in a roundabout way," he said.

"You should keep your mouth shut around the dean."

"Ah ... you heard about that?"

"Everybody heard about that."

"And now we're stuck with teaching a course about social protest."

"Ah, it won't be so bad." She grinned. "Protest is in the air, this year."

"Oh. So. Then. Is protest your—your thing—as they say?" He was looking at the studs on her motorcycle jacket.

"Oh, hell, no! My dad is a Methodist preacher, and I didn't fall far from the tree." She turned to follow his gaze. "The motorbike? I ride that because I can park anywhere on campus—that is, when the weather isn't freezing my ass off."

He refrained from contemplating D'Angelo's barely covered ass. Being suddenly in the company of an attractive young woman, who sat facing him, long legs crossed at the knee, William Henry had to remind himself that he had a daughter not much younger than this, as well as a wife—somewhere—whom he had once vowed to love and honor. For their sakes, and to fulfill the commitment he made years ago—to live quietly, as a retiring bachelor, and raise Dani as the focus of his love and affection— William Henry put prurient thoughts about those long legs out of his mind. Instead, he returned to the subject that brought him to D'Angelo's office in the first place.

"But you're not unhappy at the prospect of teaching this course?" he ventured.

"The Colloquium series is supposed to be about new ideas. You remember those, don't you, Professor?"

He had to grin in return. "I am familiar with the concept, yes."

"So we find a new twist on the same old stuff. Think of it as changing perspective and finding new relationships. Didn't the Greeks know a thing or two about protest?"

"I think they invented the subject," he agreed.

"Yeah, fighting against those Persians, and Spartans, the Romans, all those heavy hitters. And the English were out of the same mold, too, protesting interference by the Roman church, the Spanish Inquisition—"

"But it's not just invaders and foreign influences," he said.

"Oh, sure! There's also protest against stifling social forms—"

"Which means examining the basis of one's cultural traditions—"

"Assumptions about classes and power structures," she added. "Along with the evolving concepts of political and personal equality—" D'Angelo stopped short, her eyes bright. "Hey, this is going to be fun!"

"We can make it work," he agreed. "Maybe even teach them some—"

"—something about the underlying literature?" she supplied. "Sure! If social protest is a way to get my boneheads interested in reading, then I'm all for it."

"Yes." He grinned. "Me, too."

15. DAUGHTER OF THE REVOLUTION

NICHOLAS CARR WAS having lunch in a booth at The Corner Room, and for once eating out on operational funds, when that tall redhead, the engineering student, the young woman who had discovered him in the library, Danielle Wheelock, came in the front door. Carr saw her before she saw him, and he slowly dipped his head until it was out of sight below the backrest of the bench across the table. He didn't want her to see him, because he shouldn't be spending his funds socially, treating this girl in return for a breakfast she'd bought him. There he waited, head down, cautiously feeding french fries into his lowered mouth.

"Oh, hello, Nicholas!" she said suddenly from beside his table.

Carr looked up and chose a radiant smile. "Hello, Dani!"

"May I sit down?"

"Please do."

She glanced at the plates arrayed before him.

He was caught in the middle of a half-eaten hamburger, fries, bowl of chili—now scraped clean—cup of coffee, and a so-far-untouched slice of apple pie that dripped lukewarm vanilla ice cream. "Do you want to order something?" he offered.

"Not if you can't afford it," she replied.

"No, no, go ahead. It's my turn to pay."

"So did your allowance come in?"

"Oh, something like that."

When the waitress came over, Dani asked for just a club sandwich and iced tea—no side orders, no dessert. Clearly, she was being kind to his finances.

"I guess you'll be moving out of the library," she said with a grin. "Since you've got your allowance."

Carr flushed. He feared having his movements tracked, open to inspection, on the way to becoming predictable. "How did you find out about that?"

"I went looking for you, of course. No sign of the interesting Mr. Carr anywhere, but I did find his backpack and bed-

171

roll behind a row of bookshelves. We engineers are real good at two-plus-two."

"That was only temporary," he said defensively.

"Of course ... now that your girlfriend's here."

"My who?" Carr asked, drawing a blank.

"Glynda? The one I met the other day?"

"Not my girlfriend. She's just a friend."

"Okay ... I'll pretend go believe that."

"No, really. An old acquaintance."

"I said I believe you," she insisted.

"So ... do you find me interesting?" he said to change the subject.

"Well, enigmatic. Exotic. Not to mention that odd whiff of industrial hand soap from the library toilets."

"I did not smell of hand soap! I showered at the gym."

"But now you can have a real place to live."

"It's a small apartment downtown."

"Oh, wow! All to yourself!"

"Well, shared with friends ..." He wouldn't mention that one of those friends was the same Glynda Jacobs. They were pooling their resources for the cause. And besides, Dani Wheelock would never find out. "I suppose you stay in the dorms?"

"No such luck. I'm living at home with my father."

"Does he work in town?" Carr asked casually.

"No, he's a professor at the university."

A red flag went up in Carr's brain.

"Oh, what department's he in?"

"He teaches the classics."

"Ancient Greeks?"

"And Romans."

Carr sighed.

A relationship with this Wheelock girl suddenly presented him with possibilities. Her father was connected with the university, which meant she would know—or could find out—about the administration's unstated aims and intentions, the thinking among faculty members, their attitude toward the students, and any new policies they formulated in response to the coming student action. Yet neither her father, with his focus on long-dead history, nor Dani, with her engineering studies, was likely to be politically aware. Carr could ask his questions mostly straight out without worrying about arousing their suspicions. It might be worth his while, operationally, to pursue a relationship with this girl. Clearly, she was already interested in him.

While he was considering all this, the waitress brought Dani's food.

She picked up one of the sandwich quarters, unpinned its toothpick, removed half the bacon, and took a ladylike bite.

"You don't seem to eat much," Carr observed with a boyish grin. "Is that how you keep your gorgeous figure?"

Dani smiled, winked at him, and took another bite.

16. The Wreck Under the Tent

On a bright Saturday morning in late January, with the first hints of early spring and the snow on the ground going all crusty and crystalline, Dani's father asked her to go with him for a drive in the country. When she had asked what the occasion was, he only said, "I want to show you something."

"Oh? What is it?" she asked.

And he replied, "You'll see."

So they drove west along the lake shore. The pavement sparkled in the sun with melt water that oozed from the banks that snowplows had piled up earlier in the winter. The road went from high bluffs with views out across the blue water down to tiny, wooded valleys that sheltered swelling creeks. In one of these—Dani had already lost count of them—her father pulled off on a side road, went through a gate, and pulled up in front of a shed in some kind of boatyard. "We're here," he said.

As they got out of the car, a weather-beaten old man stepped out of the shed and called, "Morning, Professor!"

"Came to take another look," her father said.

"That isn't your missus?" the old man teased.

"No, my daughter. She wants to see the boat."

Until two seconds ago, Dani hadn't known anything about *a boat,* but she decided not to challenge the statement.

"I left the ladder up," the man said. "Take the keys." He tossed them to her father. "You know where the light switches are."

William Henry led her across the yard to another shed—actually a canvas tent—back under the trees. Inside was the long, white hull of a boat—or more like a small ship. On the rounded stern, in gilded letters with black edging, was the name.

"Galatea," Dani said, sounding it aloud.

"Pygmalion's mistress," her father said.

"Didn't he carve her out of stone?"

"He created his ideal woman."

"And what is this?" she asked.

174

"I don't know yet," her father said with a note of wonder at himself—or perhaps it was sadness.

He led her to a rough wooden ladder leaning against the hull. The boat's white paint might once have been bright and gleaming but now was dusty with oxidation. Up near the gunwale, patches of paint were starting to blister and crack. She picked at one with her fingernail, and the surface broke away in flecks, showing bare, gray wood underneath. Dani wondered how many seasons would pass before the entire hull needed to be scraped down and repainted.

On deck she found teak planking that had gone silver-gray from sun and water damage and was starting to show an etched pattern to the grain. Bringing it back to health she figured would take about a mile of hand-sanding and gallons of teak oil. The paint and varnish topside were in no better shape. Some unlucky person had a whole lot of weekend work ahead of them to make the boat shine—and she hoped her father wasn't thinking that "someone" would be her!

When William Henry let her into the main cabin, with its mahogany woodwork, cracked green leather cushions, stained glass, and marble surfaces, Dani tried to be nice.

"It's really beautiful," she said.

"Out of another age," he replied.

"It reminds me of Grandma's parlor in Pennsylvania."

Her father gave her a startled look. "So it does!"

He took her through the cramped "galley," as he called it, and into the engine room. The boiler at the front end of the room was a looming mushroom, black with soot and grime. The long engine block—which she recognized from the wedge shape of the cylinder case as a triple-expansion model, a classic from the Age of Steam, reproduced in miniature—was almost as bad. Unpainted iron that had turned red with rust and brass gone green with tarnish were now nearly black with accumulated dirt. The cleanest thing in the room was a toilet bowl, perched incongruously next to the block's stanchions. She touched one of the engine's connecting rods, then pushed on it, and found it loose.

The curved bends in the bronze steam pipes felt brittle, like porcelain, and she wondered how close they were to cracking.

"Pretty neat, huh?" her father said.

"I've never seen anything like it."

"The proprietor, Gibbs, says it all works."

"Yes, well, maybe … but for how long?"

He led her forward, past the dome-shaped boiler, into the wheelhouse, where tall, arched windows looked out on the foredeck and the bowsprit, exposed in sunlight beyond the far end of the tent. She could see the black paint on the spar was clearly peeling. The steel cable rising from its tip to the mast somewhere above showed several loose strands.

But her father stepped up to the eight-spoked mahogany wheel. His hands stroked the old wood and then gripped two of the spokes. His eyes took on a faraway look.

"Well, Dad," she said. "It's all very nice."

"The owner wants to sell her, you know."

"I didn't know. You thinking of buying?"

"Not really … not thinking. I mean …"

"I have no idea what you'd do with it."

"Oh, fix her up. Take her out on the lake. Hold parties aboard."

Dani decided not to mention that fixing things up, going boating on the lake, and holding parties were three things she had never observed her father doing. Not once.

"It would be a lot of expense, you know," she said.

"Yes, I know. Much too expensive, really."

"So, um, then, are we done here?"

"I just wanted you to see her …"

"I know. The boat's a real jewel."

He patted the wheel. "She is …"

17. Dani Brings Home a Friend

His daughter had set aside all of Sunday afternoon to cook dinner. When William Henry had asked, Dani said she was making a pot roast and wanted it to be "extra special." Then she remembered her mother's roasts as being particularly good and asked him if he knew what Jane did with the spices. He didn't, of course. So together they dug out Jane's old cookbook, the one full of scribbles and slips of paper, each with a twist on something in the book or with one of Jane's own special recipes. A note on the roasts page in her spiky handwriting said: "salt, pepper, garlic, bay leaf, claret, Italian seasoning."

"What's 'claret'?" Dani asked.

"Some kind of wine—I think."

"But what kind?" she pressed.

"Does it matter?" he said. "Red."

"But there are so many red wines."

"Well, pick one. It'll just cook down."

Dani looked at her watch. "I've just got time to go to the store. One of the clerks will surely know."

"You're too young to be buying wine."

"Oh, that's right! Can you go instead?"

"Well, I guess I'll have to," he replied.

"Now what are 'Italian spices'?" she asked.

"I don't know. Oregano, tarragon, tetrazzini."

"Can you ask at the store and pick some up?"

"Nobody knew what was in Jane's recipes."

"Please don't make this any harder than it is!"

His daughter seemed anxious, even distraught.

"Why all the fuss? What's going on here?"

"Someone special is coming to dinner."

"Who is it? Do I know him? Or her?"

"Him. Someone I met. Someone nice."

"And you want to show him you can cook!"

"Don't you dare laugh at me, Daddy!"

"Not my intention at all." But he was smiling.

"Oh, go, get out! And don't forget the spices!"

William Henry vacated the house and left Dani to her labors. When he returned an hour later, bearing a Cabernet Sauvignon on the advice of one clerk and a clutch of small capped bottles of basil, marjoram, oregano, rosemary, and thyme on advice of another, the house already smelled of seared meat and boiling potatoes. Dani had set the table with Jane's best china and silverware. Two tall, pale candles were set in holders, ready for lighting.

When she appeared out of the kitchen, Dani was wearing her red party dress, the one that brought out the highlights in her hair, along with hose and patent leather pumps. A white bib apron protected her finery against splatters.

"Should I dress up for the occasion?" he asked.

"Oh, you look fine." She took his packages. "Thanks, Dad."

William Henry retreated to his study, but he remained on hand if she needed him. From the smells coming out of the kitchen, the wine and spices were a success, but still he decided not to come out until Dani said she was ready. At six o'clock, long after the rattle of pans had died down, the doorbell rang. William Henry stuck his head out, but Dani was already on her way to the front door. "I'll get it!" she sang.

From across the living room, and with the angle of the door working against him, William Henry could not at first see their guest, but he noted an immediate change in his daughter's body language. With one hand still on the doorknob, she shifted her weight, canted her hips, and flared her dress. The apron, he noted, had magically disappeared.

Whoever this might be, his daughter was—did people still say "smitten"?

Dani brought her guest into the house. William Henry moved to join them. She introduced the man, for he was certainly no mere boy, as "Nicholas Carr, who's going to be studying on campus." She introduced her father as "Professor Wheelock, who teaches in the Classics Department."

The two men shook hands. Carr gave his hand a firm squeeze, a big shake, and an even bigger smile. "Very pleased to meet you, Professor!" It was like watching a doll come to life.

While Carr was certainly a handsome man, with a movie star's eyebrows and firm jawline, his mouth was small and thin lipped, almost dainty. And his hands, on reflection, were soft like a woman's. William Henry could see how a young girl like Dani would be attracted, even dazzled. Carr's face and hands were deeply tanned, and he wore a light woolen jacket—something faintly naval in dark blue—with jeans and sneakers, as if he had just come from California. He did not seem bothered by the cold.

"What are you studying?" William Henry asked.

"Oh, um … political economics."

"Graduate level?"

"You could say that."

"Sociology and Political Science?"

"Excuse me?"

"That's your department, right?"

"I guess so."

William Henry decided not to pursue the matter.

Dani took Carr's coat. It turned out all he was wearing underneath was a gray sweatshirt. It made an odd contrast with Dani's party dress. Even William Henry, without "dressing up," wore a shirt with a button-down collar and cuffs, a tie, and a cardigan. Carr did not seem to mind being the only one in sports clothes.

The man looked around vacantly, as if assessing the cottage and the economic level of the people who lived there. William Henry was proud of the cottage, small and snug though it might be. But he read in Carr's appraisal some kind of disappointment—as if he expected, or was accustomed to, better.

"Can I get you something to drink?" Dani asked.

"Vodka," Carr said, "if you've got it."

"We—um—don't, I'm afraid."

"Whatever you're having."

She ended up bringing him a glass of the Cabernet. She brought William Henry a ginger ale and one for herself.

They went in to dinner and somehow, in the flurry, Dani had managed to light the candles. She seated Carr at the end of the table, opposite her father, in what used to be Jane's place. Then she went out to the kitchen and brought in the platter piled high with the perfectly browned roast and all the trimmings, including sprigs of parsley. She went back for side dishes, then took her own place along the table nearest the kitchen. William Henry silently applauded her. The young man at first looked on and then belatedly picked up the gesture, clapping loudly.

"Did you make all this food yourself?" Carr asked.

"Well, it's from one of my mother's recipes."

"I'll bet she didn't do it half as well."

Dani blushed and ducked her head.

William Henry carved and served the roast. When he paused after filling Carr's plate with two slices of meat, the man just nodded and smiled. So William Henry added two more. Carr helped himself immediately to the potatoes, without offering to pass them, and took big spoonfuls of carrots and onions as well. The moment the plate before him was filled, Carr picked up his knife and fork, then looked around and froze with the utensils still suspended. He waited uncertainly for Dani and his host to be served. But as soon as Dani picked up her own fork, Carr began cutting into his food and wolfing it down like a steam shovel attacking a dirt pile. His napkin lay conspicuously beside his plate instead of being placed on his lap. He stopped eating only long enough to take deep draughts of the wine. The art of dinner table conversation appeared to be lost on him.

William Henry watched with disbelief.

Dani looked on with the eyes of love.

William Henry could easily forgive the casual state of Carr's clothing, because a struggling graduate student might not be able to afford better. He could less easily forgive the man's atrocious table manners, although not everyone was brought up in a gentle home. However, the fact that Carr seemed oblivious of

Dani—failing to compliment her on her dress and appearance, applauding the work she put into the meal only when forced to it, and then ignoring her completely once he started eating— William Henry found distressing.

He wanted his daughter to be happy. From the quiet evenings she spent at home—when she was not out studying at the library, even on Friday and Saturday nights—he suspected she did not have much of a social life, if any. William Henry had been pleased she was finally taking an interest in the young men around her, that she was willing to put so much effort into a potential relationship. But he sensed this man Carr was too much for her: too handsome, too self-engaged, too smooth—and yet, at the same time, too rough. William Henry sensed Dani was not going to be happy with this man.

This man was trouble.

18. Resolution of the Faculty Senate

"WHEREAS, the Theodosian Library has not been upgraded or expanded since addition of the existing stacks in 1952;

"WHEREAS, the current library structure houses more than 1,230,000 books and bound periodicals in its eight permanent collections, in addition to the general collection; and

"WHEREAS, adequate space does not exist in the current structure to house the proposed new collections for African-American Studies, Hispanic and Mesoamerican Studies, Native American Studies, Gender and Equity Studies, and Political Awareness, Civil Disobedience, and Social Protest, including appurtenant functions of acquisition, cataloguing, microfilming, circulation, and reading rooms; therefore

"RESOLVED, that the Faculty Senate support the University in building a new wing to be situated on vacant ground north of the main library structure."

This measure passed on January 24 by a vote of 186 to 0 with just one abstention. Afterward, the following comments were heard in the cloakroom.

"Well, that was easy."

"No question we need the space."

"Though I wonder what got into Wheelock?"

19. Eviction Notice

The envelope bearing the embossed seal of the University of Lake Ontario came in the mail on Friday afternoon, just two days after the Faculty Senate had voted in support of the administration's plans to expand the main library building. At first, William Henry did not connect these events because, as a faculty member, he received all sorts of letters on formal stationery. But then the return address caught his attention: "Department of Buildings and Grounds, 429 Rutherford Hall, University Station, New York."

He didn't know anyone in Buildings and Grounds.

Except for the people who sold him this house.

He tore open the letter with shaking hands.

"You are hereby formally notified that the University will begin proceedings in eminent domain against the property herein designated as Parcel 267C within the next forty-five (45) days ..."

Jane had always said there was one big problem with owning a house on campus: when you needed or wanted to sell it, you really only had one buyer. Now William Henry had discovered the other big problem: when the administration planned to expand campus facilities, you were standing squarely in their way.

He scanned down the letter until he came to the figure with five digits and a dollar sign. It was less than he expected. The person who signed the letter—over the official but ambiguous title of "Authorized Signatory"—explained that this amount represented the original purchase price that William Henry had paid in 1952, "plus twenty-eight percent (28%) to account for appreciation in the market value of residences in the surrounding community since that time." The university considered this more than fair and generous. The letter went on to state that the university would be paying only for "the building and any improvements," rather than for ground under the house. It seemed the university's trustees had been in possession of that all along in what was called "leased fee estate." In other words, William Henry had never actually bought the parcel, simply held it under a long-term lease.

All of this rang a distant bell, recalled from the heady days when he and Jane had celebrated his discharge from the army by moving out of her little apartment in town and buying their beloved cottage in the woods. The transfer papers and mortgage agreement had run to more than a hundred pages of thickly worded legalese, and William Henry had tried to read every word, because his father always insisted he read everything he signed. But when you were buying your first real home together, you tended to gloss over the legal terms and focus on size of the rooms, sunlight on the woodwork, and view out the windows. You didn't give a thought to "buyback provisions," because you were never going to live anywhere else.

Well, "never" had come just a bit early.

For the marriage, as well as the cottage.

William Henry studied that five-digit figure. Deducting what he still owed on the mortgage, the amount represented a small down payment—less than ten percent—on a house in town. Or he could bank it, pay rent every month, and live for what? Three years? Maybe four—if the apartment was small enough.

Either way, the dream cottage was gone.

And now he had damn-all to show for it.

What he really needed was a new dream.

20. Rivals of the Old Firm

When someone—and Nicholas Carr was intent on finding out who—posted flyers around campus announcing an "organizational meeting" for the "local chapter" of the "Students for Democratic Action (SDA)," he alerted Jacobs and Noyes and made their participation mandatory. Then he remembered he had a date with Dani Wheelock that same evening. Well, business had to come before pleasure.

He tried calling her at home, to cancel, but on the second ring a man answered—Professor Wheelock. "Hello?"

Carr knew instinctively that Dani's father didn't like him. Not many fathers did. So there was no point in saying he had been planning to take his daughter out but now something more important had come up. Too much to explain and nothing that couldn't be smoothed over later with a little sweet talk and flattery. He hung up the phone.

At the meeting that night, in one of the classrooms in Dover Hall, Carr entered and took a seat at the back. Jacobs was down in the front row, and Noyes in the middle. They knew enough not to sit together or even make detectable eye contact. With their own "Social Policy Forum" officially listed for Student Organizations Day, to be held in Weller Gymnasium during registration for spring semester, the three had a professional interest in other groups that might be forming on campus.

The SDA meeting was pathetic. The only visible organizers were five very young undergraduates, all neat and clean, with scrubbed faces under short hair, the men in dress shirts with blue pinstripes, the women in white blouses, and most with sweaters in the school colors of green and gold. They looked like decorated frogs.

They spoke hesitantly about "thinking it would be a good idea" to establish a way for students to "air their concerns" about "issues like the war, the draft, and racism," one of them said, "capitalism and imperialism," another chimed in, and "anything else they wanted to discuss," said a third.

If those campus flyers had generated any kind of crowd, Carr might have stood up right there, asked some kind of innocent question—the subject wouldn't much matter, under the rubric of "anything else"—and leveraged whatever answer the boys and girls gave to begin his own spiel, smoothly take over the meeting, and ultimately control the group as a sister-adjunct to his own Social Policy Forum. Then he and Jacobs could decide later whether to use the new organization or crash it.

But the turnout was actually dismal: fewer than a dozen people, barely more than the self-proclaimed organizers, not counting Carr and his core team. The hall was so thinly populated he was afraid his team might stand out for what they were—or obviously were *not,* which was students—and so give the game away.

At one point, as the scrubbed youngsters talked among themselves from behind the lectern, it occurred to Carr they might actually be shills for the administration. That would be a new tactic: setting up a tame protest group, as if trying to inoculate the student body against just the sort of wild and unpredictable notions Carr wanted to spread.

But then he realized the timing of the whole thing was too inept. Not even the dean's office, if anyone there had any crowd skills, would plan to hold the group's first meeting on a cold and lonely January night. Certainly not a Friday night, when everybody else was out getting drunk in celebration of the weekend, or attending a fraternity mixer, or whatever it was that normal people did at the end of the week. And never during the semester's last week, when conscientious types would be beavering away at term papers or cramming for finals. Better to wait for those warm and lazy afternoons that beckoned in springtime, when the itch to go outside and start shouting became almost unbearable.

Jacobs glanced back at him, and Carr lifted his chin and glanced at the exit. She nodded and tightened her scarf. Noyes caught the signal, stood up, and slipped out of his row. After a decent interval, Carr followed them out.

"Organizing this campus is going to be harder than I expected," Noyes said when they met outside.

Carr shrugged. "Tonight wasn't the night."

"Amateurs." Jacobs said with a sneer.

"We make our own opportunities."

———

Dani had arranged her study schedule so she would have the night free. After she fixed an early dinner, through which she hurried her father, he then gallantly offered to take her turn at washing dishes. That left extra time for her to take a bath and arrange her hair. She laid out her bolero jacket in fuchsia silk with embroidered dragons and then matched it with a short, black, wool dress that also went with her best pair of high black boots. She just hoped this ensemble wouldn't be too warm when they got to the dance.

She didn't expect to be ready by the time Nicholas called, but that was a woman's prerogative. She would make an entrance while he waited for her in the living room. He might even bring her a corsage.

Dani had such expectations for the evening that her father had caught the hint and knew something was going on. But he tactfully didn't ask—until, well past eight o'clock, when she finally came down in all her glory, with her hair pinned up and her eye shadow and lipstick perfect. Then she sat down in the living room and picked up a magazine.

"You're going out," he said flatly.

"I—I think so. Has anyone called?"

"Not in the last three hours," he said.

"No one at all?" She was almost pleading.

He frowned. "Well, this afternoon ..."

"Yes?"

"The phone rang, but no one was there."

"Oh. I see."

After a pause he said, "Dani, I'm so sorry."

"It was nothing."

21. Sealing the Deal

"Excuse me," said the tall man standing on the other side of the bars of Marion Davison's teller cage in the Bursar's Office. "I need some help with this." He held out a letter, a long one, two pages, dense with words.

Marion put on her spectacles and read the salutation, then jumped to the signature. "This is from Buildings and Grounds. They're three floors up." She then prepared herself to deal with the next person in line, although no one was actually standing behind this man—who was evidently the same "Wheelock" as in the letter.

"But I've just come from their office," he said. "There I met with Miss Robbins, who signed the letter. She said the process is all in motion. She even gave me a date to be packed up and moved. She said your office would cut a check for me."

Marion reluctantly examined the contents of her in-box. "The paperwork hasn't come through yet. You'll just have to wait until it does."

Although the function of the Bursar's Office was both to receive and to disburse monies, Marion belonged to the university heart and soul. That made this money—any money, actually—the natural property of the administration. It would pass her hands only when all other forms of recourse had been tried and failed.

"Could you tell me when that might be, please?"

"Now that's hard to say," she countered. "We're real busy, what with the semester ending and all. Could be a week. Could be a whole lot more."

"Perhaps someone could call me when it does come through?"

Marion sniffed. "Do I look like a telephone?"

"No, ma'am, you do not."

"Well, then …"

———

In the days since the letter had come, evicting him from the cottage in the woods, a new and different vision had been forming in William Henry's mind. He wanted to cut loose from the

188

land and the entanglements of renting or buying property, which then suddenly became encumbered with leases and liens and other legal hazards. He wanted to be free of all that. In its place, he conceived of buying himself a boat—the boat, *Galatea*. If he lived aboard her, he would be floating free and self-contained. And if anyone claimed he was infringing on their rights or standing in their path, then William Henry could just slip his moorings and sail away.

However, the notion of living on the water and one day slipping away clashed awkwardly with his vision of *Galatea*. While she was stately and elegant, reminiscent of a time when people lived more graciously, her accommodations—if he could call them that, for all her sixty-odd feet of curving white hull—would be cramped, even for one person. He realized that his dream of sailing away did not have room for a heartsick daughter. But then, Dani had talked of moving into the dorms for the past year, eager to get out of the house and probably out from under the pressure of her father's thumb. Now would be the time.

Of course, the old boat needed some modifications if he was going to live aboard. That absurd toilet bowl, for one thing, had to be placed in its own compartment. And he would need some sort of washing facilities, a tub or shower—and not set down *plunk* beside the engine, either. But all these things, he was sure, could be worked out. In fact, meeting the challenges of living afloat and adapting his life to this new reality might be fun.

With these thoughts whirling around in his head, William Henry proceeded from the Bursar's Office to visit Harold Stephenson at Farmer's and Merchant's Bank of New York. They held the mortgage on his cottage. With some luck, and a certain amount of cooperation from Stephenson, William Henry could parlay the university's check, when it came, into paying off the old mortgage, making a down payment on *Galatea* with the remainder, then taking out a new loan, with the boat held as collateral, to cover the rest of the twelve-thousand-dollar asking price.

Sitting on the hard wooden guest chairs in front of Stephenson's desk, William Henry explained all this. Stephenson watched him at first with an amused glance, then pulled his chin, and finally looked away and would not make eye contact.

"You want to buy a pleasure yacht?" the man said, finding great interest in something outside the window.

"Well, it would be a bit more than that," William Henry said.

"You'll put her in commercial service? Like a charter?"

"I was thinking more a residence. A live-aboard."

"You want a cabin on the water—like that?"

"Well, more as a home. I'd live there."

Stephenson bit his lip and at last looked him in the eye. "You want us to make a loan on this boat as if it were a house?"

"Yes, because it would be my primary residence, my house, as it were."

"But it's a boat, with no land under it—not what we call real property."

"You wrote a mortgage for the cottage, and that was just wood and shingles. The university still owned the land."

"Yes," Stephenson said. "But, in terms of collateral, the cottage was, well, *real*. It wasn't going to sink."

"It could have burned down. I had to insure it against fire."

"I don't know, Wheelock. You're a good customer, but—"

"There must be some precedent for this kind of loan. *Galatea* isn't a rowboat or a pleasure boat, more like a steamship. She's sixty feet long, for God's sake."

"Well … I guess I can talk it over with my loan officer," the man said reluctantly. "You know, of course, that we will need assurances—a marine survey, proof of licensing and inspection, insurance coverage."

"I can arrange all that."

"What about in winter?"

"Excuse me?" William Henry asked, startled.

"Can the boat stay in the water when there's ice?"

"Well, the owner has her in storage now, but I suppose—"

"Maybe there's a reason he doesn't live aboard?"

"I think that's because of his wife, actually."

"You sure you've thought this through?"

"Well, at least I'm beginning to."

———

Late in the day, with Bill Gibbs once again thinking of closing early, a crunching of the gravel in the yard made him look out. The professor's dark-blue Volvo was back. It was just over a week since the last visit, when the man had brought his daughter, and that had been about a week since the time before, which was not quite two weeks after his first drop-by. Gibbs was enough of a salesman to know these things took their own time. And the larger the boat, usually, the longer the time. But the first words out of Wheelock's mouth as he came in the door were, "Is *Galatea* still for sale?"

Bingo!

"Haven't talked to the owner in a while," Gibbs said, "but I'm sure she is."

"And is he still asking twelve thousand?"

"Yes, with maybe some wiggle room."

Wheelock paused … a long pause.

Gibbs could see him deciding.

"Well, then, I want her."

Gibbs went slow where other men might go fast. "Okay. All right. Um, do you have the money?"

"I'm working out a bank loan right now," Wheelock said. "I'll have the cash for a down payment in a week or two."

"That's good. That's appropriate. I'll call the owner tonight."

"The bank says they'll need a marine survey. Do you arrange that?"

"I've got one here somewhere. Couple of years old, but still current."

"And what about licensing and inspection?"

"State does that after she goes in the water."

"And, of course, insurance," Wheelock said.

"I handle it for most of the boats at the yard."

"Then ..." The man suddenly looked deflated. "Then I guess it's just a matter of getting the money."

"Well, not quite. She does need a bit of work before we can float her."

"I see. And is that something that you or the owner takes care of?"

"Sure ... for a price. Your boat, you decide how much to do."

"What kind of work?" Wheelock asked.

"Like I said before. Through-hull fittings need patching and caulking. Hull could do with scraping down and a coat of paint, too. And the engine requires some attention. Nothing a handy-man couldn't do himself. I've got all the tools you need here in the yard. Lend 'em to you for nothing."

"Well, I ... yes ... I suppose I should get my hands dirty."

Gibbs smiled. "Just think of it as sweat equity."

22. Resolution of the Faculty Senate

"WHEREAS, WAR IS a human travesty, unending source of tragedy, and blight upon the world, while those who profit from war by supplying the materials of destruction are the true enemies of civilization; and

"WHEREAS, peace is a blessing and the natural state of humankind in pursuit of the examined life, and opposition to war in all its forms as well as those who wage it is the highest calling of a civilized mind; therefore

"RESOLVED, that the University be declared a 'War Free Zone' and a place of refuge for any and all who oppose it and the act of conscription necessary to support it."

This measure passed on January 31 with a vote of 186 to 2.

Standing in the cloakroom adjacent to the amphitheater in Wilson Hall, while the tenured professors filed out of the session, Edward Belton could feel their eyes on him. They would briefly examine the dark-green uniform, the gold captain's bars and Infantry badge with its crossed rifles, the three rows of campaign ribbons and medals, including a Bronze Star with "V" for valor and Purple Heart. Their eyes would briefly touch on the pink, plastic-covered prosthesis where his left arm should have been—a souvenir from the Ia Drang Valley—then quickly slide away. All but one pair of eyes.

"What will you do now?" asked Wheelock, of the Classics Department. He was the only other delegate to oppose this latest resolution.

"I will stand my post until the administration tells me the ROTC program is no longer accredited on campus."

"How long you think that will take?"

"I'll be gone by June, if not before."

"Then you go where they send you."

"That's the army life," Belton said.

Wheelock started to turn away, but stopped, turned back. His hand went up to his right eyebrow, fingers stiff. It was too crisp for a civilian's salute.

He returned it automatically—then remembered. "Oh! *Colonel* Wheelock!"

"Well, I was actually just a major, and a pencil-pusher, now retired."

Belton paused. "Do you think this might all be just a phase?"

The man squinted. "Like something in the water?"

"Yeah, that. Kind of temporary insanity?"

"Maybe for the professors here."

"But for the students?"

"Bend the twig ..."

"Shape the tree."

23. Work for a Handyman

Durinc the week-long break between fall and spring semesters, the university virtually shut down, and neither Dani nor her father had classes. Normally, this would be their vacation time. But now he asked her to come out to the boatyard on the inlet and help him work on the old steamship, *Galatea*. She thought they ought to be spending the time planning and packing for the move out of their house on campus. But for William Henry, getting the boat ready to launch was the first priority. It seemed that owning a yacht was, for him, the new dream, the way forward. It was drawing all of his attention.

"But have you actually bought the boat yet?" she asked in surprise.

"Well, the bursar's check and the bank loan haven't come through."

"So there's still time to back out?"

"But I did sign the papers."

"Are they binding?"

Her father never heard the question. "Since we have the time this week," he went on, "I thought we could begin cleaning her up. The owner has agreed to let us go aboard and get to work."

"That's thoughtful of him," she said. If the deal fell through, think of all the free work the owner would get. But her father was so fixated on his dream that he missed the irony in her comment.

They spent the first two days exploring the cabin, the lazarettes, and other storage compartments belowdecks at bow and stern. They removed junk and trash, like a set of punctured and deflated rubber fenders, tangles of old rope, and mildewed life jackets in various sizes. As they went along, her father was figuring out which projects to tackle first. He dictated them to Dani, who kept a notebook in her back pocket.

A locked hatch on the fore deck, right in front of the wheelhouse, puzzled them. They tried the keys from the yard manager, Mr. Gibbs, but none of them fit the fancy brass lock plate. At their lunch break, when they asked him about it, he suggested they look in the desk in the main saloon, and there Dani found a curlicued brass key.

She took it out on deck, knelt, and turned the lock. The edge of the hatch lifted by an inch or two. She pulled on it and felt a counterbalancing mechanism start to move of its own accord. The hatch slid back and down, and out of the hole in the deck rose some kind of metal contraption. It was green and spotted with tarnish and covered in cobwebs. In the dim light under the canvas tent, which was still in place over the boat, Dani studied the thing to try and understand its purpose.

On its back side, which faced the wheelhouse, she saw a row of twenty-five flat tabs of discolored brass: fifteen of them were long, while ten were shorter and spaced at odd intervals between them. On the front side were twenty-five upright brass cylinders, set in banks of twelve and thirteen, each one taller than the last. A complicated manifold fed into the cylinders and was in turn worked by levers from the tabs. Only when she noticed the wedge-shaped slots in those vertical cylinders did she begin to suspect …

"Hey, Dad!" she called. "You need to see this!"

Her father came out of the engine room through a side door in the wheelhouse and stopped dead when he saw the contraption. "Is that what I think it is?" he asked.

"It's a steam calliope," she confirmed. "See that tube with the hinged joints? It must go back to the boiler."

"Does it still work?" he asked.

"Can't tell until we get steam up."

"By golly!" He counted the tabs with his fingers. "Two full octaves, with all the sharps and flats, just like a little piano."

"You took some music, didn't you? Can you play it?"

He shook his head. "My instrument was the cornet, back in the high-school band. But with this keyboard, you don't exactly have to be Van Cliburn. We could steam into dock tootling away, like the circus coming to town—or one of those Mississippi River steamer boats drawing into Natchez or New Orleans."

"So cleaning up and testing the calliope is a priority?" Dani prompted.

"Well, probably after getting the engine to work."

"Ah, yes, about the engine ..."

Dani had already tried to make it turn.

With a wrench from the engine room toolbox, she had first loosened the valves on the main steam line going into the high-pressure cylinder and the exhaust coming out of the low-pressure, to avoid pulling a vacuum. She disconnected the reversing gear, so that she would not be trying to turn the dead mass of the long propeller shaft. Then, wedging a broom handle between the spokes of the flywheel, she put her shoulder to it and pushed with her feet against the deck, using her full strength. All that did was break the broom handle.

Dani figured the grease on the crank bearings was certainly old and probably fouled with dirt. The bearings themselves might be shot. Without firing up the boiler and putting steam through the cylinders—and hope that all the valve links still worked—she had no way to force the connecting rods to move. Before she could do that, however, the boat had to be sitting in the water, because the boiler drew its makeup feedwater directly from the through-hull fittings, which also supplied cooling water to the steam condensers that recycled hot water back into the boiler. Otherwise, she would have to spend hours filling the system from a hose.

While Dani understood the theory behind the triple-expansion steam engine, she knew that didn't mean she was qualified to work with live steam. "Grandpa knows about this stuff, doesn't he?" she said. "Didn't he used to run a railroad?"

"Um," William Henry said. "Let's not discuss it with my father yet."

"Why not? Don't you think he'd be thrilled to see all this?"

"No, he'd box my ears for buying a steamboat."

"I guess he would. Tough old man."

"But handy," her father said.

———

During the week he and Dani put into fixing up *Galatea*—at least as much as they could before actually taking possession—William Henry kept track of everything they needed to make the boat ready for launching in the spring and then living aboard.

Bill Gibbs had spoken of scraping the hull and then repainting, but William Henry did not see the point of that. The chalky white paint above, and the dusty red paint below the waterline was still smooth and unblistered. Well, mostly smooth, as he had found some ragged patches when he walked around the boat from one end to the other, peering between the cradle frames with a flashlight. It had taken him more than an hour just going over the sixty-two-foot length, covering both sides. He imagined doing that again at the speed of a paint brush, divided the hours in his head into days, and hoped he had enough cash left over from buying the boat to hire a team of painters. As for scraping the entire length down to bare wood himself or even paying others to do it—well, one more coat of paint on the current layer wouldn't hurt a bit.

At the stern end, he ducked in under the fantail and gave a tug to the great, bronze, three-bladed propeller. It felt … loose. He put one hand on the shaft and the other on one of the pitched blades and wiggled it. The connection to the shaft was solid. Then he grasped the shaft itself in both hands. He pushed and twisted. Somewhere back under the hull, further toward the bow, he heard a sound like someone throwing a handful of sand or pebbles into the weeds. He followed the shaft up to the hole where it disappeared inside the hull and found bits of some material—decayed rubber or dried fiber—sifting out from around the shaft. Gibbs had said something about "packing glands," and now William Henry mentally added another job that needed doing before *Galatea* could float.

He walked back along the outside of the hull to those places where the stub ends of various pipes emerged. The pipes were all sawed flat and fitted with metal flanges that lay flush against the hull, sealed to the wood. Some pressure or flexing at that point of contact had cracked the red paint, which had flaked away and exposed the hull surface surrounding the flange.

It was very odd. What he saw there, in the beam of his flashlight, did not look like planking or any kind of wood grain. He went to the largest of the pipes, in the vicinity of the engine room—this one covered with a screen mesh and cupped baffle against drawing bits of weed and debris up inside the boat—and there he examined a similarly exposed area. The subsurface was gray and smooth. It reminded him of cement. William Henry supposed some kind of sealant—maybe epoxy—had been used to fit the flange to the wood underneath.

He couldn't say for sure anything was wrong.

And the marine survey would certainly have covered it.

The only thing that could stop him now was the bank's decision.

24. HELPING THEM UNDERSTAND

DANI'S COURSE LOAD was full for spring semester and her spare time would be completely committed to studying her engineering work and to the special requirements of her one elective. Still, she liked to wander from table to table in the gymnasium on Student Organizations Day and see all the extracurricular activities she would be missing.

Glee Club, Dance Band, University Orchestra ...

Chess Club, Math Club—Dani's one membership, although she was seldom able to attend. "Hello, Stephen ..." "Hey there, Dani!"

Latin Club, *Club de la Langue Française*, Spanish Club, *Soyuz Russkovo Yazyka*. The College of Engineering didn't have a language requirement, although she had always dreamed of speaking French ...

Junior Varsity Softball, Varsity Field Hockey, Judo Club, Karate Club, Fencing Club. With her long arms and legs, Dani had been told she should try out for fencing but sports were far down on her list ...

Students for Democratic Action, Organization for Social Protest, Social Policy Forum ... And there sat Nicholas Carr with his blonde friend and another man.

Dani stopped, stared, tried to back up, to disappear—and then he looked up and saw her. Carr recognized her with just his eyes, nodded briefly, then appeared to make a decision. He got up from the table, came around to the front, and approached her.

"Hello, Dani," he said almost shyly.

"I should be mad at you for standing me up."

"Gee, I'm really sorry. You know, something came up that night. An emergency. I tried to call, but ..."

"My father said someone called at the house but hung up."

"I, uh, don't think that was me. I tried your phone a couple of times, but got a wrong number every time. I must have misdialed."

"What was the emergency, that night?" she asked.

"Oh, our friend Randall there got sick." He pointed back at the table. "Vomiting and everything. We had to take him to the hospital."

"I'm sorry to hear that. He looks okay now."

"Yes, he's all better. Stomach flu."

"Is he your roommate then?"

"Yes, we share a room."

"And an interest in politics, I see. I'm glad you finally managed to enroll."

"Well, about that ..." Carr hesitated. "Turns out I applied too late."

"You're not a student?" she asked.

"I was once, back in Berkeley."

"But this is a *student* group."

"I used to be a member."

"And now you're—?"

"Just helping out."

"I don't understand. You came all the way here to New York, in the middle of winter, with no place to live, and too late for the semester, just so you could 'help out'?"

"Well, because it's important to me," Carr said. "You can only study so much. And then you have to go out in the world and do things."

"What did you study?" she asked. "Back in Berkeley?"

"Political economy—like I said. Graduate level."

"All right. And what is it you do now?"

"Raise students' consciousness."

"Consciousness of what?"

"History," he said.

Spring 1968

1. The Paperwork

When William Henry dropped by his office on campus after his third-period Introduction to Logic class, he found a message from Harold Stephenson at the bank. The subject line on the little pink form gave no indication whether the news was good or bad. He called back immediately, holding his breath as he dialed.

"Well," Stephenson said once the pleasantries had been spoken, "the bank's loan committee approved your application. We can make a mortgage for fifteen years—not for thirty, of course—and the rate's two full points above what you'd pay on a house—"

"That's wonderful news, Harold. So the payments would be …" William Henry tried to calculate them in his head and failed. "So … what would I be paying … ?"

Stephenson cleared his throat. "Four hundred and fifty dollars per month."

That was more … more than William Henry had been expecting. It was about half again more than he had been paying on the cottage in the woods. It was quite a bit more than he might pay in rent on an apartment in the nicest part of town. Still, neither of those housing options had the panache, the flair, the coolness factor of a boat on the water. It was a new life he was entering.

"That doesn't break your budget, does it?" Stephenson asked.

"No, uh, I can cover that," William Henry said quickly.

"We know it's within your cash flow, of course."

"I'll probably have to give up a few vices."

"Well, yes—but then, don't we all?"

William Henry laughed at the joke, weak as it was. Then he considered that he was also facing a whole array of new expenses. He still had to pay for materials and any extra labor to work on *Galatea*—and there would always be things he didn't think of, like rope for tying things down, or canvas for sails or awnings, or something. He would also have to make arrangements for mooring her—probably rent space on a dock somewhere down along the waterfront. And he would have to buy fuel if he wanted to move the boat anywhere. Simply "sailing away" was going to cost money.

"There was one thing," Stephenson went on. "In that marine survey you supplied, it stated the boat was fit for 'inland navigation,' including 'lake and river service.' One of the members of the loan committee asked if that meant your boat should not be taken on the ocean, and if we should write a stipulation to that effect. Another member asked if that had anything to do with the distances traveled—the fuel capacity, necessary crew, and so on—or if it referred to the kinds of wave action the hull can withstand. Do you know anything about that?"

"Only what I read in the survey ..."

"You see, it came up as a question. Lake Ontario here can whip up some sizable waves. One of our bankers has experience with boats. We thought since that hull's more than eighty years old, it might not be able—"

"*Galatea's* been safe to navigate on Lake Ontario for a lot of years."

"We understand that, but now we have a fiduciary interest—"

"Be hard to have a boat you can't take out of the creek."

"I understand, and I argued against any restriction."

"I do appreciate that, Harold," William Henry said. "And the boat will be insured against loss, of course." That was another expense he would have to support—probably at higher rates than a house, too.

"Yes, I pointed that out to the committee as well." Stephenson paused. "So the paperwork will be ready for you late this afternoon. You can stop by anytime tomorrow and sign."

"I want to thank you for seeing this through, Harold."

"It's my job, you know. *Bon voyage!*"

2. The Elective

Along with her full load of engineering work, Dani's advisor had encouraged her to take one elective outside her major during spring semester. She had tried to find a class as far removed as possible from her cerebral world of calculating gear ratios, stress factors, and coefficients of friction and thermal expansion. So she had signed up for Theatre Arts 101, Introduction to Acting.

Dani knew she was out of her league when most of the girl students—including the instructor—showed up for the first class in leotards and ballet slippers. The boys wore sneakers and sweatpants. Dani was wearing long johns under her jeans and heavy boots, because it was damned cold outside, and wondered if she had missed something in the course description.

Instead of a classroom, they met on stage at Beyer Memorial Auditorium, where the Theatre Arts Department held its productions. But now the place was barren: a floor subsurface of black-painted canvas, a back wall of red brick, with all the scenery flats and curtains pulled up into the flies, a theater full of dark seats made invisible by the harsh, white lighting on the stage.

"I'm Professor Sokolov," the instructor began, "but we're not formal here, so you can call me Elise." She smiled and mentioned the plays where she had appeared, mostly regional productions but with two that went off Broadway. The names whizzed right by Dani: *Long Day's Journey into Night, The Rose Tattoo, The Miracle Worker, Romanoff and Juliet*, and others Dani didn't catch or couldn't remember. Thinking "Romanoff" had to be a slip of the tongue, she looked it up later and discovered there was actually such a play, with Shakespeare translated to a Cold War setting in Eastern Europe.

Professor Sokolov then invited the students to give their own resumes. The class members all seemed to be aspiring actors and actresses, coming off starring roles in their high-school senior plays. All except Dani, who hadn't given a thought to acting until about three weeks ago.

The class began formally with the students sitting in a circle, cross-legged on the floor, and breathing in through the nose, out through the mouth, and imagining "a place where you are most relaxed and cared for, where you are at peace, where you are happy." Dani wasn't any good at yoga, either. She tried to think of such a place, but for her none existed. She finally settled on the satisfaction she got when an equation resolved itself into one perfect answer and all the gears of the universe seemed to click.

After a brief lecture about the various acting styles—the classical British style, where the performer learns and practices the expressions and gestures appropriate to the action; the Stravinsky Method, where the performer puts himself into the mood and feeling of the play—Professor Sokolov asked them all to choose one of the monologues from *Spoon River Anthology* by Edgar Lee Masters. Delivering it in front of the other students would be their first actual assignment in the course.

"And I have exciting news," she announced as they gathered up their things at the end of class. "The department's signature production this semester is going to be *The Persecution and Assassination of Jean-Paul Marat as Performed by the Inmates of the Asylum of Charenton Under the Direction of the Marquis de Sade.*"

The other students greeted this with great enthusiasm, but Dani was left gasping. Something about inmates in an asylum? And the Marquis de Sade?

"It will be a large production," Professor Sokolov went on, "and we need many extras, performing as nursing sisters, warders, and members of the bourgeois audience. The department has accepted my offer of students from this class to fill these roles."

This brought even more excitement from the students. Dani was still trying to sort out the play's title. And now it seemed she was going to dress up, put on makeup, and appear on stage with people pretending to be crazy—along with someone pretending to be the Marquis de Sade.

She left the theater in a daze.

Later, at lunch, she tried to describe the whole experience to Nicholas Carr. Of course he picked up on the title of the semester's production right away.

"*Marat/Sade*? You're going to be in *Marat/Sade*!"

"It's a play about crazy people," she said.

"It's a fantastic political narrative!"

"With the Marquis de Sade."

"Yes, but it's brilliant!"

3. WATCHING THE PROFESSOR AT WORK (I)

TEACHING A COURSE alongside Professor Wheelock turned out to be more fun than Agnes D'Angelo had imagined. He was so stiff and formal when you first met him; who could guess that, put behind a lectern in a roomful of students, he would light up like an old Vaudeville trouper?

On the first day in class, Wheelock juxtaposed the comedy of *Lysistrata* with the tragedy of *Antigone* to establish a key thought about social protest: that it can support either conservative or progressive viewpoints. Antigone was protesting her uncle Creon's unjust decree about leaving a fallen warrior—her brother Polyneices, who was considered a traitor against Thebes—to rot in the field rather than burying him according to the ancient rites. Antigone thus adhered to traditional values and ways of doing things against an overbearing ruler who violated existing social norms. Lysistrata and her friends, on the other hand, tried to force a peace in the long, drawn-out Peloponnesian War—which had proved debilitating to both sides—by withholding sexual favors from their men. The women challenged the existing social order and traditional values, where men make all the political and military decisions, and so were promoting a higher value and new social good.

But Wheelock didn't simply explain all this. He read out bits of each play, first in the original Greek, then in translation, putting on voices and gestures appropriate to the characters.

From *Lysistrata,* he quoted the title character as she explained her scheme, using a warbling falsetto: " 'We need only sit indoors with painted cheeks, and meet our mates lightly clad in transparent gowns of Amorgos silk, and perfectly depilated. They will get their tools up and be wild to lie with us.' " Here Wheelock paused for the class to snicker. " 'That will be the time to refuse, and they will hasten to make peace.' "

From *Antigone,* he read out the tyrant Creon's decree in a thunderous bass: " 'But for Polyneices—who came back from exile and sought to consume utterly with fire the city of his fathers and the shrines of his fathers' gods, sought to taste of kindred blood, and to lead the remnant into slavery—touching this man, it hath been proclaimed to our people that none shall grace him with sepulture or lament, but leave him unburied, a corpse for birds and dogs to eat, a ghastly sight of shame.' And note, please, how Creon manages to avoid his own responsibility for this desecration by using the passive voice—'it hath been proclaimed.' Indeed so—by him!"

The fact that Wheelock took his examples from woman-centered plays—where it was the supposedly weaker sex standing up for what they believed—had surprised Agnes. She would have thought an older man—for Wheelock had to be approaching fifty—from a department like the classics—a subject dominated by old men—might chose materials more male-oriented, like Achilles defying Agamemnon in *The Iliad*. But here Wheelock was a more enlightened fellow than he appeared.

As they worked together, preparing the course outline, each day's lesson plan, the reading assignments, and test materials, Agnes had sensed something else about the man. Although he seemed to be a fixture of the academy and socially conservative, what with his military background and such, a rebel was hiding beneath that formal surface—and not too far beneath, either. He was inquisitive and impatient, eager to put old ideas under a new light, and dissatisfied with the status quo.

Agnes also sensed sadness in the man. Wheelock was missing something—or someone—that left a large hole in his life. It sat on him like a kind of hunger. At first, from the way he sometimes looked at her, Agnes thought he was simply another man in the midst of the customary male mid-life crisis, that he was feeling dissatisfied with his faithful yet aging wife and reaching out for someone younger and more exciting. But after a time she knew that it wasn't sex he wanted. No, something in Wheelock's life had passed him by long ago, leaving an emptiness.

She wanted to tell this man to slow down, to be careful. That acting on such feelings—busting out, grasping the hot iron, burning his bridges—was almost certainly the way to get hurt. His life would change, and not for the better. But, for all their time spent working on the course, she just never found the right moment to stop and warn him.

4. Overheard at the Marat/ Sade Rehearsals

To PREPARE FOR their roles as inmates of the asylum at Charenton, the actors with speaking and singing parts, all young men and women of above-average intelligence and from polite backgrounds, were ready to smear their faces with lampblack and greasepaint, don the rags of peasant blouses, pantaloons, and billowing skirts, lie on the floor with twisted, writhing limbs, and dart their tongues about like lizards. To prepare for their silent roles as nursing sisters and wardens, members of the Theatre Arts 101 class adopted upright poses and wary frowns, folded their hands as if in prayer, or beat imaginary truncheons against their open palms. Both groups were trying to make themselves believe in a world that had gone insane, while musicians in the background practiced runs and trills with clarinet and tuba, actually trying to play out of tune and off the beat.

After the first rehearsal, as the actors unbent their limbs, stopped their leering, and washed their faces, Dani overheard the following exchanges in the green room.

"Does this strike anyone else as odd? I mean, here we are dressed in rags, acting crazy, and telling everyone we want a revolution—while our Charlotte Corday drives a powder-blue Mustang, and our Marat is a medalist and captain of the gymnastics team."

"It's just a play, f'gosh sakes!"

"*Romeo and Juliet* was a play. This is guerrilla theater."

"It did win a Tony Award."

"And it was on Broadway."

"Only 145 performances. Hardly a success."

"Yes, but on *Broadway!*"

"And it won *awards!*"

5. The First Rally of Spring

Nicholas Carr knew the weather wouldn't be right. Although the snow was mostly gone from campus by the third week of February—with only crusty rings left around the north sides of trees and ridges along the east sides of buildings—the sky could still cloud up and snow again. The lawns were brown and soggy, and no one would want to stand out in the cold wind and meager sunlight and listen to speeches, let alone march off through the mud to occupy the administration offices. But those were just the physical realities.

Political reality was another matter. The other groups had already put up posters for their rallies, and Carr's Social Policy Forum needed to kick off the protest season if they were to maintain any kind of control. So he and Randall drove Glynda's rusted-out Corvair to the loading dock behind the Theodosian Library, unpacked their loudspeakers, microphones, and amplifier from the back seat, carried them around to the front steps, and ran an unauthorized extension cord over the threshold to the electrical outlets in the vestibule.

The Mall, stretching down to the concrete arches and wrought iron fences of Strahling Gate, made a natural assembly space—not to mention a strip of dry concrete twelve yards wide and a hundred yards long, so that no one actually had to stand in the mud. At 2:20 in the afternoon, right before the change of classes, he switched on the amplifier and began talking. It didn't matter what he said now: an amplified voice drew listeners the way an ambulance's wailing siren drew spectators. But Carr liked to keep things authentic.

"The university system is nothing but a machine," he began, almost at random. "It sucks you into its maw, through the admissions tests, SAT scores, and application forms with their essay questions that make you want to feel special, so that you'll compete with each other, and climb over the backs of your fellow students, just so you can win a place here. They do that to make you feel you're somehow chosen and important. But truth is, they just need to fill those classroom seats and keep the tuition money coming! What you don't understand is the university *needs* you! The system *needs* you! Without you, they are *nothing!*"

By ones and twos, then threes, students who had been running to sixth period, either coming up the Mall from town or cutting across at right angles to get to the other side of campus, slowed down, paused, and stopped to listen.

"But the university is not the end of it all," Carr went on, "because the university is only a cog in a much bigger machine. After they process you with a degree, their stamp of approval, the university sends you out into the maw of that society-wide machine, the military-industrial complex. And there you're stuck and scrambling for the next forty-five years of your life, climbing over the backs of your fellow workers—unless that machine decides to draft you and send you off to the jungles to fight against the little yellow people who've gotten in the way of their global machine."

By tens and twenties, then—well, with the usual ebb and flow of passersby, some stopping as others moved on—the crowd settled out at a steady mass that Carr eyeballed to be about thirty-five people.

Dani Wheelock was standing in the second row. Of course, he remembered now, the engineering buildings were in this part of campus. It was only natural for her pass this way and stop. He looked right at her, touched a finger to his cheek, winked, and smiled.

"And why does that big machine need you?" Carr went on, asking the crowd rhetorically. "For profit! You make and sell their widgets—all the cars, television sets, refrigerators, all the shiny toys, glass beads that our society trades as wampum—so you can earn your widget salary and then turn around and buy your own widgets. Endless supply feeding endless, useless demand! And all so that some number-crunching banker on Wall Street can earn a few dollars and think about taking his kids to Disneyland."

Carr spoke for another ten minutes. As people started getting restless and looking at their watches, he started winding down.

"The system's got you, people! It will use you—or kill you in the jungle—but it doesn't care! The system *needs* you, because without you the system is nothing. But deep down, the system doesn't *care* about you!

"Thank you for listening! Thank you for your time and attention!"

He watched the crowd disperse with slightly dazed looks.

It didn't matter how many came out this time.

Nothing that Carr said mattered, exactly.

The message was in the emotion.

Little stabs of resentment.

Breaking them down.

Sowing the seed.

6. Repairing the Engine

"I THINK WE'VE got it licked!" Dani exclaimed aloud, finally. This was after spending most of one Saturday morning aboard *Galatea*, on her knees in the bilges, with her head down below deck level, taking apart the bearing journals and connecting rods around the steam engine's main crankshaft. The work had been both delicate and tedious.

She had started the previous weekend by reading up, in her spare time, on the mechanics of triple-expansion steam engines. She quickly discovered that when she had tried to move the engine on that previous visit, she might have used the jacking gear instead of a broomstick. So the first thing she did on this particular Saturday morning, after opening the steam lines and freeing the propeller shaft, was engage the jacking gear and try to turn the crankshaft by hand. It still wouldn't budge. But she could use what she had read to make sure the gear was engaged and locked; that way, as she loosened the bearing points, trying to shake the frozen shaft loose, it wouldn't suddenly turn on her and break bones in her hand—or worse.

The journals were located at either end of the shaft and between each of the crank throws. The rods were on the throws between the journals. Working her way down the engine bed, connection by connection, she loosened the bolts on each bearing cap or rod end. The bolts on the rod ends were difficult to reach, and all the bolts were frozen by rust and time. She loosened them with a few drops of light oil as necessary, or with the heat of a propane torch if *absolutely* necessary, and kept a fire extinguisher handy for when those two methods were used together.

After removing the cap or rod end, if the bearing surface underneath looked intact, she lifted the thin sheet of copper, cleaned it with a stiff bristle brush, and slathered it with grease. But if the material was scored or burned, she pulled it off the top of the shaft and drove it out below with wooden wedges and a mallet, taking care not to scratch the steel shaft's bright surface or crimp the copper sheet between shaft and bearing seat. Then she greased a new piece of copper, drove it into the gap around and under the shaft, reseated the bearing cap or rod end, fitted the bolts, and tightened them in sequence to equalize pressure on the bearing.

With the crankshaft as clean and pampered as she could make it, Dani climbed stiff-legged out of the bilges. She tried turning the jacking gear again She strained, the gear took up slack, but the crankshaft still didn't budge. Dani released the jacking gear and, for extra leverage, wedged a piece of hardwood into the spokes of the flywheel. She said a short prayer against the pistons being gummed in the cylinders, or the valve rods stuck in the slides and breaking against the cam surfaces. Then she set her sneakers against the deck and pushed, hard, on the stick.

The connecting rods shivered and moved slightly. The big, low-pressure piston groaned in its cylinder. One of the valves gave a metallic shriek. And then the flywheel turned. Not far and not fast, but the engine was no longer frozen solid. Dani reset the stick and pushed some more, eventually taking the crank through a complete revolution. Nothing sprang loose or fell out of the black-painted cylinder block.

That was when she declared the crankshaft job finished.

"Excellent!" her father replied.

While Dani worked on the engine, William Henry had been cleaning the boiler. At her suggestion, he first used a snake-like brush on a long handle, pushing it up through the narrow firebox door, to pull the sticky oil soot out of the fire tubes. "They don't have to be shiny clean," she had told him. "Just rake out as much gunk as you can. Otherwise it insulates the tubes from the heat. The carbon could also catch fire and burn right through the thin metal."

When he had reported that job done, she told him to fill the boiler with buckets of water and look with a flashlight for leaks in the tubes, which would show up as weepage, seepage, or a flow of water down into the firebox. When William Henry thought he had success, he invited her to stick her head through the firebox door to confirm it.

After that, she showed him how to clean the oil jets with a fine wire, to make sure they would all ignite and burn evenly. That job kept him busy for about twenty minutes.

"What's next?" he asked.

"Okay, now test the draft."

"Um, how do we do that?"

She told him to fetch an electric fan from Mr. Gibbs in the yard office and set it up in front of the firebox door. Then she lit an oily rag and laid it across the oil jets using a two-inch spanner like a toasting fork. "Now go outside and see if smoke comes out the stack."

While he did all this, she had continued disassembling and cleaning the crankshaft bearings. And then, for the last hour or so while she worked, he had fiddled about in the engine room. Mostly he had been shining up the boiler and its fittings with a can of brass cleaner and an old rag.

By early afternoon, they had taken the engine and boiler as far along as they could without actually raising steam and doing a trial run.

"Oh, there's just one other thing," William Henry said. He led her to the main steam line, where it came out of the boiler on its way to the cylinder block. On the outside of an elbow bend, where the pipe took an upward turn, he pointed to a dime-sized hole. "It kind of fell apart while I was polishing the pipe," her father explained.

"Well," she said, her heart sinking, "that looks pretty bad."

"But not as bad as here ... and over here." He showed her two more ragged holes. "Do you know how to patch these?"

"No, Dad, that's the high-pressure line. I think we're going to need a machinist to fix this."

7. Watching the Professor at Work (II)

University professors were not in the habit of auditing each other's classes, especially not at the undergraduate level. They might go to public lectures by renowned scholars, given on special occasions to colleagues of equal standing. But they almost never dropped in on classes to see how others approached the task of imparting basic knowledge. So it was eye-opening for William Henry to teach alongside Agnes D'Angelo and observe her with students.

She hardly acted like a professor at all. Instead of standing behind the lectern, she pulled the chair around from behind the desk, sat down beside the front row, and just talked to them like a fellow student, or perhaps a more knowledgeable older sister.

In part her style no doubt derived from the fact she was only a few years older than the average undergraduate. But she wasn't being self-consciously unassuming or modest on that account. This attitude went deeper. D'Angelo didn't treat teaching as an exchange between a learned professor full of knowledge and students with empty heads waiting to be filled.

William Henry asked her about this after she had precipitated a lively discussion on themes of guilt and repression in the works of Nathaniel Hawthorne and Washington Irving, whose characters D'Angelo had suggested were struggling against the prejudices of newly settled and self-conscious societies—whether in the puritan tradition of Salem or among the proud Dutch farmers of the Hudson Valley. Until this class, William Henry had not read or thought about these 19th century authors since high school, and then he only remembered Hawthorne's novels as brooding and dark, while Irving's stories were more like light fantasy or science fiction.

"You mean," she replied with a smile, "because I don't make the material sound all kinds of important and stuffy?"

"I mean, you don't seem to assume you know more than your students."

"Well, that's because I *don't*. I may have more facts, sure, but not more ..." She paused, and her eyes went distant.

"Awareness?" he suggested. "Analysis?"

She shook her head. "Authority."

"Surely, you're leading—"

D'Angelo kept shaking her head. "This isn't some bogus Socrates thing, where he kept asking all the questions but no one really doubted he knew where the answers were going. I might have a few ideas about the course materials, but I'm more like a hunting guide out in the wilderness than the ring master in a circus. I know the local game trails and watering holes, but none of us—not students or the teacher—knows just where and when we'll spot a deer."

"And the *deer* being ...?"

"An original thought."

"But that isn't *teaching!*"

"No, it's more a process of discovery."

"I'll have to think about that," he said.

"Oh, Professor!" D'Angelo exclaimed. "You mean all this time you've just been filling their heads with *knowledge?*" She made a *tsk*-ing noise, but she was still smiling.

"Well, with some enthusiasm for the subject, I would hope."

"Yeah, but they're not baby birds, waiting with open mouths. Adolescent humans are by nature hunters, seekers, takers. They only value what they can lay their hands on and make their own. If you just *give* it to them—"

"Oh, I'm not disagreeing, I just—"

"You haven't thought about it."

"Well, something like that."

8. OVERHEARD AT THE MARAT/ SADE REHEARSALS

BECAUSE REHEARSALS WERE still at an early stage, the actors didn't have to sing their lines in the songs but only recited them like poetry. And while Duperret, as a sexual deviant, was supposed to actually throw Corday down on the floor and try to ravish her, for now they let him just follow her around with a goofy leer on his face.

Afterwards, the actors picked apart the action of the play while changing from rehearsal attire—mostly leotards and loose-fitting sweat pants—into their street clothes.

"Why does she want to stab Marat? Isn't he one of the leaders of the revolution?"

"Well, he was, you see. But then he hijacked it for personal gain. The people were being denied by the revolutionary government, and then Napoleon came along."

"So now they want a second revolution?"

"No, they want the *real* revolution. The first was just a change of administration."

"Deposing the king, imprisoning the aristocracy, and chopping off their heads wasn't *real?*"

"It didn't serve the needs of the people."

"And what, pray tell, are those?"

"Freedom, justice, equality."

"Just not for the nobles."

9. SHARING HER HAPPINESS

HAVING BEEN RAISED by her father from an early age—and one who was a naturally distant, bookish man at that—Dani had little experience of the way boys were supposed to relate to girls, and girls to boys, except what she could pick up from books and movies. For the mechanics of being a female, she had relied on a long discussion with her grandmother and hints dropped by favorite teachers and the school nurse. But for how do deal with the whole love-and-lust thing, she had been pretty much on her own.

Now that she was exploring this exciting new ground with Nicholas Carr, her world was being rocked emotionally and hormonally. Sometimes he seemed so strange, making and breaking dates with her, unwilling to introduce her to his friends and not caring to meet any of hers, secretive about his activities to the point that she sometimes thought he might be a CIA spy or a Russian agent. She had never even visited the famous apartment he claimed to have in town, which he was "sharing with a friend." Sometimes she suspected, if she ever did see it, she would find there a Mrs. Carr and at least one baby Carr.

But Nicholas seemed to care for her. He took time for her. He smiled and winked when he saw her. Being a bit older, he tried to explain things to her. And if she didn't think too much about the secrets he kept, Dani could believe she was in love.

Curiously, that put her father in a new light. She realized William Henry had a hollow spot inside him—a brittle, echoing place where something important was missing. As Dani grappled with her first real, adult love affair, she suddenly understood that when her mother went crazy and ran away, all those years ago, it not only damaged her life. Jane stole away Dani's loving mother, but more importantly, she robbed William Henry of his lifelong friend, companion, lover, and soul mate. On that day, he became a kind of a shadow. In the place under the heart where most people kept their love and affection, their anchor in a stormy sea, William Henry had only painful memories.

Now that she was experiencing the happiness of drawing close to one particular person, Dani wanted to share it with her father. Of course, she didn't have the first idea about how to do that—until one day in her Theatre Arts 101 class. In the context of using life experiences to bring out the emotions underlying a role, Professor Sokolov made an unusual—for a teacher—personal revelation.

"A couple of years ago," she said, "I went through a messy divorce. It was the usual thing when you stab somebody in the heart. Out came all these conflicting feelings—pain, loss, longing, lust, betrayal, anger, fear, confusion, self-doubt. ... For about a year, I was in the perfect place to play Medea or Lady Macbeth."

Suddenly, Dani looked at this woman in a new light. Elise was an adult, yes, and a teacher, yes, but not some remote authority figure. Sokolov had just owned up to having a complex life, a history of love and attachment, and feelings that must be very like what Dani's father must be feeling. She must be guarding that place under the heart, too.

With a cool eye, Dani appraised Elise Sokolov as a woman. She was no longer what anyone would call young—maybe in her late thirties or early forties, actually not far from William Henry's age. Still, she had a pertness about her, with a bright eye and ready smile. The woman simply *felt* young, when Dani thought about it—full of enthusiasm, excitement, vivacity. And she had a youthful face with short, blondish-gray hair and a trim dancer's body.

Dani mentally placed Elise Sokolov alongside her father, talking to him, smiling up at him, touching his hand. And she placed William Henry beside this woman, sharing a joke with her, opening up to her, touching her shoulder.

Of all the unlikely things in this world, her father and her drama instructor finding love and companionship with each other was not perhaps the *least* likely.

Dani just had to think of a way to pull it off.

10. A Trivial Virtue

"Well, it's good to see the campus finally coming alive," Andrew Michelson announced at large. He was standing by the coffeepot in the break room shared between Sociology and Political Science and the Classics Department. "We're so far behind schools like Berkeley and Ann Arbor, it's been embarrassing."

Three other professors sitting nearby nodded in agreement, but William Henry lifted his head. Michelson was referring to the student rallies on campus, which had become a fixture of the early afternoons, especially in the middle of the week, especially as the weather warmed. From a sad little affair that barely drew fifty students onto the Mall in February, the bullhorns and the rhetoric were now regularly attracting hundreds.

From hints that Dani dropped all too casually, her young man, Nicholas Carr, had emerged as one of the main speakers. He appeared to be quite good at it, too. Dani was shaping her route across campus between classes just so she could look in on the rallies and listen to him. Of course, William Henry wasn't going to tell Michelson that his own daughter was involved with one of the protest movement's leaders. He couldn't bear the gleam of satisfaction that would appear on the man's narrow face.

"I'm glad to see the people are finally getting real," Michelson went on.

William Henry put down his cup. "And who are these 'people'?"

"Why, the students, of course. Our own proletariat."

"And have they somehow been *imaginary?*"

The man shook his head. "Now you're playing with words. I mean they haven't been *authentic*. Not sincere in their efforts to root out the hypocrisy of the times."

"What hypocrisy is that?" William Henry asked brightly.

"Do you really want to know?" Michelson turned suspicious.

"Please. Instruct me," he said—the dangerous invitation of Socrates.

"They've all bought into the central myth of our capitalist society," the man said. "They believe we're all free individuals, living independently, able to think for ourselves. They think they like Coca-Cola for how it tastes, rather than because the advertisers have hypnotized us all into buying it. They believe we draft young men and send them off to Southeast Asia to fight for freedom, rather than because it sells arms for Colt Industries, Bell Textron, and all the others in the military-industrial complex. They think—"

"But that's just your view of reality," William Henry said.

"No, no," Michelson insisted. "That's the way things are."

"But isn't it our job to teach them the many ways of looking at reality?" William Henry pressed. "On one hand, the Romantic viewpoint says each man is an independent spirit, imbued with free will and a destiny to pursue. On the other, the Marxist says he is only a cog in the greater society. We have a duty to lay out these alternatives and the reasons for believing them, and let the student choose for himself."

"How can you be sincere when you have no underlying beliefs?"

"Oh, *sincere*," William Henry said. "Sincerity is a trivial virtue."

"No, it's probably the most important," Michelson said.

"Really? Is the man who is *sincere* about picking your pocket superior to the man who—for any number of other reasons, whether indifference, incompetence, indecision, or a sense of personal honor—refrains from the theft? There are many more important virtues, like keeping your word and your promises, paying your bills, and taking care of people."

"Sincerity is all about being honest with yourself."

"Again, a triviality. I prefer being honest with other people."

" 'Know thyself'—isn't that what Socrates said?"

"Actually, that was inscribed on the Temple of Apollo at Delphi."

"So there you are," Michelson said triumphantly.

"Yeah—that's where the pythoness inhaled gas and spoke nonsense."

"You're just playing with me!" the man protested.

"That's what we classics scholars are good at," William Henry said smiling.

11. Mending, Bending, and Brazing

Robert Wheelock came up to Byzantium to help his son with the steamboat he'd bought. Of course, it took Willie an hour of rambling conversation, pieced together through a couple of long-distance phone calls, before he could admit to having spent his mortgage money on such a thing, or to the boat's being in such a state of disrepair that it needed expert metalwork. The boy was always close-mouthed about his private life and cautious when he thought someone might criticize. Not that Robert had ever given him cause to feel that way. Or *much* cause.

After Willie described the problems he and Danielle were having with the steam engine, Robert had packed a suitcase, selected tools from his workshop and laid them in an old carpet bag, kissed his wife Libby good-bye, and left on the four-hour drive from Roulette, Pennsylvania. He planned to stay at a motor court on the edge of town because Willie's tenancy at the little cottage on campus appeared to be precarious—and that was another long tale Robert had pried out of his son, admission by admission.

At least the trip would allow him to spend time with his granddaughter.

He went aboard with Dani, who had set aside from her busy study schedule a whole Sunday to work with him. Since the steamboat was still on chocks under a tent in the boatyard, they had to climb ladders and use flashlights to get inside.

"Isn't this fancy!" Robert said as she switched on lights in the saloon.

"It reminded me of your parlor back in Roulette," she said.

"Oh, I don't think we were ever this grand!"

"Dad fell in love with it right away."

"Your father is a romantic."

She took him through to the engine room, which was toward the front of the boat, rather than below decks or in the stern. It had the prettiest little triple expansion engine—a miniature of the workhorse that had driven luxury liners and tramp steamers all through Robert's youth. The only eyesore was a white china toilet bowl perched next to it on the deck.

"Awkward place for a thunder mug," he said.

"The previous owner had no imagination."

"And your father wants to live aboard?"

"That's the plan. Silly, if you ask me."

"Well, inconvenient, to say the least."

"Can we move the toilet?" she asked.

"Let's focus on one thing at a time."

Dani showed him the main steam line with its corroded patches, some of which had collapsed inward. He took a small ball peen hammer from his bag and lightly tapped the metal of the boiler's dome, the riveted joints, the live and dead steam lines going into and out of the engine, and the shell of the condenser. Finally he said, "We'll replace the steam lines first and pray about the rest." While Dani took notes, Robert wielded a measuring tape and dictated run distances, pipe dimensions, and the required number of elbow bends and T-joints.

After a trip to the hardware store for copper tubing and marine-grade, phosphor-bronze fittings, Robert borrowed the boatyard's circular saw and some scrap plywood to make a tube-bending jig. Then he and Dani got to work in the engine room, cutting away the old, corroded pipe, mending the clamps and holders where they could, fashioning new ones where they couldn't, then bending and brazing new pipe along the steam runs.

"Did you ever make a still, Grandpa?" she asked as he bent a fourteen-inch length of tube into a neat half-circle.

Robert squinted at her. "You do know I was a judge. An officer of the court?"

"I know you like a drink, too," she said. "And that sometime during Prohibition you developed a talent for working brass and copper."

"Now that's what we call circumstantial evidence."

"Yes, but did you build one?" she asked.

"I might have advised a few country boys on the design."

"Ah-hah!" she shouted triumphantly.

"And you, missy, have you ever smoked any of that hemp weed?"

Dani sobered right up. "Oh, no, Grandpa!"

"That's good then."

After they had finished the fabrication and let it cool, Robert went down each line, opening and closing the valves to isolate sections, then blowing into safeties and petcocks while Dani listened at each brazed joint for the thin whistle of escaping air.

"Everything seems tight," she said.

"Won't know until we get steam up."

"What do we do if we find a leak then?"

"Give me a call. I stand behind my work."

As they were cleaning up scraps of bronze and putting away tools, Robert had a chance to ask the question they'd been avoiding all day. "How's your family life?"

"You mean, without Mother?"

"Something like that," he said.

"Dad misses her, of course. I think he's really lonely. But I've got a few ideas in that direction."

"You're another matchmaker, just like your grandmother. How about yourself—'in that direction'?"

"Well ..."

"Is that 'well' as in 'pretty good'?"

"Um ..."

"Or 'well' as in 'won't talk about it'?"

"Oh, I have a boyfriend."

"Does he have a name?"

"His name's Nicholas."

"A student here at college?"

"Um—won't talk about it."

"Should I be concerned?"

"No, Grandpa. I'm good."

"Well, I should hope so."

12. Overheard at the Marat/ Sade Rehearsals

As the company practiced the "Homage to Marat," with its stirring final call for another popular uprising, one of cast members began to take exception to the wording. That set off a discussion in the green room.

"They're singing about Marat and his political career, right?" the young man said. They describe how he's going into and out of the courtroom, and then into hiding, right? They say that sometimes Marat is the hound but sometimes also he's 'the otter.' Well, shouldn't that be 'fox'?"

"Maybe 'fox' didn't fit the rhyme."

"But the word's not in the rhyme scheme."

"Maybe the line just scans better?"

"Maybe the French hunt otters instead of foxes."

"Like hunting weasels and ferrets."

"No, that's hunting snakes and things *with* ferrets."

"But aren't otters *aquatic?* So, once they got into a river or lake, then *zip,* they'd be gone. A dog couldn't even *smell* them to follow them."

"That part of the song just doesn't make much sense."

"Yeah, but the whole play's supposed to be ... well, *crazy.*"

13. BLIND DATE WITH FUSILLADE

DANI HAD BEEN totally mysterious about the whole thing, and that should have been William Henry's first clue. First, she made a reservation for two at *Le Paysan,* a French restaurant in town that was supposed to be good. The timing was for early evening—six o'clock, really too early to be eating—but she would not tell him who the other person was.

"Should I wear a red carnation in my lapel?" he asked.

"No, she knows to look for a tall man on his own."

"So at least it's a she. Is she someone I know?"

"Not yet." Dani put an envelope in his hand.

"What is this? Secret messages for her?"

Outside it said, "Open at 7:30 sharp."

"No, your tickets. It's a surprise."

"Who's paying for all this?"

"You are. So have fun."

William Henry had not been on a date in years. Come to think of it, not since his wife ran away. While he shaved, bathed, and dressed—perhaps more carefully than if he were simply going out in public—he still wasn't happy about his daughter's plans for the evening. For the past ten years he had tried to be faithful to Jane and the marriage he was keeping alive *in absentia.* Nothing had changed now, of course. But because Dani had already involved a second person in this rendezvous, William Henry felt an obligation to the mystery woman. He was too much of a gentleman to hurt another person if he could avoid it.

The restaurant was cozy and dark inside, with the drapes drawn against the late spring dusk and candles lit on the intimate tables. Somewhere in the back, gentle string music was playing on a stereo. The air smelled of wild flowers and uncorked wine.

William Henry gave the maitre d' his name.

"Ah, *m'sieur,*" he said. "Your guest is waiting."

The man led him to a table in the back. The woman seated there had ash blonde hair cropped close to her head, lapping like petals across her brow and around her ears. She had nicely

232

wide-set eyes of a deep jade green that brightened when she caught sight of him. As he walked toward the table she stood up. She was short, no taller than Jane had been, with a slender, well-muscled body. She wore a black dress of simple cut, low in front and still lower in back, that was hemmed well above the knee. She left a shawl of yellow silk draped across the back of her chair.

It flashed obliquely across William Henry's mind that his daughter had good taste in women. Then he realized he'd seen this woman somewhere before.

She offered her hand. "I'm Elise."

"I think I know you." He took her hand.

She smiled. "You may have seen me on stage."

"It was a campus production, two years ago—"

"*The Cherry Orchard,* Madame Ranevskaya."

"But I remember your hair—" he blurted out.

"Short hair goes better with a life in wigs."

"It's still very nice," he finished lamely.

She smiled at that and let him reseat her.

"You're teaching my daughter in the drama class," he guessed.

"Yes, she's a beautiful girl. You've raised her well."

"Sometimes she gets crazy ideas—"

"Like setting you up on blind dates?"

"This is the first time, believe me."

"I never thought anything else."

They chatted over wine from a bottle the sommelier recommended, ate a dinner of succulent meats and steamed vegetables in savory sauces, and finished off with tiny cups of darkly roasted coffee. During that time, William Henry discovered Elise's name was Sokolov but she wasn't Russian—that had been her husband's name. He wasn't Russian, either, and besides he was well out of the picture. She said that with a charming shiver and shake of the head to imply she wasn't sad about it. When it came time to reciprocate and tell Elise about Dani's mother, William Henry hesitated.

"If it's too painful …" Elise began tactfully.

"No, it's just difficult to explain. Jane—she ran away. Almost like a child running away from home. She got sick—in the head. She crashed the car, stole a policeman's gun, took some shots—at me, I think, but she was very confused at the time. She was in the hospital for a while, a mental hospital, and then, she just … disappeared."

"My word! What, did she break out?"

"Or slipped out. No one could say."

"You tried to find her, of course."

"Police bulletins, missing persons, everything anyone could do. But, apparently, she did not want to be found. We've not heard a word, not a phone call or a note, in ten years."

"How did Dani take that?"

"Hard, I think." William Henry realized how inadequate that sounded. "She goes quiet when we talk about it. She was old enough, at the time, to know something wasn't right with Jane. I've tried to make sure Dani knows it wasn't her fault."

"That was a wise thing to do. Dani seems remarkably well adjusted."

"Or she's just a natural actress." He paused. "Not that I'm trying—"

"To fish around and find out how she's doing in my class?"

"Well, something like that. But you don't have to—"

"Most young girls are curious about the stage."

"Not Dani. This class was a big surprise."

"She has a future—in engineering."

"I hope so. She's good at it."

When 7:30 came around, William Henry took out the envelope and opened it. "Dani said she bought us tickets, but I don't know—oh, no!"

"What is it?" Elise asked. "Some amateur theatrical in town?"

"Worse, it's the latest movie. *Bonnie and Clyde.*"

"Has she *seen* it? They end up dying in a hail of bullets."

"I believe she thinks it's some kind of love story."

"Do you suppose she's trying for an 'A' in my class?"

"Or a spanking …" he said with a grim smile.

"What say, we pass on it and go for a walk?"

So they walked on campus, side by side, without actually touching. They talked about their work as teachers, about young people, about the rallies on campus—Elise being in favor of them as a positive expression—and about their lives in academia. They walked until the night air turned cold, the dew began to fall, and Elise's shawl was not enough to keep her warm. Then he walked her back to her car. They said good night casually, with no mention of meeting again, and Elise drove off.

William Henry breathed a sigh of relief. The whole experience had not been too dreadful or too awkward. Actually, it had been rather pleasant, spending time with an attractive woman in an intimate setting. But he sensed Elise was not eager for more dates and, in truth, he felt the same way. He was a poor choice for such a sparkling companion.

In the years since Jane left, although he made sure Dani understood that Jane's breakdown was not her fault, William Henry harbored a feeling he himself might have been the cause of it. The fact was, he had held onto that snoopy neighbor's letter for far too long but never confronted Jane with its supposed infidelities—technically, because the letter did not constitute proof of anything and, emotionally, because he secretly feared to tread in that area. That kernel of suspicion might have contributed to Jane's growing paranoia. And then, the last time he spoke to his wife, without her being under sedation, she had tried to shoot him. That didn't speak well for his ability to deal appropriately—maturely, emotionally, equitably—with any woman.

Besides, so far as William Henry knew—technically, legally—he and Jane were still married. He had never filed for a divorce, or tried to declare her dead, and he still didn't know where Jane might be. So serious involvement with a new woman was—maturely, emotionally, equitably—simply out of the question.

14. WEAK AT THE KNEES

ON THE FOLLOWING weekend, Robert drove up to Byzantium, fighting the Friday evening traffic through the suburbs of Rochester, and checked into the motor court with the lumpy beds. The next morning he and Dani tackled the old boat's plumbing and that awkward toilet bowl.

While they pried up floorboards and traced the piping for fresh water from an on-board storage tank and waste disposal through a hull connection, his son worked on the outside of the boat, scraping, sanding, and painting. When Dani asked why Robert hadn't invited Willie to join them in the work, he thought about it for a moment. "This isn't his kind of job," Robert said finally. "Your father may be very smart, clever, even diligent about the things he does. But he's just not handy."

The positioning of that freshwater tank and the through-hull fitting had originally dictated placement of the toilet on the starboard side of the engine—which sat directly above the keel on the boat's centerline. And so it would be simplest to move the toilet to the engine room's starboard corner toward the stern. During the week, Robert had busied himself with sketching first a simple stall, then a full cabinet with latching door, that they could erect around the bowl. He'd visited several lumber yards to obtain some nice pieces of mahogany to build it in more or less the style of the nineteenth century. And from the hardware store he bought suitable pipe, petcocks, and new plumbing seals.

As soon as Robert and Dani had disconnected and were lifting up the toilet bowl, Willie stuck his head into the engine room. "That's going well, I must say."

"Just getting started," Robert said.

"Oh, good. Then, while you're at it, could you put in a shower?"

"Yea—ah … what?"

"You know, someplace to take a bath," Willie said. "I'd ask for a tub, but I don't think there's room."

"There's barely room for the toilet."

"Well, could you see about it?"

Robert stared into the corner of the engine room, mentally pacing off feet and inches. Luckily, the slope of the cabin top provided just enough headroom. And he had bought enough lumber to expand his cabinet design. If Robert turned part of the floor into a teak grating, with a pan made of galvanized sheet-metal underneath to catch the runoff, which could be plumbed into the waste line ... and if nobody minded a dripping plastic shower curtain that would crowd the toilet bowl while in use ... then making the toilet stall into a full bathroom was just possible.

"I suppose you want a sink for washing up?" he asked.

"And a mirror for shaving, so I don't have to use the galley."

"We'll see." Then he grinned. "You know what it will cost you."

"I'll happily double your salary."

"Which is still nothing."

"Thanks, Dad."

When his son had gone back to working outside, Robert turned to Dani. "You free next week? Looks like we've got a two-day project on our hands."

She grinned. "He forgot to ask for a light over the sink."

"We'll have to give it to him then, won't we?"

Together they started removing floorboards in the corner where they would build the new cabinet. When they had opened up the floor, Robert took a flashlight and, with Dani holding onto the back of his belt for safety, knelt to explore the realm under the deck joists. He probed the darkness with the beam, over to the keel, out to the vertical inner slope of the hull, fore and aft toward the ends of the boat. Right away, he noticed an oddity.

"Have you or your father looked into the bilges?" he asked his granddaughter.

"Only when I worked on the engine bed," she said. "Seemed pretty clean."

"Well, spacing of the ribs is odd right in here. One, two, two, one, two."

"Let me see." Dani took the flashlight and dropped down into the hole.

From above, he saw her swing the beam, pause, swing it again. "You're right. Looks like fresh wood alongside the older ribs."

"They're called 'sister ribs.' They help shore up broken ones."

"Got it. But there's no visible crack or break in the old ribs."

"None at all? What do the older ones look like?"

"Gray. Kind of mottled or ... clotted," she said.

Robert's heart sank. "Help me down."

With his granddaughter to steady him, Robert slid into the hole. He was careful about placing his feet in the narrow spaces between the doubled-up ribs. Dani had been right: the difference between the new ribs and the old was striking. The old ones seemed to be covered with thick paint—until he touched one with his bare hand. The surface was cold and smooth, like porcelain. He rapped it with his knuckles, and a patch scaled off and fell into the bilges. The old ribs were covered in portland cement, mixed thin, without aggregate, like gray icing on a cake.

Robert took out his pocketknife, opened the smaller blade, and stuck it into the aged wood where the patch had fallen off. The knife point sank in easily, like probing old cork. He stared into Dani's uncomprehending eyes.

"What is it, Grandpa?" she asked anxiously.

"Dry rot. Plastered over to keep it from spreading."

"Is that as bad as it sounds?"

"In an old wooden boat? Worse."

It took a bit of maneuvering for Robert to climb out of the hole. Dani helped him steady his feet on one of the fresh ribs with his head above the deck, then lithely climbed out herself and lifted him to the point where he could get a knee up. "Whew!" he said, sitting on the deck with his legs still dangling in the hole. "Go call your father. He has to see this."

Two minutes later Willie returned with his daughter. "Dani says you two found something interesting."

"You've got dry rot in the bilges."

"I see. Now, what is that, exactly?"

"A fungus gets into the wood and eats out its strength," Robert explained. "Turns the wood into shaped sawdust. You've had some ribs attacked, and someone tried to fix it by putting in fresh wooden ribs and covering over the others with portland cement."

"Well," his son said, "it must have worked."

"Why do you say that?" Robert asked, nonplussed.

"The marine surveyor gave her a clean bill of health, notarized and everything. *Galatea's* ready to float as soon as the inlet clears."

Robert bit his lip. He wasn't any kind of expert on ship design, wooden hulls, or repair techniques. He only knew that what was going on down below looked jerry-built and temporary. But he also didn't want to contradict the judgment of a professional in the field. And Willie was so proud of his new toy.

"In that case ..." He made a decision. "I guess she'll hold for a season or two."

"Of course," Willie said. "Everyone agrees about that."

"Just keep an eye on the situation, hear?"

"Certainly, Dad. Thanks for checking."

15. Too Much Too Soon

Nick Carr's famous apartment was smaller than Dani had expected: just a single room on the second floor of a converted house, with three unmade mattresses on the floor, along with two piles of dirty laundry and a Calrod hot plate. She asked about the other door into the room, and Carr said it was a walk-in closet—but from the way he hesitated, she thought either he had never looked or possibly it was something else. Then she asked if she could use the bathroom, and he told her it was down the hall and be sure to knock before entering.

When she came back, there was no place to sit except on one of the mattresses. At once Carr dropped down to sit beside her, leaning heavily on the hand he had planted behind her back, his chest brushing her shoulder, his face close to hers. When she turned slightly, to see him better, Carr took that as an invitation to kiss her. She smiled under the pressure of his lips.

It wasn't Dani's first kiss. She had been on dates with boys before and knew what to expect. But she hadn't been out with a man, or alone in his room, or sitting on a bed—well, a mattress on the floor. That was a new experience.

Carr's free hand came up to her opposite shoulder and cupped it. He pressed with his lips, pushed with his chest, cradled her with the supporting arm, guided her backward with his hand, and suddenly she was lying on the mattress with him practically on top of her.

Dani opened her eyes in surprise.

He drew back and looked at her.

"What are we doing?" she asked.

"This." And he kissed her again.

Just kisses were not enough for him. Soon his mouth opened and his tongue was pushing between her lips, seeking entry. She held her jaws together and tried to think, briefly, about what was wise. But he was so sweet, so tender, with features so beautifully formed, and yet a mature body hardened by rough living. She really did want more than chaste, shy-girl, close-mouthed kisses with him. She relaxed her jaw and gave his tongue the slightest gap between her teeth.

It instantly thrust inside her mouth, exploring the pearls of her teeth, the ridges of her palate. She tried to block him with her own tongue and suddenly there were two snakes wrestling in her mouth. She felt her throat close against the commotion. She tried to draw back but her head was already pressed into the mattress. While she tried to free her mouth to breathe, Carr's hands were running frantically up and down her front, over her breasts and across her ribs, down to brush her thighs. It was a good thing she had chosen a heavy, cable-knit sweater and blue jeans—rather than the silk blouse and wrap skirt she had been considering, which would have offered much easier points of access.

"Urk!" Dani made the noise in her throat—not a moan, definitely not moaning, more like an angry hum.

Carr's tongue withdrew, his hands stopped moving over her body. His face, his beautifully formed, passionate face, with heavy-lidded eyes like veiled sapphires and those perfect eyebrows, hung above her, barely in focus, with a questioning look.

"Umm," she said. She did not want to send the wrong signal, or put him off. But still …

"Isn't this what you wanted?" He sounded sulky.

"Oh, yes, I want it." Dani said. "But not—not so fast."

He smiled. "I understand, go slow—" His mouth drew close.

"But please, just for now, let me breathe."

Carr gave a little sniff and rolled away from her.

Dani closed her eyes, wondering what she should do next.

The door of the room opened and closed. When she looked, he was gone.

"Damn it!" She lay there a moment, angry with him, more angry with herself.

Then she rolled off the mattress and stood up. Maybe he had gone down to the bathroom—"to take a leak," as boys said. Maybe he had gone out for a walk in the cool spring air. Maybe he was coming back. Maybe she should stay and wait for him.

Dani was confused, her head all turned around. She wanted to stay, to talk with Nicholas, to try and make up with him. But she also wanted to get out of there, to spend some time alone, to think through their relationship. She found her purse where she had dropped it on the floor by the door. Her coat was lying by one of the piles of laundry. She didn't mean to snoop, but as she picked up her coat, the pile shifted and rolled apart.

Where she had expected to find old socks and Jockey briefs, like the laundry her father put out each week, she discovered a black lace bra with a decent-sized "C" cup and a pair of see-through black nylon panties, cut to ride very high on the hip. They seemed about right for the woman she had seen that day on the Mall, the one with the blonde ponytail and the tight black jeans, Glynda Jake-something.

Maybe Carr had simply agreed to do her laundry, but Dani doubted it. And there was a third mattress in the room—what was all that about?

She felt like such a fool.

16. Overheard at the Marat/ Sade Rehearsals

THE MARQUIS DE Sade had a couple of long, glowering, self-absorbed soliloquies. As he practiced them, the rest of the cast had to listen, feigning rapt attention. He was, after all, the voice of the playwright. Later, someone wondered about this.

"Hard to think of the Marquis de Sade as a revolutionary."

"Well, he survived the revolution, didn't he?"

"I guess. But he was also a nobleman."

"The maquis were French guerrillas, weren't they?"

"Listen to yourself! That's *maquis,* with a 'K.' And he was a *marquis* with an 'R.' That automatically makes him an aristo."

"Actually, it was maquis with a 'Q,' you know."

"But de Sade had the 'R.' I know he did."

"So he was aristocrat and revolutionary, both?"

"He was able to save his skin, that way."

"It also helped that he was crazy."

17. The War of the Squirrels

As William Henry was crossing the campus on his way to class, he paused to watch a gray squirrel that was nosing among the exposed roots of a oak tree. The squirrel sensed it was being observed and kept one eye on the human while it dug around in the packed earth. William Henry guessed it was digging up an acorn cache left from last autumn.

Sure enough, after a minute or two the creature pulled up a dark-brown nut and broke it open with its teeth, all the time watching William Henry for signs of hostile intent. So engaged, it did not see the two squirrels—larger animals with brilliant, burnt-orange fur—coming across the lawn from the other side.

The two intruders never paused but rushed at the gray, rolling it on its back. The half-eaten nut went flying, and one of the reds dashed to recover and devour it. Its partner faced off with the lone gray. The two tussled, rising on their hind legs, and William Henry clearly saw the red bite the gray on the nose, making it squeak. Then the injured squirrel feinted to the left and ran around the tree. Ten seconds later it stuck its head over one of the lower branches and scolded the red: "*Chih-chih-chih!*"

The two red squirrels ignored it. They went poking about in the earth between the tree's roots and quickly found the nut cache. They had won it by outright aggression.

William Henry remembered seeing an article in the school newspaper, written by a graduate student in biology, about these red squirrels invading the campus. Evidently, some predator had arisen in woodlands to the east—the writer thought it might be either house cats or hawks—and was driving the reds westward. The campus, which was free of predators and a rich feeding ground, with both plentiful oak trees and food scraps dropped by careless students, was a prime environmental niche where the population of grays had grown fat and lazy. Encounters between the two species—the plentiful *Scurius carolinensis* and the marauding *Tamiasciurus hudsonicus*—would make for interesting observing conditions on campus this spring. Neither species, the writer hastened to point out, was endangered or in decline.

William Henry now considered that article in light of what he had just seen with those three squirrels. He suddenly had an eerie sense that, descending all around him, like grimly silent paratroopers, strange forces were about to set his world into frantic motion. New, invasive, disruptive influences were at work everywhere, stalking the old order of things, turning everyday life on its head. This sense of undefined pressure pushed in on him from all sides, from the changing school curriculum to the protests on campus. And here it was repeated in the realm of nature!

Then he shook his head. Just because the university administration had eminent-domained his home to expand the library, and because trends in academic fashion were driving him out of the subjects he liked to teach, that was no reason for him to become all … apocalyptic!

It was a beautiful spring day. The birds were chirping, the squirrels were fighting over nuts, the trees were in bud, and the flowers were about to bloom. He should try to relax and enjoy himself.

18. Reflooting Galatea

ABOUT A WEEK after Robert and Dani had finished replumbing the bathroom fixtures, and after Willie had declared himself done with all the scraping and repainting he intended to do on the hull and cabin exterior, the Lakeshore Yard folks were ready to put *Galatea* in the water for the season. Robert had extended his stay at the Byzantium motor court, partly to join his son for this happy event, and partly so he could offer advice where he might if things were to go terribly wrong.

Bill Gibbs maintained a self-propelled bridge crane with two canvas-backed steel slings to lift the hulls of his other customers—the sleek sailboats and squat cabin cruisers, all modern constructions of aluminum or fiberglass—out of their cradles and lower them into the water from a pair of concrete piers. On a couple of mornings Robert had watched that monster machine in action and gauged the various lift points with his eyes. Then he remembered the cement-slathered ribs he'd seen in *Galatea*'s bilges and he shuddered. Those straps might lift a thirty-foot hull, but they would cut through an old wooden boat, especially one sixty feet long, like a knife through cheese. And besides, the crane wasn't tall enough to clear the two masts, and no one had said anything yet about unmounting them.

When the Wheelock family arrived at the yard on a crisp Saturday morning in April, Gibbs's crew had already cleared away the tent. The old steamboat sat in a narrow glade among leafy trees, her white hull sparkling in the sunlight, her mustard-yellow cabin with its arched windows trimmed in hunter green recalling a gentler, more gracious time—an era that Robert, at his age, could almost remember. As a parting gift, Gibbs had paid one of his men to shinny up the masts and out along the bowsprit on a bosun's seat to paint them a deep and glittering black.

"Now, how are they going to get her out of there?" Robert wondered.

"I don't know, Dad. But Gibbs swears they managed to get her in."

246

As it turned out, the yard handled *Galatea* the same way Pharaoh handled blocks of granite—with rollers. Although Robert had never studied the hull's support, and Willie had never inquired, what looked like individual cradle frames weren't separate at all, but one massive trestle structure that was nearly as long as the boat itself. Hidden in the weeds underneath were pieces of telephone pole cut into twelve-foot lengths.

The crew hooked the chain from a Caterpillar tractor—which Gibbs mentioned was rented for the occasion at the rate of a hundred dollars a day—to the cradle's stern end and started pulling. The telephone poles creaked, some of them crunched, and the old steamboat began rolling over the packed earth. As the cradle cleared open ground, teams of men—also hired for the day—ran forward two-by-two, picked up the poles exposed at the bow, ran them back toward the stern, and shoved them under the moving cradle. It took two hours, occasionally shifting the tractor to the bow or stern, depending on the direction of travel, to maneuver the boat to the head of the concrete ramp that sloped down between the piers to the inlet.

"Here comes the tricky part," Gibbs said.

Robert glared at him, and Willie looked nervous.

The tractor couldn't precede the boat down the ramp into the water, dragging it along. And there was no way a chain could be anchored at the end of the pier with some kind of pulley arrangement because, as the cradle structure sank, the chain would tend to cut upward into the hull. Instead, the crew fixed ropes to the cradle and drew them back along the road. They took two of the telephone poles and set their cut ends against the crosspiece at the cradle's stern end. The tractor inched forward, under the delicately curved white transom, and dropped its shovel blade to the concrete. Still moving forward, it scooped up the ends of the two poles while the men kept them aligned with the cradle. Then everyone—Willie and Dani included—took a hand at the restraining ropes, which kept the cradle and boat from sliding too fast into the water. As the rollers came out from under the cradle, two men worked them free of the pushing poles and ran them forward, into the water, and lodged them as best they could under the front end of the cradle. The tarry, weather-treated pieces of wood sank like stones.

"Be a bitch, grappling them off the deep end of the ramp," Gibbs said.

Foot by foot the old hull entered the water. Until natural buoyancy took hold, the sharp cutter bow and forward gunwales sank further and further. Just as everyone thought the boat would nose under, she lifted from her cradle and floated free. Two men with lines in hand jumped aboard from the piers and walked her around to the yard's floating dock.

"Like I said," Gibbs summed up, "we've done this before."

The manager invited the Wheelock family aboard *Galatea* as a yard launch towed her out to a mooring in the inlet. Willie stood proudly in the bow, hands on his hips, his face in the sun. Robert and Dani hung back to give him his moment.

Before they climbed over the side to go back to the dock with the launch, Robert slipped below into the engine room. He took a flashlight and pulled up the hatch that he and Dani had built into the deck planking where that naked toilet bowl had been. For a long minute he stared into the bilges, listening for evidence of water coming in: a musical trickling, or even a steady dripdrip. He heard nothing. That was a good sign, but he vowed to himself to return the next day and check—just in case.

"Well," he said as they all stepped out on the dock, "I guess it's time to go back to Roulette and tend my garden. Think I'll head out, say, Monday?"

Willie took his hand. "Thanks for coming, Dad. You've been a great help."

Dani gave him a hug. "Don't go making any more stills, Grandpa."

Robert grinned at her. "You keep your nose clean, missy."

19. A Night of Watching

WHEN AGNES D'ANGELO and William Henry stepped out of their joint class on the History of Social Protest, they walked into a crowd of students that had spilled over the Mall and flowed into the lanes and byways between classroom buildings. This was the largest demonstration Agnes had yet seen on campus, but it didn't make her nervous. While the noises coming from its head, up by the Theodosian Library steps, did sound angry—shouts echoing from loudspeakers and a buzz of response from students up and down the Mall—the tone in the backwater where they were standing was more like students on a holiday: quizzical, hectoring, and glad for an excuse to be out in the sun. She sensed nothing overtly hostile about them.

"Shall we work our way around the edges?" William Henry suggested.

"What?" she asked. "Don't you want to join in this social protest?"

"I'm content to *teach* Antigone. I don't actually want to *be* her."

"She does come to a bad end. Hanged herself, didn't she?"

"After being sentenced to burial alive. It was faster."

"Ah! 'My life hath long been given to death.' "

"Morbid little girl," the professor said.

As they moved along the fringes of the crowd, William Henry suddenly touched her elbow and pointed toward an older man, wearing shirtsleeves and tie, who appeared to be wandering in a daze.

"What's wrong with him?" Agnes asked.

"Victim of a time warp, I think."

"And your meaning, sir?"

"You haven't heard his story? Leonard Salkind's a colleague of yours from the English Department. I can't say how talented he might be, but for years most of his class load has been teaching what the students call 'bonehead English.' "

"I know the term," she said shortly.

"Well, the story around campus at the time was Leonard found his students too uninvolved, too sleepy, too *bourgeois*. So he tried to enliven his classes and awaken them politically by doing things like playing that Beatles song 'Nowhere Man' and injecting radical insights into the books he taught, pointing out the totalitarian aspects of Plato's *Republic* and the elitist anarchism implicit in Dostoevsky's *Crime and Punishment*."

"Did it work?"

"Look around you," William Henry said. "And now look at Leonard. I suppose he thought he was going to lead his students somewhere, with him striding at the forefront, waving a burning brand. But he's out here at the edges, like the rest of us, fifteen hundred feet from the microphones. He probably thinks he started all this. Now I'll bet he wishes the students were back in class and Plato was just another dead Greek."

"You're not feeling very charitable today."

"I'm no fan of mass movements," he said.

"And why is that? Too exciting for you?"

"So much raw energy can get out of hand."

"Sometimes a little chaos is good for the soul."

"No, really, it's not. Chaos can get you killed."

Agnes tried to absorb that in silence. She genuinely liked this older man, but his mood today had become way too heavy. To change the subject, she asked, "So tell me about 'Wheelock's Folly.' "

He smiled. "You heard about that, did you?"

"The whole campus has heard."

"Am I a laughingstock?"

"That depends on what you're trying to do."

"I ... I think I've fallen in love."

"With an old steamboat?"

"No, with an idea."

He tried to describe his feelings, with words like "freedom" and "independence" coming more and more frequently. Agnes gathered that he felt boats were little worlds "whole unto themselves," creating a defined space of water around a separate way of life. With a boat, a man could pack up everything he owned, cast off the ropes that held him to the shore, and sail off to some other place that suited him better. It sounded very much like Ayn Rand, and Agnes wasn't a fan of Randite rhetoric.

"But why a steamboat?" she asked.

"They're the most charming of boats. Stately, slow moving, gentle ... enduring. The steam engine whistles and chuffs and just putts right along. Didn't you ever see *The African Queen*?"

"Sure, and she gets blown up by the Germans."

"Actually, blown up trying to *sink* the Germans."

"Still blown up. Is that going to happen to you?"

"Oh, no. I don't have any enemies."

"I hope you can keep it that way."

———

When the protest had started, Dani stood about three feet back from the bottom of the library's steps. But then, as more and more people crowded in, the pressure increased and pushed her forward. Soon her toes were being crushed against the granite risers. But when she took a step up, one of the rally organizers moved down to intercept and push her— gently, at first—back onto the flat area at the top of the Mall.

These organizers were all men, all young, all wearing black leather jackets. They had serious expressions on clean-shaven faces. They did not look up toward the speakers at the microphones or join in the cheers and chants of the crowd. Instead, they watched the mass of people with stony eyes. As the afternoon wore on, they seemed to multiply in number, and soon these men formed a cordon around the entrance to the library, arms linked, swaying and pushing back against the pressure of the assembled students. Dani tried to excuse herself when she accidentally stumbled into one of them, and he only grunted and looked away.

"Hold that line!" someone above them—not one of the main speakers—called out. It sounded like the cheer at a football game, so stupid under the circumstances that Dani searched among the two dozen or so people gathered around the microphones to see who might have said it. And up there, looking down at her, was Nicholas Carr's blonde roommate. The woman gave a little nod, not in recognition but as if she had somehow put Dani in her proper place. Dani had only come to hear Carr speak, but so far he had not appeared.

Finally, around five o'clock, after all classes had let out for the day, and the crowd had swelled to bursting, the library's bronze double doors opened by a narrow crack, and Nicholas Carr came out. The person at the microphones paused, looked back, and stepped aside. Carr confidently took his place.

Dani knew all along he was some kind of figure in the campus protest scene, but she never guessed how important a leader he was. Here the whole campus was waiting for him—the main speaker, the man of the hour. And he was also her beau, her boyfriend, her special guy! Deep down, she knew Carr probably didn't feel the same way about her, but she still couldn't keep her heart from swelling with pride.

He raised his hands, looking out over the crowd, and the mass of people hushed obediently. Even the hum of chatter from its far edges seemed to go quiet.

"What are we here for?" Carr shouted, his amplified voice echoing back from the surrounding buildings.

"Peace!" suggested a lone voice in the crowd.

"Out of Vietnam!" called someone else.

"End the draft!" said a third voice.

Carr nodded, smiled, and lifted his palms, inviting more calls.

"War no more!" bellowed one of the serious young men.

Carr raised his fists and repeated, "War no more!"

The crowd picked it up: "War no more!"

"What are we here to study?" Carr asked them.

"War no more!"

"What do you tell your teachers?"

"War no more!"

"What do we want from the government?"

"War no more!"

Half of the people at the top of the steps raised bullhorns, previously hidden in a jumble of equipment, and shouted back at the crowd: "War no more!"

The people behind Dani were suddenly in fluid motion, seething, swaying, milling around. The people with the bullhorns, led by the blonde roommate, now spread out and descended the steps, mixed with the young men in black jackets, and began corralling sections of the mass, dividing it, shaping it into two lumpy sub-masses.

Carr went on through the loudspeakers: "What are you gonna march for?"

"War no more!"

"What are you gonna *fight* for?"

"War no more!"

"When are you gonna get it?"

"War no more!"

"*No!*" Carr roared. "*When* do you want it? *When* will you get it?"

"*NOW!*" the crowd roared back. "Get it now! Now!"

Someone with a bullhorn shouted: "Make peace now!"

The crowd picked it up immediately: "Make peace *NOW!*"

Suddenly Dani understood the orchestration. Half the organizers, off to her right, were using their bullhorns to lead that part of the crowd into sustained chants of "War no more!" The others, to her left, led their side in "Make peace now!" The maneuver was beautifully done, like synchronized swimming or a choreographed stage production.

"Go tell the administration!" Carr shouted.

"War no more!"

"Go tell the government!

"Make peace now!"

And just as suddenly Dani knew that, whatever was going to happen, she didn't want to be part of it. She could feel the pressure all around her of hands, elbows, chests, and knees, moving, writhing, pushing, squirming. The handlers were going to lead them off somewhere. If Dani didn't make her escape now, she would be pulled along. And if, along the way, she did not keep her footing and fell down, the mob would trample her to death.

She ducked, fought, pushed against one of the black leather jackets, stuck her own sharp elbow into his throat, then spun her body around. The mob spit her out onto the granite steps. The handler reached out to pull her back, but already the mass of people was moving off, and he was swept along.

In less than a minute, Dani was standing alone on the Mall. Above her, standing away from the microphones, Carr was giving quiet directions to his lieutenants. Then he looked down, saw her, left his friends with a flurry of little fist bumps and back slaps, and came down to meet her.

"Let's go," he said quietly.

"Are we going after them?" she asked, nodding at the mob's rag-tag end.

He hesitated, shook his head. "That ... would not be a good idea."

"Where are they going? To the administration building?"

"Maybe. Eventually. First Randall and Glynda will swing them around campus a couple of times."

"Why?" Dani asked.

He stared. "You really don't know why?"

"No. What do you get from all this?"

"It proves a point, doesn't it?"

"Okay, um ... *What* point?"

"That the students are on our side."

"And whose side is that, Nick?"

"Haven't you been listening?"

"I've done nothing but listen for a couple of weeks now," she said. "Can you stop the government from fighting the Vietnam War? From here? On a campus by the lake, halfway to Canada? You've got—what, four or five thousand students? And they're only angry because the draft might get them. Do you think the university administration can stop the war?"

"You really are an engineer," he said with a private smile.

"What's that supposed to mean?"

"Apply *X* foot-pounds of force, get *Y* feet of movement."

"Yes, so?"

"It works in engineering, but not in politics. Think of emotion—in this case, raw human outrage and anger—as a force-multiplier. That's not just five thousand individual people out there. It's an expression of sentiment. To anyone standing outside the campus gates, they're not just a fraction, however large or small, of the student body. They're the *whole* student population, rising up, on their feet, and moving forward."

"And all to stop a far-off war in Asia," she said.

"No, to stop *all* wars. To end national conflicts."

"So now all wars are bad—just by definition?"

"Poor people get killed. Capitalists grow rich."

"You do know my father was a war hero?"

"There are no heroes in war, only fools."

"He fought for what he believed in."

"He'll just have to be reeducated."

"I don't think he'll agree to that."

"*Everyone* will be reeducated."

"I don't like the sound of that!"

"Look—are you hungry?" Carr checked his watch. "Let's get something to eat. We can talk politics later."

"I don't think I want to talk politics at all."

"That's fine, too."

————

As dusk was falling, the phone rang at the cottage in the woods. When he answered it, William Henry heard a man's voice say distractedly, "Oh ... you're there!" It took him a moment to recognize the voice of his department chairman, James Littlefield, recently appointed after Peter Lombardy retired.

"What can I do for you, James?"

"I think you'd better leave."

"Oh, and why?"

"The peace marchers are still parading around campus," Professor Littlefield said. "The local police are on high alert, and the administration has called out the New York National Guard."

"Oh, my!"

"The marchers are said to have torches. Rumor has it they mean to burn down the administration building. At the very least, everyone expects a riot."

"But do you think that's likely?"

"I don't know, in this climate ..."

"Then I think I'd better stay here."

"We want you safe, William."

"I'm waiting for my daughter."

"Ye gods, she's not out in that?"

"She's usually studying over at the engineering library at this hour," William Henry answered slowly. "I expect she'll be coming home soon. I want to be here when she does."

"I understand. Well ... take care of yourself."

After he hung up the phone, William Henry went to stand outside the front door. It was a quiet spring evening, deep in shade under the pine trees. But in the distance he could hear a growing hubbub, many voices, but rising and falling in cadence. It sounded ominous.

He walked back to his office and drew from the desk drawer his old service automatic, a well-worn Colt .45. He had taken it from his footlocker back when Jane discovered that damning letter. Without analyzing his reasons, he had cleaned the pistol, bought ammunition and loaded it, and put the thing aside, ready to hand. Upon reflection he supposed the confusion and anxiety of those days, just before Jane disappeared, had something to do with this decision. But he never did unload the pistol and pack it away.

Now he took it into the living room, settled himself in what once had been Jane's favorite chair—facing the cabin's front door at a distance of fifteen feet, which was well within accurate range—and laid the pistol across his lap. He debated with himself about going out, trying to find Dani, and bringing her home safely. But, in truth, he did not know where she was. He could only pray she wasn't mixed up in the rambling riot that was apparently building on campus. And although it was no longer his, he still felt compelled to defend this cottage—and perhaps the great Theodosian Library that lay beyond it—against vandals and arsonists. So he sat and waited and watched.

The light outside the windows faded to black. The hum of voices faded to silence, except for the wind in the trees. William Henry waited and watched.

At some point he must have dozed off. He awoke with a start when the furnace gave its usual *click* and *thump.* He listened hard in the darkness. A rush of air came from the register and he heard a voice whisper faintly, *"Fish knives."* Or perhaps it was just a noise that sounded like those words.

He looked at the glowing dial of his wrist watch. It was after midnight. If Dani had been in danger, that was now long past. Even the hardiest protesters could not keep up a march this long after dark—although he suspected it might have stopped somewhere and turned into a bonfire, a pep rally, or a beer fest, and perhaps all three rolled into one. He put his head outside the door again but didn't smell smoke or see any telltale glow against the sky.

It was time to go to bed.

Let tomorrow take care of itself.

———

Nicholas Carr was still riding his wave of euphoria from the afternoon's demonstration as he and Dani walked back from getting hamburgers at the White Castle in town. He could hear echoes of the chanting still coming from the campus. Three times during their walk, police cruisers passed at speed with dome lights twirling. That reminded him of another triumph.

"When we met with the Dean," Carr told Dani, "the administration tried to control the language that we would use during the march. He didn't want inflammatory words. So I suggested we chant 'Off the pigs,' and explained to him that 'pigs' are the police." He giggled. "And the man agreed!"

The girl seemed mystified. "Why was that particularly clever?"

"He didn't know 'off' is the protest term for 'kill.' He thought instead that we meant 'lay off' or 'keep off.' So our people are out there yelling to kill the police, and he thought we meant 'leave them alone.' Brilliant!"

"Uh, yeah," Dani agreed quietly.

Carr wasn't going to let her bring him down.

When they arrived at the apartment, his roommates were once again conveniently absent—this time reaping the whirlwind Carr had sown. The room still had no place to sit except on the mattresses, and as soon as Dani sat and pulled her feet up, he was down beside her. He put one hand on the pad beside her hip and pressed her slowly but firmly backward with the other—just as before, except this time he met less resistance.

Once again, Dani let him kiss her and then opened her lips to him. His tongue played around inside her mouth for a while. When she predictably drew back, he bent to kiss her chin, the soft underside below her jaw, and started downward. As he went, he helped her out of her lightweight jacket and began unbuttoning her blouse.

She stopped him with a hand. "I don't know …"

"Dani … You're so beautiful." He kissed the hollow at her throat. "And we've grown so close."

When he lifted his head to see how far he could still go, she was staring up at him with soft, confused eyes. Her lips were wet and slightly parted.

Carr kissed those lips briefly and, at the same time, unfastened one more button. She didn't move to stop him this time—but then, she didn't move at all.

He kissed the sharp little vee between her collar bones. She moaned deep in her throat, rumbling against his lips like a cat's purr.

Yes! he thought.

With the front of her blouse hanging open, his hand moved to stroke gently at the straining lace of her bra. He progressed from stroking to lifting the straps with his fingers and working them off her shoulders, pulling one cup down off her breast. And still she let him.

While he massaged her exposed nipple with his lips and tongue, Dani lay quietly, no longer moaning but not protesting either. His hand went further down, unfastened the buckle of her belt, pulled the loose ends free. When she still didn't resist, he unsnapped the copper stud at the top of her jeans and pulled at the zipper tab of her fly.

Tonight was definitely the night!

————

As Nick Carr stripped her in the horrible little room he shared with his radical girlfriend and the mysterious third person, male or female, who seemed to be in residence, Dani's emotions veered from excitement and curiosity to fear and alarm, and then back to anticipation and wonder. Finally, the dominant thought was, "At last I have a boyfriend, and he finds me beautiful!"

Dani had never thought of herself as beautiful. She knew she was plain, awkward, unattractive to men. In the last few years, as she matured into womanhood, her father had tried to tell her how important and valuable she was as a person. Words like "beautiful," "smart," and "talented" had played their part in his praise, but those were the things every father was supposed to say to a daughter.

Here was a handsome young man—not a boy, not a child, but a man of some experience—who shared this room with an attractive, mature, sophisticated woman—and yet he found Dani "so beautiful." He wanted Dani in preference to the other women he could have with the most casual word. This godlike male creature had chosen *her*.

When he had exposed her breasts and belly with his probing, it seemed silly just to lie there, half in and half out of her clothing, and still wearing her boots.

She sat up long enough to unbuckle the boots, let him remove them and pull down her jeans, and whisk away her blouse and bra. She made a feeble attempt at unbuttoning his shirt and pushing down his jeans, but his hands moved more quickly and soon he was naked beside her except for a pair of gray briefs.

Dani lay back in just her pristine white nylon panties, wondering what came next.

He went back to kissing her, fondling her above and now below, and then his fingers snagged the waistband of her panties and pulled downward.

"I'm …" she said. "I don't have … um … protection."

"Don't worry about that. I'll use a condom."

The kissing, fondling, stroking, and probing continued. At first it was with his fingers, which were hard, bony, jointed, busy in their action, but cold in their touch. Then she felt something much larger, smoother, boneless but still hard, softer than a fingertip, moving clumsily, but hot and dry to the touch. She understood that condoms were made of rubber, latex, slick and gummy, but this felt more like naked skin.

She tried to swim up through the cloud of pure sensation, reaching for a harsher realization. "Haven't you …?"

"Don't worry. Just a taste. I'll pull out in time."

The act, when it happened, was like being stabbed. None of the fantasies she had entertained for the past half-dozen years had prepared her for hard, sudden reality. His pelvic bones were thudding against her, and the thrusts of his male organ against her insides hurt. She opened her eyes wide, to see Nick's face above her, no longer kissing her, no longer even seeing her, but twisted in some kind of grim experience all his own.

The hard, sharp thrusts continued for six, seven, eight times—and stopped.

Nick hung there above her, his face intense, confused. Then he sagged. His head came down beside hers. His chest lay heavily across her flattened breasts. His hard belly pressed her down into the mattress. Dani was pinned there.

Suddenly, for no reason she could explain, her mind went back to her freshman chemistry class, thinking of the phase change in a supersaturated solution. Out of swirling liquid, solid bits—seed crystals—combined and grew into grains and flakes, a metal salt rained down inside the beaker.

One thing changed and became another.

Liquid changed and became packed with solids.

Virgin girl became—what? Woman? Hussy? Whore?

Dani only knew she wanted Nick off her, out of her, away from her. She began pushing at his chest, beating on his shoulders, rousing him from his sudden collapse.

"All right, all right," he said and rolled off her.

Naked and ashamed, she gathered up what she could find of her clothing and fled down the hall to the bathroom.

20. Overheard at the Marat/ Sade Rehearsals

THE PRODUCTION MOVED from rehearsal on a barren stage, with the actors sitting on boxes and folding chairs, to elements of the finished set design for the Charenton bathhouse, with faux concrete, iron bars of painted doweling, removable drain grates of painted wood, and slatted benches which, surprisingly, were real benches from a garden supply store.

"Is there going to be water in the bathtub?"

"No, that would make it too hard for Marat to get in and out."

"But he never appears except in the bathtub."

"Yes, but I mean for the actor."

"So it's *pretend* water?"

"Well, it's a pretend skin disease."

"Will the dagger leave pretend wounds with pretend blood?"

"No—I mean, yes—we'll use fake blood."

"Just asking."

21. Testing the Engine

William Henry had spent the morning driving around to service stations and auto repair shops with a dozen jerry cans bought from the army surplus store. At each stop, as Gibbs had predicted, the owners were glad to have him take waste motor oil off their hands, because the new environmental awareness and a raft of recent township and county laws on dumping had made disposing of the oil a headache for them. By noon he had about forty gallons, which was all that *Galatea*'s fuel tank could hold.

He and Dani loaded the jerry cans into a rowboat they had borrowed from Gibbs at the yard, took them out to the steamboat at her mooring, and carried them through the saloon and forward to the engine room, where the holding tank was situated under the deck.

"This seems like a lot of work," Dani said, "when you could just putt-putt over to the fuel dock and fill that tank with a hose."

"You told me the engine doesn't run on gasoline," he said.

"Gibbs sells diesel there, too. She'll run fine on diesel."

"Yes, but for thirty-five cents a gallon. This is free."

"Only if my drudgery costs nothing," she said.

"Think of it as 'sweat equity,' " he replied.

They loaded the feedwater tank using the petcock on a pipe through the hull. Then Dani worked a hand pump on a siphon to charge an initial volume of cold lake water into the boiler. She primed the boiler's oil jets with another hand pump that was built into the fuel line. She explained to William Henry that, when they had steam up in the boiler, a tiny single-cylinder steam engine with its own flyball governor would drive a fuel pump to pressurize the jets.

"That's very ingenious," he said, "having the steam work everything."

"That's the way they did things in '85. But when the boiler's cold you'll have to adjust and pump it all by hand. Are you sure you're up to the task?"

"I guess I'll just have to be, won't I?"

She bound the torn edge of a cotton rag to a stick with a piece of wire and dipped the cloth into the fuel tank. Then she capped the tank, lit her improvised torch with a match, and thrust it into the firebox. She opened the valve on the oil jets, and the spray ignited with a *Whump!*

"Excellent!" he said. "How long until we have steam?"

"I … don't know," she said. "We'll know when she starts whistling."

It turned out to be forty-odd minutes by William Henry's watch. During that time, metal creaked and groaned as everything heated and expanded; the boiler made random thumping noises; and the various pipes attached to it gurgled and spat. Dani ran here and there, opening and closing valves and petcocks that dumped handfuls of sputtering water out onto the deck. He tried to follow and memorize her actions—until he suddenly understood that she was just chasing the flow around and relieving pressure wherever the pipes were rattling the hardest. He decided he could do that, too. Finally, the relief valve on top of the boiler's dome popped and let out a breathy howl.

"There we are!" she said. "Now we close this, this, and *this*"— she worked the valves in order along what she and Robert had called the main steam line—"and we get … *that!*" She pointed at the engine just as the connecting rods attached to the crankshaft in its bed started to move.

William Henry understood that the live steam was supposed to progress from the small high-pressure cylinder at one end of the engine, then exhaust into the intermediate middle cylinder as steam volume increased, and finally into the largest cylinder, the low-pressure cylinder, at the other end. So he expected the different connecting rods would actuate in order, with two of them waiting for the first one to move. But of course, he saw now, they were all fixed firmly to the shaft. That meant the smallest piston had to force the whole gizmo into motion before passing steam to the other cylinders so they could add their effort to the work.

The engine started, hesitated, rattled briefly, turned again, and settled into a steady rhythm, with all three drive rods moving in unison. The push rods which operated the steam valves inside the cylinder case rose and fell between them. The exhaust steam from the low-pressure cylinder was fed back into the condenser, although a portion—as Dani had explained—went up the stack from the boiler to improve draft through the firebox. Still, a disconcerting amount of steam escaped from the cylinders and valves, fogging the windows in the engine room.

As the engine worked, William Henry felt the deck surge under his feet. The room was moving. No, the whole *boat* was moving forward. *Galatea* came up snug against her mooring buoy and started a stately dance in a circle around the inlet.

"Oops!" Dani said. "Forgot to put in the clutch."

She worked a lever and the boat stopped moving.

They spent the rest of the afternoon with Dani in teaching mode and William Henry in the role of student. She explained the theory of the engine, and the purpose of each valve and petcock. He made a mental note to get a bunch of wired garden tags and make her go back through everything, putting written notes on each handwheel and spigot. Next, she showed him how to adjust the engine's speed with the main steam valve and how to work the reversing gear to turn the propeller shaft so the boat moved ahead and astern or, in an emergency, disconnected the shaft from the engine entirely. Finally, she explained the linkages that would let him perform these basic functions from up in the wheelhouse.

"Now, do you think you've got all that, Dad?" she asked.

"It really doesn't look very difficult." He tried to smile. "This is an amazingly complex piece of machinery!"

"But you explain it all so well," he said defensively.

"Yes, but I won't be here when things go wrong."

22. Moving Day at the Cottage

ONCE AGAIN, DANI spent a day helping her father haul heavy loads. With eminent domain hanging over their home, the place the family had called "the cottage in the woods," they had to move out: William Henry to his new lodgings aboard *Galatea,* which was tied up to a rented berth on the municipal dock at the foot of Water Street; Dani to a dorm room obtained late in the semester through her father's status as a professor.

Neither living arrangement was sized to accept a lifetime's— at least, from most of Dani's life—accumulation of furniture, clothing, books, paintings, cherished curios, dishes, cookware, and family heirlooms. So they spent the days leading up to the actual move separating their possessions into three sets of boxes.

The first held books and papers necessary to William Henry's immediate work, as well as volumes he would deeply miss, like his leather-bound Homer. Into these boxes also went his shaving things, the meager contents of his medicine cabinet, a selection of dishes, pots and pans, and flatware to complement the boat's tiny galley, and seasonal clothes that would fit into the tiny cupboards. As he cleaned out the drawers in his office, Dani saw him lay an automatic pistol on the desk blotter.

"I didn't know you had a gun," she said.

"Just a relic left over from the war."

"Are you going to get rid of it?"

"I think I'll take it aboard."

"And that's because …?"

"Because you never know."

The second set of boxes held Dani's clothes, schoolbooks, and a few childhood souvenirs, like a Little Miss Revlon doll that she had absolutely adored as a girl.

"Aren't you going to get rid of that?" her father asked with a grin.

"Never, never, never, Missy Rev!" she replied in a six-year-old voice.

The third and largest set of boxes they filled with personal and family possessions that had no immediate use, like winter coats and boots, the skis Dani had once used to schuss around the pine woods in back of the library, as well as books, clothing, and mementos too important or familiar to donate to charity or leave behind for destruction. These items, along with the beds, chairs, dining room table, and other furniture, would go into storage that William Henry had arranged with a moving company in town.

In cleaning out the attic, Dani saw her father put his olive-drab army footlocker among that third pile of boxes. She had never looked inside it, had never discussed her father's war experiences, but she guessed the pistol had ultimately come from that dark green box.

Also in the attic were piles and piles of old magazines, complete sets bound with string, now deep in dust and the litter from a long-ago squirrel invasion.

"Do we have to move all those?" she asked wearily.

"I think they still have some value," he said.

"Would you really pay to store them?"

"Well ..." he said, biting his lip.

"Garbage!" she exclaimed.

That left one closet from her father's bedroom.

"What do we do with Mother's old things?"

"I'd hate to just throw them away."

"Donate them to Good Will?"

"She might come back."

"Dad, you know ..."

In the end, they boxed Jane's clothing and shoes and set them aside for storage. It occurred to Dani that she might have asked to try on a few outfits—although she now stood a head taller and wore two sizes larger than her mother ever had. But even aside from those practicalities, she thought the request might hurt his feelings. So she let the collection of well-made tailored suits and beautiful party dresses go into the darkness.

Just as Jane had gone, so many years ago.

23. Time to Wind Things Up

"Did you *see* them?" Glynda Jacobs asked excitedly as she came through the door of the room they shared. "I had to take the back way just to get home."

"I've been watching them swarm all morning," Carr said. He turned briefly from the window, where the edge of the landlord's tattered paisley curtain had concealed his outline.

Starting just after nine o'clock, when Carr first looked out, he had seen one blue Chevrolet head up the street, then a second Chevrolet, this one black but the same two-year-old model, drive down the street. He missed the plates on the first one, but the second was definitely a U.S. government designation: G14, which was the classification for a standard sedan. That didn't tell him which branch of the government had come to town, but the possibilities were depressingly few. The second sedan had been coming into the sun, and so Carr had seen a narrow slice of the driver's profile: mid-thirties, crew cut, wearing a white shirt, tie, and dark suit.

The chances that the first car was some kind of civilian and the second just a General Services Administration accountant, possibly out scouting sublets for a daughter enrolled in summer classes, became vanishingly small.

"Where's Noyes?" he asked Jacobs. "He was with you."

"I don't know. He left the café before me."

"Did he have any errands?"

"Not that he said."

"Damn!"

Carr made a decision, one that he should have made an hour ago. He went to the closet, took out his backpack and bedroll, and began stuffing laundry—clean and dirty alike—into the main compartment. He put his shaving kit on top and zipped up.

"You don't think they're after us?" Jacobs asked.

"It doesn't pay to think any other way."

"But this is good news, isn't it?"

"We made an impression."

"You bet! Big time!"

"Time to leave."

She went to the closet and got out her own luggage: a leather satchel like an old-fashioned lawyer's briefcase and a carpetbag which was actually made out of carpeting in a flowery design and probably belonged to her grandfather. She, too, gathered up clothing and cosmetics and randomly stuffed them in either bag.

"Do we wait for Randall?" she asked.

"Has he ever been arrested?" Carr replied.

"I don't—I think so. Why do you ask that now?"

"Because he'll be in their database. They'll have his photo."

"Oh, yes, of course," she said. "I think I'm in their database, too."

Carr went over to Jacobs's satchel, where he'd seen her put the beige knitted cap, dug it out, and handed it to her. "Put that on," he said.

"But it's eighty degrees outside."

"Pull it down over your face."

"Oh." She flattened her ponytail under the cap. "Where do we go from here?"

"Wherever they send us." He went back to the window.

"Should we leave a message for Randall?"

"Of course not—oh damn!"

Down below, Noyes was walking toward the building's front entrance. Just as he stepped off the curb to cross the street, the blue Chevrolet came into sight, drifted into the oncoming lane, and double-parked right across his path. Carr wondered briefly if under COINTELPRO the Feds could bust a civilian for jaywalking. But did the nature of the charges really matter?

"What?" Jacobs asked.

"Forget about Noyes."

"What's happening?"

"They've got him already. They'll be here in a—" From two stories above, Carr saw Noyes glance up at the window, a move that the Feds could not possibly miss. "—in less than a minute. Go out the back way."

"Do we travel together?" she asked.
"Are you trying to be funny?"
"You know I love you."
"Don't be absurd."

24. Nowhere to Be Found

Dani spent four days trying to avoid Nick Carr in all the usual places they would meet up, and then for three days she actively tried to find him. Finally, in desperation, she worked up the nerve to go back to the room he shared with his friends. When she knocked on the door, it was opened immediately by a pretty, dark-haired girl—not the blonde she had seen with him on the Mall.

"Is Nick Carr here?" Dani asked.

"Who's that?" the girl answered.

Dani looked past her, into the room. It was neat and clean, with a braided throw rug and the corner of a regular bedstead visible in the angle between door and jamb. The bed was made up with a ruffled spread. The pigsty had become a middle-class girl's room.

"Three people used to live here ..."

"I don't know about them," the stranger said. "I rented this room two days ago."

"Oh, they must have moved."

"Look, if I get mail for them, should I call you or something?"

"I don't think they get mail."

"All right then." The girl closed the door.

Dani stood in the hallway, undecided. Coming here had been the last thing she could think of doing. Perhaps, if she tried hard enough, she could find the landlord and see if he had any word of Carr and his friends. But Dani knew how student housing operated, which was strictly by bulletin board postings and weekly envelopes of cash left with a trusted tenant somewhere in the building. She intuited that the only notion the owner would have about Carr and company was when the cash stopped coming and the premises were suddenly abandoned. That was the *modus operandi* of a young man who hid out in libraries with a backpack and a sleeping bag.

She had known all along it was stupid to invest so much of her time—so much of *herself*—in a boy who was so unreliable.

Beautiful, charming, knowledgeable, exciting, yes, but essentially not serious. Oh, he was serious about his politics, about whatever kind of mission he had been on, about staking his claim to "the fulcrum of history"—if she even knew what that meant. But Carr was just a user, a casual picker-up and putter-down, of people and places. And now he was gone, disappeared, abandoning both her and the university students he had tried to shape for some purpose that remained a mystery to her.

Stupid, stupid, stupid!

25. The Persecution and Assassination of Jean-Paul Marat as Performed by the Inmates of the Asylum of Charenton Under the Direction of the Marquis de Sade

To attend Dani's first play, William Henry sat in the fifth row of an intimate little theater on campus that had no more than six rows banking steeply away from the outthrust stage in each of three different directions. "Theater in the Round," the program notes called it. What that meant, in the case of a play as energetic and enthusiastic as *Marat/Sade,* was the characters on stage were hobbling and flopping around right in front of the knees of the audience in the first row, and when they screamed, the spittle flew through the hot beams of the klieg lights toward the heads of those sitting in the last two rows.

After about fifteen minutes, William Henry decided the play itself was a mess. It didn't seem to be *about* anything, except misery, hunger, madness, and the desire for a totally destructive revolution—more complete and ruinous, apparently, than the one that had given France the Reign of Terror and a push toward Napoleon's dictatorship. About halfway through, he detected a plot line based on the determination of the young country girl, Charlotte Corday, to murder the wily old revolutionary, Marat. But even this simple action was obscured by too many songs and soliloquies and too much insane muttering. The whole lacked, as Aristotle would have insisted, any kind of organic growth.

He supposed, charitably, that the songs and speeches were intended to mimic the choral odes of a Greek play. But he wondered what an Aeschylus or Sophocles—brought forward twenty-five centuries, attired in tweeds and oxford cloth, and taught English—would make of the muttering and rambling, not to mention the self-absorbed musings of the play's supposed author, the Marquis de Sade, who sat on the stage and took some part in the action.

273

It required a certain amount of what Coleridge had called the "willing suspension of disbelief" to see in all these healthy, handsome, and athletic young people the wretches of an early nineteenth-century madhouse. Disbelief depended on generous applications of black eye makeup, gray face paint, rouge in smudges like recent bruises, and costumes consisting of bare feet, ragged peasant blouses, and twill breeches for the men—except for the pink silk and a waistcoat on de Sade—and voluminous wool skirts for the women, plus an overwrought acting style based on rolling eyes, writhing limbs, and stuttering delivery. But, really, all William Henry sensed was the illusion of spiritual neglect mixed with howling confusion. He thought back ten years to his only personal encounter with madness—the locked ward where Jane had been held briefly—with its starched nurses, looming orderlies, neat blue bathrobes, and zombified quiet. The Charenton depicted on stage was, in contrast, totally out of control.

For all that she had just spent thirteen weeks in acting class, Dani did not seem to have a speaking role. And perhaps that was just as well. She appeared to be some kind of ward sister, dressed like another of the women on stage in a black nun's habit and white cotton wimple. Along with two men dressed in blue uniforms like Victorian railway or bank guards, their only function was to pursue and catch any of the inmates who made a break for the exits and now and then to pick up and revive any actors too badly mauled in the fights on stage. Dani pursued these tasks with utter seriousness. During the music and the philosophical musings, she sat quietly on a bench along the back wall as if nothing was happening.

If it had simply been his money at stake in the ticket price, William Henry would probably have left at intermission—if there had been an intermission. He would have hesitated to leave during the performance because then Dani or one of the guards might have tackled him. But, out of support for his daughter, he stuck with the play. And at the end he rose to his feet as part of the standing ovation that was expected at such college productions.

After taking their bows, the actors turned as one and pointed to someone down in the front row. Only then did William Henry see Elise Sokolov, Dani's drama teacher and the woman with whom his daughter had sent him on a dinner date. A spotlight swung to catch Sokolov, and she reacted by smiling angelically and placing fingertips against her clavicles as if to ask, "What? Me?" Then she rose to take a bow. The good-looking, older man sitting next to her beamed, clapped harder, then reached forward and touched her elbow. William Henry realized the man must be her escort and felt a twinge of wholly unwarranted jealousy. One of the young actresses on stage brought Sokolov a bouquet of red roses, and she did a little curtsy to receive it.

A woman sitting above and behind William Henry in the sixth row asked her companion, loud enough for him to hear, "How long does this production run?"

"Three nights and two matinees, through Sunday," a male voice said.

"Well, I should think they'll all be dead by then."

26. THE LEVELING OF A LIFETIME

DANI AND HER father both cut their classes for the day to watch as the university began work on the new library wing. The day before, Dani knew, a team of professional loggers had made quick work of the pine trees, and now the three identical cottages stood in an open field of brown duff spotted with yellow stumps oozing resin. While the groundsmen worked with chains behind a Caterpillar tractor to remove stumps along one side of the field, a single bulldozer approached the first of the cottages—but not yet the one where she and William Henry had lived.

The machine aimed its blade just above a corner of the concrete foundation, at the lower edge of the matchboard walls, and started pushing. Old, dried boards cracked and snapped. Paint flakes and wood splinters flew, and the sturdier internal beams groaned. The little house jumped a couple of inches on its footing and started to sag. The roof began to slide, expelled a handful of its shingles, and collapsed. The operator, sitting inside an iron cage built around his control seat, didn't change expression as he lifted the blade and rolled the heavy tractor forward and backward over the remains, turning boards, window frames, and joists into so much kindling, ready to be scooped up and discarded.

When the job was done, the bulldozer rolled on. Dani watched it cross a space among the stumps of three large trees. Only she knew it was crushing a lifetime of small graves—two hamsters, five goldfish, a parakeet, and an old tomcat—all of whom she had buried ceremoniously and with genuine tears.

She and her father were already holding hands. She gripped his harder as the machine reached the corner of their own cottage. It went down quickly in the same way, except that when the roof split open, it disgorged from the attic pile after pile of bound magazines with the distinctive, yellow-bordered covers of the *National Geographic*, the black-and-white photography with the large, red logo of *LIFE* magazine, and the Norman Rockwell paintings of *The Saturday Evening Post*.

In five minutes the house where Dani had grown up was reduced to rubble and the machine was heading for the third cottage. A big part of her childhood had just vanished.

Her life might be changing, her childhood ending, in another way, too. By her own calculations, she was now three days overdue. When Dani left her father and the construction site this afternoon, she was going down to the university medical clinic to have some tests done. It might all be a mistake—well, either way it was a *mistake*—but she wanted to make sure she had nothing to worry about. And if something *was* there, then it put her whole carefully planned future in doubt.

27. Homecoming

THE FIRST INKLING Jane Wheelock had that something wasn't right came as she followed the concrete walkway around the corner of the Theodosian Library and missed seeing the pine trees which once loomed above the building's roofline. She remembered how those trees shaded the family cottage. The resolute click of her high heels faltered. She moved slowly toward that empty skyline. Turning the corner, Jane found a fence of rough boards that stretched away in two directions. Something big and empty obviously lay beyond—and it wasn't her home.

Jane crossed the margin of grass along the walkway, onto the sticky brown dirt churned up by construction activity, and put a gloved hand against the fence. She tried to see through a crack between the boards, but they were too tightly fitted. She walked one way then another, and finally found a knothole at eye level. She moved her face close—careful not to smudge the heavy layer of pancake makeup that was part of her working appearance—and looked through it.

Where the pine forest and three cottages had once stood, she found a hole that was a couple of acres wide and at least thirty feet deep. On the far side, a dirt ramp led down to the bottom, and there stood two yellow bulldozers. They were apparently done for the day, having taken a chop out of the earth as square and level as if God had punched the ground with a giant cookie cutter.

So Willie was not at home.

Their home no longer existed.

What was she going to do now?

Well … after all this time, Jane was nothing if not resourceful. Since Willie was a professor, kind of a public figure at a university, surely someone would have his current address. If she hurried, she could probably call at the Classics Department or the Bursar's Office before they closed for the day.

278

William Henry was experimenting with cooking a formal dinner in *Galatea*'s tiny kitchen and had invited his daughter to share the results. He had put on spaghetti sauce—his own robust recipe, based on olive oil, garlic, onion, mushrooms, hamburger, canned tomatoes, and dashes of various spices selected mostly by their smell—to simmer at four o'clock. On the second burner he now boiled water for the pasta. Without an oven, he had to make garlic bread by searing store-bought rolls in a pan on the third burner.

Dani had offered to help, but he made her wait in the saloon. He did let her set the table and retrieve and open a bottle of wine from the cool recesses of the aft lazaretto.

"I really do have something important to tell you, Dad," she insisted.

"It's tricky making all this come together. Can you wait till we eat?"

"Sure—I guess."

Finally, he brought in plates with halves of the butter-browned rolls, went out and came back with a tureen of spaghetti and sauce with two big serving spoons.

"What, no salad?" she asked.

"This is Italian. Pasta *il primo,* salad *il secondo.*"

"If you say so."

He served their plates. She poured the wine.

"What I need to tell you," Dani said, "is that I went to the clinic the other day, for some tests—"

She paused, and William Henry felt it, too. The boat had rocked as if a weight were added on the dock side. It wasn't a large motion but went counter to the gentle back and forth that the town's breakwater admitted from the vigorous wave action out on the lake. They heard the scuff of shoe leather on teak planks: someone had stepped aboard from the dock and was now walking across the back deck.

"Are you expecting someone?" Dani asked.

"No, it's just us for dinner," he said.

"I'll go see," she offered.

Before he could stop her, Dani went down the length of the saloon, dodging past tufted armchairs and casual tables, to the glazed double doors which opened out onto the deck. She peered through one of the windows but shook her head. With the cabin lights turned on inside, William Henry guessed all she saw was her own reflection. She reached for the doorknobs.

"Wait! Don't!" he called, but it was too late.

She opened both doors to a small figure, revealed by the spill of light.

"Oh, my God!" Dani stepped back. "It's Mother!" And she stepped back again.

"Hello, darling," Jane said, coming into the room.

With a sense of *déjà vu*—more like a dislocation—William Henry saw his wife wearing the same belted trench coat, the same black leather pumps with spike heels, her hair in the same bell-shaped coiffure the color and scent of darkened red honey, her face the same sweet oval with wide-set gray eyes, the same person with whom he had fallen in love, now twenty years ago, in a drug store in Roulette, Pennsylvania. She came slowly up the length of the cabin, her hands deep in the pockets of her coat, her hips swaying confidently around the obstacles of furniture where Dani had dodged them like a linebacker.

William Henry stood up. He had an urge to rush forward, but somehow his legs locked him in place between the dining table and his chair.

"They told me up on campus you'd bought a boat," Jane said. "Your department chair, that nice Professor Littlefield, called it 'Wheelock's Folly.' But I can see why you love it." She withdrew a hand from one pocket. She was wearing gray suede gloves. She ran the tip of one finger across the marble top of a claw-footed table. "It looks just like the parlor back home." She looked around. "Gaudier, though."

"The boat is from the same era," he said inanely.

"Of course," Jane conceded. "Is it just me, or is this whole thing *smaller* on the inside than it looks on the outside?"

"It's—" He managed to move the chair and take a step toward his wife. "—an effect of being on the water, I think." More inanity.

"Rather toylike, actually," Jane said with a sniff.

"I live here now," William Henry said.

"Of course you do, Willie."

"Mother—" Dani began.

"My, you've grown up into a beautiful young woman."

"Mother, what are you *doing* here?"

"Why, I've come home."

"Here? To live?"

"Of course, dear, aren't we a family? Although, now that your father has bought himself a yacht, we can all sail away together. Wouldn't that be nice?"

SUMMER 1968

1. THE REASON WHY

THE KILOGRAM OF heroin was, to Jane's practiced hand, the appropriate weight—a bit more than a two-pound bag of sifted flour. It might have been cut with fillers, but their supplier had never done that to them in the past. Still, the only way to tell if the powder was pure was to open the bag, take a sample, and test the product, and Jane wasn't ready to do that yet. The powder had been prepared for transport by being packed into a nitrile-rubber pouch, sealed with epoxy, scoured with steam, and sewn into a stiff canvas sack. It was supposed to be undetectable by the dogs that sniffed out drugs. But unpick the stitching and slice the rubber, and she would have white powder all over the place.

The canvas sack was the size of a small bread loaf or a very large salami. It might have contained anything, from rice flour to cane sugar. The squiggly printing in red ink on the outside supposedly said some such thing, but whatever the language—Burmese, Thai, Vietnamese, or Laotian—Jane could not read it. The only way to be sure she was not just carrying flour or sugar was the testing that she was not prepared to do.

For now, the bag lay at the bottom of her suitcase, hidden under several changes of clothes, a second pair of shoes, and her cosmetics case. Even there, the package made her nervous. On the West Coast, in Los Angeles, she could conceivably claim to have just visited an Asian specialties market to satisfy her baking needs. Here, in Upstate New York, carting around two pounds of Vietnamese-labeled rice flour was suspicious.

So the first thing she needed to do, on moving into a rented room in Byzantium, was find a place to stash her prize. The bureau drawers were too obvious, because any narcotics agent would empty them first. Beneath a layer of trash in the wastebasket was too dangerous, because she couldn't know when the landlady emptied it. Under the bed was too exposed, because the antique four-poster stood too high on its spindly legs. Her roving eye fell on the air duct for the house's central heating—

now switched off in early summer. The ornate iron grate was down low on the wall. She could get to it in a minute.

Jane took a steel nail file from her case, twiddled the screws holding the grate to the wall, and lifted it off. She coughed at the sight of the dust bunnies—more like dust *wolves*—that lurked inside the opening. Clearly, Mrs. Bronson's housekeeping stopped at the edge of the visible world. Jane got some wet toilet paper from the bathroom and cleaned the floor of the duct as far back as she could reach, then placed the package in the shadows just short of the elbow bend that plunged down to the basement. As she fastened the grate, it crossed her mind that an earthquake might shake her heroin loose and send it into the household furnace. But then, they didn't have earthquakes on the East Coast, did they?

For the twentieth time since leaving Los Angeles, Jane realized that stealing the key of heroin had been a mammothly stupid decision. It exposed her to real risks from both sides of the law—deadly risks in the case of Eric Bell, who operated on the wrong side. And, like most decisions in her life, Jane had no way of walking it back, pleading stupidity or temporary insanity, begging his forgiveness, and returning their relationship to what her long-lost husband would have called the *status quo ante*.

One of Jane's reasons lay in her makeup case. To pick up the drugs from Eric's intermediary in Seattle, who actually did import foodstuffs from Southeast Asia, she had to travel as a woman of business, a buyer for a major California supermarket chain. She had the business cards and carried a case filled with rice flour samples to back up her story. She wore business suits, hose, and heels to look the part. And when her eyes were blackened and her face and arms bruised, she patched up her appearance with layers of pancake makeup. Before embarking on this double-cross, Jane had simply decided she no longer wanted to take the punches. No one would ever hit her again.

A second reason was the sheer monetary value of the powder she was carrying—although that had never been quite so powerful an attraction before her decision about being hit. At street prices, that key would easily fetch more than half a million dollars. That was before Eric and the club cut it with milk sugar, baby laxative, or anything else a person could snort, smoke, or shoot up without lethal effect. Before the cut, at wholesale, that two-pound sack had enough cash value for Jane to run far and run fast. Afterwards, at retail, she would have enough to live on, comfortably, for the foreseeable future. Either approach looked to her like a workable deal.

Of course, there was Eric. If he would hurt her for talking back, or thinking out loud, and sometimes just for his own brute pleasure, then he would kill her, chop, bang, dead, for stealing half a million of the club's dollars—even if the up-front exposure had only been a fraction of that. Given the state of their relationship lately, he had probably been ready to kill her just for leaving any white powder residue inside the rubber bag.

No, it was time to get out, risk and all.

The only question was, would he follow her here?

Yes … probably … eventually. But looking for Jane in Byzantium would not be his first thought. She hadn't mentioned the place in ten years. Eric might not remember just where, along his famous cross-country motorcycle jaunt fueled by gasoline, grass, and alcohol he had picked up his passenger in a blue bathrobe. And, in the time they had been together, she and Eric had traveled to, talked about, or dreamed of visiting so many different places. No, in her wake Jane had left, not just a trail of clues, but a continent-wide jigsaw puzzle.

Now all she had to do was find a way to turn two pounds of white powder into a ton of folding green paper. And what better place to do it than a college town?

2. Getting to Know You

Dani had agreed to have lunch with her mother at a little restaurant in town that offered "al fresco" dining along a stretch of sidewalk penned in by a black iron railing. When a waiter led her through the gate, she found Jane already seated, holding a glass of white wine and smoking a cigarette. Jane was wearing the same formal business clothes as the night before—a tailored jacket of navy-blue wool, matching straight skirt cut just above the knee, white silk blouse with a ruffle, nylons, and high heels. By comparison, Dani felt dumpy in her sandals, jeans, and strappy top.

"Hello, dear," Jane said, rising from her chair and offering her hand. "I'm so glad we could get together."

Who was this person? Why was her own mother speaking to her like some kind of business associate, or maybe a client? Dani took the hand, then dropped it and sat down.

The waiter hovered, and Jane dismissed him by ordering a second glass of wine for her daughter.

"I can't legally drink that, you know," Dani said.

"Oh, well," Jane replied. "One more for me."

Dani was already feeling about nine years old, the age when she last saw her mother. But here Jane just casually assumed her daughter would be drinking wine at lunchtime. The context—the "vibe," as the students would say—felt all wrong.

"Why are you here, Mother?" she demanded.

"Why, to get to know my grown-up daughter, of course."

"I mean, why now, after all this time. And just where have you been?"

Jane pursed her lips and took a larger than ladylike gulp of wine. "As to *now,* I'm officially on leave."

"Oh? From where? The asylum?"

Jane flinched as if slapped. "No … that was … a mistake. It was long ago."

"And in all the time since, you've been …?"

"On assignment."

"Assigned by who?"

"One of the agencies."

The way her mother said this, after looking around to see who might be listening, made Dani suddenly suspicious. "Are you saying you're *a spy?*"

"Phh-bbtt!" Jane made a tiny spitting noise. "It's military intelligence, if you must know. I've been working out of California the last couple of years."

"Prove it," Dani challenged her.

"You mean, with a badge or a business card?"

"Show me something you couldn't do before."

"*Moya sobstvennaya doch' nye vereet m'nye.*"

"What is that?" Dani asked. "Russian?"

"I said, 'My own daughter doesn't believe me.' "

"You learned to speak Russian."

"At the Defense Language Institute in Monterey."

"And you've been spying on the communists?"

"Well, tracking their smuggling operations."

"Oh? And what have they been smuggling?"

Again that look around. "Narcotics, mostly."

"The Russians are smuggling dope into this country?"

"From Laos and Vietnam. They bring it in through Canada."

"My mother is an international expert on dope smuggling?"

"Hard to believe, isn't it?" Jane agreed.

Dani considered. "Not really."

After they ordered lunch—a small steak for Jane, fish for her and a glass of iced tea—Dani answered her mother's questions about life in Byzantium during the past ten years, all the time avoiding the big news, the news that would shortly change Dani's whole life. Jane applauded her daughter's choice of engineering as a career, although she warned it would be harder to work in a field so completely dominated by men. Jane expressed regret that she had not been able to return and become more of an influence in her daughter's life. Also, that her leaving had cost William Henry so much grief. She marveled at his choice of selling the cottage for an antique yacht, and together mother and daughter agreed the steamboat was both impractical and yet somehow wonderful. Jane said she could see Willie's eyes shine when he talked about the boat—or "steam launch," as he called it—last night.

But for all that they seemed to be chatting so cozily, Dani noticed Jane's attention never fully settled on her. Jane's eyes never stopped roving the street, examining passing vehicles, studying pedestrians on the sidewalk outside the railing.

"I've seen that car twice now," she said suddenly, pointing at a mud-brown sedan without lifting her hand off the tablecloth. "Government plates, too."

"Friends of yours?" Dani asked.

"Most likely from the Bureau."

"The FBI is here in town? Really?"

"They have domestic jurisdiction."

"Jurisdiction over what?"

"Just about everything."

"So, do you want to wave them over for a chat?" Dani asked facetiously.

"No, I think we ought to take our business off the street."

Jane waited until their waiter passed through again and stopped him with a hand. "I'm finding the sun out here is too strong. I'm getting a headache."

"Really, Mother?" Dani said with concern.

Jane ignored her and continued with the waiter, "Could we move our plates to a table inside?"

"Certainly, madam." And he lifted Dani's plate right out from under her fork.

"That's ever so much better," Jane said, standing up and retrieving her wine glass.

3. Extending Her Horizons

Finding so many federal eyes active and alert on the streets of Byzantium had made Jane nervous. Her good old clinical paranoia was one thing, but this police presence tweaked senses and skills she had developed in half a dozen years of transporting large volumes of serious contraband from one distant place to another. She was acutely aware, too, that she still wore the persona and carried the identity of someone who had flown across country just the day before, straight from a routine pickup. Routine was the enemy of security, or so Sergeant Lighthorse had always said, and her meeting with the Seattle food importer might easily have been spotted or snitched, infiltrated or observed, and tracked onward. It was time for evasive maneuvers.

Jane found a store on the backstreets of Byzantium called "The Rag Shop," which sold cheap clothing both new and secondhand off the same racks. In half an hour she was outfitted in the style to which she was more accustomed: black jeans, ankle boots with stacked heels, flame-red nylon camisole with a peek-a-boo neckline, and olive-drab army fatigue jacket with a rainbow peace symbol sewn onto one shoulder and a marijuana leaf embroidered on the other. With her new wardrobe—and traces of pancake makeup and eye shadow left to conceal the age lines on her face—Jane would could fit right into the local scene as a grad student or teaching assistant or something. She changed in the back of the store behind a curtain and carried her business suit, purse, and shoes out in a crumpled paper bag, which she promptly dropped in a garbage can.

In the purse were the cards and boarding passes of the person who had flown into Syracuse from Seattle twenty-four hours ago. Jane's own identity—which was not much better but at least did not trace back to the pickup—was concealed in the lining of her suitcase at the boardinghouse. Carrying her driver's license and credit cards on a run was stupid. It was something she never did under normal circumstances, but nothing about this trip was normal.

Jane spent the rest of the afternoon reacquainting herself with the town. Not with the upscale shops, chic restaurants, Faculty Wives Club, and Maple Street Elementary School she had known ten years ago as an actual wife and mother—those days were long gone. No, now she drifted in and out of coffee shops, bookstores, and the Student Union. She listened to the chatter and asked offhand questions, impersonating that grad student or teaching assistant, who was looking to score some magic mushrooms or maryjane. Oh yeah, or some of that white powder!

After a couple of hours of this, her heart was sinking fast. If the market for dope ever went down, it was in a college town at the end of semester and the start of the long summer vacation. But maybe, just maybe, not for the harder products. Weed smokers and hash tokers moved with the population. Heroin junkies tended to stay put throughout the year and peddle their ass, steal, and shoplift to stay alive. At least, that was the pattern in Los Angeles and San Francisco.

By four o'clock she had a pretty good idea of the territory, but by then it was too late to make any serious moves. And she still had one more thing to do, connected with severing her ties back to Seattle. She wasn't ready to give up her room at the genteel boardinghouse off Main Street, but at least she could sanitize it. A sixth sense told Jane she had to move that kilo now, physically, get it out of her lodgings, away from anyone who might have seen a red-haired businesswoman come to town.

She went back to the house by a roundabout route. First, she stopped at the local A&P and picked up a load of groceries as pretext. Next, she went to her room, changed the army jacket for her trench coat, and retrieved her prize from the air duct, burying it under the groceries.

Jane took a taxi down to the town dock. Upon arrival, she sat in the back for a few minutes to watch the old boat before committing to action. When she had convinced herself Willie was still off somewhere doing his end-of-term scholarly duties, and Dani was nowhere to be seen, she paid off the driver and went aboard. The doors to the rear of the main cabin were closed with a lock plate that must have dated from the previous century. In her mind, she saw an ornate brass key with teeth the size of fork tines. She could pick that with a hairpin, and did.

She walked through the saloon and set the bag of groceries on the dinette table. She removed the sack of rice flour and looked around. Nothing in the room suggested a hiding place, not under the sofa cushions or behind the books on the pretty little built-in bookcases. Jane went forward, into the galley, and found the choices there even more barren. Three drawers and a cabinet door under the stone counters and two facing sets of overhead cupboards hardly made for a secret stash. And putting her powder among actual foodstuffs could lead to a horrendous mistake. She plunged deeper, into what must have been the engine room, with toilet and shower off to one side in a closet. The engine was a fully exposed piece of machinery, with no obvious place to hide anything. She pulled open the door to the firebox under the boiler, which was dark enough and had plenty of nooks and crannies, under the grate and up around the fire tubes, to hide her sack. But she realized that if Willie ever lit the boiler to go someplace, it would be the most expensive trip anyone ever took.

Next to the engine, embedded in the deck planking, was a brass ring on a recessed swivel. She studied it for a moment. From cut lines in the deck four feet square around the ring, she guessed it was a hatch leading to whatever lay below. She hooked her finger into the ring and pulled. Nothing happened. She twisted the ring impatiently, and that must have released some kind of latch, because she heard a sharp, metallic *Click!* The hatch came up on counterweighted hinges.

She didn't have a flashlight. And not much ambient light was coming through the little arched windows in the walls along either side of the boat. She bent and put her head through the hatch. It was even darker down there and smelled of mold, but she could make out a set of steps or the rungs of an angled ladder. She climbed down and let her eyes adjust to the gloom. A certain amount of light was coming down through the pieces and parts of the engine, which was anchored below deck level, in the bottom of the boat, right across what must have been the keel.

Jane suddenly realized she had found the perfect hiding place. No one had any business down here—at least, not during the boat's regular operation. She moved slowly, balancing from one rib of the old hull to the next, until she was crouching alongside the boiler, which also had its foundation below deck. A nest of valves and pipes went every which way, some of them even going out through the side of the boat. One of the latter penetrated the hull beyond the far side of the boiler and was thick enough to conceal her package behind a right-angle bend. She wedged the sack there against the hull planking. Anyone would need a flashlight, and be intent on looking, to find her stash.

Jane climbed out of the space under the deck—from the rank smell, she supposed she had just discovered "the bilge"—closed the hatch, and twisted the ring to latch it. She went back into the galley, where she washed her hands in the sink and dusted her knees and the smudged edges of her boots with a damp paper towel. Then she examined the three-burner stove with its propane valves and noted the prominent box of matches. She had worked something like this when she and Eric went camping.

She checked her watch. It was late enough. She fetched her groceries from the main cabin and started making dinner.

4. Dinner with the Family

WILLIAM HENRY RETURNED aboard *Galatea* toward six o'clock in the evening, after listening all afternoon to students complain about their grades for the semester. He found the aft cabin doors wide open and the main saloon filled with cooking smells. His nose quickly identified pork chops, sauerkraut, and fried apples—things you could prepare on a stove top, and one of Jane's old signature dinners. In the galley he found his wife and daughter leaning against the soapstone counters, drinking red wine and laughing together, while pans of food sizzled and snapped on the propane burners. They stopped laughing when he appeared in the doorway.

"How did you get in?" he asked. He'd once offered Dani a key but she refused.

"Oh," Jane said, "I've learned a few things about locks over the years."

"Yeah," Dani said. "Don't you know my mom's with the CIA?"

"Please," Jane told her. "Military intelligence. On leave."

For some reason, that set them both laughing again.

William Henry did not know what to believe.

He had passed the entire day, or at least the past twenty-two hours, all the way back to the moment Jane had reappeared in his life, in a cloud, trying to understand what he was feeling.

Part of him was supremely happy to have his wife back, on any terms, and despite whatever might have happened in the years since she disappeared. Part of him resented the fact that she could leave and return, inexplicably, mysteriously, willfully, without his having any say in the matter. Part of him hoped for a future in which he and Jane were reunited, in which they could live as a family with their daughter. And part of him feared this was all some cruel trick and that Jane was no more substantial, standing there in his kitchen, wearing tight black jeans and a slinky red top, drinking a glass of red wine, than some ghost or spirit or half-remembered memory.

Military intelligence? CIA? Some kind of government agent? What did all that mean? And he was afraid to ask, to probe the illusion too deeply, unless she might vanish in smoke and lies.

Ten years ago, just after Jane was diagnosed, William Henry had started reading about mental illness, in particular schizophrenia, trying to understand what was going on in her mind. Although the books and scholarly papers were circumspect, even vague, in discussing any prognosis, he gathered that the disease manifested itself with two distinct types: early and late onset. The early-onset form started in the teenage years or, especially in females, the twenties. A seemingly normal child suddenly fell apart and suffered disorientation, delusions, and hallucinations, ending in a wild psychotic episode followed by hospitalization. The late-onset form followed much the same pattern, except the first signs of deterioration and the psychotic break came in the patient's late thirties or forties, even in middle age. That form was often confused with a nervous breakdown due to accumulated stress and fatigue.

People with an early onset tended to experience a lifelong, debilitating condition, marked by gradual deterioration of the personality, loss of interest in the world, and lack of joy in life, all punctuated by fits of screaming violence. These patients needed constant care and medication until, sometime in middle age, they just burned out, becoming vacant husks.

Late-onset patients usually had a better outcome, going through a short, florid stage of the disease with hallucinations, paranoia, and addled thinking, followed—with the right treatment and medication—by almost complete remission and resumption of a normal life. Some psychiatrists thought this better outcome had something to do with the endurance of a more completely formed personality and presence of "socio-demographic characteristics"—whatever that meant.

To William Henry's mind, much of this analysis was irrelevant, because Jane had been diagnosed somewhere in between, just before her thirtieth birthday. So she fit in neither category—and in fact she had escaped from the hospital before the doctors could even complete an initial evaluation. Just possibly, she had turned herself in somewhere else for treatment—but then, the new doctors would surely have identified her and sent her back to Byzantium.

So maybe Jane had really experienced the late-onset form, gone into some kind of spontaneous remission, and sobered up. But then, what had she been doing for the last ten years? William Henry could imagine—and fear—a thousand and one possibilities. But training with a government agency and working as some kind of a spy? ... No.

All of this passed through his mind while his wife and daughter recovered from their laughter. Jane took a fork and tested the chops. "These are done," she said. "Dani set the table. Let's eat!"

———

Jane cut around the sections of her pork chop with a wooden-handled paring knife and a stainless steel fork from the galley. Both utensils she remembered as belonging in the drawer by the sink in her old kitchen. She wondered where the family silver had gone—probably to a box in storage someplace, although it was possible Willie had sold it to help pay for this extravagance of a pleasure yacht.

Willie was an enigma to her—at least on the level of spoken language. Last night, when they had finally met after all the years in between, he talked in generalities: changes to the campus, changes in his workload, losing the house, buying the boat. But never one word about her, or himself, or them as a couple. He never said anything about loving her still, or hating her now, being glad she had come back, or needing to know the terms of her return. Either he simply accepted her return—or he rejected her. And she couldn't tell which it was.

But that was just from his words. Jane had known instantly, when she first walked into the room, from the look on his face, that he was as deeply in love with her as always. Even now, sitting at the end of the table, he was stealing looks at her. So the old magic of sight and sound, smell and touch still worked. That was something to build on, at least.

Jane herself did not know what she expected to come from this trip. A reunion? A final dissolution? A brief stopover on her flight to somewhere else? Those were questions for later. First thing was to figure out how to lay off that stolen kilo of heroin. When she had enough money in her pocket—and the evidence of her crime was gone beyond reach, into the anonymous flux of trade that ended in the veins of nameless people—then she could relax and consider the future. Until then, her future was on the far horizon with a dark cloud—a nexus of probabilities— raised in front of her.

For now, she determined to be content, eat her pork chop, and deal with tomorrow when it came—just as she had been doing for the past ten years.

Dani could remember meals like this from her childhood. The pork was done just right—still juicy, not dried out like her father cooked it—and savory with spices in the measures and propor- tions only her mother knew. The apples were fried in butter with a tablespoon of sugar, to give them the taste and consistency of apple sauce, but warm and with the red and yellow skins still attached. The dead-brown sauerkraut was from a can, but Jane heated it with chopped onion and a touch of nutmeg, which leavened the acrid flavor. The meal took her back to snowy nights at the cottage in the woods, when everyone was snug and warm. Everyone was safe.

But that was only a memory. While the food might be the same, the setting was different: the gaudy cabin of a nineteenth- century steam yacht, floating on a sleek hull filled with rotten timbers, tied to shore by a couple of frayed ropes, likely at any minute to be swept out to deep water and sunk.

The people were different, too. Instead of the mother who had loved and raised her, Dani was sitting across from a bright and brittle woman, some kind of professional, maybe even a spy, who spoke in riddles and treated her like a stranger. Instead of her father who, distant and absent-minded as he sometimes was, had always paid attention to her, shared his thoughts, and asked for her help, the man sitting now at the end of the table wore a glazed and imbecilic expression. Dani tried to figure out if he was happy or sad, scared or angry, or simply perplexed about Jane's return. A bit of everything, she guessed. But it was clear that, right now, he wasn't hearing a word anybody said.

Dani still had her own secret. With her old mother and father, she might have had the courage to tell it, to seek their advice, to face the choices that lay before her. But now she felt so alone. Her old dream of finishing college and working as one of the first female engineers—all that was somewhere out on the horizon. Between her and that distant time loomed a dark cloud that represented the improbable burden of her bearing a child out of wedlock and trying to raise it as a single mother. Becoming pregnant was something Dani had gotten into on her own. Now she had to see it through on her own.

Suddenly, the pork was dry and tasteless in her mouth, the apples sweet but slightly rotten, and the cabbage bitter and sour.

5. Doing a Deal

THE NEXT MORNING Jane waited until a decent hour—closer to noon, actually—and went to a store she had spotted in the back-street neighborhood the day before. Her intuition was supported this time by word of mouth, but she just as easily might have followed her nose. The window sign said "Beads 'N Things" and below, in smaller letters, "Incense, Burners, Lifestyle." Jane fluffed out her hair with her fingers, hooded her eyes, and stuck out her lower lip in what Sam Lighthorse called her "hard core" expression.

"How ya doin'?" said the girl behind the counter.

"S'alright," Jane replied noncommittally. The place was empty but smelled like a combination of dirty feet and Indian spices. She idly examined a display case of tiny pipes made variously of clay, stone, and glass.

After a few moments, the girl drifted over. "Can I help you?"

Jane looked up slowly. "If I wanted to move some weight, would I talk to you?"

"Excuse me? I don't think—"

"Well, think now. Are these pipes for smoking *tobacco?*"

"Gee. I guess some people might try—"

"Nonsense, dear. These pipes are for smoking *product*. Now, if instead of pipes, I wanted the product itself, who would I be talking to?"

"What? Are you a narc?" the girl asked.

"Do I *look* like a narc?" Jane replied.

"An old lady trying to be hip? Yeah."

Jane gave a bitter laugh. " 'Old lady.' Good one!"

"Maybe you should talk to the manager."

"Maybe I should," she said equably.

The girl disappeared through a cascade of hanging beads. A minute later a man in his late twenties, with a droopy expression, frizzy ponytail, and a tie-dyed shirt, came out. "I hear you're looking to make a connection."

"That's the story."

"Are you *trouble?*"

"Only if I get it first."

The manager grimaced.

"Look, I just flew in from the coast," Jane continued. "I need to do some business. I've got weight to sell. If not to you, then point me. No blowback. Guaranteed."

The man considered. "Maybe you can help out some friends of mine."

He went over to the old-fashioned brass cash register, flipped up a panel, pulled out six inches of blank paper tape, and tore it off. He scribbled two lines in pencil and handed it to Jane. It was an address on the other side of town.

"Ask for Jodie or Diane. Tell them you talked to Boz. See if we can break this thing. But you treat them right, now! You stiff them, or anybody comes back looking for trouble, and I'll have Peaches here"—tipping his head at the counter girl, who scowled—"find you and beat you to death."

"My word on it," Jane said and left—not exactly sure what sort of "thing" she was supposed to break.

The address was across from campus and heavily invested in student housing, not like the quieter neighborhood where she had taken a room. With the end of the semester, she counted three vans and a dozen cars parked with their doors and trunks open. People from both sides of the street were loading boxes of books, suitcases, chairs, small tables, and stereo components. Everything was coming out, nothing going in.

The apartment in the address was on the third floor. While doors up and down the hallway hung open and the staircase resounded with the pounding feet of moving day, this one door remained closed, the space beyond it dead quiet. Jane knocked anyway.

No response for three heartbeats.

In the glass bead set in a brass ring at everyone else's eye level, but just above Jane's head, a dark shadow blocked the light filtering from inside. She waited impassively to let them inspect her. From behind the door came a shout in a female voice, "Yeah?"

Jane rolled her eyes. "Is anyone home?"

"Who wants to know?" was the reply.

"Your fairy fucking godmother!"

Another pause. Then, "Oh, shit."

The door opened on a retaining chain. If the girls inside thought a little thing like that would stop any kind of determined enforcement action, they were more amateur than Jane probably wanted to deal with. An eyeball appeared in the crack, partially obscured by a hank of dirty blonde hair.

"Just me," Jane said, holding up her hands.

"What you want?" the girl asked suspiciously.

"Boz sent me. Thought maybe we could do a deal."

The eyeball looked her up and down again.

"We ain't got any," shouted another female voice from inside the room. The head attached to the eyeball nodded. "Yeah, we're tapped out," the attached mouth said.

Jane smiled. "Then this is your lucky day."

"Who the hell is it?" bawled the voice from inside.

The mouth removed itself from the door crack. "Some old lady."

"Some old lady," Jane corrected, but quietly—so the whole building didn't hear, "who's holding a kilo of the Golden Triangle's finest. Yours if you want it."

The door closed, the chain rattled, and the door reopened. The blonde girl stepped briefly into the opening but was immediately pushed aside by an older woman with dark ringlets. She was heavyset where the other was slender. Neither of them was particularly attractive or well groomed. "We don't want any," the new woman said.

"Your friend Boz implied otherwise."

"Yeah? Well, Boz don't know shit."

Jane's antennas were twitching now, but she was still desperate to unload the kilo before real trouble showed up. This was the one good lead she had. "All right, forget Boz. I think I can help, is all. I've got some product to move—prime stuff—and everyone says you two are the local movers. Jodie and Diane, right?"

The dark one looked at the blonde, shrugged. "C'mon in." And as the door shut behind Jane, she said softly: "Your funeral, bitch."

Inside, the apartment was a mess. The two facing couches and the armchair between them all sprouted white stuffing from splits in the upholstery. Random articles of clothing—both women's and men's—lay scattered on the floor. Food containers, dirty plates, glasses, and beer bottles crowded the coffee table. Flies buzzed slowly back and forth. Jane didn't expect two women to live like an order of immaculate nuns, but these girls wallowed in filth like teenage boys. And yet ... something about the room also felt unlived-in. Like these people and the trash were just passing through. The phrase "crash pad" occurred to Jane. She'd seen a few of those in her time, too.

"Show us what you've got," the dark-haired woman said.

"You think I brought it with me?" Jane said. "If we can reach—"

"That isn't the way it works!" shouted a new voice from across the room.

Out of a short hallway that led God-knew-where, two young men appeared. Like the slender girl, they were pale and skinny, about eighteen years old, and looked seriously underfed. They wore black leather jackets and crew cuts. They stood their ground like street fighters. Neither one of them had the slightly off-center, unfocused look which Jane associated with habitual drug takers. These boys were razor sharp and itchy. They stared at her with chiseled, almost Aryan expressions but dead eyes. Nothing going on in those eyes.

In three long steps, they came into the room and positioned themselves on either side of Jane. The blonde girl shrank away, and the dark-haired one backed off slowly.

"When will you bitches learn?" asked the one on the left, who had a wispy little beard. "*Nobody* moves drugs in this town except through us!"

"Sure, Jake," the dark woman said. "We weren't thinking anything else."

"No-no-nobody asked her," the blonde girl said. "She—she just came by."

"Then she's a narc," said the other boy, whose baby cheeks had dimples.

"Yeah," agreed Wispy. "Let's take her down."

Dimples moved in front and grabbed Jane's arms just above the wrists.

Bad move. Jane knew at least three possible counters and chose the easiest one. She flexed her arms outward, pressing hard against the inside of his palms, to make him step in closer and tighten his grip, pushing against her pressure. Jane instantly reversed the flow, drawing her hands inward and past each other, her left hand spread wide to catch Dimples's left wrist just above where he had taken hold of her right hand. The force caused the weak side of his grip—the fingers and opposed thumb—to snap open.

It took an opponent with extreme bodily awareness not to confuse the grip she now had on him for the grip he had lost on her. Dimples had no such awareness. With her right hand free, she struck him twice in quick succession: rising uppercut to chin, then back fist at peak to bridge of nose. As soon as he let go of her left hand, she raised it to shoulder height and chopped into his collarbone. Thank God for the sergeant's *jujutsu* lessons.

As Dimples sagged away, Jane slipped past him and angled her body to face Wispy. She did a neat step-slide to close the distance, jacked her trailing right knee like a lever on a spring, backward then forward and up, slamming it into his groin. As he bent to cover himself, the heel of her left hand struck upward just under his nose. More broken bones, this time with a gout of blood.

She danced away from the danger space between the two men. Her eyes swept the room and located three potential weapons among the clutter on the table: glass ashtray, beer bottle, cheese spreader. But it turned out she didn't need them.

"What the fuck!" said Wispy, trying to catch the blood from his nose.

Dimples staggered over to a couch and threw himself down.

"Who *are* you?" Wispy asked, still bent over.

"Just a businesswoman," Jane said.

"What do you want?"

"As I was trying to explain to the ladies, I recently flew in from Seattle. I actually do have a key of heroin to unload—at bargain prices, if necessary. I was practically going to make them a present of it, but now I don't think so."

"Heroin?" Wispy croaked. "Who's dealing heroin?" He waddled to the couch and sank down beside Dimples.

The dark woman shook her head at Jane. "This is a hick college in the boonies. These are all middle-class kids. Heroin's not their thing. We're strictly weed and hash."

Jane looked from her to the slender girl, who shrugged in return. "So you just move soft stuff? That's what all the ruckus is about?"

"There's a lot of money in marijuana," the dark woman said.

"Oh yeah," Jane scoffed. "If you're moving a couple *tons* of it."

"Monthly buy in horse around here is like ... three, four grams, tops."

Jane considered that. The woman had just popped her prospects of a sale.

"Okay," she moved on. "So I get you're Jodie 'n Diane. Which one are you?"

"Diane," the woman said. "She's Jodie"—pointing at the blonde.

"Right, and who are Wispy and Dimples here?"

The girls giggled at the nicknames Jane used.

"They're the enforcers for our local distributor."

"Really? These guys are supposed to be *muscle?*"

"I know, it's pitiful. This place is winding down."

Jane sighed. Now wasn't that the truth? ... All over.

"So who did they represent, when they meant something?"

"They're a local branch of the student-run Social Policy Forum."

"Politics?" Jane was aghast. "You sold drugs to support a political party?"

"It's kind of a two-fer, with the right crowd. The rest don't care."

"That's not even a workable business model," Jane said. "Shit!"

She eyed the two boys, both of whom were still breathing, although they didn't seem to be grateful for the fact. The problem was to get out of the room without drawing any kind of last-minute, face-saving retaliation. But she decided they were tame. Wispy's nose was still bleeding, and Dimples's right arm hung at an angle.

"Right," she said. "I'll be leaving now."

"Please, just go!" Dimples bawled.

"And no one follows me out."

"Are you kidding, lady?"

Jane got through the door and ran down the stairs. She was counting seconds until either of the boys—or even the dark-haired woman—thought to pick up a weapon and pursue her. But when she got to twenty, which coincided with the bottom of the staircase and the building's front entry, she figured they weren't coming. Still, she made sure to go off *down* the street, not back the way she had come.

From what Diane had said, Jane had no hope of a wholesale deal in Byzantium. And if she settled down to retail that kilo, she'd be a grandmother on a pension before she saw the last of it. No, the safe thing to do—the sane thing to do—was take the dope down to the lake and pitch it in. Or flush it down the toilet. But then Jane would have no leverage when Eric came after it, nothing for a bargaining chip.

And that was just as dangerous.

Maybe even more so.

6. A Summer Cruise

WHEN WILLIAM HENRY returned home after his last day of regular office hours, closing out the spring semester, he found Jane had already come aboard. She was sitting in the saloon with her feet up, a glass in her hand, a bottle of red wine open at her elbow, and a third of it gone. He supposed she had picked the lock again, because he certainly had not given her a key.

"Hey, Captain!" She toasted him with the last gulp in her glass.

"Hello, Jane." He set his briefcase aside and took off his jacket.

"Why'n'cha rustle yourself up a glass? This-ss a good Cabernet."

"Oh, thank you. Nice of you to bring it."

"But I didn't … found it under a hatch."

"Please, do make yourself right at home."

She refilled her glass and toasted that with another gulp.

"Jane …" He paused to sort out his priorities. "Why are you here?"

"I thought we'd already got clear on that." She put down the glass and folded her hands in her lap, as if for recitation. "I've been working hard the last couple of years. I—my team, that is, we—just wrapped up a big case. Army's given everybody some well-earned leave. I thought I'd come home and spend it with my family."

"You've been in the army?" he asked carefully.

"Well, military police. An adjunct position."

"Um, what's your rank?"

"Group I'm with isn't big on ranks and protocol."

"I see. What was the case?"

"I'm not supposed to talk about it."

"Dani says you're tracking Russian dope smugglers."

"That was supposed to be confidential."

"So you told a college girl?"

"I told my daughter."

"Oh, of course."

William Henry went into the galley to fetch a glass for himself. Out of Jane's sight and away from those watchful eyes, he paused to consider. If Jane really had been working on a big case for the army, then someone would know about it. After all, he was not without resources himself. He took a glass from the cupboard and returned to the cabin.

"Look," Jane said, "what have you got planned for the summer? Are you signed up for any classes yet?"

"No, my course load has been getting pretty light." He poured a measure of wine and tasted it. She was right, it was a good vintage, something he'd been holding onto for a special occasion.

"Then let's go somewhere!"

"Go where? Like on a trip?"

"You've got a boat, for God's sake! It's not tied to the land—or well, it's only tied, not bolted down. So let's use it! Let's go somewhere!"

That was the whole reason he had bought the boat, he remembered now, rather than a bungalow in town or a farmstead out in the country—to be free of the land. To be able to just pack up, cast off, and go. For the last year and more he had been feeling hemmed in and trapped, nursing his frustrations and resentments against the university, the changes in his teaching assignments, the narrowing climate of opinion on campus, and the relative tedium of a professor's life. The steamboat was an undeclared statement. Why not make it out loud?

"Where do you want to go?" he said with a grin.

"Anywhere! There's a huge lake out there," she said, pointing out the window and across the breakwater. "Let's just find the other side and get lost exploring it."

Having planted her seed—and none too soon—Jane left Willie to think it over by offering to go make dinner. Earlier, she had found a leftover pork chop in the icebox, along with half a dozen eggs, an onion, parsley, and some bread. She could do a nice omelet and toast for the two of them.

When she came out with their plates, he had taken up the surface of the dinette table with a big rolled-up map. It was beige and baby blue—mostly a broad expanse of blue—and he was studying it intently. While she stood there, he pushed the map aside and unfurled another, the new one was mostly beige with just squiggles and blotches in blue.

"What's all this?" she asked.

"Oh! Sorry!" He rolled up the maps and dumped them on the settee.

Jane put down the plates. "But what's with all those maps?"

"Charts," he corrected. "I'm just planning the trip."

She smiled at him. "So where are we going?"

"Well," he said as he cut into his omelet. "Just steaming around the lake would be pretty boring. There's not much to see along the north shore—just lots of farmland between Toronto and the Saint Lawrence River."

"That's in Canada, right?"

"Uh, right," he said. "But if we go across to Trenton, we can get into the Trent-Severn Waterway. That's a canal system cutting through a whole bunch of little lakes and ending up in Lake Simcoe. From there we cross into Georgian Bay on Lake Huron."

"Sounds nice."

"Then we go down through Lake Saint Clair and the Detroit River to Lake Erie, back up lake to Buffalo, through the Welland Canal to Lake Ontario again, and back home to Byzantium."

"How long would we be gone?"

"Three or four weeks." He shrugged. "All summer if we want."

"That would really be fun. But ... we pass through Detroit?"

"Yes, we'd have to. It's on the river. Is that a problem?"

Eric Bell still had contacts in Detroit. She and Eric had spent an ugly summer in Detroit. So ugly, in fact, that Jane had enrolled in the *jujutsu* classes right afterward. She could not go back to Detroit—not and be seen or identified. Detroit would be the first big city that Willie's little trip came to, returning to the States from Canada. That meant they would pass through U.S. Customs, with paperwork, declarations, maybe fingerprints, and possible police involvement. The outstanding warrant against her was an old one—but who knew what these newfangled computerized filing systems might dredge up? Eric's contacts there also had contacts with the police.

Still, a lot could happen between now and Detroit.

"No," she said. "No problem. Just wondering."

William Henry was determined to get to the bottom of Jane's stories. That second night after her return, when she had picked the lock on *Galatea*'s cabin door to fix them all a family dinner, and Dani had mentioned her mother being in "military intelligence," the notion was so vague and fanciful that William Henry had automatically dismissed it. But now, with more details having come to light—some big case, military police, dope smuggling, Russian involvement, probably in the Far East or Indochina—he wasn't so sure.

He tried to think of someone he could call, an old service connection, who might help him verify Jane's story. Of course, everyone William Henry knew would be fifteen years out of date and likely retired by now. But then he remembered a young lieutenant from Fort Dix, when he was passing through during the Korean War, a young hotshot named Hamilton, went by "Scooter" but the first name was actually Alfred. He had been transferred out of the Quartermaster Corps and into the Judge Advocate General's office when it was discovered he had a law degree.

With the excuse of having errands to run, packing in supplies for their impending cruise, William Henry returned to his office on campus and started making phone calls. On the fifth try, on a long-distance call to Washington, D.C., he tracked down the man.

After brief exchanges to catch up, William Henry asked Scooter—now a full colonel—what he knew or could find out about a military police operation, probably run out of the West Coast, to catch Russian dope smugglers. More specifically, was it headed by a woman, possibly a civilian contractor, named Jane Wheelock?

The line went quiet for a long time. "You know that's going to be classified," Hamilton said at last.

"I imagined it would be—but if you could peak around the edges—?"

"Yeah, Russians. ... Maybe at the top, at the executive level, just to get the ball rolling, you understand? But the mules, they're going to be American, our own guys—soldiers or, like you said, military contractors. That's the way to get contraband into the country. The whole Military Ocean Terminal system—that's been a leaky sieve."

"I understand," William Henry said.

"No, I don't think you do. An operation to catch American soldiers trafficking in dope? You'd have to infiltrate, make dummy buys, even carry product for them ... work way under the radar. That team would be juggling kryptonite, Willie. Deadly poison. You don't risk spreading it around. They're going to bury that one so deep, not even the brass will have access. ... Even if I knew, I couldn't tell you."

"Oh, well, thank you anyway, Scooter."

"Wait a minute! Isn't your wife named Jane?"

"Uh, yes."

"Jane Wheelock?"

"Yes, but we've been separated for quite a while."

"So, you checking up on the little woman?"

"Well, it's something on that order."

"Yeah, good luck with that."

"Thank you, Scooter."

7. Bon Voyage!

To celebrate the start of his summer cruise, Dani's father had decided to hold a party aboard the old steamboat at the town dock and invite all their friends. Being practically the only girl in the Engineering Department, Dani didn't have many friends from school, because the boys usually didn't want to be just friends. She might have invited two of the girls she had gotten to know from her Theatre Arts class, but they were gone on summer vacation. So Dani was left to herself in a corner of the saloon cabin when she wasn't trying to help her mother prepare plates of hors d'oeuvres in the tiny galley.

At one point her father came by. "I'm sorry it's not your kind of crowd," he said. "Whatever happened to that young man you were seeing—the one who was getting his masters in history? I had hoped you would invite him."

"He had to leave town," she said carefully.

"You were seeing a boy?" Jane asked.

"It wasn't serious," Dani replied.

"He did seem a bit unreliable," her father said.

You don't know the half of it, Dani thought.

If Jane had any friends at the party, Dani couldn't identify them. She supposed her mother knew some of the faculty wives, from the time when she had been one herself, but none of them came over to give her an arm's length hug and kiss on the cheek, the way women did to each other. Despite the fact that Jane was by far the most attractive woman there, having resurrected from storage a stunning red satin cocktail dress, which she set off with a flaring black leather belt, the other women pretended not to know her and the men instinctively stayed away, as they would from a glowing rod of uranium.

So William Henry's friends, which meant his colleagues from the humanities and their wives, dominated the party. Dani had been to some mixers among the engineers and found them to be a fairly sober, even boring, group. But these liberal arts types were big on jokes and puns, political argument, and drinking.

Dani kept hoping her drama instructor, Elise Sokolov, would show up, but since her mother had come home maybe that wasn't such a good idea. One young woman spent an unusual amount of time talking to her father, practically following him around. She came dressed in leather pants and a studded jacket, carrying a motorcycle helmet, and Dani tried to figure out if she was one of his students or a teaching assistant. The woman was pretty enough that Dani suspected something might be going on between them. She noticed that William Henry made no effort to introduce the black-clad woman to the older professors from the Classics Department and subtly, but effectively, kept her from meeting Jane.

Everyone wanted a tour of the boat, although there wasn't much to see besides the saloon, galley, engine room, and the wheelhouse. Dani led a couple of these tours herself. She was especially proud of the old steam engine and all the work she and her grandfather had put into restoring it. But aside from a few clumsy remarks— "What kind of gas mileage does that thing get?" and "What an ugly lump of iron!"—no one seemed to notice the engine, much less the squat, dark dome of the boiler. Liberal arts types. If this had been a group of engineers, they would have been all over the propulsion system with calipers.

As she took her father's guests through the engine room, Dani straightened—for the third time—the rug that Jane had brought aboard that morning as a "boat-warming present." It was a faux Persian with tessellated edges that just fit the deck space down one side of the engine between its support stanchions and the inner hull. "To cover up that ugly scar in the floor," Jane had said—meaning the hatch that Dani and her grandfather had cut for easier access to the plumbing in the bilges.

By ten o'clock the party had both thinned out and become noisier. The motorcycle woman had gone. Jane was in the galley washing glasses. And Dani had retreated to the smoke-free air on the front deck, where she sat on the stub end of the bowsprit and listened to the waves lapping against the hull.

"This a big sucker," said a voice behind her.

She turned to find a man—one of her father's friends, introduced to her hours ago as Professor Michelson—standing at the wire railing that ran around the edges of the fore and aft decks just above knee height. From the unsteady way he moved, Dani guessed he was more than a little drunk.

"Damn … but Wheelock bought a *big* boat," he said.

Dani didn't know what to say, so she kept quiet in the dark.

Michelson leaned over the rail. "Can't even see the water from here."

"Sir!" she exclaimed. "You don't want to stand too close."

"Stuff must be down there … somewhere."

He leaned out farther, bent to peer down—and tumbled right over the wire. He never even called out and made very little splash going in.

Dani leapt up and ran to the spot. "Man overboard!" she shouted. But the party was going on more than thirty feet away, back beyond the darkened wheelhouse, whose windows were closed, back past the engine room and galley. No one heard her.

She was wearing her second-best party dress, the gown her father had bought her for the high-school prom, which she had since simplified by removing ruffles at the waist and hem, but it was made out of silk and still worth something. She was also wearing high-heeled pumps that were no good for swimming. Dani kicked off her shoes, slipped out of the dress, and dove over the side. As she crossed the wire, she recalled that the water along the dock was probably deep enough to float a pleasure boat but not for diving from a high point. She unsteepled her arms and tucked her body into a roll, so that she landed on her back instead of knifing into the water. She came up quickly and splashed around trying to find the professor.

"What're you doing?" came a voice in the darkness.

Michelson was hanging on a boat fender that was slung over the side.

"This'us no time to go swimmin'!" he said thickly.

Dani paddled over and steadied herself on the fender. "Are you all right?"

"Course I'm all right," he protested. "I'm just ... wet."

"There's no ladder up here," she explained. "But the free-board's lower toward the stern. We'll swim down there, call, and someone will throw us a rope."

"Lead on, my dear," he said with mock gallantry.

When they got alongside the open windows of the saloon, Dani's calls attracted a group of partiers to the back deck. Her father quickly retrieved the old mahogany swim ladder from the lazarette and put it over the side. Michelson climbed out dripping water from his wool pants and jacket, followed by Dani in just her underwear and pantyhose.

"Odd time for a swim," her father said disapprovingly.

"Professor Michelson fell in," she replied.

When the two of them had returned to the light, it became apparent Michelson had somehow gashed his forehead in the fall and was bleeding freely. Jane brought dish towels and William Henry produced a first-aid kit. Her mother cleaned the cut with Mercurochrome and applied a bandage.

"He'll need stitches," Jane said. "Can someone drive him to the hospital?"

That effectively broke up the party, as a solicitous group left for their cars.

Jane turned to her daughter. "And you, young lady! Cover yourself with a towel, at least."

———

After their guests had left and their daughter had gone back to her dorm room—where the university was letting her stay while she waited for the summer term to open—Jane and Willie were cleaning up from the party. She washed dishes while he collected the paper napkins and empty bottles. For some reason Jane couldn't figure out, he was delighted with the way their *bon voyage* party had ended.

"You remember Michelson, don't you?"

Jane shook her head. "Colleague of yours?"

"Arrogant prick in the Sociology Department."

"Oh," she said. "So what's the joke?"

"Well, you see, *Galatea* never had a proper christening when we launched her in the spring." He grinned. "But she got one tonight, when we cracked a Sociology professor's head on the bow."

"But he might have been killed."

"Yeah … no such luck."

When the boat was all tidy and it was time to turn in, Jane pulled out one of the suitcases she had brought aboard that afternoon, full of clothes bought especially for the trip. She unfolded a brand-new flannel nightgown with a high neck and low hemline. It wasn't her normal sleeping attire—in midsummer in Los Angeles she usually went bare-assed naked—but it seemed appropriate, given the circumstances. In order to get out of town, she was going to be living a lot closer to her husband than they had for the last decade.

Jane retreated into the tiny bathroom closet—which Willie was teaching her to call the "head"—to change out of her party dress, clean her face, and brush her teeth. On returning, she found that he had pulled out a convertible, queen-sized bed from the settee and was making it up with sheets and a blanket. She eyed it with amusement.

"I don't suppose you have another of those," she said.

"Sorry, this is the only one," he said casually. Then he flushed. "Oh!"

"Yes. 'Oh!' " she deadpanned. "How are we going to deal with this?"

"I guess I could make up a hammock or something in the engine room."

"Do you *have* a hammock? Or a something?"

"Not really. I could put two chairs together …"

"We should be adult about this," she said. "We used to be married. I don't snore. And you don't fart in bed—or you didn't used to," she added with a grin.

Willie nodded. He bent to retrieve the settee's seat cushions that he had stacked against the wall—which she was learning to call a "bulkhead"—and arranged them under the covers, down the center of the bed. They weren't any kind of a hindrance, more of a suggestion, should either of them start to feel frisky. But they were a reminder of Jane's and Willie's currently estranged state. "Oh!" was all she could think to say.

"All right?" he asked.

"Yeah, sure."

8. Crosswise in the Trough

IN THE DAYS since *Galatea* slid into the calm waters of the inlet at the boatyard, William Henry had piloted the old boat on a few trips—suggested by Bill Gibbs as "shakedown runs"—up and down the lakeshore. He had taken her ten miles west from the Byzantium town dock on one mild Saturday under blue skies and warm sun, then fifteen miles east under overcast and light drizzle. These tentative runs, after much reading in *Chapman Piloting & Seamanship,* and with Dani acting as his first mate, had familiarized him with getting up steam in the boiler, opening valves and petcocks in proper sequence to start the engine, handling bow and stern lines as they left or approached the dock, and operating the controls in the wheelhouse. It all seemed straightforward enough.

Now William Henry was embarked on the great adventure, a whole summer-long cruise, and he was learning how much more there was to know. The first leg was the longest passage, straight across Lake Ontario to Presqu'ile Bay and the western end of the Murray Canal, which cut across a narrow neck of land and took them into Trenton, the official start of the waterway leading up into the heart of Ontario Province.

He had spent the morning of the day before their departure with the chart spread across the dinette table, comparing map bearings and magnetic deviation on the compass rose printed in the chart's corner. Then he used a pencil and ruler to draw a bold, black line to the northwest across all that empty blue space. He figured that the distance on a heading of 315 degrees would be just sixty-six and a fraction miles. He wasn't worried about overshooting, because the far shoreline lay directly across his course. When he did finally see land on the horizon, the only trick would be figuring out from the chart where it was he was actually making landfall. At a cruising speed of six knots, *Galatea* should complete the passage in about ten hours—an easy, if full, day's work.

Once he was out on the lake, beyond sight of land in deep water, the waves were coming directly at the bow, driven by a stiff breeze out of the northwest. The crests were just tall enough, and the troughs between them long enough, that William Henry found he could increase the engine speed a bit, climb up the face of an oncoming wave, then back off the throttle as the hull's center point crossed the crest line, and ride easily down the back side. It was almost like surfing—but with a bathtub instead of a surfboard. It was actually fun ... until the engine suddenly died.

The rhythmic throbbing in the engine room behind him went still. Without thrust from the propeller, the hull wallowed and slewed at an angle on the long slide toward the trough between waves. The side of the bow slapped hard at the oncoming wave, sending a shower of spray up over the wheelhouse.

"Whoa!" he said, mostly to himself.

Without forward momentum, the wheel swung idly, the rudder unable to bite into the water. In three heartbeats, the hull had turned sideways in the trough and began to roll with the waves instead of crossing over them.

"Jane!" he shouted. "Hang on!"

Wherever she was, back in the galley, or further back in the saloon, she probably didn't hear him. Because none of the controls seemed to work anyway, William Henry abandoned them and went through the door at the back of the wheelhouse and down the three steps into the engine room.

The place was full of steam. It jetted from the pressure release valve on top of the boiler and billowed down from there, hiding everything else in the room. William Henry batted at the clouds with his hands, trying to clear a space in front of his face, but that didn't help much. He staggered across the rolling deck to reach the windows on the upwind side of the boat. He thought to open them, letting fresh air in and driving the steam out. But when he wiped away the condensation covering the glass, he saw the bottom of the wave trough rise to within inches of the deck's edge and the window sash, then fall away and disappear as the hull rolled through an arc of at least ninety degrees. He realized that if the old boat rolled too far and then took a rogue wave—or something like it—over the gunwale and against the side of the cabin, water flooding the interior might sink the boat. Even if he didn't open the windows, the water pressure against those old wooden sashes with their pretty little window panes might smash through and sink her anyway.

He was trapped in a thickening cloud, on a rolling deck, amid a nest of hot pipes, among machinery that was nothing but sharp edges, in the middle of a crisis. The situation might have been funny if it weren't so deadly serious. Suddenly, all his dreams about making himself free of the land and roaming the wide world had come up against hard reality.

"Willie! Willie!" Jane called from the far end of the room. "What the hell's going on?"

"Bit of an emergency!" he called back. "Stay in the galley!"

Think! he told himself. *What to do first?*

Stop making more steam!

He remembered Dani showing him the valve that regulated steam pressure to the fuel feed pump under the boiler. Shutting it off would certainly extinguish the boiler's fire and stop the pressure buildup—but then, when he had fixed whatever was wrong, he would be faced with trying to prime the pump, relight the oil jets, and rebuild steam while the boat rolled frantically from side to side. No, the better choice was simply to reduce the flames as much as possible and let pressure in the boiler subside rather than collapse entirely.

Without burning himself too badly, William Henry groped his way to the front of the boiler, ducked under the escaping jet of live steam, and found the valve wheel on the feed pump line. It was too hot to touch, but he pulled out and wadded his shirttail to protect his hand. Bracing a knee against the rolling deck, he peered through the layered-mica port in the firedoor and watched as he turned the wheel. The parallel rows of long, bright, yellow flames flickered and fell into tiny, dim, red smudges. By guess and by feel, he stopped turning just before they disappeared entirely.

In a minute or two the whistling jet above his head shrank to a petulant, popping gurgle that was mostly hot water. Soon after, the clouds of condensation in the engine room began to subside.

———

Jane had been on boats before. She was almost sure of it. Sometime in her life, maybe as a child, she had taken a ferry ride. She had thought she was prepared to cross a body of water as big as Lake Ontario in a vessel as substantial as *Galatea*. As soon as she finished handing off mooring ropes at the dock, and the boat headed out beyond the breakwater, Jane settled down in the saloon with a book and a glass of iced tea, leaving the technical details of navigation and steering to Willie.

But when they got out of sight of land, and the room began its peculiar rocking-horse motion, she had difficulty focusing on the page. For all its mahogany and marble, the cabin was not the parlor back in Willie's father's house in Roulette. Instead, it was attached to the fun house at an amusement park.

Jane tried looking out the windows for a bit and focusing on the horizon. But from where she sat, all she saw were the frothy tops of the waves rolling past. This view only served to emphasize the degree of motion and the disconnect between what she saw—the level surfaces and vertical planes of the familiar room all around her—and what her inner ear was describing—a kind of lunging, whirling acrobatics.

She wanted to light a cigarette, but when she did the smoke—normally so rich and soothing—suddenly tasted thick and sour to her, like burning leaves, and clotted in her throat. She stubbed out the butt, gagging.

She took a sip of her iced tea, and all that icky sweetness and tart acid collected at the back of her mouth, the top of her throat, and her stomach gave an experimental heave.

She took heavy, panting breaths and suddenly wanted to go up on deck, get some fresh air, feel the stiff breeze on her face.

Jane stood up, and the world changed about her again. The familiar thumping of the engine and the rhythmic creaking of the timbers paused. The cabin seemed to sag sideways, then came to a stop with a hard, slapping jolt. In the immediate silence, the room gave up its awful fore-and-aft pitching and took on a much worse side-to-side rolling. She got to her feet, holding unsteadily to sliding chairs and toppling tables.

Going up on the back deck now—with only those two precious railing wires, threaded between chrome-steel posts along the edge of the hull, to keep her from tumbling off into the water—was no longer a good idea. Jane reversed course and made it to the galley door, which was flapping back and forth on its hinges. Luckily she had already washed the breakfast dishes, so loose pans and crockery were not flying off the kitchen counters. She thought Willie must know what was going on, and went to the door to the engine room on her way to the wheelhouse. As she put her hand on the knob, it occurred to her that the head, with its wide and inviting toilet bowl, might be a useful stop along the way.

When she pulled open the door, however, she plunged her face into a billowing madness of hot steam that smelled like oil and heated brass. Her stomach did a flip-flop right there, and she had to start swallowing mouthfuls of watery saliva really fast.

She saw someone flailing around in the steam, and knew it must be her husband. When she could get breath to speak, she called out, "Willie! Willie! What the hell's going on?"

"Bit of an emergency!" he answered calmly. "Stay in the galley!"

That was all the incentive Jane needed. She stepped back, slammed the door, turned around, and vomited into the sink.

———

As the boiler's relief valve sputtered above his head, barely hinting at the dragon sleeping inside the pressure dome, William Henry tried to understand what had gone wrong with the system as a whole. He had only theoretical knowledge of the steam engine. His father or his daughter would have known how to fix it immediately, but he was stumped, facing a complicated repair aboard a rolling vessel far out of sight of land. Well ... he still had his brain. He was, after all, the professor of logic. He could figure it out.

Some instinct about starting from first principles told William Henry to begin with the boiler. It was obviously making enough steam, too much steam, in fact so much steam that the pressure release valve had popped. Therefore, it was more steam than the engine and all the auxiliary systems, like that fuel feed pump, were currently able to use.

This implied a blockage somewhere, a plugged line or a closed valve, rather than any kind of leak. He checked all the valves he knew about and found them in the same positions he had left them on starting the voyage. The problem was therefore a blockage. But that implied something solid in the pipes, when all the boiler produced was high-pressure steam: a lot of punch but without even the substance of liquid water. It was just possible that the makeup water for the condensate feed had sucked in some trash from outside the hull—a fragment of paper or bit of weed—that had made it past the filter screens, been pushed up inside the boiler, and then blown out into the live steam line. To test this, he opened petcocks along the line, and they all showed residual steam and hot water right up to the engine.

At the engine block itself, he could find no sign of trouble: no leaking steam, no dribbling water, but no indication of movement, either. The flyballs attached to the speed governor on the crankshaft hung limp and still. Whatever was plugging the system must be somewhere up in the block. Since so much of the activity there was hidden under a surface of black iron, William Henry was reduced to examining what he could see from outside—which wasn't much. His eyes traveled downward, along the support stanchions, to the exposed crankshaft and connecting rods, which alternated with the cams and guide rods that actuated the internal slide valves for each cylinder. These valves, as Dani had explained, ducted live steam into either end of the double-acting cylinders during the expansion cycle and exhausted dead steam at the end of the compression cycle.

Except ... the cams working the high-pressure cylinder were jammed. The Persian carpet Jane had brought aboard had somehow shifted with the rise and fall of *Galatea*'s plunging ride across the waves. One of the tassels had caught in the cam, and that pulled in a corner of the thick fabric, jamming the mechanism. As soon as the high-pressure cylinder stopped, the intermediate- and low-pressure cylinders were deprived of its exhaust steam and they also stopped.

Mindful of the damage to his hands if all those cams and rods suddenly started moving again, William Henry shut off the steam line to the engine entirely. He took a grip on the carpet's corner and pulled. The fabric at first held fast but then, when the boat rolled and added the backward pull of his body weight to the strength of his arms, it came free and he fell back against the bulkhead. Pushing the carpet aside, he cut away as much of the tassel that was caught under the cam as he could with his pocket knife. When only a few inaccessible threads were left in the works, he opened the steam valve to feed the engine. He went to the boiler and opened the fuel feed to build up steam, then returned to the engine to see what would happen.

The cam stuttered and worked to mash out those last bits of thread.

The crankshaft turned. The flyballs whirled and came up to speed.

Pure logic and intelligent observation together had fixed the engine.

William Henry went forward to the wheelhouse to regain control of his boat, but first he scooped up that errant carpet. He dumped it in the space between the binnacle and the wheelhouse windows, where it couldn't get into any more trouble.

With the propeller providing thrust and the helm answering, he swung the bow around into the wind, added speed to meet the next wave, and continued on a northwest heading toward the Canadian shore.

Every voyage was destined to experience some kind of crisis, and William Henry figured they had just gone through theirs. He was relieved the problem could be fixed so easily.

9. Change of Name

Jane's stomach remained queasy and her skin clammy through the rest of the afternoon. She lay slumped on the settee in the main saloon with a damp washcloth across her forehead and a bottle of really cold water at hand to keep it wet. Then she simply endured the agony, waiting for this damned voyage to be over. And when it was, she intended to go ashore, find the next bus out of wherever it was they landed, and continue her journey alone.

In late afternoon, with the western sun just beginning to strike her face through the cabin's low windows, the old steamboat's awful rocking motion eased and then died away entirely. Jane lifted her head and looked out. Rather than an endless horizon of rolling waves, she saw perfectly flat water and a near shoreline—near on both sides, like a river, but as straight as if drawn with a ruler. She remembered Willie saying something about a canal before they reached their destination. So her torture was almost at its end.

"Jane?" came a distant call. "Jane!"

She must have dozed off. When she sat up, her head was clear, her stomach settled. In fact, she felt pretty good.

"Jane?" It was Willie, calling from the wheelhouse.

She went forward and stepped up behind him. The bowsprit was pointed at a space of green lawns and trees, like a public park—with the addition of wooden docks sticking out into the river.

"I need you to handle the lines," he said, "while I bring us alongside. Do you feel up to that?"

"Sure," she said.

Jane stepped out the side door and walked up onto the foredeck. A twenty-foot length of white nylon rope was already tied to a cross-shaped post in the middle of the deck. The rope was an inch thick, pale gray with dirt, and softened by sun and abrasion until it felt like silk in her hands. She fed it through the chocks set into the edge of the hull—careful to go *under* the wire railing like Willie had showed her—and coiled the free end in her hand.

Then she waited, standing like a statue, while Willie sent the boat forward and back, turned and twisted the wheel, and edged into the dock against the current—just like parallel-parking a car.

When the boat was still twenty feet out, a young man down the dock noticed and came toward her. He was in his twenties, wore blue jeans cut off at the knee and frayed, and a red nylon tank top that was three sizes too small. The rest of him was bronzed skin, etched muscles, and sun-bleached golden hair.

"Help you with that?" he asked casually.

"Oh, yes, please," Jane said with a smile.

She tossed him the line, and the man pulled in the bow. Jane tore her eyes away from him and ran down the narrow catwalk alongside the cabin to the back deck and the other rope. When Willie kicked the stern in, she jumped down onto the dock, looped the end of the rope around the nearest cleat, and tied it off with the only knot she knew—a double granny.

Suddenly the young man was kneeling beside her. "That won't hold," he said.

"I, ah, no, um, please, show me," she replied.

He untied her knot, spun the rope a couple of times around the base of the cleat, made a loop, twisted it, hooked it over one horn of the cleat, and pulled it tight.

"That's all?" she said. "It's so easy!"

"That's it," he said. "Welcome to Canada, ma'am."

The boy smiled, stood up, and sauntered away, flexing his muscles and leaving Jane feeling deflated by that respectful "ma'am."

Willie appeared through the saloon doors. "Nice job," he called.

"Wasn't he, though?" she replied.

"You feel up to some dinner?"

"Sure. Buying or making?"

Before Willie could reply, an older man in a dark blue uniform with red-and-white maple-leaf shoulder patches and a silver shield came up the dock. "Evening!" he called out. "Does that yacht run on genuine steam?"

"That she does," Willie said. "Built about eighty years ago."

"Well, we sure don't see many like her up here."

"We just crossed over from New York."

"Right, Captain. I'm with the Canadian Customs—Officer Brandt. Do you want to show me your registration and documents?"

"Why don't you come aboard?" Willie said.

While her husband talked to the man in the saloon and spread out paperwork on the dinette for examination, Jane retreated into the galley, cleaned out the sink, and considered what she might cook for dinner. Within a minute, Willie stuck his head around the door.

"We need to show identification," he said. "Do you have your driver's license?"

Jane paused. "Is that absolutely necessary?"

"Yeah—in lieu of a birth certificate."

She retrieved her purse, dug out her California license, and handed it to him.

Willie took it, glanced at the picture—a good one, taken eight years ago, before the bruising started—then froze. "Whose name is this?" he said, but quietly, so that Officer Brandt wouldn't hear.

"Mine," she whispered back.

"You're 'Jane Bell' now? Where did *that* come from?"

"It's just a name. It's like, you know, out of a hat."

" 'Wheelock' wasn't good enough for you?"

"It was too easy to find," she said.

"We'll talk about this later."

"Please, let's not."

William Henry had decided back when Jane first reappeared that his best course would be to move cautiously, probe her stories and past history only gently, and prepare to withdraw quickly when challenged. He had already seen, years ago, how badly Jane could react to suspicion and criticism, and he had no reason to think she had changed in that regard. Perhaps his suspicions and his probings had been the match that ignited her first psychotic break. Best to put off any confrontation for now.

10. Filling Up

THE FOLLOWING MORNING William Henry gathered his jerry cans from the lazarette, took them across the park to a pay phone, and called for a taxi to take him into town. When the cab arrived, the driver helped him load the cans into the trunk. Then the man turned to him, "Where to, sir?"

"I need to buy fuel for a steam engine," William Henry replied, pointing toward *Galatea,* which was tied up at the dock and just visible through the trees.

"What's she run on, coal?"

"No, she burns oil."

"You mean diesel oil?"

"Any kind of oil."

The man stared. "So … you got a boiler in there?"

"Yes, for a steam engine. Oil fed, with nozzles and a pump."

"You can't buy diesel at the marina, you know. It's not for working boats."

"I know that, but any kind of oil will do. If you've got a garage in town, I'd like to buy their used motor oil. That burns just fine."

"There's a couple of garages, but they don't sell diesel, either."

"Just waste oil—from engine tune-ups. I'll take it off their hands."

At the first stop, an Esso station, the mechanic wanted to know if William Henry was bothered by metal filings at all, because some of the engines he worked on were pretty old and worn, and customers sometimes reused their oil filters.

William Henry thought there was a filter in the fuel line but wasn't sure. He took the oil anyway. How likely was it that a tiny grain of metal would float in the oil, make it through the feed pump, and clog more than one or two of the jets? He didn't know but, according to Bill Gibbs, the previous owner burned anything and everything, including cooking oil.

At the Petro-Canada station, the manager asked if he would take synthetic oil.

"I guess so," William Henry said. "It burns, doesn't it?"

"Well … get it hot enough and it smokes."

"But is the oil flammable or not?"

"It's supposed to be safe."

"Then I guess not."

It took four more stops and a lot more questions—the last stop a hamburger joint which was just about to drain its french-fryer for fresh grease, before the lunchtime crowd—but finally William Henry had his forty gallons. And all it cost was twenty dollars in cab fare.

11. Appreciation for Galatea

While Willie was off on his errands, Jane stayed aboard. She stowed their bedding and made up the settee in the saloon, cleaned up the breakfast dishes, and kept herself busy with small chores. As it was a hot morning, she left windows open along both sides of the cabin. Occasionally, as people passed by out in the park, she could hear their comments. Most of them were simply admiring, but one exchange gave Jane pause.

"What a pretty old boat!" said a woman's voice.

"More of a yacht, dear," a man answered softly.

"Yacht, then. I wonder where it's going?"

"Boat like that doesn't have to be *going* anywhere. They're probably just out for a cruise, like all the other pleasure-boaters."

"I wonder how far he's going, then. Maybe all the way to Lake Huron?"

"If so, he's in for a surprise. He'll have trouble with the marine railway, if not with lift locks at Peterborough and Kirkfield. I doubt they can take a hull that long."

"Hush, dear. The owner must know about things like that."

"Not many of them know what really lies up ahead."

How much, Jane wondered, did Willie know?

Then the couple passed out of hearing.

12. First Hurdle

JUST TWO MILES upstream from Trenton, they came to the first lock on the waterway. While the river curved away to the right, toward the ominous white wall of a dam in the distance, a narrow channel to the left led up to the lock gates. They were closed, showing massive, stacked beams of black timber that angled inward toward the lock basin. In the bright morning sunshine, William Henry could see that the seams between the timbers wept with dark streaks of water from the pressure behind them.

He maneuvered along the downstream concrete quay, and Jane leapt ashore to tie up. The lockmaster came out to greet them both, and William Henry heard once more the familiar exclamations about *Galatea*'s heritage, her graceful lines, and her antique means of propulsion. The man explained that the lock was currently draining and would open momentarily. He said the full cycle took about thirty minutes, and while they waited he collected the lock fee. The amount was based on boat length and, considering *Galatea*'s waterline plus bowsprit and the overhang at the fantail, approximated a commercial barge rate.

When the gates finally opened, swinging back against the inside lock wall, Jane was ready to cast off and climb aboard, but William Henry motioned to stop her. Before they could enter, the traffic coming downstream had to exit: two cabin cruisers, a small sailboat with its mast unstepped, and three canoes whose occupants were too tired or too lazy to unload and portage around the dam. Then William Henry stepped back into the wheelhouse, engaged the engine, signaled Jane to cast off, and steamed into the lock.

They were suddenly facing a wall of bare, wet, algae-covered concrete that stood at least twenty feet high. William Henry angled toward it on the starboard side, where earlier that morning he had strung out a row of air-filled, vinyl boat fenders to protect the hull's clean white paint.

Jane was standing on the foredeck with the docking line in her hand, looking up at the top of the wall. "What do I do now?" she called.

William Henry cut the engine and leaned out the wheelhouse doorway. "You go back and fend off the stern. I'll handle the bow."

She passed him, heading for the catwalk alongside the main cabin. In the narrow space she turned sideways so as not to get her white shorts and blue-striped sailor top smeared with the algae.

"Take a boathook," he called after her.

"Yes, Captain," she replied.

The gates had already swung closed behind them. Almost immediately the water's surface inside the lock began to churn and bubble as the lockmaster opened the sluice gates and let the chamber from the upstream side. *Galatea*'s hull was pushed toward the wall.

Jane, on the aft deck, leveled the point of the hook against the concrete. She turned and called forward, "Just hold her off?"

At the same moment, the bubbling water came up between the hull and the wall, pushing them out toward the lock's center.

"Well, watch that we don't drift out, either," he called back.

"How do I do that?" she yelled.

William Henry had already found one of the steel cables that descended from the top of the wall and were evenly spaced about every twenty feet along it. He had looped a length of bow line around and under the nearest cable. He found he could control the hull's position by alternately pulling on the cable and pushing against the concrete.

"Hold on to that cable right next to your head," he told her, pointing.

"Eww! It's all slimy!" she cried, touching it with her fingertips.

"Use a rope." He held up the excess bow line. "Like this."

Jane dropped the boathook, got the stern line, and looped it around her cable. Then she retrieved her hook, couched it under her right arm like a knight's lance, and pushed bravely. William

Henry saw that she was working too hard, trying to keep tension on both the cable and the hook, so that the hull never strayed more than a foot from the wall. But he thought better of trying to explain everything to her inside the first half hour of their travels on the waterway. Her method worked well enough.

When they got to the top of the lock, he was glad they did not try to hold on to the cable itself, because the edge of the wall where it went over was now a couple of feet below *Galatea*'s gunwale. The water stopped churning, the surface inside the lock turned smooth, and the lockmaster went forward to crank open the upper gates.

As those gates went flush against the outer wall, beyond the end of the chamber, the lockmaster motioned them through. William Henry and Jane let go of their ropes and she jumped ashore. Jane walked up to the center point of the hull and pushed off—just as William Henry had shown her when leaving the dock—then grabbed the handrail along the cabin top and scrambled aboard.

Soon Jane joined him in the wheelhouse. He noticed that she had a streak of green algae on her forehead. He wiped it off with a fingertip and showed it to her. She grinned at him.

"Only forty-four more to go," he said.

"Oh, joy," she said, rolling her eyes.

13. Sister, Wife, Whatever

When Eric Bell rolled into Byzantium, he knew he was days late and shit out of options. First off, it took a day or two for him to even know he had a problem. When his old lady didn't show at the Orange County airport as planned, Bell waited for the phone call. Rule was, the cops, the narcs, the feds had to give you one phone call, and that call went to the club—not to your lawyer, your bail bondsman, or your mommy. The club came first.

But no phone call came, so Bell had lost a whole day and a half right there. And then, when he finally figured out Jane hadn't been picked up but instead had done a number, he made the mistake of arranging a private meet with the Hell's Legion MC president, hoping to negotiate his way past their problem. He told Hawker, "Your horse, your problem." To which Hawker took three long, raking bites out of his yellow-stained mustache with that snaggle tooth of his and said, "Your bitch, your problem. Deal with her. If not, you *both* become our problem."

Trouble with that was, Bell had no way of knowing where Jane had gone. So he spent another day tearing through the apartment and all her things. Maybe she'd left a letter, a postcard, phone number, receipt—even a matchbook—anything for a clue to the theft she must have planned far in advance. But nothing.

Bell knew Jane had no friends outside the club and had never heard her talk about family, no mother or father, no old boyfriends, no entanglements. He spent another day tracking down her judo instructor, Sam Lighthorse. The redskin wasn't surprised Jane had split. In fact, he seemed pleased she had taken a big chunk of the club's product with her. Bell would have punched Lighthorse out for that—except he'd tried doing it once before, for the way the man looked at Jane, just on general principle, and it didn't work. Bell couldn't land a blow. Sneaky injun fought dirty.

That left Bell with just two clues, both of them more than ten years old. First, the little town in Upstate New York where he'd picked Jane up as he came west on that first road trip: Byzantium. Second, the name she had copped to but changed soon as

335

she got to California: Wheelock. Those two facts weren't much to go on, but Hawker was getting serious, and Bell had no better answers and was starting to look like an accomplice. So it seemed a good idea to get out of town. The next day he lit out on a cross-country iron butt, twenty-seven hundred miles in ninety-four hours, just hanging onto the handlebars and keeping the throttle wide open. And here he was.

A fast cruise up and down the main and cross streets showed Byzantium was a college town. Bell didn't think Jane had the smarts to be a student, much less a teacher—more likely a waitress or barmaid. That gave him an idea, and he pulled the big Electra-Glide in at the first bar he found, a place called the Ace of Spades.

"You look thirsty, friend," said the bartender, eyeing his dusty leathers.

"Could do with a beer," Bell admitted, levering his butt onto a barstool.

The man drew a glass from the tap and set it before him.

"What brings you to town?"

"Looking for someone."

"You got a preference?"

" 'Scuse me?" Bell said.

"Is your preference for a female someone—or male?" The man leered at him.

"Nothing like that. Looking for my"—well, what *was* Jane?—"my sister."

"She got a name?"

"Wheelock."

The bartender's head jerked up and the leer was gone. "Short woman, reddish hair … about forty now, but still awful pretty?"

Bell put down his beer. "You've seen her?"

"Not lately, but I heard she's around."

"Any idea where I could find her?"

"Hooked up with her husband."

"Uh-huh. What's his name?"

The man shrugged. "Wheelock?"

"Okay, so where do I find this guy?"

"He's a professor, over on the campus."

Bell laid a dollar on the bar and stood up.

"Tell her …" the bartender began. "Tell her Lou says 'Hi,' "

The campus was deserted, wide green lawns and empty buildings. Bell guessed that, it being summertime, the students were all gone until fall. But professors and their wives, they were permanent residents, right? So he still had a chance of finding Jane. But where to look? Even when school was out, one place would still be open for business—wherever it was they handled the money. It took Bell ten minutes with the campus map, and a search of his memory back to the year he tried a semester of college on the GI Bill, to locate the Bursar's Office. And there the gray-haired woman inside a brass-barred cage knew the Wheelock name right away.

"He bought that funny old steamboat," she said.

"What did he want a boat for?" Bell wondered.

She shrugged. "Because they tore down his house?"

"All right. So, where does he keep this boat?"

The woman looked him up and down. He guessed his leathers, denim, and layer of road grime were putting her off. "Why do you want to know?" she asked.

"I'm looking for Wheelock's sister," Bell said casually.

"Didn't know he had one." The woman squinted at him.

"What? No, I mean … *his wife!* He's married to *my* sister."

"Oh? Yes, I heard about her. She came back."

"So they're both on the boat?" Bell guessed.

"Probably," she said. "But it's gone now."

He screamed inside. "Uh, where did it go?"

"Out on the lake somewhere, most likely."

"Well, does anyone know where they went?"

"I don't know. Maybe their daughter does."

"They have a daughter? Okay, where is she?"

"Here on campus. They gave her a dorm room."

"Well, can you direct me?" Bell asked nicely.

"You sure you're her uncle?" the woman said.

"Positive!"

With the name of the dormitory, Durrell Hall, and the room number, 301, from the Bursar lady, Bell checked the map and went off to finally get a straight answer. He walked through the building's front door, right past the sign saying "No Men Upstairs." Like the rest of campus, the place was deserted, so who was going to challenge him? He climbed the stairs and knocked on the door.

"Who is it?" came a girl's voice from inside.

"Delivery for Miss Wheelock," Bell lied. He figured claiming Jane was his sister and explaining to this Danielle person that it made her his niece wouldn't wash. Not with a real relative who would know the score.

There was a rustle from inside the room. "Uh, you're not supposed to come up here," said the voice. But he heard the click as she unlocked the door anyway.

Bell figured charm and persuasion weren't going to work. And he was tired of making nice and getting bull crap in return. He planted his size thirteen boot on the door next to the latch and shoved hard.

The door exploded inward and he was treated to the sight of a tall, pale girl, all legs and arms, wearing just running shorts and a tee shirt, flying backward through the room. She landed halfway across the single bed, bounced once, and fell behind it on the floor. But she was spunky, and by the time he got into the room she was back on her feet to face him.

Bell knew how to deal with spunk. He took two boxer's steps forward and put the old pile driver right in her breadbasket.

The girl whooped, bent over, and went down clutching herself.

Now that they had established who was boss, they could begin making progress.

————

Dani knew she'd made a fatal error the instant her hand finished turning the lock. But before she could secure the door, it crashed open. The knob smacked her hand away, breaking some of the long, brittle bones. The door's edge cut into her face alongside her nose and up across her forehead. The force of the blow threw her back over the bed. She scrambled up to meet her attacker, but before she could raise her arms, he had leapt inside the room and punched her hard in the stomach. She went down in a heap and actually left the world for a little while.

When she came back, she was sitting upright in the desk chair. Her arms were tied at her sides and against the chair back with several pairs of her nylons knotted together. She tried to move her feet, but they were tied to the legs—with more nylons, she guessed.

The man, a hulking brute in dusty black leather and faded denim, stood in front of her and stooped over to look directly into her face. He had eyes the color of storm clouds set in sunburned skin. His beard and hair were long and might once have been blond but were going gray—although that might also have been from the dust.

"You awake now, Danielle?" he asked.

"Who the hell are you?" she demanded.

"A friend of your mother's."

"*You're* military intelligence?"

"What? Huh? She told you that?"

"Or are you a Russian drug smuggler?"

"Russian?" he said. "Oh, that bitch tells lies!"

"Be careful what you call my mother!" Dani said.

"And *you* be careful about anything she tells you."

"All right, noted. But still, who the hell are you?"

"The guy she's been living with for ten years."

"Oh ...!"

Wherever Jane had been, whatever she'd been doing, Dani never stopped to think she might have taken another man into her life, other than Daddy. And if Dani had been told about such a person, she would never have imagined a middle-aged biker wearing outlaw colors. In the mirror on her closet door, she could see the gaudy embroidery across the back of his leathers—with "Hell's Legion" on the top rocker, then an army of skeletons in Greco-Roman battle gear parading through the middle, and "Motorcycle Club" on the bottom rocker. The notion of her mother spending any time at all with such a person was just too bizarre ... too lower class, white trash, *Sturm und Drang* ... too silly.

"You've got to be kidding me." She laughed out loud.

"It's not a joke." He punched her in the face.

Dani went away for a while again.

When she came back, he was still standing there. "Look, I know your mother's on a steamboat your old man bought," he said. "Just tell me where they went. It's important I find her."

"If I tell you, then you'll go and hurt them."

"Yeah, and if you don't tell me, I'll hurt *you*."

He punched lower down, in the stomach again.

Dani felt something soft tear open inside her.

Suddenly she had blood between her legs.

"Oh, God!"

"God ain't here to help you, little girl."

He hit her twice more before she told.

"Canada. Ontario," she said at last. "North of Trenton. Canal."

"Where exactly?" he asked softly. "Show me on a map."

"I don't ... Not hard to find ... follow the waterway."

"Up a canal? That's it? Then where do they go?"

"Around the lakes ... Superior ... Erie ..."

Dani went away for the last time without being hit. When she woke up, he was gone. Her bonds were cut and she was lying on the bed. But she was still bleeding.

14. AGE TURNS TO BEAUTY

JANE HAD BEEN sharing a bed with Willie for three days now—four, counting the night before the crossing—and he still hadn't touched her. Sure, on the narrow foldaway that pulled out of the saloon's settee, they occasionally brushed elbows and knees, and once she'd awakened to find his stomach lodged comfortably against the small of her back, but these contacts had led nowhere and to nothing. Their relationship was not amorous. Not even a good-night kiss.

That bothered Jane. Not that she craved a renewal of their previous, hotly sexual relationship, but its absence left her in doubt about what Willie was thinking and feeling. She knew she was walking a knife edge here, and that somewhere ahead, perhaps in days or a week, probably not more than a month from now, her past would catch up with them. When that happened, she wanted Willie on her side, bound to her with every tie she could weave during this tranquil in-between-time. And she knew instinctively the strongest tie of all for binding a man to a woman.

So, as the old steamboat made its slow, thumping way down the rivers and up the narrow lakes that knit the canal system together, with the high summer sun beating down on the hard, blue water that led between fresh, green fields, Jane decided to pull out her big guns. While Willie handled the controls up in the wheelhouse, steering the boat down a long, straight stretch that promised no more locks for another hour or two, she carried her suitcase back into the saloon. Among the clothes she had bought for the trip, Jane spent a good hour over one purchase. She had tried on a dozen candidates for size, shape, color, and fit, examining herself critically in the store's three-way mirror with each one.

Now she took out the tiny pink bikini that had been her final choice. It was hardly an item of clothing—more like four small triangles of stretchy fabric held together with straps and strings. She quickly stripped off her shorts, blouse, and underwear. Working without a mirror, it took her a bit longer than expected to get everything in place and all the knots just right. But finally she was ready.

She went through to the engine room and picked up a bath towel from the cabinet at the back by the head, then walked casually into the wheelhouse.

"I'm going to get some sun out on the front deck," she told Willie. "All right?"

He turned around from tending the big ship's wheel, glanced at her, stopped, dropped his jaw, and stared.

"I won't be in your way," she said. "Will I?"

The boat was already veering off its heading, toward the shore, toward the side where Jane was standing next to him. She reached forward, pretending not to notice when her breast brushed against his arm, and straightened the wheel. "Will you be okay?"

"Yeah, sure," he sputtered. "You go ahead. Get some sun. Good idea."

Jane smiled at Willie, turned, and walked out through the side door. She went forward to the clear space on the deck and spread her towel. She dipped one knee and then the other, knelt on the edge of the towel, launched herself forward slowly onto the palms of her hands, and lay down—conscious all the time of the view she was presenting to the wheelhouse.

In a minute she was up again and went inside. "Forgot my suntan lotion," she explained as she passed through the wheelhouse. When she came back, she repeated the kneeling and leaning performance, with the added attraction of spreading the lotion and rubbing it into her skin wherever she could reach—and she had a lot of exposed skin to cover.

When all that was done, Jane lay quietly, face down, and smiled.

Let him grumble and frump and pretend he didn't notice.

Girls won. Every time. It was the law of nature.

———

It was just lucky, William Henry knew, that the waterway ran straight, wide, and empty at this point. He wasn't sure he could handle any tricky steering or traffic to dodge. He tried to keep his eyes on the channel, but every few minutes they drifted down to Jane's figure, barely covered by the triangle of pink cloth stretched tight across her buttocks and the string knotted just below her shoulderblades.

God, she was a beautiful woman!

She had kept her figure all these years.

That body showed no hint of flab or wrinkle.

He tried to remember the woman who had left him ten years ago and how she had been, right at the end: the dull apathy, the glaring anger, the frenzied accusations, the confusion, the fear. He could recall the snarling woman in a blue-serge bathrobe, the demented woman who pulled a policeman's gun on him—but failed to pull the trigger, he reminded himself—and the confused woman who crashed their car and wandered in the woods with their frightened daughter. But he could also remember, although more dimly, the years of happiness, of sharing silly jokes, of cuddling before crackling logs in the fireplace, of chopping and stirring and tasting as they made dinner together, of making mad, frantic love in the bedroom upstairs. He remembered Jane as once being the smart, capable, no-nonsense, wisecracking woman who had put the chairman of the Sociology Department in his place and faced down the president of the Faculty Wives Club.

He missed that woman, William Henry realized. Her departure had left a giant hole in his life. He had not really smiled in all the time she had been gone.

But who, he had to ask himself, had come back now? The mystery woman, the secret agent, Russian speaker, member of an army group so elite they could dispense with rank and protocol? To be sure, she carried Jane's old style and dash, the cocky attitude, the offhand sense of confidence. But she had something more now, a gleam of frenzy in the eyes, a barely suppressed anxiety, a brittle quality, like a spring wound tight to the point of snapping. Maybe Jane wasn't crazy anymore, had overcome or burned through her paranoid schizophrenia. Maybe she had gained control of herself and turned all that negative energy into something strong and powerful, enabling her to live a better, more useful life than that of a faculty wife and mother. But maybe, too, Jane had progressed to a deeper, more disturbed stage of the illness, living in full-blown fantasy, fueled by God knew what lies and reckless acts pursued over the years, heading for a breakdown that would make their tussle in the emergency room seem calm and civilized by comparison.

William Henry didn't know what was going on with Jane.

He sensed it was important for him to learn the truth.

But, damn! His wife was still a beautiful woman.

15. ALERTING THE AUTHORITIES

DANI LAY IN one of the five beds in the university health clinic. She was their only patient, and after official business hours—which had ended at five in the afternoon, because they were between semesters—the clinic was echoingly deserted, except for Dani and a night nurse. The woman, whose badge identified as "Cheryl," told Dani she was on call in case of emergencies, but Dani suspected the nurse was only there to check on her.

Supposedly, Dani could not be moved for fear of a possible concussion. But other than a slight headache, that was the least of her injuries. Her left cheekbone was broken where the edge of the door had struck her face, and she was scheduled for surgery in a day or two to have the break "decompressed" and repaired with a steel plate. Meanwhile, the blow had given her a massively blackened left eye. The cut on her forehead had taken eighteen stitches—the tiny, precise kind that doctors used on the layers of muscle and skin when working on a woman's face. Her right hand was broken in three places and was now in a plaster cast. And finally, as one of the doctors had explained with great sadness, she had "lost the baby." However, they had managed to stop the bleeding and given her a dozen more stitches, all deep inside.

Lost the baby that nobody knew about.

That meant no longer pregnant.

No longer a problem.

Dani had bigger concerns right then. A dangerous lunatic, an outlaw biker, was chasing after her mother and father. Dani had only the haziest understanding of why he was so angry. But if he was willing to tie her up and torture her just to find them, he probably wanted to kill them. Kill Jane or kill Daddy? In his state of cold, psychotic rage, the one implied the other.

"Can you help me make a phone call?" she asked Cheryl.

"You're not supposed to exert yourself."

"This is important, life or death."

"Who do you want to call?"

That was the question.

William Henry and Jane were off cruising a couple of hundred miles of lakes and rivers. They might be anywhere by this time. Dani understood that the waterway had a series of fixed points, "locks" that changed the water level, and these were run by special people called "lockmasters." She might leave messages for them to be on the lookout for *Galatea* and warn her mother and father, but she had no idea how to contact a lockmaster. That left the police—except they were called something else in Canada. Mounties?

With Cheryl holding the phone to her ear, and the campus switchboard making the connection, Dani was soon talking with a dispatcher—more likely a public relations spokesman—at the Royal Canadian Mounted Police in Ottawa.

"I'm trying to contact my parents who are vacationing in Ontario."

"Where exactly in Ontario are they, ma'am?"

"That's just it. They're cruising on the Trent-Severn canal."

"I see. Now, where exactly on the canal, please?"

"Somewhere between Trent and Severn, I guess."

"Port Severn's a township. The Trent is a river, not a place."

"I don't know *where* then," she said. "They're just cruising."

"Thousands of people use the waterway this time of year."

"Can you leave word with the lockmasters or something?"

"You want them to look for two people among all those—"

"They're traveling in an old steamboat, very recognizable."

"I see. And what's the name of this riverboat?"

"Steam launch, actually. Named the *Galatea*."

"*Gal of* Who? No, wait, *Gala* … *Gala* What?"

"*Galatea*. She was a Greek goddess."

"Never heard of her. Spell it, please."

"G-A-L-A-T-E-A. It's the Pygmalion legend."

"Pig-what? Pigmies? What about pigmies?"

"Nothing about pigmies! I need to get word to my parents!"

"No need to shout, miss. … All right, give me their names."

"Professor William Henry Wheelock. And Jane Wheelock."

A pause. "Very good, I have that. And what's the message?"

"A maniac is coming after them. He's going to kill them."

"I ... see. And what's this maniac's name, please, miss?"

"I don't know his name, but he shouldn't be hard to spot."

"Oh, and why is that? Is he raving? Foaming at the mouth?"

"No, he's one of Hell's Legion. You'll recognize him by the army on his back, all skeletons wearing Greek or Roman helmets and holding round shields and long flaming spears. He's very dangerous and I think he's—"

"Thank you, miss. I see. We'll get word out to the lockmasters right away."

Just as the connection broke, Dani heard the *rip* and *crackle* of paper being torn and wadded.

16. Appreciation for Galatea

While they waited to go into Lock No. 13 at Campbellford, an elderly man approached as Jane stood on the quay holding the stern line. "That's the prettiest boat I've seen on the waterway in a long time," he said.

"Do you want to come aboard?"

"Oh? Um, no … I'd better not."

"I'm sure it's safe," Jane said. "And I don't think you can hurt anything. *Galatea* is old, and she's been through a lot, but she's still here."

"No, it's just … I don't want to get the sickness again."

"Do you get seasick? But this is just a canal—all flat water."

"I mean the sickness of loving boats too much. They're like a beautiful woman. They call to you. They entice you. And then they steal your soul."

"Is that what women do?" Jane purred.

"Not all of them. But a fine old boat like this … it does."

17. Couple of Days Behind

FOLLOWING A ROUTE he traced on road maps picked up at gas stations along the way, Eric Bell raced around the eastern end of Lake Ontario, threaded a path from bridge to bridge through the Thousand Islands, and worked his way back west again through Canada to the town the Wheelock girl had mentioned: Trenton. He went right down to the municipal dock and started looking for boats.

He found plenty of boats—speedboats, sailboats, houseboats, pontoon boats, cabin cruisers, rowboats, kayaks, and canoes. None of them fit the description of any "steamboat" he could imagine.

After parking the Electra-Glide on a side street, stashing his vest with the Hell's Legion club colors, and trying not to scowl too much, Bell started asking people on the waterfront.

"Excuse me, sir, I'm looking for an old steamboat."

"Have you seen a steamboat come through lately?"

"My sister and her husband are vacationing up here on the canal."

"Yes, I'm supposed to meet up with them. On a steamboat."

"Has anyone seen a *God-damned, fucking* steamboat?"

A couple of people thought they might have seen one.

One old man assured him steamships used the Seaway.

Someone tapped Bell on the shoulder. He whirled around, crouching and reaching for the nine-millimeter Parabellum he kept tucked into the backside of his jeans. When he saw the blue uniform with the silver badge and the maple leaves, he tossed his head, shuffled, grinned, turned the reach into a scratch, and then laughed out loud to show how loose and friendly he was.

"I understand you're looking for an old boat?" the officer said.

"Yeah, my sister and her husband are vacationing up here—"

"Elegant old yacht? White hull? 'Bout eighty feet long?"

"That sounds about right," Bell agreed, still dazed.

"I processed their paperwork—but I couldn't say as those two were married. His name Wheelock, driver's license issued in New York. Her name Bell, out of California."

"That's them. When did you see them?"

"Couple of days ago … maybe a week."

"Where were they headed?" Bell asked.

The man shrugged. "Up the waterway."

"Thank you, officer. Thank you kindly."

Bell got himself a chart of the Trent-Severn Waterway at a shop in town and compared it with a roadmap of the state—except they called it a "province" here—from a gas station. The roads through the region, what he could find of them, were mostly set in a grid angled toward the northwest. The waterway, or the rivers and pieces of canal that linked up a series of slender lakes, angled toward the northeast. He couldn't find a lot of places where the two of them came together. But Bell spread his chart and the map on the table in a diner where he wolfed down two burgers, some fries, and a piece of pie. By the time he was finishing his coffee, he had marked a route that would take him back and forth to likely points of intersection.

Sooner or later he would catch up with the "elegant old yacht."

The yacht would have Jane and his kilo of heroin.

Then the fun would begin in earnest.

18. HALFWAY MARK

JANE WAS NOT having as much fun as she had thought it would be, cruising the canals in a pleasure boat. For one thing, they seemed to be going nowhere with a maximum amount of trouble and fuss. Days were spent chug-chugging up one tiny lake that hardly made a blob under Willie's finger when he pointed it out on the map. Then they turned around and chug-chugged back down another lake. And like as not, between the one and the other, they had to work their passage through a lock or two—or three—which meant Jane was hanging on cables slimed with green algae and pushing off walls dripping with still more algae and mud. In between such times of excitement, Jane put on her tiny pink bikini, wiggled her fanny up and down the deck, and lay on her bath towel. But, so far, all that got her was one hell of a sunburn.

When they came to the town of Peterborough and Lock No. 21, Jane suddenly felt uneasy. She had a premonition about the place but couldn't put her finger on just what it was.

Instead of the usual wooden gates that trickled at the seams and hinges, Willie steered the boat into a basin of still, green water dominated by three stone piers, each more than sixty feet tall, like the ramparts of a castle. Between two of them hung what Jane could see, as they swung around in the channel, what looked like a huge bathtub boxed in trusswork and balanced on a massive steel piston.

Now she remembered: someone at the dock back in Trenton had warned someone else that the lift locks at Peterborough, both there and someplace else as well, were not long enough for *Galatea*'s hull. That Willie's voyage would come to grief right here.

Standing beside him in the wheelhouse, Jane wanted to warn him that the boat wouldn't fit, that they would have to turn back. Up at the far end of the nearer bathtub, which on their side was sunk in the water of the basin, she could see a sheer stone wall marking the dead end of the upper channel. She could imagine the steamboat's delicate bowsprit pushing forward, lodging against the stone blocks, then snapping off when the lift tank started to rise. The steel cables that braced the first of *Galatea's* two masts would give way, and the mast itself would fall right across the wheelhouse, killing them both.

"Come forward, Cap'n." The lockmaster, standing on a walkway inside the truss, motioned for Willie to keep moving, then held up a hand for him to stop.

The bowsprit wasn't within twenty feet of the stone wall.

"You want to go tie on?" Willie asked her.

As Jane stepped out on the back deck, she could see the stern was well inside the dimensions of the tank. As she looped her line around a cleat along the walkway, a gate slowly rose from the bottom of the channel and sealed them inside the tank. Without so much as rippling the surface of the water, the tank hoisted them into the sky while the entry basin and surrounding land fell away.

So much for the opinion of strangers overheard back in Trenton.

When they stopped moving and Willie signaled her to cast off, Jane looked ahead. Already the gate at the far end of their tank was subsiding into the channel, and beyond the bowsprit lay a long, straight stretch of canal.

"Lock twenty-one," Willie said as she rejoined him in the wheelhouse. "Almost halfway. Isn't this fun?"

"Yeah," she echoed. "Fun."

Better than dodging bullets.

19. First Time in Ten Years
... and Counting

When it was over, William Henry could not quite say how it all happened. They had tied up for the night below Lock No. 26 at Lakefield, planning to go through first thing in the morning. While Jane kicked the fenders over the side and tied off fore and aft, he went through the engine room opening valves and twisting petcocks to release steam pressure and drain overflow from the hot well. With these chores done, they met up in the galley.

Jane had obviously been planning to get more tanning done that day, because she put on her bikini right after lunch. But then they entered a string of five locks in a row, starting with Nassau Mills, all spaced just a mile or two apart. So she spent the afternoon running around the deck, jumping ashore with lines, fending off, holding on, and all the time wearing no more than a sun hat, sneakers, and two strips of pink cloth.

Now, in the heat of late afternoon, she stood in the galley, half bent over, facing into the open door of the icebox. William Henry had thought Jane was checking what she had on hand for dinner, but then he saw a wisp of fog drift out. Jane scooped it with her closed fingers and pulled the bit of moisture toward her throat and chest. Then she ran the hand, cupping whatever coolness it held, down her stomach and over her thighs. She pulled a bottle of beer out of a six-pack, touched it briefly to her forehead, then rolled it slowly across her belly below the navel.

It was the most sensuous performance he had ever witnessed.

Without a thought for consequences, William Henry moved forward, touched her shoulder, ran his hands down her back and under her arms, held her by the hips. Jane reacted without haste, setting the bottle on the counter, stepping back into him, reaching her arms above her head. He buried his face in her hair and pulled her close. From there, the encounter could only have one ending.

Ten minutes later they were lying drenched in sweat, side by side on the cork mats which covered the galley's varnished floor, with the icebox door above them and no longer exuding mist or cool air.

"What did we just do?" he asked quietly, feeling something was now lost.

"What men and women are supposed to do," Jane replied.

"I'm not sure it's such a good idea—"

"Hush," she told him.

In another ten minutes Jane rolled toward him, threw her leg across his hips, and started them on a second round. Whatever she had planned for dinner, it was going to be late.

20. A Miss by Less Than a Mile

As *Galatea* pulled away from Lock No. 31 at Buckhorn, Jane stood on the back deck trying to coil her rope in a neat spiral, the way sailors did it in the movies. It was harder than she had imagined. The rope had a certain way it wanted to bend, and in the direction she was coiling it, the loops were trying to lift up from the deck and flop over. She was becoming more and more frustrated with her efforts, when suddenly a silver flash caught the corner of her eye and her ear caught an all-too-familiar roar.

Jane straightened and turned to look. A big, black motorcycle, all glinting chrome and stuttering exhaust, bounced over the green lawn behind the lock's apron, climbed up onto the cement quay, and slewed to a stop at the water's edge. The rider dismounted and ran down the quay to where it ended above the mud and brush of the canal bank.

Even at this distance, just less than a mile, she recognized the cut of the rider's leathers and the fading blond of his hair and beard. However he had managed it, Eric had traced her, followed her, and found her. And if Harley's could roll on water, he would have caught her, too.

Careful to give him no sign she noticed, Jane bent to continue her rope trick, fudged with it a minute more, then casually went down into the main cabin. Only then did her knees start shaking. She realized she might be a day or less away from being killed.

She suddenly focused on the charts Willie had left spread across the dinette table that morning after planning their day's run. Instead of the mess and nuisance she usually considered them, Jane now realized the charts might tell her what she needed to know so desperately. As a passenger on this cruise, she had no idea what roads and towns connected with the canal system. Specifically, how easy was it to go from one point to another over the land? Or rather, having found them in Buckhorn, did Eric have an easy ride to the next lock or lift bridge? These were the main stopping points, where the boat might be held up for a hour or more, making them a likely target. Or was his route more complicated and delayed?

She studied the chart on top for ten minutes and concluded it was no good. Each section of canal or lake dealt mostly with the buoys, navigation hazards, and sight lines over the water. It showed only an inch or so of land on either side of the bank, with the towns sketched in as fuzzy patches beyond the water-front and roads mere stubs leading off into white paper.

Well, her husband would know about all that—but how to ask him?

Jane went through the engine room to the wheelhouse.

"Hi," she said, stepping up to stand beside him.

"Hello yourself. What's up?" he asked.

"I was just wondering how far it is to the next lock ..."

"A ways. Pigeon Lake, then Buckhorn Lake, and on to Bobcaygeon."

"Oh, thank God!"

"Uh, why so glad?"

"I'm just getting tired, is all." She punched him playfully. "You're working me too hard on this voyage, Captain."

Eric Bell watched the boat head off down the channel. It was a steamboat, all right. He could tell from the tall stack and plume of black smoke. And, from the size and what he could see of the gleaming white hull and the gay yellow-and-green trim on the cabin, he guessed it could pass for the description of a yacht.

He'd been chasing rumors of an old steamboat on the canal for days now, back and forth across western Ontario, and always arriving a few hours or minutes after it had already left. This was the first time Bell had actually seen the boat.

He could also see someone standing on the back deck. It was hard to tell at this distance, but he thought it might be a woman, dressed in white shorts, pink halter top, and sun hat. If he looked real hard, he could convince himself she was rather small and had reddish hair.

Bell pulled the map out of his back pocket. It was more than twenty miles by water to the next lock at Bobcaygeon, but only fifteen miles by road. So he could get there in twenty minutes, well ahead of the old boat. Maybe too far ahead, though. Like as not, they might tie up someplace for the night. So then they could be two days getting to Bobcaygeon. And if Bell sat on the dock there, waiting, for a couple of days, all day long, he was sure to attract attention. He'd already drawn stares from the small-town cops and been pulled over on the road a couple of times by the sheriff's deputies. Country people generally didn't like motorcycles. And they for sure didn't understand the Legion of the Damned on the back of his leathers. If he was in jail, he could miss the old boat again. So close …

Ah, the hell with this! Bell thought. He knew where they were going. The girl had said so. Why did he want to chase Jane and her new boyfriend all over Ontario? He could wait in comfort up ahead, where he would have allies and resources, people to do the watching for him. Let the old boat come to him.

Bell walked back to his bike, maneuvered it down off the concrete strip, away from the water, and shook the dust of Ontario from his boots.

———

William Henry noticed that Jane looked really happy when he suggested they stop for the night in a cove on the east side of Fox Island. Not just happy, she seemed to be shaking with relief, skipping about and cracking jokes. She was so distracted she almost threw the anchor and its cable *over* the bow rail—instead of passing it under, as he'd shown her—before he backed the steamboat slowly away to hook the flukes. Then, as she was making dinner, a simple meal of bacon and eggs, she fumbled around in the galley. When they arrived at the table, the edges of the eggs were burned while the bacon was rubbery and sopping with grease.

"What's wrong?" he finally asked.

"Nothing. … Everything's just perfect."

"That's why you're like a cat on the griddle."

Jane stared at him, and the stare went on too long.

"You can tell me," he said gently.

"I think I saw someone. At that last lock."

William Henry waited for her to continue.

"In fact, I'm *sure* I saw someone," she said.

"Not a good someone?" he suggested.

"No. A drug dealer from Los Angeles. He's also one of those Hell's Angels. Very short temper. Extremely violent."

"What would he be doing here, in the middle of rural Ontario?"

Jane stared at her plate. "I think … he's probably looking for me."

"Did you arrest him—while working with the military police?"

She looked up startled. "What? Oh, yes … he was arrested …"

"But he escaped."

"He must have."

Right then, William Henry knew everything was a lie. This new Jane, secret agent Jane, international woman of mystery, busy tracking Russian dope dealers or American soldiers smuggling drugs across the Pacific, leading a select team of military police, or FBI, or CIA—it was all a fantasy. The reality was going to be a lot less complicated.

"Is his name 'Bell'?" he asked gently.

"Yes. … His first name is Eric."

"Is he your new husband?"

She paused, hesitated. "Nothing that formal."

"But you took his name," he observed.

"I took a lot of things from Eric."

"Should I be afraid of him?"

"He's not a nice person."

"I would guess not."

Jane was staring at her plate again. Eventually, she picked up her fork and started poking at her eggs. The conversation was apparently finished, but William Henry had to ask anyway: "Do you want to talk about it?"

"No," she said.

21. Appreciation for Galatea

When they arrived at Lock 32, in the middle of the village of Bobcaygeon, Jane studied the quay before stepping ashore with the bow line. She saw no sign of a motorcycle, no sign of Eric Bell and his angry scowl. But she remained alert and attentive all the time she was off the boat.

She suddenly realized she could overhear a couple sitting on a nearby bench.

"I remember seeing boats like that on Lake Ontario," said the man, who was gray-haired and gaunt. "Summer of 1902, it was. I was twelve."

"You were ten," said his wife, who was equally gray. "I was twelve."

"Owned by the millionaires, they were. All of them up from New York City."

"They mostly kept to the Thousand Islands, though," said the wife. "That's where rich folks had their summer homes."

"True, true. You never saw steamboats this big on the canal here—not unless they were hauling cargo or making repairs. This one's more of a yacht than a working boat."

"I saw a yacht go all the way up to Lake Huron, once."

"Any rich people live on Lake Huron back then?"

"Maybe a few. Nice place, Georgian Bay."

That was someplace up ahead of them, Jane realized. She was about to tell these nice old folks *Galatea* would be going all the way to Georgian Bay. But before she could open her mouth, Willie signaled her to get back aboard for heading into the lock— and a good thing, too. With Bell around, Jane had to watch her mouth. A pair of gabby old folks like these two would tell him everything.

22. Squall Line

UNDER GOLDEN SUNSHINE, *Galatea* glided down a long stretch of canal that ran straight as a country road, three long miles interrupted only by three evenly spaced, shallow locks—the last of them Lock 41 at Gamebridge. After that, the old boat slid past a wharf and jetty and left a shoreline that faced out toward open water. For two weeks the system of lakes and canals had enclosed William Henry's horizon with endless fields and forests, hills and islands. Now dark blue water stretched beyond sight to the west.

He had to consult the chart to make sure they had actually arrived at Lake Simcoe, which was all of perhaps a dozen miles across, rather than Georgian Bay itself with the vastness of Lake Huron spreading beyond it. The chart showed about sixteen miles of easy steaming north by west up to the Atherley Narrows, which marked the entrance to a smaller body, almost a bay, called Lake Couchiching, and then on to the start of more canal work. He figured they could dock for the night in Orillia, fill up the fuel tank and icebox again, and even have dinner ashore.

As the boat cut across the lake with the throttle wide open, he became aware of a mass of white clouds—"thunder bumpers" his father would have called them—that was building off to the west. Minute by minute, the clouds rose higher and stretched farther to the north across his course. The pretty, white billows had a dark underside that deepened in hue as they rose above him. Soon William Henry could see slashes of rain etched between the clouds' bottoms and the lake surface.

The first little gust hardly moved *Galatea* at all. The hull rocked gently as the wind took her on the port beam, pushing against the sheer side of the long hull and cabin top. He corrected with the wheel and kept on course.

Nothing prepared him for the sudden wind that came just before the storm hit. The wheelhouse heeled over at an angle—worse than that day crossing Lake Ontario—and the bow slewed around to the east. The sky closed down around the boat. The bright afternoon became a twilight of mist, slashing rain, and wind. Visibility shrank to just a few feet beyond the tip of the bowsprit. The waves rolling under the keel felt as big as any he had felt out on Ontario.

William Henry tried to hold course for the narrows, but the bow was being driven around. Whatever he did, he could not force the compass card to swing northwest again or bring her heading into the wind, which was the safest option in a squall. He suddenly faced the kind of hard choice that all boatmen dread: whether to cut his engine and drift more slowly toward the unknown eastern shore, where he was now rushing at full throttle—but that would also put his vessel completely at the mercy of wind and wave—or maintain power and forge ahead under power, even though he could not see where he was going and did not know how far he had to run. He could sense that shoreline, like some dark green line on an old radar screen, and felt it was not far at all.

Having already experienced the terror of trying to relight the boiler and restart the engine while rolling *in extremis,* he opted to continue under power.

Jane came into the wheelhouse. "Are we in trouble?"

"Thunderstorm," he said. "We're caught in a squall."

"So ... where are we going?"

"With the wind." He pointed.

"Is that safe?"

"No ..."

William Henry continued battling with the wheel. Jane tried to help by wedging herself against the doorway that led out the port side to the front deck. The wind had been rattling it so savagely that the panel seemed about to fly off its hinges. Jane's weight stabilized the door, but he could see that the rain coming in around the edges was soaking her hair and clothing.

She was trying to smile at him, but white skin showed around her eyes.

He smiled back, and as soon as he looked away, disaster struck.

Like coming out of a fog bank, the view beyond the bowsprit suddenly cleared. Instead of a distant vista of blue-gray water, William Henry saw wet, green grass right under the boat's fore-foot. The hull lurched up over a short beach of sand or gravel and stopped.

He lost his hold on the wheel's spokes, rebounded from its curved mahogany arc, and fell sideways to the deck.

Jane was thrown from the doorway, clattered against the frames of the forward windows, and went down on the far side of the binnacle.

In the sudden stillness, he could hear the engine still beating and the propeller churning up stones and mud.

———

Morwenna Daffyd looked out from her veranda at the storm that had been brewing for the last half-hour and finally arrived. Dark sheets of slanting rain now obscured the view of the lake—at one point obscuring the edge of the lawn! The summer heat had vanished and temperatures had dropped perhaps twenty degrees since the storm swept over. That and the spray bouncing off the railing had driven all of her guests inside—except for the Tollivers, who stood a few paces away, obviously enjoying the violence of nature in all her glory.

Morwenna had a different purpose in standing out there and getting wet and wind-blown. She was trying to count the skiffs at the end of her dock. As veils of rain followed one another ashore, she came up with a different count each time: once she thought she had identified all six, but mostly it was just five. Five was not a good number.

She did not think any of her guests had taken out that last skiff. But with twenty-three of them pursuing the various pleasures of *Crwydro Gorffen* at peak season—outside playing at bocce ball and croquet on the lawns, swimming off the float deck, or simply wandering about the gardens and woods; inside playing cards in the parlor, or pool and billiards in the paneled lounge in the basement; upstairs playing other games behind the closed doors of their rooms—it would be difficult for Morwenna to call for a nose count. One of the skiffs might simply have broken loose in the storm and would be found later somewhere down the shore.

Then again, all the hulls were painted a dark hunter green, the decks a tasteful pebble gray—her late husband Richard's choice of colors, not hers—so that, under bare poles with sails taken in, the little fleet bobbing against the dock and plunging through the green-foaming waves was nearly invisible. Perhaps she had consistently miscounted, and six really was the true number.

Just as Morwenna was about to turn away, an apparition materialized out of the driving rain: a long, black lance, an elegantly curved bow, and a long, white hull that over its length faded back into the mist. The ship's prow rode through the waves, then rode up across the gravel strand, and finally cut a wedge into the lawn.

"*Fy Duw!*" she exclaimed. "My God!"

"Did you *see* that?" said Jack Tolliver.

"Right onshore!" said his wife Maggie.

"We must help them!" Tolliver said and ran down the stairs to the walkway.

"Yes, of course," Morwenna said. Still, she hesitated. She saw no sign of anyone in distress—just this large sailboat, yacht, steamship, or whatever it was that had stranded itself on her lawn. It might as easily have broken away from its moorings somewhere as come here under its own power. It certainly was wedged tight and not going anywhere. But then, Morwenna was the mistress of this house, owner of *Crwydro Gorffen,* and she dared not hang back when one of her guests charged out into the storm.

By the time she herself was running through the rain, Tolliver had reached the hull and was looking for a way to climb aboard. With the red-painted bilges fully out of water, the edge of the deck hung six or seven feet above the grass, within his reach but too far to pull himself up.

"Perhaps with a chaise?" she suggested, pointing back up the lawn.

"Good idea," Tolliver said. He raced back, retrieved one of the folding wooden chairs, and set it at an angle against the bow. It gave him the height he needed to clamber aboard.

By then Maggie Tolliver was standing beside her, and both women were drenched to the skin. "Jack may need some help," she said.

Maggie was dressed in shorts and quickly climbed after her husband.

Morwenna was wearing a full skirt, however, which made such gymnastics not only difficult but unladylike. But it was no time to stand on dignity, she decided. Tucking the skirt up around her waist, exposing her knickers for all the world to see, she followed them aboard.

By the time she got up on deck, climbed over the railing, and ran down to the pilothouse—which, she noted, had three charming cathedral windows toward the front—the Tollivers had already found the doors and gone inside. Jack was helping a tall man, who seemed to be about Morwenna's age, rise from facedown on the floor. The man was looking around with a dazed expression, then put a hand on the big mahogany wheel and felt the throbbing they all could feel.

"We have to stop the engine!" he said.

"Show me how," Jack replied.

The man shook his head, reached into a nest of brass pipes and push rods on the rear wall of the pilothouse, and fiddled with a couple of valves. The throbbing subsided, and from somewhere farther back Morwenna heard the hiss of escaping steam.

"See about Jane," the man said.

Maggie was helping a small woman with reddish hair who had collapsed in front of the pilot station. She was soaking wet, and the water streaming from her hair was tinged with blood. Maggie lifted her to her feet, but the woman was barely aware of her surroundings.

"What happened?" she asked vaguely.

"You've run your boat ashore," Morwenna said.

"Where are we, please?" the man asked.

"Oh, lying halfway across the beach and about fifteen feet into the back lawn," Morwenna said. "But we'll worry about that later. I think for now you should come up to the house. We can get you both dry clothes, medical attention for your wife's head, and a nice cup of tea."

23. INTERLUDE ASHORE

IT WAS STILL raining that evening when William Henry and Jane walked into the dining room of the resort-hotel where *Galatea* had plowed ashore in the storm. The tall, dark-haired woman who had come aboard as part of their rescue now met them at the hostess station, so he assumed she was a hotel employee. She led them across to a table tucked into a cozy bay window. The view out the westward-facing casement showed a stretch of green lawn down to the shoreline pierced by the steamboat's sharply curved bow, now canted at an angle. The rest of the hull was lost in a haze of dancing raindrops.

Neither of them had been able to go back aboard for clothes. Jane was wearing a long skirt donated by a much taller woman, probably from among the guests. She had to roll and tuck the waistband to keep from tripping on the hem. Her voluminous peasant blouse obviously came from the same wardrobe, because she had pulled the ruffled neckline tight and cinched it with a safety pin to keep the folds of gaily embroidered cotton from slipping off her shoulders. She also wore sticking plaster on her forehead to cover a row of tiny stitches put in by the hotel's doctor on call from Beaverton. William Henry was wearing a wool suit, dress shirt, and tie that were said to belong to the owner, and they were a better fit.

The hostess took their order for drinks. She was a beauty of indeterminate age, as William Henry noticed for the second time—once when she came aboard disheveled and bedraggled by the storm, and now when she had her hair combed out and wore a cocktail dress of dark-blue satin with a firm bodice and full skirt—the sort of clothes Jane used to wear. This woman was stunning either way.

William Henry ordered domestic beer for himself. Jane asked about the hotel's selection of white wines and chose a Pinot Grigio, which sounded expensive. The hostess handed out menus and left them alone.

William Henry stared for a long minute at the name blazoned across the menu's top, in bright red type inside an oval, next to a drawing of a winged dragon with one claw raised: "*Crwydro Gorffen*." Below it, in smaller letters, were the words "Hotel and Spa." He tried to wrap his tongue around the name and finally gave up. That intruding "w" defeated him.

When the waitress came over with their drinks and to take their food orders, he pointed to the words. "How do you pronounce that?" he asked.

The girl, who was young enough to be one of his students, smiled and shook her head. "It's just some Welsh," she replied. But William Henry had already guessed that much from the dragon.

Jane ordered grilled salmon, William Henry *boeuf bourguignon*. The prices were high enough to qualify, in his book, as "fancy dining." That assessment matched the desk clerk's suggestion that they "dress for dinner," followed by the concierge delivering their borrowed clothes. After the waitress had left, William Henry said quietly to Jane, "I don't know how we're paying for all this—the hotel room, the meals—such expenses were not part of our travel budget."

"Oh, relax!" she said. "It's just for one night. Besides, I'm tired of cooking three meals a day on a camp stove."

The table where they sat was big enough for four people, and while they waited and sipped their drinks the waitress stopped by and without explanation set a third place between them. Just as the food arrived—three plates now—the hostess came over, asked if she might join them, and introduced herself as the hotel's owner, Morwenna Daffyd.

William Henry pulled out the chair for her, and Jane gave her a sideways glance and the briefest of nods.

The woman pronounced her surname as "DAH-fid"—with the long "A" as it was pronounced in Latin, French, and other continental European languages—rather than the more familiar "DAY-vid" with the vowel-shifted English "A." Putting that together with her lilting and slightly archaic speech patterns, and the symbolism on the menu, William Henry supposed she was a direct transplant from Wales. He was also mildly surprised, having seen a placard at the front desk identifying the proprietor as "Richard Daffyd."

"Will Mr. Daffyd be joining us, too?" he asked, indicating the empty place at the table.

"No, my husband died last winter. Of the cancer."

"Oh, I'm so sorry to hear it!" William Henry said, suddenly realizing that he was wearing a dead man's clothes. "Then I'm in your debt for—" He plucked the lapel of his jacket. "I hope it's not too painful for you."

"Not to mind. I've done my grieving," she said simply. "Besides you two were wet through." She turned to Jane. "And you wear that blouse much better than I ever could." That explained the mismatch in sizes between Jane's small frame and the borrowed clothes—for Mrs. Daffyd was nearly as tall as William Henry himself.

Jane grimaced and thanked her in a mumble.

"I was wondering about the hotel's name," William Henry said. "It's Welsh?"

"Ah!" The woman's dark eyes flashed. She said something that sounded like Latin, but with accents in all the wrong places: "*Quid rigor ven.*"

He tried to repeat it, and she corrected him. "But what does it mean?" he asked.

"In the English, it might mean 'finished the wandering,' or, if you like, 'done with roving.' Richard and I wanted this to be a place our guests come home to—a place to rest and refresh their spirits."

"That's a lovely thought," William Henry said.

He glanced at Jane and saw her make a face.

"I'm sorry we had to crash onto your lawn like that," he continued. "I'll find some way to—"

"No harm done!" Mrs. Daffyd shrugged and tossed her raven-black hair, which fell in glistening waves below her shoulders. "You only dug up a few square yards of sod that needed tending anyway. I'm more afraid for the damage done to your beautiful old boat."

"I don't expect she's hurt too badly," he replied. "But we'll know more in the morning when I can get someone to drag *Galatea* off the beach."

"Galatea? That's from a Greek legend, isn't it?"

"Why yes, it is!"

William Henry related for her the Pygmalion legend from Ovid's *Metamorphoses* as if he were teaching it in class. That story lead to his telling her about the circumstances of his finding and buying the boat, and then the work that he, his daughter, and father had put into restoring *Galatea* that spring. He ended with the summer cruise he and Jane were taking along the Canadian waterways. In all of this detail, he left the exact nature of his relationship with Jane vague—for some reason finding himself self-consciously avoiding the word "wife."

Telling all of his stories and answering Morwenna's—Mrs. Daffyd's—sometimes oblique questions took the conversation through dinner and into coffee afterward. By then the dining room had emptied out and it was time for him and Jane to go up to bed.

———

It was still raining in the evening after the crash when Jane and Willie walked into the hotel's dining room. The black-haired Gypsy woman, the jezebel who had come aboard that afternoon flaunting her bare legs and flashing her scarlet nylon panties, was now manning the hostess station in a cocktail dress and led them over to the best table in the room with a view of the lake. She was all smiles and courtesy and practically draping herself on Willie's arm.

Jane felt silly because the clothes she had to wear—charity from some Amazon warrior-woman, who had to be at least as tall as this one, perhaps even the bitch herself—were three sizes too big and hung about her shoulders and waist in billows. She felt like a little girl playing dress-up. Besides, her head ached from the crack she had taken when the boat went aground, and the stitches hurt whenever she tried to move her eyebrows. In contrast—wouldn't you know it?—Willie looked terrific in the clothes the hotel staff had borrowed for him.

Willie seemed unusually interested in everything here. The resort's impossibly mangled Welsh name so fascinated him that he asked the waitress about it. And when the poor girl didn't know, that painted hussy—who also, it turned out, happened to own the place—rushed right over, sat herself down between them, and gave Willie a language lesson.

"Crud-rigor-morphine" was some kind of rest home and amazingly expensive. Willie agonized about the prices and then apologized all over himself for taking the woman's clothes and plowing up her beach. And she played the great lady and waved it all away. Served her right for putting her hotel so close to shore on a lake that was subject to such violent storms.

Jane was no dummy. Within a minute of sitting down, the woman let slip how her husband had died. So now the grieving widow was trolling for a new man.

Then Willie started telling this strange woman his whole life story. He gave her one of his old Greek legends and told about finding this beautiful old boat, about how he had restored it so lovingly, and about the wonderful time he was having on her lake. The Daffyd woman just kept smiling, batting her eyes, and asking for more. And not once did Willie mention Jane, their long and happy marriage, or the miraculous way she had come back to him after all those years apart. He and this Welsh woman just ignored her completely—until Jane, in her clownishly floppy clothing and with that stupid bandage covering half her face, disappeared right into the draperies.

It was enough to make her want to claw somebody's pretty eyes out.

———

The morning after the storm, the man with the stranded boat, William Henry Wheelock, professor of classics from some college town in Upstate New York, asked Morwenna if he could use the office telephone to call about having his boat removed from her lawn. He said he felt awkward calling from his own room, because his wife was still abed, poor thing, with an aching head. Also, it was likely to be a long-distance call, and he wanted to take care of the charges.

Morwenna offered to send up some aspirin. But when he started on his calls, she stayed by her desk, fiddling with her ledgers, in case he should need any help with the local authorities, making identifications, taking directions, and such.

"Someone on this lake must have a tugboat," he suggested.

"We don't ever get the big cargo ships up here," she said.

"Well, then a powerful launch maybe? From a marina?"

"There might be a few of those up around Orillia."

Between her notions of what a "marina" might be and listings in the phone book, he was able to call half a dozen such places. Each time, from his end of the conversation, with shorter and shorter questions and briefer pauses for the responses, she learned that none had any kind of launch or workboat capable of pulling a sixty-foot steamship off the land.

"Have you any notion of helping yourself?" she suggested gently. "Perhaps some movement involving the engine …?"

"I went down early this morning, got up steam, and went full in reverse."

"Did you have luck with that?"

"She didn't budge. But I'm afraid you now have a new sinkhole and a sandbar in the water right off your beach."

"I'll put up a sign for warning the swimmers."

After that, he called the Trent-Severn Waterway authority, which was part of the Parks Canada Agency. He started with the capital phone number, in Ottawa, and worked down through the waterway headquarters, in Peterborough, to the closest administrative office, in Kirkfield, trying to arrange for the use of one of their workboats. Such a boat did exist and could be provided, it turned out, although the cost would be high and its current schedule of assignments was long. Professor Wheelock could not expect help for another week.

"I'm afraid we'll have to impose on your hospitality for a while yet," he said.

"Or ... you could just deed your vessel over to me," Morwenna said sweetly. "I can always use it for a steam-heated bathhouse. Or perhaps a gift shop?"

From the professor's horrified look, she knew her teasing had gone too far.

"We'll pay for our room and board, of course," he said.

"Of course. Although it's the high season, you understand, I do have an available booking." When she mentioned her holiday rates, however, his head jerked slightly. "But I'm sure we can work out some arrangement," she said at last.

———

William Henry finished digging out, with a slight undercut, the embankment that defined the resort's side yard to the north. He had spent the previous day removing the last bricks of the old retaining wall and stacking them carefully on a tarpaulin to protect the grass underneath. That grass had been specially seeded and rolled flat over the years for lawn games like badminton and *bocce*, which he saw guests playing like some ancient version of marbles, except with large stone balls.

Now he selected a small, round boulder from the load that Morwenna—or "Mrs. Daffyd," as he should call her—had ordered for this job. He wedged the stone into the hallow below the bank, and followed it with a row of others, keeping them well back of the wall's original line. There, according to the references he had consulted, the boulders would provide drainage and relieve pressure on the wall from the natural creep of the soil behind it. Once he had rebuilt the wall against this backing of boulders, he would shovel gravel into the spaces between them to finish the job. He would probably be done by the end of the week.

He was proud of his handiwork. And it was the least he could do for Morwenna to repay her kindness.

When he had learned how long *Galatea* might be stuck on her property, and she had quoted the daily rate for the room he shared with Jane, William Henry must have shown his hesitation about the costs. Morwenna instantly dismissed the idea of payment but instead described the hotel's sad state of repair. Since her husband died, she had been without any real help in the upkeep. "The place does want a man who's handy with a scraper and paintbrush," she had said.

William Henry was glad that, for a few days at least, he could be that man—or serve her in any capacity. Morwenna—Mrs. Daffyd—made him feel shyly grateful to be a fully functioning male again and not as old and withered as he'd imagined for the last ten years. She herself was a compellingly beautiful woman: tall and graceful, with masses of hair that fell around her face, and flashing eyes that pierced him like a hoplite's spear thrust. He had found himself instantly stricken—as far back, he realized now, as that afternoon she came aboard the boat—and he could only hope he was concealing his feelings for her better than he had hidden his concerns about money.

The strange thing was, she had never asked him to rebuild the wall. He himself had noticed the way the bricks bulged outward at the top, seeming about to fall over, and mentioned it.

"Oh, it's held that shape for twenty years," she said. "Don't trouble yourself."

But that evening he pulled out a gardening book in her library, and the following morning he began poking around behind the bricks with a shovel. Later that day, a truck mysteriously arrived from the local nursery with the right choices of stone and gravel, confirming his suspicion that Morwenna had already studied the job and knew everything that was required. Their minds seemed to work together like that.

———

Jane was becoming less and less amused. Yes, annoyed, even though the David woman—however she spelled her married name—had been extra nice to her. Morwenna asked about the stitches on Jane's forehead every two or three days, and promised to summon the doctor when it was time to remove them. She always commented on how nice Jane looked, no matter what old thing she was wearing. But all the time the Gypsy woman was making a play for Jane's husband.

Now she had Willie out in the yard, ripping apart an old wall—and letting him think it was his own idea—to pay for their lodging while they waited for the boat to get pulled off. And the woman was already talking about the peeling paint on the back porch and what color did Willie think would look right with the rest of the old hotel's trim?

"Crudrow Gordon?" What kind of a name was that? "It means you're done with roving, sweetie." In a pig's eye! It was gibberish, meaning the black-haired old witch just wanted to lay her bony hands on his carcass.

And Willie was lapping it up like cream! Just like a man—to fall for the first flash of thigh some strange woman gave him. Jane hadn't been so dazed by her hard landing in the wheelhouse that she didn't notice how the cunning old witch had tucked her skirt up into her belt and swayed her hips to show off her butt with every other step.

When Jane called Willie on his behavior, he got all defensive and denied it. He was just being nice to the woman, he said, because they had plowed a dent in her lawn that would cost her something to repair. But the last straw was when he suggested Jane might help out in the kitchen or wait tables in the resort's dining room.

Sure she would, Jane thought—serve them ground glass and chopped garbage.

Rather than become anymore beholden to the woman, Jane had moved out of the room set aside for her and Willie. She took her suitcase and moved back aboard *Galatea*. The head didn't work, not with its outside hull fittings stuck in the grass. And to come and go Jane had to climb over the makeshift ladder that one of the guests had arranged by stacking a couple of old lawn chairs against the bow. But at least she was on her own turf.

And besides, every minute she spent ashore had been nerve-wracking. Jane had left half a million dollars in contraband just sitting out there in the old hull, waiting for someone to come along and find it. Or worse, for another storm to pull the boat off the beach and sink her with Jane's package still aboard.

Whatever Willie and his new lady friend were getting up to, up at the house, did not bother Jane in the slightest. Let her make eyes. Let him fawn. Let them rut like pigs, for all she cared.

Jane was spending her days aboard in relative idleness, reading books from the steamboat's library full of Willie's school texts, cooking what she could in the stranded galley with no draw on the water tank and no ice in the icebox, making her way around the perilously tilted deck, and staring out at the lake through the slanting line of windows in the main saloon.

She took to sleeping later and later each morning—until the morning that a funny little tugboat, the *Trent*, which was painted a carnival blue and yellow, stopped just in back of *Galatea*'s stern and hailed her. Jane stuck her head out of the cabin door, still wearing her nightgown.

"What do you want?" she called.

"You the people need a tow?"

"Ask up at the house."

"This the boat?"

"Well, yes."

The mate or deckhand or whoever he was jumped for *Galatea*'s taffrail, hung on the outside for a second, then hauled himself aboard. He had a line tucked into his belt and used that to pull across a heavier piece of rope.

"Wait a minute, please!" Jane called.

"Ain't got all day," the man said.

He hauled in about fifty feet of line from the *Trent*, dropped a loop of it around one of the big, cast-iron stern cleats in *Galatea*'s deck, went over and made fast to the other cleat, and signaled to whoever was piloting the tug.

Jane climbed out onto the back deck with the breeze flapping her nightie around her thighs and pulling a rat's nest of tangles out of her hair.

"Hang onto something," the man told her.

The *Trent* backed away in reverse, churning water. The rope stretched taut, then started to vibrate like a guitar string. It shed cupfuls of the water it had absorbed while lying slack in the lake.

Galatea didn't budge. The cleats Jane normally used for tying up to the dock now groaned in the deck timbers, which made snapping noises like repeated pistol shots. But they seemed to hold. Suddenly the hull jerked under her feet, almost throwing her off balance. The bottom made a terrible scraping noise, grinding through the sand and gravel of the shoreline. Jane could also hear a deeper groan, where sixty-odd feet of keel and planking and the ribs that connected them took up the strain.

And then the boat was free, sliding smoothly backward through the water.

"Took a little weed off your bottom there," the deckhand said with a grin.

"Now what?" she asked. Jane was conscious of being alone with the old boat out on the lake: no one in the wheelhouse to steer, no steam up—and so no way to maneuver in the first place.

"We'll tie onto that float over yonder," the man said, pointing to the swimming dock anchored a hundred yards offshore.

"Swell," Jane replied. She went to arrange the fenders and get one of her own lines out. That was something she knew how to do.

With *Galatea* held to the dock by one cleat, her bow hanging free and pointing generally out toward the horizon, the man went over to the *Trent* and came back with a clipboard.

"Sign here," he told Jane, handing her a pen.

"What is it?" she asked, peering at the paper.

"My work order—and your promise to pay."

The amount was more than two hundred dollars!

"I ... I can't just sign this!"

"You in possession of the boat?"

"Well, I guess ..."

"Boat's off the land?"

"It appears so."

"Sign here."

As she scribbled her name by the "X," Jane heard someone shouting from a distance. She looked over and saw Willie running across the resort's lawn, waving his arms and stopping every few paces to jump up and down.

She sure hoped he still had two hundred dollars in his bank account.

24. Scraper

THE NEXT-TO-LAST LOCK on the Trent-Severn Waterway wasn't a lock at all, in the sense of a rectangular basin that filled with water to lift or drop a boat from one level to the next. Instead, it was the Big Chute Marine Railway—a specially built, flat-bedded rail-road car, twenty feet wide, built on stilts with high sideboards. When *Galatea* arrived at the far end of the upper lake, the transport car was already in the water. The lockmaster signaled William Henry to come ahead, maneuver between the boards, and stop his engine.

Jane was standing out on the front deck with her line. "Should I tie on, or what?" she asked the man.

"No need," the lockmaster told her. "But you'll have to come ashore, ma'am. No passengers, other than the captain."

William Henry had put *Galatea*'s bow as far forward as pos-sible, practically right up on shore between the exposed railway tracks. Now he stepped out of the wheelhouse and looked back. About a third of the hull extended beyond the transport's side-boards. He pointed this out to the lockmaster. "Should I be wor-ried about the overhang?"

"No, Cap'n. She's fine. We take the big boats all the time." With that, the man stepped down off the walkway and turned to operate the transport controls.

Slowly, slowly, at a rate of mere inches per second, the side-boards rose around the boat. Then William Henry felt the bed come up under her keel. *Galatea* settled on her port side with an induced list of two or three degrees. The transport kept rising steadily, and the water fell away.

The hull let out a great, hollow groan, timber grinding on timber, echoing through the bilges. William Henry looked back along the rail to the stern. He thought he could see a slightly convex curve to the gunwale and an outward bowing, where normally the sides of the hull curved up and in—but the differ-ence from the lines that he had become familiar with for the last couple of months was so small that he really could not be sure.

If ever the stern was going to crack and drop away, this would be the moment. Finally the groaning stopped, and the hull remained intact.

Within minutes, the bed of the transport was standing five or six feet above the ground. William Henry looked over the side, down to the pavement of a public road that ran around the end of the lake and across the railway tracks. It was blocked with lift gates and flashing lights, just like a railroad crossing, while a line of cars waited for *Galatea* to pass. When he looked ahead, however, the ground dropped away. According to the chart, the railway descended fifty-eight feet over a distance of more than five hundred. Working it out in his head, William Henry arrived at a grade of eleven percent—pretty steep.

As the transport went over the top and headed down, he heard a crash from the cabin behind the wheelhouse. It sounded like crockery, and he imagined Jane had left the breakfast dishes on the counter—nothing that couldn't be cleaned up later. Then he heard a lamp fall over in the main saloon. When nothing more fell, he was relieved that was the extent of the damage—until he heard a horrendous grinding and scraping at the stern, and the deck jarred and shifted under his feet.

"What the hell's that?" he called to the lockmaster.

The man looked back along the length of the boat. "Probably tapped your skeg at the top of the grade."

"Well, is everything all right?" William Henry asked.

The man shrugged. "You can't hurt the dirt."

"Not the ground! I mean my hull!"

"Know when she floats."

Now William Henry looked forward as the bow approached the water. With the steep angle of entry, the bowsprit dipped lower and lower, finally lying almost horizontal with the surface. The water rose around the hull toward the gunwale. Just as he thought the bow might go under, the hull shifted and began to float.

After twenty minutes of total transit time, the transport car was fully submerged in the lower lake. With his heart in his mouth,

William Henry started the engine. He listened for the thump and clatter of a bent propeller or, worse, a bent shaft. But the engine sounded no different and the boat maneuvered normally.

Jane had followed the transport down the long slope. Now, as William Henry angled the bow over to the quay, she jumped aboard.

All in all, he was glad they would not have to come back this way.

25. APPRECIATION FOR GALATEA

ONE DAY, WHILE poking around under the deck hatches, Jane had discovered that *Galatea* boasted a two-octave steam calliope. She had asked Willie if it still worked, and when he said he didn't know, she begged him to let her test it. And so, as they crossed the couple of miles of open water in the arm of Georgian Bay that separated the last lock at Port Severn from the nearest big town at Midland, when they were well out of earshot of anyone who might object, Jane pulled up the keyboard with its two banks of steam whistles, Willie opened some valves, and she started to play.

Unfortunately, Jane had never studied piano, and her repertory was limited to an enthusiastic rendition of "Chopsticks" and a slower and more hesitant "Yankee Doodle." She played both repeatedly and with gusto until they pulled up to the town dock.

After Jane had tied up, an old man approached. "I couldn't help noticing … those pipes there. Is that really a steam calliope?"

"You bet!" she said. "Raise the dead with it."

"I heard you out on the bay. … May I come aboard?"

"Certainly." Jane helped him over the rail. "Do you play?"

"Not one of these, but I play the organ at church."

"Want to give it a try?" she offered.

"Maybe just a bit of Bach. Do you know the 'Toccata and Fugue'?"

"Well, I never …" she said doubtfully, then brightened. "Oh, yes! Please!"

The man settled on the little box seat and poised his fingers above the brass keys. "They're warm!" he exclaimed.

"It's powered by live steam."

The man tentatively touched the keys, making a few random shrieks, then began tapping his fingers in earnest. The first stately phrases, repeated at three different levels, burst out of the pipes, followed by rising and falling sequences—the word "arpeggio" occurred to Jane—which echoed off the surrounding buildings and the distant hills. The old man grinned as the music picked up speed. People on the street across from the dock were coming out of storefronts and doorways to listen. And then, when the music had reached its peak, the steam whistles stuttered, warbled, and began to spit hot water.

"What happened?" he said. "We've lost pressure."

"I guess my husband cut fire in the boiler."

"That would do it," he said. "Oh, well ..."

"Thank you for the experience."

"Not at all, m'dear. Thank *you!*"

26. Catching Up With the World

William Henry had designated the Canada Post in Midland, Ontario, as his forwarding address until the end of July. And so, the morning after they arrived in town, he walked over to collect his mail. Returning on board, he dumped the stack on the dinette table and began sorting. Jane wandered in from the galley with a cup of coffee in her hand.

"Nothing for me, I'm guessing," she said.

"Who knew you were back in town?" he asked.

"Other than Eric?" She paused to think. "No one."

"That's probably a good thing then."

Jane made a face at him.

William Henry set aside the anticipated findings—his scholarly journals, the few magazines to which he still subscribed, two monthly statements from his bank, the charge for dock rent in Byzantium for June and July, and a couple of leftover utility bills from the cottage. After that, he had just two envelopes in his hand.

The first of them had the return address of "The Chairman, Classics Department, University of Lake Ontario." William Henry tore into it, expecting a chatty departmental letter from Professor Littlefield hoping everyone was having a productive summer and outlining the course plan for the academic year ahead. The contents were quite different.

The opening sentence leapt out at him: "In light of the evolving nature of the University's educational mission, the interests and needs of our incoming generation of students, as well as budgetary considerations in the College of Liberal Arts, your services with this Department will no longer be required." The rest was instructions about his final paycheck and termination of benefits through the Bursar's Office. The letter made no mention of William Henry's scholarly achievements, academic standing, or position on the tenure track. No recommendation. Not even a good-bye.

"Well," he said aloud, "they've let me go."

Jane came to his side and studied the letter. "Can they do that? What about job security? Aren't professors supposed to have that tenure thing?"

"I was in line for it. Didn't get it."

"What will you do now?"

He stopped to think, still absorbing the situation. "What I've been doing anyway, I suppose. Continue sailing on around the lakes. Tie up at Byzantium again. Start sending out my *curriculum vitae*."

"Pretty late in the year for that, isn't it?"

"I expect I'll have a few lean months."

The second envelope was written in an unrecognizable hand with a return address of "D. Wheelock, 301 Durrell Hall, University Station, New York." He opened that one to find three pages of hastily folded notebook paper covered in ballpoint scrawls that bore no relation to Dani's usually neat script.

The opening sentence screamed in block capitals: "Mother and Dad, Watch out! There's a madman coming after you!" The rest of the letter described Eric Bell down to his beard and biker leathers with a patch on the back showing a horde of skeletal soldiers. Bell seemed to know all about the old steamboat *Galatea* and wanted to know where Dani's parents had gone on their summer cruise. She described how he forced his way into her dorm room and tied her to a chair to make her tell. "Mother, he says he's your boyfriend from California, but I can't believe you know anyone like that." He was crazy and mean, Dani wrote. He was also violent, because he punched her a couple of times. "Beware this man!" Her letter concluded that they were not to worry about her. She was really all right. She was getting out of the hospital today and would be going back into the dorm to work on her summer courses.

"Out of the hospital!" Jane exclaimed when he showed her the letter.

"She *says* she's better now and back in school," he said, studying the text again carefully. "This letter is at least three weeks old, so the whole experience is now in the past. She makes it sound like cuts and bruises—but still, I don't know. Her handwriting is all loopy and strange."

"Bruises you fix with a bandage and ice. 'Hospital' has got to be serious."

"Right. We should go back to make sure she's okay—and take care of her if she's not." William Henry tried to envision a return without reference to his charts. "Now, it would take a couple of weeks to thread our way back through the lakes and canals, using the same route we followed out here. The faster way has to be going forward from this point: down Lake Huron, through Lake St. Clair and Detroit, up the length of Lake Erie. Then we cut through the Welland Canal into Lake Ontario and east to Byzantium. It's a much longer distance but mostly open water and clear steaming. We can be there in five or six days, I guess, if we push hard."

"Forget that! I'll take a bus and be home in a day."

"But I still have to go with you," he said quietly.

"No, she needs a mother's care," Jane replied.

William Henry refrained from pointing out that for ten years their daughter had grown up without a mother. She could recover from a beating in the same way.

"You don't understand," he said. "If you go back, I'm stuck here in Midland. I can't handle the boat without you. It's a two-person proposition, trying to steer, operate the engine, and handle the lines all at the same time."

"Then you can afford to wait here for a couple of days."

"Bell's still out there, and he's looking for this boat."

"He's looking for me," Jane said, "not for you."

"Yes, but if you leave and Bell finds me, then he ties me to a chair and beats me until I tell him where you've gone. That leads him right back to Dani."

"Look, we've had no sign of Eric since we saw him—since I saw him—back at Buckhorn," Jane pointed out, almost reasonably. "Now I know he's not going to give up the search"—from the way she said this, so positively, William Henry wondered what hold this man had on her—"but maybe he went back to

Byzantium anyway. Maybe he's planning to torture Dani—or hold her hostage—or—"

"Wait! Stop! Did he see *you* back at Buckhorn?"

"I ... I think so. He was staring right at the boat."

"So he knows he found us—but he couldn't *get* to us."

"That sounds right," she said. "What are you implying?"

"He probably got tired of chasing around the waterway, trying to catch us at each of the locks or in one of the small towns. I guess, then, he would decide to go on ahead, try to intercept us at the other end ... someplace like here, in Midland."

He watched Jane work through this thought, her face shifting from angry scowl to some deeper, darker emotion.

"Then we both of us have to leave," she said. "Right now. Abandon the boat here. And after we see Dani we fly off to someplace unexpected. Head out west, maybe, or go to South America or Europe. We need to lead the trail away from Dani for a while. And we get away from this stupid old boat, too. Just disappear."

"I suppose ..." William Henry felt himself go cold inside. It seemed incredible that his *Galatea,* the dream of freedom on the water that he had pursued for half a year—although it seemed longer now—the renovation project he, Dani, and his father had labored over, the elegant yacht for which he had traded his home, even traded his future, and to which he had dedicated the rest of his life, might slip away so easily. He imagined leaving her tied up here in Midland, boiler cold, bilges slowly filling up without the daily pumping out, cabin secured by that antiquated brass lock plate and prey to the first group of teenage hooligans or souvenir hunters to come along. He imagined her stripped and broken and sinking at the dock.

He couldn't let it happen. That Jane could suggest this so casually showed she never really understood what the boat meant to him. He stared at his wife. *She really did go away for good,* he realized, *all those years ago.* She was a stranger to him now.

For Dani's sake he might agree to leave *Galatea* in Midland, let the gallant old girl take her chances for a few days or a week.

But then they would come back—he would come back—and somehow bring her safely home.

"Give me a day to make arrangements," he said at last. "I need to find a berth, flush the boiler, change a few locks, shift some stores …"

"All right, but let's do it quickly."

27. Change of Plan

Jane was relieved to be free of this interminable cruise. The fresh air, the blue water, and the green fields had all been a pleasant change. For a couple of days perhaps. Maybe even as much as a week. But a little of the country life sure went a long way. And, as Willie pointed out, Eric Bell was likely to be waiting somewhere up ahead. From the return route Willie had described to her, Jane worried most about the big cities. Detroit was the big choke point along their way, the place *Galatea* would have to pass if they ever went back to Lake Ontario. It was a dense, urban place where Bell could lose himself, hole up, and keep an eye on the waterfront—or set spies to watch—lying low until the distinctive shape and colors of the old steamboat one day showed up on the river.

No, it was better for her and Willie to abandon the boat now. Get out and go somewhere that Bell would never expect, never know to look for them. Jane was sure she could talk Willie into it. Oh, they would spend a day or two in Byzantium, checking up on Dani and making sure she was really okay. But then they were free.

Willie didn't have his teaching job anymore, so he wouldn't be tied down to the university. The world was wide open. They could pick where they wanted to settle. And university professors could find work almost anywhere, couldn't they? Especially one who taught ancient history and spoke only dead languages like Greek and Latin. His future really had no limits—not like he would be trying to teach American history, say, or English literature in someplace like Italy or Argentina. And Jane herself had pretty good survival skills, too—on both sides of the law. She also had a nest egg tucked away behind that pipe down in the bilges. The only trick now was for her to secure the package and hide it in her luggage without Willie finding out and getting concerned. Eventually, one day, she could arrange some kind of deal in a big city like Florence or Buenos Aires—or more likely in an American city like Chicago or Milwaukee—and they could live happily ever after.

Or that was one plan—if Willie would go along with it. If not, then she still had the dope and her freedom and her options. Eventually, even Eric Bell would give up the chase and return to California.

Willie had spent the rest of the day, after receiving Dani's letter, in finding a safe harbor for leaving *Galatea*. He paid to berth her at a marina on the other side of the point and asked the manager to keep an eye on the old boat. Willie obviously thought they would be coming back, maybe in a few days or a week. But he would get over it.

Once they tied up at the new dock, Willie spent the following morning putting hasps and padlocks on the cabin door and on the hatches in the deck that covered deep storage places, five steps down inside the hull, which he called "lazarettes." Then he and Jane shifted some of the boat's contents around, disposing of perishables and stowing loose items of furniture and house wares. Jane took her turns lugging stuff out of the cabin, carrying it belowdecks, and stowing it at his direction. She gave him a big smile each time they passed.

While Willie was down in the forward lazarette arranging cookware and stacks of china on a shelf, Jane happened to look across the water and spot a large cabin cruiser, at least forty feet long, with a steep cliff of white freeboard at the bow. This new boat was approaching the berth next along the dock behind *Galatea*. It was coming in fast and at a sharp angle. Jane could tell from the startled expression on the face of the pilot, an older man on the bridge behind the wide, raking windshield, that he had misjudged both his speed and the remaining distance. She grabbed her boathook and raced to the other side of the deck in an attempt to fend off a collision. The open hatch of the aft lazarette was right across her path, and she leapt over it.

Jane herself misjudged, catching just the toe of her sneaker on the far edge of the coaming and feeling it slip off into empty space. The boathook in her hands touched the deck first, striking hard, crosswise in the hatch opening, and the hardwood shaft caught Jane under the ribcage. The impact broke her fall. It also knocked the wind out of her and flipped her body around, ass over crown. She landed on her back at the bottom of the storage compartment, hidden in the shadows below deck level.

Stunned and unable to move, Jane waited for the crash of the big boat hitting *Galatea*'s exposed quarter. It never came. Instead she heard the roar of powerful engines and the frothing of water being beaten by great bronze propellers. Then both sounds were chopped off, leaving relative silence.

From a distance, from out of the other lazarette, Willie's voice shouted, "What the hell?" She then heard him stomping up the steps and imagined Willie finding himself alone on deck.

From closer at hand, from the other boat, which would by now be hanging right off their stern, she heard a strange voice calling, "Sir! Sir! Your wife just disappeared!"

"What do you mean 'disappeared'?" Willie shouted back.

"She was there on deck a minute ago—then gone!"

She heard a scuffling that had to be Willie's sneakers, up and down the teak planking, obviously looking for Jane over the side. She wanted to call out to the square of daylight five feet above her head that she was all right, not to worry, she was just down in the hold. But she could not draw breath to do so much as whisper.

———

William Henry returned from the Georgian Bay General Hospital in Midland, where the ambulance had taken Jane after the medics had carried her out of the aft lazarette. In the emergency room, the doctors taped her chest three times around with an Ace bandage and wanted to keep her overnight to watch for signs of internal bleeding. After that, she would just have to lie low, taking shallow breaths and her pain medications, allowed to do no strenuous physical activity for up to six weeks. Clearly, traveling by bus back to Byzantium, let alone heading out on the great escape Jane had talked about, was out of the question now.

He looked around *Galatea*'s main saloon. Well, Jane could lie on the settee during the day, and he could make it up as a bed for her at night. William Henry could sleep on an air mattress on the floor, or something, to avoid jostling her as she slept. He would cook for her, bring her books and magazines and otherwise keep her entertained, and help her into the head as needed. He spent the morning unpacking the house wares and buying food for the icebox.

The boat was still immobilized, because he could not handle the engine, steering, and docking all by himself. He would have to extend the terms of their stay at the marina here to cover Jane's convalescence. And that left them a sitting target for Eric Bell, when he came—especially after the entrance into town they had made two days ago, complete with "Chopsticks" on a steam calliope!

William Henry went to the forward lazarette, under the front deck, and retrieved a box full of stuff he had not wanted to put in long-term storage when cleaning out the cottage back in Byzantium, mostly financial records and family memorabilia. He set it on the floor in the saloon and began digging down. Near the bottom he found what he was looking for—his service automatic and a spare clip, both loaded. The old, faintly stained gray metal of the pistol, with the worn checker pattern on its oiled wooden grips, fit easily into his hand. The weight of those blunt-nosed, copper-jacketed bullets in their bright brass casings, each as big around as his fingertip, was suddenly comforting. William Henry was a soldier, after all—more than a match for any outlaw biker.

The Colt Model 1911 would no longer live in a cardboard box, that was certain. But he still couldn't just leave it, fully loaded, on a table or tucked between seat cushions. He looked around the cabin. The shelf with his favorite books. Behind the thick leather-bound spine of *The Iliad,* he thought. Perfect cover for a grim tool of war.

———

For three days Jane lay on her side and took shallow breaths. The doctors had told her to try a deep breath at least every hour or so—this was to ward off pneumonia or a collapsed lung, they said—but it hurt too much. She found that, paradoxically, it was easier to lie on the side where the ribs were broken, and she assumed this had something to do with the way her spine worked between her shoulders and hips. The best times, of course, were right after Willie doled out her Vicodin, and then she could float free of her spine, her ribs, and pretty much everything else for a while.

She could see he was getting restless. Yes, he was attentive. He cooked for her, and sometimes the food he brought her even tasted good. He read to her, when she was tired of leafing through the magazines he bought, and she began to get a feeling, if not an actual liking, for some of the old Greek stories and plays out of his bookshelves. When she started asking questions, he switched tracks and read to her from Edith Hamilton's *The Greek Way,* and then from Will and Ariel Durant's *The Life of Greece* to improve her general knowledge. Jane amused herself by letting him think she was interested, and then she found she really was interested.

But still, Willie was restless and anxious, and she knew the name of that anxiety. Eric Bell was still out there somewhere. So long as they stayed in Midland, they were not safe.

On the fourth day, Jane sat up, opened her bathrobe, and unfastened the steel clips that fastened her elastic bandage, or at least all those she could reach. She asked Willie to take out the two that were far down her side toward the back.

"Are you sure we should take the bandage off?" he said.

" 'We' don't have to put up with it. I do," she replied. "I can't breathe. The damn thing itches. And frankly, my dear, it's beginning to smell. So take out the damn clips!"

He helped her pull the robe down off her shoulders, unfastened the clips—only hurting her a little when they caught and tugged on the bandage. He unwound the springy fabric from around her torso and under her breasts. She took a breath, then a deeper one. She scratched all over, wherever she could reach, where the elastic ribbing had marked her skin.

"Better now?" he asked, helping her back into the robe.

"Much. Thanks."

He hesitated.

"What?"

"I was wondering if you felt better enough to travel."

Jane considered. "Not jolting around on a ten-hour bus ride."

"How about sitting right there—but with a little more wave action?"

"What are you suggesting? Moving the boat? But I thought you couldn't—"

"I can work out something," he said. "It won't be fast and it won't be pretty, but I can get us away from the dock. I've looked at the chart, and Georgian Bay has hundreds of islands, coves, and inlets north and west of here. We could go places only a boat can reach, keep away from the towns, and Eric Bell would never find us. Cruising the lakes was always part of this trip anyway. We might as well enjoy it."

"Oh," Jane said. At least it was a plan, and it might even keep them alive. "It sounds like fun."

To prepare for the voyage, Willie spent the next morning shopping at a grocery store in Midland, brought it all back by taxi, and enlisted the driver's help in carrying his prizes aboard. Jane watched them parade through the saloon and into the galley with bags and cardboard boxes of canned fruits and vegetables, sardines and those little cocktail wieners, cured hams, condensed milk, powdered eggs, ten-pound bags of rice and flour, boxes of crackers and dried pasta, coffee and tea, and two extra tanks of propane for the stove. Jane could see hours in the galley for herself, when she was up and able to hobble about, trying to turn all that stuff into actual meals.

He spent the afternoon buying jerry cans at the hardware store and going around to local service stations to get more motor oil for the engine. It was like they were never going to touch land again.

While Willie was out, Jane got paper and pen from the chart box, propped herself up at the dinette table, and wrote a letter to Dani. She acknowledged her daughter's letter, hoped

Dani's hurts were not too severe, thanked her for the warning, and wrote they were on the lookout for this Bell person, whom Jane knew slightly from California—no need to go into detail on *that*. She wrote that they were now headed out for a cruise "on the lakes"—without being specific about which lakes or for how long. The less Dani knew, the less she could tell if Bell showed up again in Byzantium. About her own broken ribs or Willie's lost job, she kept quiet. Those were details they could discuss later, in person, or perhaps with a phone call—if *Galatea* ever came near a phone.

For now, Jane had written what she could without alarming her daughter. She signed the letter, left it on the table, and tottered over to the settee to rest. Willie could add a postscript later, if he liked, and mail it before they departed.

Jane was too tired to think about it anymore.

28. Georgian Bay

It took William Henry a couple of days to figure out how to handle the boat by himself. He learned to plan ahead and move quickly. He worked out a system for bringing the boiler up to steam, setting up the engine so that one valve adjustment would take the shaft to slow, steady revolutions, and singling up the dock lines so that the hull was secured by just one rope at the bow. Then he could quickly cast off, push the gunwale away from the dock with one leg up and poised, scramble aboard over the rail before the gap became too wide, run back to the wheelhouse, and apply thrust and rudder to catch her momentum and take her out into the channel.

He thought getting back to the dock would be just a reverse of this process, aided by that same momentum as the hull coasted with the engine at dead stop. Setting out the anchor and taking in were also possible. It would all work, so long as he wasn't fighting a strong current or a cross wind.

With that, on the fourth day after Jane was released from the hospital, he cast off in Midland and headed out into Georgian Bay. He had no specific destination, just a chart that extended as far north and west as Cockburn Island and the international boundary. He had no goals, other than to get lost among the thousands of islands, peninsulas, and inlets that decorated the eastern shore of Lake Huron like the lace on a lady's neckline.

————

While Willie steered the boat through the long, sunny days of late July and early August, Jane reclined on the settee in the saloon, her shoulders and neck propped up against the mahogany woodwork with cushions, and watched the world pass by the cabin windows.

It was a beautiful world, like a picture shot in Kodachrome, except it was real and close enough to touch. She had never thought water itself could be so bright and blue. The little bays were like sapphires when the sunlight struck them one way, like lapis lazuli when it struck another. The islands were like boulders lying on top of the water, great masses of rock, gray and brown, washed clean of dust and dirt. But they must have hidden dirt somewhere, because each island had its cap of dark green trees: evergreens, cedars, spruces, firs, all kinds of Christmas trees but without the decorations. The air that poured through the cabin windows was so clean it was like breathing crystal. Occasionally, Jane saw a plume of black smoke curl down from *Galatea's* stack and regretted they had to leave any tarnish on this pristine landscape.

Jane fell in love with Georgian Bay. When they returned to one of the small towns like Midland, Owen Sound, or Wharton for supplies and fuel oil, she asked Willie to buy her a book on the region. "Buy two books," she insisted. "No, buy me a whole armload."

And so she lay on the settee, surrounded by books, comparing the pictures and descriptions with the real life unfolding outside her windows. And when they anchored for the night in some quiet place, after Willie had cooked dinner and done the washing up, she told him everything she had learned. How the recent geology, all those rocky islands, had been pushed around by the glaciers—of which the Great Lakes these days were just little puddles left over from the melting and runoff of the last Ice Age. But even the Ice Ages were recent history, in a way, because the faulting in the Georgian Bay District went back to tectonic plates and the collision of Peru with southern Labrador in some distant place called Gondwanaland, about two billion years ago.

"When the world was young," Willie said with a smile.

"Are you making fun of me?" she asked, getting angry.

"Not at all. I'm glad to see you're enjoying the trip."

"It's because for once I've got something to teach you."

"You always had one more thing to teach me, Jane."

" 'Had'? You mean, I don't anymore?"

"Sorry. It was a slip of the tongue."

"I am endlessly fascinating, sir." She batted her eyes at him.

"Yes," he agreed, "you certainly are."

———

Toward the end of August, William Henry found himself beginning to tire of paradise. Each of those islands, rocky and tree-
crested, like a bonsai come to life, while beautiful in its own
way, began to look like every other island. He had sampled all
the different shades of blue the waters of Georgian Bay could offer and identified and exclaimed over all the shapes the clouds
of the sky could take.

When they anchored at night, Jane stopped talking about the
landscapes she had seen during the day. And when he paused
at lunchtime and brought her a sandwich, he often as not would
find her reading in one of his histories or a novel as one of the
tour books he had bought her.

She was also healing. After the first couple of weeks, she began getting up from the settee in the saloon during the day and
going to sit in a folding chaise on the front deck. And after that,
she began wearing the bikini again and lying out on a bath towel. But her actions now were less provocative and more casual.
And they did not return to intimacy after her accident.

William Henry was getting restless. Endless cruising with no
goal was not his purpose in life. Not to mention the fact that
soon the money would give out. While the steamboat might run
indefinitely on donations of used motor and cooking oil, it still
cost something to dock her, and they needed to buy provisions
like food and ice. And, even though the sun still shone and the
wind was warm, he could feel the days getting shorter and know
that autumn was not far off.

Anyway, by now, after nearly a month of aimless cruising
among isolated islands and landlocked coves, he thought they
were well rid of Eric Bell and whatever murderous obsessions
he harbored about Jane. Without actually discussing the matter
with her, William Henry believed it was safe to continue their
original plan, to return on the great circle route around the lakes
and back to Byzantium.

It was time to begin sending out inquiries about teaching positions. At this late date, he could not hope to secure a place anywhere for the fall semester, but winter was still a possibility. For

that he would need a reliable mailing address and a telephone from which he could make and receive calls. Although he was now separated from the University of Lake Ontario, aside from the mechanics of picking up a few checks and signing a few forms, Byzantium was still his home base.

And so one morning he sat down at the dinette table with his charts and plotted a course westward, out of Georgian Bay, then southward down the length of Lake Huron, to where the imaginary line of the international border cut inland along the St. Clair River, separating the State of Michigan from the Province of Ontario. The route home led down that river to Lake St. Clair, then past Detroit, and into Lake Erie. But it started at a town called Sarnia.

29. CATCHING UP WITH THE MONEY

ERIC BELL HAD been running on luck, and it was finally running out. He had already run out of time. After three months on Jane's trail with nothing to show, his status at the club back in Los Angeles—if he ever bothered to keep in touch, and who needed that grief?—had surely degraded from "Bring in the dope" to "Come in for judgment," and now Bell probably hovered between "Lose yourself" and "Left for dead." Hawker was the kind to settle debts with blood if the money wasn't on the table.

Bell was starting to think he had made a tactical mistake. After chasing all over lower Ontario looking for the antique yacht belonging to Jane's old man, he had instead settled on the waiting game, watching the one place he knew, both from the daughter and from the map, that Jane and the money had to pass. If they were going back to Byzantium at the end of the summer, then they would show up in Sarnia sooner or later. And, after cruising down the length of Lake Huron, with no other ports in sight, they would have to *stop* there—rather than sailing on up the river—if only to stock up on fuel, food, and whatever else they needed to keep going.

Lately he began to think maybe the boat wasn't taking the route the daughter had described. Or maybe Jane wouldn't stay with the boat. It was a big world, and a lot could happen in three months. Besides, the bitch was tricky. But then, he decided, she had gone off on that boat in the first place for some kind of reason. And if she'd left, she left, and he was a dead man.

So Bell had rented a room in Sarnia and made friends with mechanics at each of the four local docks and marinas. He traded Harley stories, helped with their engines, and sprung for beers after work so they would keep an eye out for any foxy mama traveling with a scholarly gent in a real, live—would you believe it?—old steamboat. To add spice and urgency to the story, he told the boys how his hoity-toity sister had stolen money from their dad. He really wanted to catch up with the bitch, and he let them think there might be a reward for finding her.

Late in the afternoon on the last Saturday in August, one of these friends, Tom Wilders, called Bell from a pay phone. He was all excited because he and his family were out on a picnic at Waterfront Park and what did they see pulling around the point and entering the river but Bell's steamboat. Or something like it, with a long, curving white bow and a tall black stack blowing smoke. And on the front deck, lying sprawled out on a deck chair, was a redheaded woman wearing, swear to God, a little pink bikini. That had to be the sister, didn't it?

Bell told Wilders to get in his car, follow the boat up river, and to stop and call again as soon as it made a definite move to land someplace, or even if it just kept going out of town. Then Bell sat by the phone, passing the time by checking his weapons, wiping down his automatic with an oily rag, clearing the chamber and reloading the clip, and running a whetstone along the edge of his knife.

Wilders called back in half an hour to say the old boat had just rounded the spit of land that separated the harbor from the river and seemed to be headed for the wharf at the foot of Exmouth Street. Bell thanked the man, slipped the knife back into its sheath, and ran down the stairs to get out the Electra-Glide.

———

Jane had just finished tying off the stern line and was about to hop back aboard when she heard in the distance, beyond the trees, a stuttering roar. She paused. The loping rhythms of that engine woke something familiar in her brain. Then she dismissed the notion. Here it was a sunny and warm Saturday afternoon. A lot of people were probably out riding motorcycles. And a lot of motorcycles on the road were bound to be Harleys.

But the sound was getting louder, coming closer.

Jane looked around and saw nothing to attract any casual riders. *Galatea* was tied up along an old cement wharf, one of several that jutted out from the wooded shore at intervals, interspersed with pylons that stood in deep water twenty feet out from the rock-clad embankment. It was clearly a working dock, where ships would load and unload cargo, although none were anywhere in sight. Jane didn't see any services for a boat like theirs, either—no shore power, water spigots, or fuel pumps. So Willie must have chosen this as a temporary stopping place while he arranged for a berth at one of the marinas in town.

When she had gotten up from her deck chair to handle lines, Jane had thrown a short robe of thin, white cotton over her bathing suit and slipped into her sneakers. Now she pulled the robe's belt tight and bent to lace up her shoes. Something told her she wanted to be ready to fight or fly.

The engine noise crescendoed, and a black Electra-Glide, gleaming with chrome, rounded the corner. Without braking at all, it rolled up onto the dock and came straight toward *Galatea* and Jane. All she had time to say was, "Oh, shit!"

———

William Henry had secured the engine, but he kept steam up in the boiler and had not yet blown down the hot well. His chart showed they were now inside "Sarnia Harbour"—using that odd British spelling—and the cover notes suggested several places nearby that might cater to pleasure boats. But, from the channel, all he had been able to see were these commercial wharves. He wanted to stop and get his bearings before proceeding to their mooring for the night.

He walked from the engine room, back through the galley, to the saloon with the intention of discussing the choice of marinas with Jane. She wasn't in the cabin, however, which meant she was either out on deck or still tying up.

The rumble of a heavy engine drew his attention, and he looked out through the cabin windows. Jane was standing on the dock with a motorcycle bearing down on her. It slewed sideways to a stop and the rider—a burly young man, dressed in denim and black leather, with long blond hair and ginger beard—kicked out the side stand. He was off the bike in one fluid motion and crossed the three or four feet of space to where Jane was standing.

Eric Bell had just caught up with them.

Before the man could reach her, William Henry saw Jane drop into some kind of exotic fighting stance: feet placed at right angles and knees bent, arms cocked and hands curled into stiff claws, head held high and alert. And before she could move out of that stance, Bell casually swung the back of his hand and cuffed her. Jane flew sideways, landed, rolled, and before she could get back up, Bell was on top of her. He planted a knee between her shoulderblades, holding her down. With his left hand he gripped the back of her neck, pushing her face to the ground. Jane wriggled and kicked backward, like a scorpion pinned to a board, but she could do nothing to help herself.

William Henry went over to the bookshelf, removed *The Iliad,* and withdrew his service automatic. He slipped off the safety, racked the slide, and stepped out on deck to defend his wife.

Bell was drawing back his free right fist, clearly meaning to punch Jane's skull—a killing blow against the hard cement surface. He was grinning like a demon.

"Stop right there!" William Henry shouted, taking a bead.

Bell glanced up, unconcerned. His grin didn't change.

"Or what?" he said. "Are you gonna shoot me?"

William Henry aimed between the eyes. "Yes."

"Go ahead."

Every instinct told William Henry to squeeze the trigger. This was a man about to commit murder. This was a beast that needed to be put down. But William Henry was a civilized man, even if Eric Bell was not. He relaxed his stance, dropped his aim an inch to the side, and said, "Just don't hit her again."

"Oh, no, Professor! I won't *hit* her."

Bell rose from his crouch over Jane's body in one swift movement, dragging her along with him. The hand on her neck shifted around to her throat, pinning her head back against his chest. From out of nowhere a pistol appeared in Bell's right hand and aligned itself with Jane's right eye.

"This bitch is slightly more use to me alive than dead," Bell said. "But dead won't grieve me a bit. Now, do we see who can shoot first?"

William Henry took aim between the man's eyes.

Bell shook Jane's body like a doll, then loosened his fingers around her throat. "Tell him, bitch. Will I kill you?"

"Yes," Jane grated. "Believe him, Willie."

William Henry hesitated, and in that instant Bell swung his fist outward, with the barrel of his gun following, and shot him.

The bullet felt like a hard punch, somewhere on his right side, between shoulder and hip. Under the impact, William Henry stepped back in a half-spin, his arm flew up, his hand opened of its own accord. He heard the clatter of his service automatic crossing the deck and, sometime later, a splash over the side. But he didn't feel any pain.

He tried to be ready when Bell—dragging Jane along, folded over his arm like a topcoat he'd just shed—leapt the rail and landed on the deck. But William Henry was becoming confused, trying to sort out the numbness in his side—no, more like a cold-ness, and wet, like fog seeping through him. He could only stare foolishly as Eric Bell stepped in close, drew back his gun hand, and smashed the side of William Henry's head.

———

Jane had tried to defend herself, but she was out of shape. Three months away from the *dojo,* with no place to practice and no sparring partners, had made her stiff and slow. And three broken ribs, although mostly healed and adequate for casual activity, had made her tender. Eric's first blow, attacking sideways and collapsing her arm into her ribcage, had knocked the wind out of her. Then he knee-dropped her spine and she felt at least two of those ribs crack. The fight was over.

She was only half-conscious when Eric had taunted Willie, threatened her own life, then shot and clubbed her husband. In a way, the confrontation with her ex-lover was everything she had been expecting, everything she deserved. She had been a fool to come between Eric and the Hell's Legion Motorcycle Club by coming between the club and its drug supply. She had acted impulsively, without foresight or planning. She had made stupid mistakes—stupid mistakes all her life. But she was wiser now, and if she survived the next half-hour, she would make no more mistakes.

Once Willie was out of the way, Eric dragged her down into the cabin, dropped her in one of the green leather wing chairs, and lifted her chin almost tenderly.

"Where is it?" he asked softly.

Jane thought for one second about playing cute, playing for time, pretending she didn't know what he meant, denying she knew anything about any heroin. But those tactics would just earn her a broken jaw. This encounter was going to be painful enough.

"I've got it hidden," she said.

"Where?"

"Here, aboard the boat."

"Tell me where."

She took a painful breath, and somehow that made her brave. She dared to bargain with him. "Then will you let us go?"

"What?"

"I give you the kilo. You take it and leave. We're quits."

His lips twisted into a smile. "I get no retaliation?"

"You shot my husband and broke my ribs."

"And you think that makes us square?"

"Doesn't it—short of killing us?"

"I could still shoot you both."

"Too much legal trouble."

"Yeah, you're right."

"So ... it's a deal?"

"Sure." He smiled.

Jane did not trust him, of course, but she didn't have a choice. She started to stand up, and he shoved her back.

"I have to show you," she said.

When she moved again, he let her up.

"Through here ..." She took him into the galley, then beyond into the engine room. The boiler still chuffed and gurgled, and somewhere down below a small piece of machinery hissed and clicked. She pointed to the hatch beside the open metal framework of the engine. "Down there."

"Open it," Eric said, gesturing with his pistol.

She knelt, lifted the ring bolt, twisted it, pulled up the hatch, then stood back.

"Nuh-*uh!*" he said. "You go first—but slow."

Jane climbed down into the semidarkness. The belowdeck space reeked as before of mold and decay, but now she also smelled hot oil and damp steam. At the bottom she tried to stand on the ribs of the hull but lost her footing and stepped into cold water, the residue from Willie's morning ritual of running the bilge pump.

Eric followed her down. If the deck overhead was low enough that Jane had to duck walk, he was positively crawling.

"This way," she said, heading off toward the bow, threading the nest of pipes.

He followed, cursing whenever he bumped his head or touched something hot.

She crouched beside the boiler, feeling its dry heat like the sun on the side of her face and shoulder. She pointed beyond it to the large pipe that took a right-angle turn before disappearing through the hull. "There," she said.

"Where? I don't—?"

"Right there. Behind that pipe."

"Just get it for me."

Jane moved forward, reached behind the pipe, and felt for the canvas sacking. She dug into it with her fingertips and pulled. Nothing. The package was wedged harder than she remembered.

"It seems to be stuck."

"Come on! Get it!"

She pulled again.

"Won't budge."

Eric pushed her aside, reached in, felt around, and grappled with the package. He couldn't dislodge it either.

"Son of a bitch!"

He turned his shoulders, reached up to take hold of an overhead deck beam, and swung his butt around until his legs were forward in the empty space. He took aim at the bend in the pipe and kicked once, twice, three times. It snapped off its fitting in the hull. A spray of water like a fire hose came through the hole. The canvas sack slipped down from behind the pipe and shot forward on the spray. Eric caught it one-handed and hugged it to his chest.

Jane eased out of the open space, back toward the ladder, and Eric came after her fast. They both could hear water splashing into the bilges and lapping against the base of the boiler, where it sizzled until the metal started to cool. She was still trying to work her way gingerly over the hot pipes when he passed her. Clearly the scorching pain in those pipes didn't bother him through all that leather and denim the way it burned through her thin robe to her bare skin. She emerged from the nest a few feet behind him, and he was already at the ladder. He half-turned and kicked her in the chest, sending her back over one of the ribs, where she planted her fanny in the cold bilge water.

By the time she got her feet under her and reached the ladder, he had climbed out and slammed the hatch shut. She heard the latch click as he set the ring bolt.

Jane slammed a fist into the hatch's underside.

"Eric!" she shouted.

No response.

"Eric!"

She stepped down off the ladder and looked around. The water—which before had come up to her ankles—was now lapping her shins.

She worked her way forward again, beyond the boiler on the near side, toward the area under the wheelhouse. She ran into a rough wooden bulkhead. She felt above, where it joined the deck beams, and below, where it touched the hull's ribs. Her fingers found plenty of gaps but nothing wide enough for her to wriggle through.

She went aft, toward the plumbing under the new toilet and shower, and found the same kind of obstruction. Under the teak grating of the shower stall was a shallow tin pan, and she scrabbled at it with her fingers trying to tear it loose and beat on it with her fists to dislodge it. The thing was too well made.

Now the water was up to her thighs.

Jane was starting to be afraid.

———

William Henry woke up to the sound of distant pounding. He was lying facedown on the teak deck. When he moved his hands under his chest to raise himself, his right hand slid through a patch of something wet and sticky. He brought the hand up to his eyes and saw red paint. It took a moment for him to realize it was blood. His own blood. And then he felt the pain in his side. A deep, throbbing pain. Where Eric Bell had shot him.

The pounding continued, an urgent thumping and rattling. It sounded like the day the squall took them on Lake Simcoe, when the wind was shaking the wheelhouse door, and Jane was struggling to hold it closed. ... Jane. She was in trouble again. Eric Bell ...

He climbed to his feet, holding his right arm against his side to clamp down on the pain. No one was on deck, and the big, black motorcycle was gone from the dock.

He lurched into the cabin and found it empty. But the pounding was clearer and more insistent, coming from somewhere forward. He went through the galley, which was empty, and into the engine room, also empty. He remembered leaving the boiler with steam up and expected the pounding would have something to do with the building pressure. But the boiler was inert and cold, and he missed the hiss and click of the fuel pump. Then the pounding started again, right at his feet. It was coming from the hatch his father and Dani had cut into the deck.

"Willie!" called Jane's voice, thin and hoarse, between the bouts of pounding.

William Henry had no idea she even knew about the bilges under the engine. Only Dani and his father had ever been down there. But that seemed to be where Jane was. He knelt, unsnapped the ring left-handed, and pulled up on the hatch.

"Oh thank God!"

Jane's pale, upturned face was swimming in black water just ten inches below the edge of the deck. He reached down with his good left arm, and she clung to it. He pulled her over toward the ladder until she could get her feet on the rungs. As she climbed out, still clinging to him, the water rose to the level of the deck, fountained slowly as the last of the air leaked out from below, and started to spread.

William Henry and Jane supported each other as they hurried back through the galley, where the cork mats were starting to float. In the main saloon they splashed across the oriental carpet, which was already saturated. When they got out to the back deck, the edge of the wharf was already above them rather than below. The deck was listing at an angle away from the dock. They climbed and crawled up onto the concrete apron.

The bow and stern lines groaned as they held the sodden weight of *Galatea* to the wharf's bollards. William Henry looked down, and the large bloody patch on the teak where he had lain was slowly washed away.

With a sound like spaced pistol shots, first one line then the other parted. The boat righted herself briefly and settled slowly into the greenish water. In less than a minute, all he could see above the surface were the two masts, the funnel, and the wheelhouse roof.

30. Treatment for a Gunshot Wound

Jane left Willie on the dock and walked down the road looking for help. His side was still bleeding, although not so much as before, and he seemed kind of dazed, which was likely from the clobbering Eric had given him. Willie probably felt bad about the steamboat's sinking, too, but that would be more emotional than physical pain. Right then, she wasn't sure he even knew *Galatea* was really gone.

She hobbled down a long stretch through the trees, a quarter mile or more, past a couple of empty driveways, until she came to a proper cross street with traffic. She shuffled out into the street waving her arms. She figured a half-naked woman in a tattered bathrobe that barely covered her thighs—who was at once bent over and limping but dancing around and acting crazy—would attract more attention than a plaintive cry for help. Sure enough, within thirty seconds a siren blipped behind her, and she turned to see the flashing lights of a police car. She lurched up to the driver's window.

"You've got to help me! My husband's been hurt!"

"Ma'am, you'll have to get out of the street."

"You don't understand. He's been shot!"

"Ma'am? You mean, with a gun?"

"Down there!" She pointed.

The officer put her in the rear seat and drove back down through the trees to the wharf with his lights and siren still going. Only when he saw Willie and the blood on his clothes and on the concrete did he radio for an ambulance. "Hospital's close," he told Jane, "just over on Mitton Street."

Willie was still breathing when the officer let her out of the car, and she stayed with him until the ambulance team put him on a stretcher and loaded him up. Then she rode in the police car following the ambulance to a hospital called Bluewater Health.

"How did it happen?" the officer asked. "I mean, your husband shot, you beat up, and the boat sunk at the wharf back there."

"We were attacked," she said.

"Yeah. And who was it attacked you?"

"I don't know. Some wild man on a motorcycle. Hell's Angel type. He wanted our money and my jewelry."

"And then he sank your boat? Big boat, too!"

"I guess we didn't have enough money. Or jewelry."

"Okay. Let's get your husband fixed up—and yourself looked after—and I'll be around later to take your statement. In the meantime, we'll put out an alert on the Hell's Angel."

Jane thought about the package the police would find if Eric were stopped—and the story he could tell them.

"Yeah. Sure," she said. "I think he said something about going over the river into the States. Back to Detroit. Or maybe it was Lansing."

"Well, we'll look for him anyway."

She had to leave it at that.

In the emergency room, they put Willie in one treatment bay and her in another. The team on the other side of the curtain was calling for transfusions and surgical prep. On her side, a nurse looked at the bruising on her throat and back, prodded the bruises on her ribs, and rubbed ointment on the second-degree burns across her arms and legs.

"What's happening with my husband?" she asked.

"He seems hurt pretty badly," the nurse said.

"But he's not gonna die. I mean, is he?"

"I'll go check with the doctors."

"Muscle damage and loss of blood," the nurse said when she came back. "He broke a rib where it stopped the bullet. It seems to be lodged in the pleura, just under his right lung."

"Oh, that's a relief. When can I see him?"

"Well, they're taking him into surgery to remove the bullet. It'll be a couple of hours yet. Do you need some clothes? Do you have someplace to go?"

Jane was released with directions to a nearby rooming house and a clothing store. She still had to figure out what to do about money, because her purse was at the bottom of the harbor. Perhaps she could ask the hospital administration for Willie's effects and see if he had been carrying a wallet.

That thought raised a bigger question. She had to keep Willie—when he came out from under the anesthetic and could see visitors—away from the police. He would know it was no random "Hell's Angel" from Michigan who assaulted them. He knew Eric's full name and would deny the attack had anything to do with money and jewels.

But what did Willie really know? She had never told him about the kilo of heroin. For all he knew, Eric was simply a jealous and violent ex-lover who followed Jane from California. Eric's actions were extreme: beating up Dani, shooting Willie—well, Willie *did* come out of the cabin pointing a gun, didn't he?—and then locking Jane in the bilges and trying to drown her by sinking the boat. But those were the things a crazy California biker was *supposed* to do, weren't they?

Her story depended, then, on what Eric might have told Dani, back in Byzantium. Her semi-hysterical letter had mentioned a "boyfriend." But if he had told her anything about a stolen kilo of heroin—stolen by Jane, the drug mule, which his club wanted back because it was worth half a million dollars to their traffic—well, Dani certainly would have mentioned it. And her letter would probably have used a much more judicious, even sanctimonious, tone.

So Jane was in the clear. She had her story. And she could make it stick—so long as she kept all the players apart.

31. A Hazard to Navigation

It was three days after his surgery, and William Henry was fully awake now. He had shed the grogginess of the anesthetics and the painkillers they gave him for the wound in his side. It still hurt to breathe, but his mind was clear.

Jane had been there the first day, Sunday, during visiting hours, smiling down at him as he woke up in the morning sunlight. She had told him everything was all right, that the surgeon had got the bullet out, and he was going to get completely better. The doctors and nurses had told him the same thing the night before, when he came to in the recovery room.

"How are you, Jane?" he had mumbled, still feeling the drug vapors.

"Oh, I'm great! Good as new. Just a few scrapes and bruises."

"How's *Galatea*? Were you able to shut down the boiler?"

"Um, you *saw* her, Willie. … She sank at the dock."

"Oh. Yeah." *Lines breaking like pistol shots.*

He had fallen asleep after that exchange.

Jane came the next day, Monday, which was Labor Day, which they celebrated in Canada the same as in the States. She sat quietly by his side during visiting hours, sometimes holding his hand, sometimes just looking at him. He would ask for a glass of water. She would give it to him. The nurses shooed her out when he rang for the bedpan. And she left when it was time for his pills and dinner. He had something he wanted to ask her, but he could not think it through, could not arrange the words in his mind.

But now it was the third day, Tuesday. His mind was clear, and his question was ready. The chain of reasoning went like this: Who was Eric Bell, really?

At one point, Jane let him think Bell was someone she arrested during her career with the military police, supposedly while tracking down drug smugglers. But William Henry was pretty sure that was a fairytale. The closest Jane ever came to the military life was the day she had rummaged around in his footlocker back in Byzantium, a few days before she went crazy.

Then Jane suggested Bell was someone she knew personally, perhaps intimately, at least close enough that she used the man's name on her driver's license. In that case, he probably came after Jane—not out of revenge for arrest and incarceration—but because of thwarted lust, jealousy, or a sense of possession. But if so, he would want to take her back to California, not kill her. It would have been William Henry he wanted to kill.

And yet Bell had held a gun to Jane's head and dared him to shoot first. Bell had bragged she was as good as dead to him—no, rather more use *alive* than dead, "but dead won't grieve me a bit." William Henry was remembering everything exactly now. The man had been in the grip of a powerful emotion, one strong enough to draw him clear across the country, beat up an innocent girl, track a boat he knew only by its description through the waterways of Ontario, and then endure months of watching and waiting for it to arrive. It was a fearsome emotion, but it wasn't anything related to love or even lust.

And then, when William Henry had been merely shot and stunned, rather than killed outright, Bell had dragged Jane belowdecks, locked her in the bilges, and sunk the boat just to drown her. As an execution, it was fairly convoluted and uncertain of result. Why not just shoot her when he had a gun in his hand?

No, William Henry knew he was missing an important piece of this puzzle. He intended to ask Jane outright when she showed up for visiting hours.

But when eleven o'clock came, the nurse ushered in a stranger rather than Jane. She introduced the man as Mr. Martin Duquesne, the harbormaster at Sarnia.

"How do?" the man asked, reaching across the bed to shake hands. "Are you the registered owner of that old steamboat at the commercial wharf?"

William Henry shook with him. "Yes, that's me."

"You know she sank at her moorings, right?"

"Yes, I was present when it happened."

"And you didn't think to report it?"

William Henry waved his left hand, indicating himself lying in the hospital bed. "I've been rather preoccupied."

"I see," Duquesne said. "Was anyone else hurt?"

"Just my wife, a few scrapes and bruises."

"Is anyone *dead*? Still *down* there?"

"No, of course not." But William Henry added in his own mind, *so far as I know*. Eric Bell was unaccounted for. He might be down in the bilges, having drowned where Jane did not. But then, who had locked the hatch on her? And who had ridden away on Bell's motorcycle? No, Bell was gone, but not that way.

"You know you have to move the boat, don't you?"

"I … haven't gotten that far yet. I suppose she can be raised."

Duquesne dipped his chin and frowned. "My people tell me the hull is more than sixty feet long, made of wood. And when was she built?"

"Last century, in the mid-eighties."

"Old timbers. Does she have a big, heavy engine?"

"Triple condensing," William Henry agreed.

"Uneven weight distribution," the man said.

"What does that mean?"

"A lot of money, sir. Three, maybe four derricks, two of them on barges. Maybe have to build a crib around her to keep from breaking her back. Certainly a cradle after they pull her from the water. Survey for all this will take a week or two, with another week for fabrication. Then you have to locate and hire the derricks and bring them in—we don't have anything like that in Sarnia."

"How much money?"

"Twenty, twenty-five thousand. Minimum."

"Ouch!" William Henry said.

"You carry insurance, sir, certainly."

"To pay off the mortgage. About half that."

Duquesne sighed. "Then we'll have to demolish the hulk in place. She's a hazard to navigation. And we do run a busy port here."

"I see." Visions flashed through William Henry's mind of the boat into which he had poured his love, energy, and money for the last seven months, to which he had mortgaged his entire future. He saw surfaces of old brass and iron, mahogany and marble, teak and varnish, tufted leather and stained glass. All turned in an instant to scrap and rust and waterlogged wood. "And what will that cost?"

"Oh, I haven't worked it out yet. But—off the cuff, mind you—about a tenth of the salvage cost."

"And there's no alternative?"

"None, sir."

"I suppose I should thank you."

"No need for that."

Duquesne then let himself out.

William Henry brooded through lunch and the early afternoon. Eric Bell had shot and clubbed him but hadn't killed him. Instead, he—and working through him, Jane—had changed the course of his life completely. Well, it was not just them but also the evolving nature of scholarship and his declining fortunes at the university. And, to be honest, William Henry had to admit a hand in his own destruction, because he might have been a bit more gracious about the new curriculum and eager to show his worth in a changing world.

Still, he had much to discuss with Jane when she finally came for her visit.

Along toward four o'clock, when she still had not arrived, he asked the nurse to make a call for him to the boardinghouse where she was staying.

The woman came back ten minutes later. "I'm sorry, sir. They say she paid up and checked out this morning."

"Well, did she leave a forwarding address?"

"Not that anyone there knows of."

"Oh … well … then …"

"I'm truly sorry."

FALL 1968

1. Mother and Daughter

JANE HAD BEEN back in Byzantium for two weeks before she tried to see her daughter. She needed that time to find an apartment and get a job. With the start of the semester and the university coming back to life, the one was harder to do than the other.

At first she thought she would have to settle for her old job schlepping cocktails around in fancy dresses, but the owner of the bar where she first applied—a place called Third Base, on Bacon Street—wanted her to try mixology. The pay was better, he said, and Jane was sure she could do the work, because she'd seen Lou Fiacco mix enough drinks, even the hard ones requiring a delicate hand. It was only after she'd been on the job a week and seen the youth, beauty, and short skirts that he favored in his waitresses that Jane finally understood. If there was going to be an older woman in the house, he wanted her behind the bar and pretending to listen to the customers instead of flirting with them out front. Well, that suited her. And if things got tough, she could always go back to the Ace of Spades and double-team with Lou—except she had vowed it would be a year of Sundays before she set foot in that place again.

After getting an income stream, Jane had finally found a one-room bed-sitter that was three flights up in a not-so-good neighborhood. At least the building was walking distance—although a long walk—to her work. The bus routes went too far out of her way and, at the wages she was making, she couldn't afford a car for a couple of years yet—if she was even around that long. It all depended on how things went with Dani.

She knocked on the door of 301 Durrell at four o'clock on a weekday afternoon. Jane had chosen the time carefully to leave an hour before she had to go on shift. That would be long enough for them to catch up, and it gave her an excuse if the conversation turned ugly.

"Who is it?" asked a voice from behind the door, an older version of Dani's voice, cautious and low.

"Your mother."

"Oh!"

Jane heard locks click and the door opened a crack. One eye inspected her, and then the door opened all the way.

Dani's face had a dark-eyed, sunken look, especially on the left side, where the surgeons had repaired her cheekbone. Her daughter wasn't quite so pretty anymore. Well, she would just have to work on restoring Dani's inner glow of confidence, which was the true source of a woman's beauty.

"May I come in?" Jane asked.

"Sure." Dani stepped back. "I didn't think I'd see you again."

"Oh? And why not?"

"Dad called weeks ago. He said you'd split and left him to pick up the pieces, like before. I just figured I was one of the pieces."

"Nonsense, you're my daughter. I want to help you." Jane moved into the room and sat on the bed. She patted it for Dani to sit beside her.

"Is it really true that the boat's been sunk?" the girl asked.

"Yes, up in Canada. But your father and I got out first."

"And that this Eric Bell, your old boyfriend, did it?"

"I guess you could call him my boyfriend. Yes, that fits," Jane said. "But the sinking was just a terrible accident. That boat was full of old pipes, rusted stuff, rotten wood. You've been down there, Willie told me, helping fix up the engine. One of those old pipes just broke."

"Yes," Dani said thoughtfully. "It could happen that way. Except Dad said Bell locked you in the bilges."

"That was another accident."

"What were you doing down there?"

"Trying to stop the leak. Water was—"

"Was this before or after Bell shot Daddy?"

"Eric was a jealous man, angry and violent. Things got out of hand." Time to change the subject, Jane decided. "So ... has your father returned to Byzantium yet?"

"He's still picking up the pieces."

"Oh, well then, he'll be along soon."

"Are you two getting back together?"
"I hope … we can live as a family."
"And is that crazy biker really gone?"
"I swear you'll never see him again."
"How could you know a man like that, Mother?"
"Eric was like … a force of nature," Jane said.
"Yeah, a tornado. He was a psycho."
"We all have one of those in our past."

2. Done Roving

WILLIAM HENRY HAD debts to pay. First was the bill from the hospital for his surgery and two weeks of recovery and convalescence. Then came the costs of demolition to clear the hulk that once was *Galatea*. He remembered having carried a pretty fair sum in cash and traveler's checks, with at least one blank check on his bank in Byzantium and several credit cards. But somehow his wallet went missing in the emergency room. So he stayed on at Sarnia to work off what he owed.

For two months he did odd jobs. He mowed a hundred lawns and then raked a ton of leaves. He painted two complete houses, three porches, and a garage. He repaired a tar-and-gravel roof and cleaned out rain gutters. He posted a card on the bulletin board at the St. Clair Community College, over in Port Huron, Michigan, offering to tutor in Latin and Greek, history, drama, and English composition. He ended up substitute-teaching a course in remedial algebra and geometry, drawing heavily on his memory of working out problems in operations research back in Korea.

He wrote letters to Dani in Byzantium, where she was deep into the fall semester of her junior year. From her replies, he learned she was studying harder than ever. Oh, and Jane had come back to town—again. She was working at a bar just off campus, living in a one-room walkup, and trying to become a mother. Dani thought they might make it work—Jane playing at being the loving mother, Dani the dutiful daughter—at least for a while, at least until the wanderlust or the craziness took over Jane's brain again and she departed for who knows where. He decided his daughter had grown up to be a realist. He promised to try to come visit them over the holidays, if he could get away.

William Henry finally paid off every cent he owed and even had a few extra dollars in his pocket. But he suddenly was without a goal or a thought in his head. "I am Diogenes," he whispered to himself, "but without the lantern—or a barrel to live in."

So he went to the bus station and bought a one-way ticket. What had taken weeks to cover by boat was just four and a half hours overland by road. And when the bus arrived in town, he hailed a taxi and gave the driver the address as best he could remember it. "Certainly, sir," the man said. "Take people there all the time."

The taxi stopped at a gate defined by two pillars made of raw, gray granite chunks set in mortar. They defined a gap in the hedge of mountain laurel that ran along the road. The gate bore no sign, no markings. William Henry hesitated, because he had never seen the property from the landward side, having only come upon it by water.

"You're sure this is the place?"

"Yes, sir. No other like it."

William Henry paid the man, shouldered the satchel that contained everything he owned—a change of clothes, dry shoes, a razor, toothbrush, and soap—and walked down the crushed gravel driveway.

Morwenna Daffyd must have been looking up from the registration desk and spotted him through the beveled glass in the doors of the entry hall. She stepped out onto the portico and waited for him to cross the graveled circle.

"Is it a paying guest you are now?" she asked when he was close enough for them to speak without shouting.

"No, but coming down from the road I noticed the retaining wall in your south yard is about to collapse."

"Oh, it's held that shape for twenty years." But she was smiling.

"Yes, and it might go in the next heavy rain. Certainly with the spring thaw."

"Do you do better stonework than the last man who fixed my wall? He was a scholar and not much else."

"Oh, I do a bit of everything these days—" He held up his hands. "—and have the calluses to prove it."

"Well, the old place could do with a bit of mending. Come in and we'll discuss your rates over a cup of tea. Mind you, I'm a poor widow and can't pay much."

"I don't need much," he said. "Not anymore."

About the Author

Thomas T. Thomas is a writer with a career spanning forty years in book editing, technical writing, public relations, and popular fiction writing. Among his various careers, he has worked at a university press, a trade-book publisher, an engineering and construction company, a public utility, an oil refinery, a pharmaceutical company, and a supplier of biotechnology instruments and reagents. He published eight novels and collaborations in science fiction with Baen Books and is now working on more general and speculative fiction. When he's not working and writing, he may be out riding his motorcycle, practicing karate, or wargaming with friends. Catch up with him at www.thomastthomas.com.

Photo by Robert L. Thomas

eBooks and Paperbacks:
Coming of Age, Volume 1: Eternal Life
Coming of Age, Volume 2: Endless Conflict
The Children of Possibility
The Judge's Daughter
eBooks:
Sunflowers
Trojan Horse
Baen Books and eBooks:
The Doomsday Effect (as by "Thomas Wren")
First Citizen
ME: A Novel of Self-Discovery
Crygender
Baen Books in Collaboration:
An Honorable Defense (with David Drake)
The Mask of Loki (with Roger Zelazny)
Flare (with Roger Zelazny)
Mars Plus (with Frederik Pohl)